MAN-KZIN WARS XII

MAN-KZIN WARS XII

♦ ♦ ♦

CREATED BY

LARRY NIVEN

Man-Kzin Wars XII

This is a work of fiction. All the characters and events portrayed in this book are fictional, and any resemblance to real people or incidents is purely coincidental.

A Baen Books Original

Baen Publishing Enterprises
P.O. Box 1403
Riverdale, NY 10471
www.baen.com

ISBN 10: 4165-9141-9
ISBN 13: 978-1-4165-9141-2

Cover art by Stephen Hickman

First printing, February 2009

Distributed by Simon & Schuster
1230 Avenue of the Americas
New York, NY 10020

Library of Congress Cataloging-in-Publication Data

Man-Kzin wars XII / created by Larry Niven.
    p. cm.
  ISBN-13: 978-1-4165-9141-2 (hc)
  ISBN-10: 1-4165-9141-9 (hc)
  1. Science fiction, American. 2. Kzin (Imaginary place)—Fiction. 3. Life on other planets—Fiction. 4. Space warfare—Fiction. 5. Science fiction, Australian. 6. Science fiction, Canadian. I. Colebatch, Hal, 1945– II. Harrington, Matthew J. III. Chafe, Paul, 1965– IV. Niven, Larry. V. Title: Man-Kzin wars 12. VI. Title: Man-Kzin wars twelve.

  PS648.S3M3754 2009
  813'.0876208—dc22

                        2008043892

10 9 8 7 6 5 4 3 2 1

Pages by Joy Freeman (www.pagesbyjoy.com)
Printed in the United States of America

CONTENTS

ECHOES OF DISTANT GUNS

◆ ◆ ◆

Matthew Joseph Harrington

I

Silent Partners

Quartermaster noticed the Named were getting upset again, and quietly set his subordinates and their slaves to checking fabrication procedures and inventory. A few days later, his guess proved right, but far beyond his expectations: Commandant's Voice announced that a Hthnarrit would soon be arriving on Fuzz, bringing a fleet to be supplied.

This was exciting. Quartermaster had never seen a Patriarch's Companion, nor met anyone who had. He signed out a disintegrator to keep the landing field clear, it being seeding time again, but otherwise stayed out of the way and let his staff do their jobs. Clearing the field was the only entertaining part anyway—the tufty airborne seeds that everything threw out burned spectacularly when their molecules started breaking up.

When Gnyr-Hoth's own ship had set down, and all formal courtesies had been exchanged, the Companion's first question was, "Who arranged the fireworks display while we landed?"

"Oh, that was only Quartermaster clearing debris off the field," replied Hur-Commandant. "The local plant life produces large amounts of fuzzy seeds on a regular basis. He ignites them with a disintegrator."

"Clever. Take us to him." Gnyr-Hoth turned to pick out a couple of kzintoshi from his entourage, waved the rest onward, and turned back to say, "Which way?"

Hur-Commandant hadn't earned his partial Name by being slow to adapt. "That building, Gnyr-Hoth." He was extremely startled when the Hthnarrit immediately began sprinting toward it, but promptly followed suit.

3

Quartermaster saw the group approaching, had no idea why, and told his staff, "Disperse throughout the warehouse. Fabrication Chief, if I'm in trouble, you're in charge. Wait in the office."

"Yes, sir. —They don't seem hostile, sir."

"Thanks," said Quartermaster, who had no *ziirgrah* sense at all. "Go anyway." He turned to face the door as his deputy left. When the Hthnarrit entered, Quartermaster came to attention and saluted, then waited to be addressed.

Gnyr-Hoth didn't particularly look like one of the 2,048 deadliest kzinti alive. He was a little smaller than average, not very heavy, and had no interesting scars . . . though that last fact suggested that most of the scars from his duels had been left on other, larger, kzintoshi. He set his feet very lightly, as if concerned about damaging the concrete floor, and his movements were almost decorative. "You're Quartermaster?" he said, having noted Quartermaster's inspection.

"Sir, I am."

"Tell me what you're thinking. Be informal."

"I . . . was wondering if you'd ever danced in a play, sir."

Hur-Commandant's ears folded about halfway shut. (But nobody else seemed disturbed.)

Gnyr-Hoth didn't object to the implication that he might have been *employed*, and as an entertainer at that. "No. One of my combat instructors sent me to a school for dancers. I was walking too loudly. Innovative teacher, won the Name Kchula."

Quartermaster's ears opened wide with surprise for a moment, then he went back to rigid attention.

"Remain informal, Quartermaster. You knew him?"

"Possibly, sir. The exec of our division on Chunquen-aga was Named Kchula. He had very dark stripes, and a little hole just near the bottom of the fan of his left ear, sir."

"I'm flattered he never had it fixed. It was as close as I ever got—lost my temper with him one day. Worst beating I ever had. You were Second Battle Specialist of the 4416th Infantry?"

"Why, yes, sir. Were you there?"

"No, in those days I was in the Grand Admiral's Guard. But that's a distinctive scar, and everyone in the sector heard about the Hero who fought on with the hole in his head. Tough opponents there, constantly practicing."

"That was *you*?" Hur-Commandant asked in astonishment.

"Yes, sir," Quartermaster replied, the scar between his right eye and ear suddenly itching horribly.

"Why don't you have a Name?" Hur-Commandant wondered.

"After I got out of regeneration I had no urge to fight, sir," Quartermaster said. "Some kind of brain damage."

One of the Hthnarrit's entourage spoke: "He needs to scratch."

"Go ahead," Gnyr-Hoth said.

Quartermaster scratched the scar gratefully and thoroughly, and took the opportunity to inspect the new speaker surreptitiously.

This one was built the way Quartermaster had expected a Patriarch's Companion to be: heavily muscled, one of the biggest kzintoshi he'd ever seen—except that his eyes were faintly bloodshot with purple capillaries. A telepath.

A remarkably healthy telepath, and not a timid one, either.

Gnyr-Hoth said, "Do you still hunt, at least?"

Both local kzinti acquired identical disgruntled tail droops. "The biggest prey here is smaller than my head," Quartermaster said.

"Unless you count God's Hairballs," Hur-Commandant joked.

"Count *what*?" exclaimed Gnyr-Hoth.

"A local animal that settles in one spot at maturity," said Quartermaster. "They seem to have a lure scent for food, or something. Basically a big pile of hair, about this high, like God's been grooming without brushes and hasn't been getting any fat in his diet. *Horrkkk*."

Amused, Gnyr-Hoth said, "Edible?"

Telepath suddenly whirled about, and looked all around frantically. Gnyr-Hoth whipped out sidearm and *wtsai*, ready to kill the detected foe, but after a few moments Telepath straightened up and said, "I'm sorry, sir. I don't know what made me do that."

"Better wrong than surprised," Gnyr-Hoth said. "So, are they good meat?" he resumed as he put away his weapons.

"I've never had any, but I understand the flavor is disgusting," Quartermaster said.

"I seem to recall reports that the initial settlement had some food-poisoning cases, too," Hur-Commandant tossed in.

"Urr, well, we should be bringing you some better prey in a few years. Scouts have discovered new aliens. When this fleet is refitted it'll be taking one of their worlds. Shouldn't be hard, they keep trying to talk rather than fight," Gnyr-Hoth said. "They're some kind of primate, so they should taste pretty good."

"Will we be getting them as slaves?" Quartermaster said hopefully. "Primates have good hands."

"*What was that*?" Telepath screamed, making everyone but Gnyr-Hoth leap a considerable distance into the air. Telepath began lashing out wildly, as if blind.

Gnyr-Hoth swept a foot under Telepath's legs, knocked him down, rolled him over, tore open Telepath's medical kit, selected a pressure hypo, and administered it. Telepath stopped thrashing almost at once, and Gnyr-Hoth rose and said sadly, "He was really good, too. Very sensitive. . . . Perhaps that's why he broke so young."

Quartermaster gestured for his staff, and a Kdatlyno came up with a cart and loaded Telepath onto it. "Medical, now," said Quartermaster, and the slave departed at full speed.

What did you do that for? one Grog asked the one who'd acted.

He kept noticing whenever we had to make adjustments. Besides, those new aliens may be worth getting to know, the latter Grog told her. *They seem to* like *to talk to new people, and we could certainly use some good hands.*

What does that have to do with— began the first, then stopped as her neighbor revealed her plan. *Oh, I get it.*

Yes, he'd have noticed the little altered spots in everyone else's memories, no matter how often we made him *forget.*

I'd better pass this on, the first commented. *Someone may land with one of those mind readers at one of the bases we can't reach from here.*

Good thinking.

Quartermaster's top crew went through the biggest vessel, sure to be designated the flagship, with exacting care, bringing everything up to specifications. The ships had been collected from all over the Empire, and each had been whatever could be spared from a given station. Most needed considerable attention.

He went through the ship continuously, inspecting the work himself. He carried a gamma-ray annealing beamer, to restore temper to spot welds.

Down in the auxiliary power room, which had required commendably little work, he checked what his Jotoki had done, squirming between monocrystal support struts to get a look at the fusion waste disposal manifold. It was fine. He got back out and looked over the struts, which were naturally in perfect shape—they couldn't be repaired onsite, only replaced, and the old ones recast. They had to be all one piece.

Quartermaster took his annealer and directed it about a third of the way up one of the main struts, causing the monocrystal to separate into trillions of microscopic domains, like ordinary metal. In a space battle, the struts had to be utterly rigid. Now, though, the proper shear stress would tear the strut, rip the manifold, spray plasma through the power room, and with any luck blow the bottom third of the ship clean off.

It could be years before it happened, but there were other things that could be done to other spaceships. Things that would increase casualties. Things that would give the primate-type aliens a chance. They couldn't be all the same, or somebody would notice the pattern. Somebody out of range.

Out of range of what? Quartermaster suddenly wondered. Then he remembered the manifold was fine, and he had many more inspections to make.

There was a war on, and everyone had his part to do.

II

Donderbeck

Like everyone else, she'd learned in school that it had been centuries since humans were uncivilized enough to commit murder.

When she joined the ARM she learned different.

The information wasn't all that useful at first.

"That's him?" said Lancaster.

"That's him, ma'am," Dr. Fisher told the ARM agent. "Please

be cautious. We were ordered not to sedate him . . . not that he responds that well to drugs anyway—"

"Yes, I need him alert," she said absently, still a little incredulous. "All right, let me in. I'll be jamming the pickups, so don't come rushing in in a panic."

"We could just shut them off," he said, startled.

"Only the ones you know about."

"You think someone may have bugged *us*?" he exclaimed.

"I have no idea. I don't care. As I say, I'll be jamming the pickups. Doors, please."

In an era when anything was fixable, Ralston Muldoon was extraordinarily ugly: crooked and protruding teeth, popeyes, a nose that looked smashed to one side, an asymmetrical skull. He was sitting with his hands carefully folded, looking at the table before him.

When Lancaster came into the room, Muldoon turned his eyes toward her, looked her down and up, and glanced at several different areas, then settled on her face. Lancaster was in the habit of looking people over in just that way herself, and she developed the sudden conviction that Muldoon now knew exactly how she was armed, what she could do unarmed, and where she depilated. "Hello, Ralston," she said, and showed her ident. "Agent Lancaster, ARM."

"Strange," he said. (Later in her career she was to reflect often on the fact that this was the first thing she ever heard him say.) "I'm brought in without explanation, then kept waiting for several hours with nothing to occupy my mind, and I'm greeted by my given name by someone who gives only her surname. It's as if someone in the loop thinks dominance needs to be established, which would only make sense if I had something remotely resembling a negotiating posture. How do you do, Agent Lancaster?"

Was he *humoring* her? Humor him back. "My name's Karen, if you prefer," she said.

"Thanks. Though I doubt we'll be seeing one another socially."

She thought over the secondary implications of that remark while she was spraying fogger on the observation mirror, then sat in the chair on the other side of the table and said, "Muldoon—" he nodded appreciatively—"one of the colony worlds has encountered a carnivorous animal, very strong and fast, that doesn't go into shock when injured. All the lethal weapons in ARM records are designed for killing Terran animals, and the situation is getting worse. You're the only weapon design expert we know. What do you want that we can give you?"

He looked into her eyes for several seconds, but wasn't focused on them. Then he said, "Two errors of fact. First, every lethal weapon more complex than a fist ax was designed primarily for killing humans, not animals. Second—well, A, you said 'encountered,' not 'discovered'; B, the only way any animal can't be dealt with by present weapons is if the survivors come looking for revenge; and C—appropriately—the time lag between here and the nearest colony makes the cover story you were assigned absurd. Someone has met intelligent aliens, in space, and they're warlike. The lack of shock is not good news. It suggests hundreds of generations of practice at mechanized warfare. You need a donderbeck. I'd like pencil and paper."

He must have been hard to take, for the staff here: He reasoned very like an ARM. "Certainly. Anything else?"

"I meant now."

He'd surprised her again. She got both out of her carryall, and he began drafting, smoothly and swiftly.

"What's a donderbeck?" she asked, after a minute or so of watching precision diagrams appear.

"Something I thought of but never needed. Easy to make. Here." He turned the drawing with hands that had become shaky once more. "The breech mechanism is from the Thompson, an early twentieth-century light machine gun. The round casings are cast nitrocellulose, no debris, nothing to eject. Solid propellant continues accelerating the rounds after they leave the barrel. The slugs are clusters of glass needles in a teflon matrix, each needle tipped with a heavy metal. I recommend tungsten."

"Uranium's cheaper."

"You'll be needing uranium for other things. The needles strike a target, the metal punches through armor, the needles slide out of the matrix and diverge, and the glass shatters as they tumble. That'll tear things up. Huge holes. If these folks don't have physical shock, they must have circulatory cutoffs, so this should trap a lot of their blood where it's no use to their brains. Knock 'em down and keep 'em there. What do the aliens look like?"

"Uh, large feline bipeds, eight feet and up. Here." She got out a display flat and passed it over.

He looked at it. "Ears like dragons."

"Dragons?"

"Mythical creatures. They were in the library the cops confiscated, if you're curious. I'll need to see autopsy data for further designs."

"We've made anatomical diagrams."

"Those will help, but I mean the autopsy films."

"Can you handle that? Never mind," she said, remembering who she was talking to.

"I'll manage," he said, not unkindly. "I'll need to be undrugged for a few days while I work on this, and I could do with a fabricating shop and a remote operating system for it."

"Why remote?"

"To save time. Otherwise someone will argue about whether I should be handling weapons. This way, I won't be."

"Good point. Anything you want for yourself?"

He thought. "One thing they might not take back, after I'm done, is a manual shutoff for my chair. I really hate being whisked off somewhere by remote control, and it's not as if the staff here has too many inmates to look after to send someone to get me."

"The ARM could get you out of that chair," she said. "That's actually something I'm authorized to offer."

"I won't take transplants," he replied. "Organ banks are morally wrong."

Her mouth fell open. "This from someone who by the age of nineteen had methodically assassinated a hundred and sixty-two people?"

Muldoon shrugged. "As far as you know."

"You mean there were *more*?" she said, aghast.

"No," he said, and made an odd soft sound that turned out to be laughter. (There was something wrong with his larynx, too.) "Sorry. I killed a hundred and thirty-one people for being needlessly cruel. I wasn't myself. The rest were sloppy kills, where people died in great pain or took more than a few minutes to die. *Those* weren't mine." He spoke with quiet, regal pride.

"Didn't you ever tell anyone?"

"Such as who? The police and prosecutor certainly knew already; they were using me to clear their files. Besides, I thought a couple looked like they'd been done by police officers, and I had no particular desire to be found hanged in my cell."

Lancaster absorbed this, narrowing her eyes. There were going to be some fresh investigations. Then she said, "There are non-transplant procedures—regenerative—available in limited cases."

"They won't be limited for long, I think. You'll need them for soldiers."

He was right. "I guess you'll be the first. Do you need anything else right now?" she said.

"Dinner. High thyroid, I'm always hungry."

"I'll see to it," she said, and left.

They could fix him up. Without transplants.

Ralston reached up and felt the dents in his skull through his thinning gray hair. He hummed through his nose, a children's song from a more realistic time:

> Now dogs and cats
> And even rats
> Will nevermore be seen—
> They've all been ground to sausage-meat
> By Donderbeck's machine.

It felt good to be needed.

III

Second Front

Ucomo was what his friends called him. Among the Smart People, one's full name was essentially a capsule biography, and as Ucomo was unusually Smart his full name was getting pretty long.

He was working on an interesting intercept when Dabak, his longtime facilitator and good friend, let himself in and took a deep breath. "Ucomo, the air in here is overburdened with carbon dioxide, and moist enough for a Stupid. This cannot be good for your health, nor by extension your rest, your work, or your consequential prosperity. I am opening the blackout screen." Dabak went to the office window, exposed the outside view, gasped, and said, "I am closing the blackout screen." Once he had done so, he took a moment to recover, then turned and said, "You should get an office that doesn't have a view of the moon, so you can get some fresh air in." After a pause, Dabak added, "I hate that thing."

"Not really," Ucomo remarked. "Oras, our ancestral homeworld, is in almost the same orbit as a similar body, Agad, and every few hundred orbits whichever one is closer to their sun catches up with the other. They interact gravitationally, the closer speeds up and moves into a wider orbit, the other slows and moves in, and they separate for a few hundred more orbits. During each period of interaction, conditions on Oras are beyond belief, and that's just the precursor of a massive climatic shift.

"Unfortunately, this means that you and I are descended from ancestors whose response to the sight of a nearby body in half-phase was *never* to remain calm and await developments. Since every colony world has a moon, we have blackout screens at every window."

"Are you recording?" Dabak said anxiously.

"Constantly, but that conclusion was already known."

"Too bad, it sounded lucrative."

"It was. What did your Mother think of my strategic plan?"

"She sent me with an invitation to donate."

Startled, Ucomo picked up a currycomb and said, "How much?" as he began instinctively to brush himself out.

"I would suppose however much you normally produce," Dabak said.

Ucomo gestured as if to throw and exclaimed, "I mean what's the bid, you fish!"

Wriggling with satisfaction—he was almost never able to get a joke in on Ucomo—Dabak said, "No bid. You're *invited* to donate." At Ucomo's gasp, he added, "I also overheard her discussing how much her latest brood of sons could be lent for bids when *you* turn female. She's very impressed with you."

"I don't know if I want to be a Mother myself," Ucomo reflected. "It takes up so much time."

"Everyone says that, but we keep settling more planets, don't we? You'll just do what the Founding Mother did and look for the Smartest mates. —What's wrong?"

"*All* her mates must have been Stupids. I don't know how a Mother can stand talking to anyone but another Mother. We must all seem like Stupids to them."

"I doubt that's their primary interest in us anyway," Dabak observed.

It was a good point. Only the survivors of male-phase competition became Mothers. Typically about one male out of every eight or nine born lived long enough to resume development, so everyone was descended from Mothers who had preferred to be continuously pregnant. "Did your Mother send a container?"

"No. I believe she intends to invite you home."

"What, like a war hero?" Ucomo said, flustered.

"If that plan works, you *are* a war hero. And how's your analysis coming?"

Ucomo was immediately all business. "The kzinti are still unaware that we can monitor their message lasers by observing trace effects on interstellar dust and gas. Their encryption remains uninspired. I believe I've figured out why they always call us Smart; the prisoners they take naturally address one another formally, being mutual strangers at peace with one another, and kzinti speech lacks the overtones needed to distinguish the word Ally" [*pi'rrin*] "from the word Smart" [*Pierin*]. "Given that the words undoubtedly have a common origin, this is not unreasonable."

"It certainly makes more sense than the theory that they're being polite," Dabak agreed. "Is there any sign that the kzinti can monitor us?"

"I believe there would be no sign if they could," Ucomo said. "To combine clarity with brevity our communications are in Ancestral mode. We are descended from creatures that spent some time living in shallows, before the oceans became too dangerous, and our brains still possess structures designed to grasp 3-D sonar pulses. This is why it's so difficult for most males to express a thought unless it's completely formed, but it also means that we get far more information out of holographic data than any alien could. If they broke our encryption, the kzinti would obtain only linear and visual information from our messages. Even their sonar-using slaves use it primarily for vision equivalence. Incidentally, I'm convinced the kzinti believe our females are nonsentient, like theirs."

Dabak went rigid with amazement, and stayed immobile for at least ten heartbeats. Then he said, "*Why?*"

"Because they never see them."

"They never see them for the same reason *we* never see their Patriarch!"

"Of course. But it's well for an enemy to have false beliefs. Oh, and they've found another alien race. Quite numerous, apparently. A fleet is being assembled to invade one of the aliens' planets, and since the force we face is the largest they have deployed, it will be contributing the largest number of ships. I intend to recommend to your Mother that we strike just as the convoy is formed, to maximize disruption."

"What are the aliens like?" Dabak wondered.

"I couldn't find anything about that. The annoying thing about spying on carnivores is they don't give enough information to each other, either. However, 'the enemy of my enemy is my weapon,' after all. Whatever else they're like, they're *useful*."

"True," Dabak said. "Well, maybe they can keep the kzinti distracted for a few years."

AQUILA ADVENIO

◆ ◆ ◆

Hal Colebatch and
Matthew Joseph Harrington

Prologve

Jegarvindertsa gestured with two of their arms at small details in the center of the picture the ship's roving cameras presented. Another of their arms enlarged the section, filtering out the vast plume of black smoke and ash clouds.

Under the organization of uniformed members of their own species, the surviving bipeds from the towns the volcanic eruption had destroyed were lining up to receive food.

Others, with weapons and without, were setting up temporary wood and fabric dwellings with material being unloaded from primitive oar- and sail-powered sea vessels and beasts of burden. Some bipeds, evidently injured, were being carried on litters. Details could be seen clearly.

In the days of their trade empire the Jotoki had dealt with many worlds, and not all the knowledge of sapients' behavior which they had accumulated then had been lost in the generations of long and terrible war. Following age-old procedures that had become almost reflexive, they had sent down camouflaged cameras and listening devices among the aliens, had translated their speech and recorded their organization, economics, sociology. There were still a few among the Jotoki remnant whose trades included the once-proud occupation of alien sociotechnician. Despite these beings' unpleasantly suggestive appearances and primitive technology, it was obvious to the watchers what was going on.

"They cooperate. They have organized disaster relief as well as a military caste. This is a civilization."

Jufadirvanlums's mouths formed into shapes venomous with disapproval: "You would still have us recruit *more* alien mercenaries."

It was a statement. An accusation, not a question, part of a long-going debate.

Jegarvindertsa raised themselves on two arms. Their gesture was in the affirmative. "What else are we to do? Half the gun mountings in our fleet are unserviced. Our asteroid miners can still fabricate infantry sledges, and we have no infantry. Do you think we can fight a war against the cursed ones without troops to ride them into battle? A war of machines? Have our failures shown you nothing?"

"And have you learnt nothing? 'The finest security force the spiral arm can give,' our ancestors said when in their mad folly they trained the cursed ones."

"These are different."

"How can another Iron-level culture whose members revel in killing one another be different? They even look enough like the cursed ones to suggest they come from the same spores!"

"These are omnivores. They have cities of a sort. And laws."

"So had the cursed ones, when those-whose-names-are-obliterated first recruited them, to our ruin."

"These are, we maintain, different. See how these organized ones even seem to feed their own poor and unfortunate. They have rudimentary medicine and public works. Like our own ancestors, they are seagoing, and you will observe that some of those ships, at least, are built for carrying cargo—they are for trade, not war."

"They have no shortage of war."

"What use would they be to us if they were herbivorous pacifists? But their military culture is not only tough and versatile, it's well disciplined. Institutionally disciplined. The fact they have uniforms shows that: Their ranks are indicated and they depend on more than mere physical strength to see orders are obeyed. They give their slaves rights: They cannot be killed or mutilated without process of their courts."

"In theory!"

"In theory, at least. They have art and poetry—a little—that is more than merely battle songs." Their voice changed as another segment took up the argument. "Also, they have administrative ability, unlike the cursed ones."

"All of which will make them more dangerous enemies, when they turn against us."

"Have you no more sense than when you were tadpoles? Our progenitors dealt with many races in peace, successfully and to the benefit of all. Our civilization was not for us alone. And long it endured. Here, on a barbaric planet, we see others who have a civilization." They fiddled with the viewer. "Now *there* is something interesting!"

They increased the magnification: "You see those beings that have a place of honor, the trumpet players. What is it they wear about their upper segment? The skin of a creature that bears a strong resemblance to a certain other creature we know too well."

"You would have us risk too much. Better to flee at once with all of our kind that are left."

"We have no choice. We must have more troops!"—repetition had always been an important arm of rhetoric for Jotoki when both speaker and listener had five brains, one or more of which might be distracted—"We have fought for millennia as the cursed ones gathered strength, suffering defeat after defeat, losing planet after planet. Only the size of space has saved our remnant so far. Our whole civilization trembles on the verge of extinction. And we, we are its trustees!" Their arms waved in frustrated anger. "Look at this ship! How many dry and empty breeding and sleeping ponds does it contain? How many of our guns and machines are work-ing with jury-rigged servomechanisms? We expect mechanisms to make combat decisions! Our machines can build us more ships, as long as computer memories function and there are planets and asteroids with metal in them. *We* cannot reproduce so easily, or train tadpoles in a single cycle! We spread ourselves thinner and thinner among our escorts, our gun turrets, our fighters. We are a fleet of shell crews propped up by mechanisms."

"If we had the Trade Council—"

"The last of the Trade Council, may we remind you, has long been eaten. We and our dwindling armsful of worlds remain. The last of the Jotoki to stand."

"The last we know of."

"It comes to the same thing. What choice do we have?"

"And do you think iron-using primitives can help us in space battles?"

"Eventually, yes. We also need to hold planets as well as take them. That means infantry, and it is infantry that we lack."

"If we must take them, we must take them from somewhere remote. Leave no witnesses to tell the cursed ones when they come of our presence."

Jegarvindertsa gestured at the scenes of devastation the cameras were still recording.

"Did you see the boat that was nearly destroyed when it rowed too near the eruption? It was one of their more elaborate and ornate craft. Were those on board actually *investigating* the eruption from abstract curiosity? The one who went ashore from it, who walked toward the eruption and died on the beach: He was richly dressed by their standards, and had attendants. We wish we had picked up his last words . . . Did we see a primitive martyrdom for science?

"They fight wars to stop barbaric customs among the tribesmen on their own frontiers," they continued. "They actually expend their own soldiers for an abstract idea of civilization."

"And enslave those they conquer."

"Doesn't every intelligent race before it learns economics? But they allow some of their slaves freedom eventually. They are traders, like us. Real traders. Merchant ships, warehouses, currency, courts. We say these beings actually care about civilization."

"They care about gold."

"So do we. So do you. Those who care about gold we can deal with. But we will say another thing. These beings are resilient. Their barbarians beat them occasionally but they always come back. We have a little time. We can watch them awhile."

Both Jotoki entities were using all five of their linked brains. The argument went on, as the world turned beneath them.

I

AD 2554

"Basically, I am a dealer in exotic slaves." The tall kzin drank with an expression of relish from the goblet of *vatach* blood his host had offered. "Like that one."

He gestured to the shackled female human who squatted,

trembling, at his feet. The creature flinched at the gesture, its wide terrified eyes darting back and forth between the great felinoids as if it was trying to understand their speech. There were drops of skin-excreted liquid on its face, and its chest heaved. Both kzinti could sense its terror, a stimulant to kzinti senses.

The Marquis Warrgh-Churrg, largest landowner of the planet of Kzrral's main northern continent, regarded his guest with a look of moderate surprise. He reclined at ease on a couch, like a smaller, softer, indoor version of the stone *foochesth* that were a feature of some kzinti parks.

"Between worlds? I would not have thought there was a living in it. We have not found much trade along those lines worthwhile since the war losses to our spacecraft." There was nothing obviously threatening in his words or the tense he employed, but lying half-curled on the *fooch* his huge bulk dominated the room and all within it.

"It is not necessarily a good living," replied his guest. "These are difficult times. The Patriarch has said that a Hero's duty now is to survive and the duty of us all is to rebuild our strength as a race for the . . . future. Noble and Dominant One, I trade"—the Hero's Tongue carried an inflection of distaste—"in other high-value items too, precious stones, rare elements, W'kkai puzzles, silk from Earth, even bulk gold if there is enough *marrgin* in it. Liquors, perfumes, and cordials too, at times. I hope that before I leave I may present you with a few samples and recipes in some return for your noble hospitality . . ."

The magnate inclined his great head.

"But rare slaves are the mainstay," his guest continued. "Trained, clever ones. As you are aware, the prime sources of monkeys are lost to us."

"You profit from the misfortunes of our kind? Do you have bulk gold in your ship at this time, then?"

"I make a living from mitigating those misfortunes, enabling Heroes to live as Heroes should despite the worst the monkeys can do. Though we were long ago driven from *Ka'ashi*, we still have upon some of our own worlds a few breeding colonies of such slaves who were brought there before the truce. It is a trade the *humans*"—the Hero's Tongue carried an even stronger inflection with that term, black lips drawing back to show a collection of daggerlike fangs—"would not approve if they knew of it. But yes,

Noble and Dominant Marquis Warrgh-Churrg, I have a little gold. Largely monkey-minted coins. You may imagine how I acquired them. Not all humans are sufficiently wary of us in these times."

"What if humans should come upon you in space?"

"Space is large. There is little chance of that. And after all, we are in a state of *truce*. But should they do so, I trust I have not forgotten the heritage of my Sires."

"You have kittens? Surely they would grow old and die while you were between worlds. You would not see them."

"My kits must fend for themselves for long, as in the olden time. As I say, and as we all know too well, these are difficult times for many of our kind. But there are ways to save time."

"You have a hyperdrive?" There was a sudden sharpness in the other's question. There was tense silence for a moment between the two, broken only by the splash of water from the fountain that dominated the court: a great golden bowl, held aloft on the sculpted backs and shoulders of four golden humanoid slaves. The wide-eyed human flinched and sweated. The off-world kzin twitched ears and tail expressively, replying in a tone submissive but urbane:

"Not I personally, Honored Host. You have seen my ship. But yes, your observation is shrewd and correct. My principals on my homeworld have access to one of the few hyperdrive units which the humans allow us and are aware of, though whether they know the use we put it to is another matter. We pay them a large bribe not to take excessive interest in us—monkeys, as you know, have little or no honor—but it sadly inflates all our operating costs. However, it makes long journeys feasible. At present it is parked several weeks away."

"You are not your own master, then?"

"Only as far as ship captains usually are. I report ultimately to others."

"A telepath could show us your superluminal ship's location."

"Only if he could read a mechanical brain. It is encoded in my own ship's computer. And that will self-destruct if tampered with by anyone unauthorized."

"Such difficulties have been overcome before."

"I doubt they would be in this case, my principals are very security-conscious. Perhaps even overly so. But my alive and physiologically healthy presence in my ship is necessary for it to respond to the activating code words and pattern-recognition logic. Coercing me or using parts of my dead person to gain access would be futile."

"The Patriarch has few hyperdrive ships. We lost most of our ships in the wars, and the accursed UNSN has informed us what their response would be to any large-scale rebuilding program."

"The Patriarch's Admiralty keeps such things for military purposes, and its security is strict. It has, I am sure, a building program for a fleet that will one day enable us, at last, to . . . Urrr. The humans allow us a token fleet, presumably thinking that such a scrap will satisfy us. . . ." His voice trailed off. After the Second War with Men, humans had greatly restricted kzinti access to the hyperdrive again, but any kzintosh knew what the Patriarch's fleet would be looking to do one day.

"However, Dominant and Feared Warrgh-Churrg, if I cannot offer you the technology of the hyperdrive, I can perhaps offer you a profitable trade. On my way here I noticed human slaves in the streets. As other visitors have told me, you have *kz'zeerekti* on this planet."

"*Kz'zeerekti*? Yes."

"Like this one?"

"The same sort of thing, yes." Warrgh-Churrg made a negligent, regal gesture with his tail at the sculptures and to one of the floor mosaics, showing somewhat stylized humanoids and other beasts arranged with hunting and leaping kzinti amid fylfots and patterns of battlements and teeth. His tail wave also took in a couple of stuffed specimens bearing another golden bowl and one posed in a fighting crouch with its puny fingers extended and its mouth open to scream. His hall was further adorned with the heads of several species, kzinti among them, but also a fair-sized troop of simians. "Got a few live ones around too." His gesture also took in a live simian in slave's drab peering at them from a distant archway. It turned and fled from sight.

"You hunt them?"

"Oh, the wild ones, yes." Warrgh-Churrg indicated his trophy belt, adorned with a proud showing of dried simian ears along with kzinti ones, taking in as he did so the similar but smaller collections on his guest's belt.

"Are they intelligent?"

"They are trainable, clever like trained Jotoki, but less reliable.

Unless caught as infants, they are not trusty slaves. But," he added, "trained up young they can be useful."

"Where do they live? In the forests?"

"Mainly in the south. The forest belt and the hot savannah beyond. Probably also in the badlands."

"Are they common?"

"I have not counted them. I chased them when I was a kit, as my own kits do now, and still I hunt there sometimes when I visit my southern estates. Some southerners hunt them regularly." Warrgh-Churrg's body language indicated that while he was pleased to display the visible signs of affluence in his palace, his interest in the *kz'zeerekti* habitat was less than overwhelming. His guest adopted a tense-of-polite-request, humble but not too humble.

"Forgive my curiosity, Noble Host and Marquis Warrgh-Churrg, but my interest is professional. How did they get here?"

Warrgh-Churrg shrugged his ears in a dismissive gesture.

"We had Heroes in the first fleet to *Ka'ashi*. Some may have returned with *kz'zeerekti* slaves. I had relations among them. And other Heroes came later. Possibly new slaves mixed with the locals . . .

"Some of the landowners want to get rid of them altogether. As slaves, the adult-caught ones are never very reliable. We tried castrating them and removing their teeth and fingernails, but we found that, often enough, that only made them more savage. And, eunuchs being eunuchs everywhere I suppose, they often joined with our own kzinti eunuchs in the harems and elsewhere to plot and spread disloyalty."

"Still, on other worlds human slaves can command a very high price now," Trader told him. "My principals have the resources to buy many if they are suitable—whole troops of them. They would send ships to collect them. They are still popular on Kzinhome."

"Even after the monkeys burnt our fleets and took *Ka'ashi* back?"

"They took more than *Ka'ashi* in the First and Second Wars. But exactly. That is a large part of the reason why human slaves are in demand, apart from the sport the best of them can give in the hunt. It reminds us in these unfortunate times that they are not all-conquering, and that times can change. You may have a great source of wealth here."

"I have much wealth already, Trader." Warrgh-Churrg again gestured expansively about the room, heavy with gold, hung with lustrous purple, panels on floors and walls bedizened with intricate stones, their tiles slanted minutely to catch the shifting sunlight in changing pictures and patterns.

"Feared Warrgh-Churrg, that is plain from the magnificence of your abode and of your hospitality. Still, perhaps there are things I can offer . . . with trade between the stars so limited by the cursed *kz'zeerekti* . . ."

Warrgh-Churrg nodded, his ears and tail twitching thoughtfully.

"Urrr. I will speak to Estate Manager. We will perhaps discuss this later. Now I shall prepare for the entertainment tonight."

"I am looking forward to it. I respectfully seek your leave to return to my ship and prepare on my own account, that my apparel and grooming may be less unworthy of your hospitality."

Trader bent while Warrgh-Churrg sprayed a little urine on him, an archaic lordly gesture signifying to all kzinti that he was the magnate's guest and under his protection. Trader exposed his throat and belly in the equally ancient ritual gesture of submission and Warrgh-Churrg dismissed him with a gracious flick of his tail.

The offworld kzin departed with decorum, striding through the great doors and down the wide snowy street toward the space port, the bowed, shackled human scurrying behind on its lead.

II

The inner door of the airlock closed behind the kzin and the human. Both moved differently as they stepped into the main cabin. The gravity-planer, running with a low, continuous purr, reduced gravity here to 61 percent of Earth, the gravity of Wunderland in which both had been born and grown up. The human removed her shackles and they sat down together in the control cabin. A touch on a keyboard opaqued the windows.

"Ginger, did I do all right?" asked the human. She rubbed her chilled bare feet, and slipped out of her brown slave's robe and into a modern fabric overall.

"I thought you acted convincingly scared," said the kzin in Wunderland-accented English. "A veteran couldn't have done better."

"I wasn't acting! I was bloody terrified!"

"I know. So was I. It's a scary job. You'll get used to it."

"I couldn't feel I'm much of a replacement for Simon."

"Simon was good. A good partner as well as a good friend. But you'll learn. . . .

"There's a first time for everyone, Pet. First time for piloting an air-car solo, first time for a soldier in battle, first time for walking into a kzinti palace on a kzinti world with a lie. You'll get used to it.

"Bloody *vatach* blood! I need a civilized drink," continued the kzin as he dialed a bourbon and ice cream, "I think you do too. . . . You followed all that, Perpetua?"

"Pretty well," said the woman. "So you've got a party on tonight."

"By the Fanged God! If he wishes to test his son, I hope I can survive it! And *Zianya*! If the Bearded God also loves me, let there not be *Zianya*!" *Zianya* were semi-intelligent animals, highly esteemed as a delicacy on kzinti worlds. The important thing was that they be torn to pieces alive at table. Their antici-patory terror and subsequent death-agonies with the first tearing bites set up a hormonal reaction that gave what was generally considered a particularly delicious flavor to their meat. "They make me sick!"

"But that's hardly the important thing."

"No. There are *kz'zeerekti* here, even if he's a bit vague about them."

"He's obviously not too interested in monkeys."

"His body language suggested he may be more interested than he lets on. He wants to establish it's a seller's market. But he said of the slaves from Wunderland that 'they mixed with the locals.' Odd. Very odd. They would hardly have just let slaves go to breed in the bush."

"Perhaps they escaped."

"Even so. But odder than that . . . 'mixed with the locals'? What locals? Convergent evolution? And mixed how? Could they interbreed? From different planets? Have you ever heard of such a thing?"

"No, never. But is that what he was suggesting?"

"I thought it was ambiguous," said the kzin, "but if he means the humans from *Ka'*—from Wunderland . . . mixed with the locals . . . It sounded as if he meant 'interbred.' I'm aware of problems with dialect, but yes, I think that's what he meant."

"You know, he didn't specifically say that they'd brought Wunderlanders back. Maybe he was just getting your interest up. I mean, convergent evolution can hardly be *that* convergent! Creatures from different planets—different stars!—can't interbreed."

"Well," laughed the kzin, rippling his ears, "Simon and I always said we could trust each other with our wives." The laughter ended.

"How is his wife?" the human asked.

"I saw her before we left. I think she'll be all right. She's strong. But he's a loss. Simon the Simian."

He touched a pad on the control console with a black, ripping-chisel claw and a hologram of the planet shivered into shape above it. Kzrral's polar and subpolar continents were colored green, with ice fields in the polar regions and mountains. It was 1.2 times the diameter of Earth, but with a smaller iron core giving it comparable gravity. It was warmer than Earth overall, though with extensive temperate zones in the high latitudes. A telltale far in the north of the largest continent marked the main kzinti settlement and their own position. At latitudes lower than 30 degrees savannah and then jungle belts were indicated, turning to wastelands while still many degrees from the equator; there, the seas steamed, and only a few mountaintops rose above ceaseless convection storms. The south pole was landless, though there was a small cap of water-ice sitting on the shallow seafloor, and some minor landmasses in the southern ocean. The planet was mostly hotter than Earth or Wunderland, much hotter than Kzinhome. Perpetua thought for a moment how fascinating a human biologist might find life-forms adapted to live in or pass through those near-boiling equatorial seas and steam-heated lands.

"In the tropics there could be anything," the kzin commented. "Kzinti wouldn't have much interest in it."

"Unless population pressure forced them into the tropics." Perpetua was tentative. A human-historical specialist, transferred out of academia as human Space geared up for another possible war, kzinti culture was all still largely academic for her. She had, she felt, reason to be tentative. Her experienced predecessor had either overestimated his own knowledge of that culture or been unlucky.

"Not a problem here. There are about a thousand estates on this continent, and they haven't yet occupied all the prime hunting territory by a long way yet."

"Quite a small population."

"About twenty-five thousand males in the whole northern hemisphere. Plus several times that number of females, of course, and kittens."

There had been quite a lot more before, and there would be again, as soon as the kittens grew up. Kzrral had lost a lot of males in both wars, as well as most of its spaceships. The economy was still a long way from recovering from that loss. The kzinti had come as colonists with their own spaceships, and before the wars they had never needed to build a great new spaceflight industry with the communication that led to.

"Always a backwater planet, relatively poor in mineral production—nothing to attract a huge population, and a good incentive to the kzinti already settled here not to welcome others. Why open up your world to competitors for territory?"

"Military security? A bigger population means you can support a bigger army."

"Against whom? We met everything in space and swallowed it up. No one was going to attack *us*! Worse luck, a lot of kzinti thought—no space-traveling races with the warrior skills to give us good sport. Well, we know better now. As for the Patriarch's regular forces, there would be no point in building up armed forces to defend against *them*. If they wanted such a planet they could take it. No doubt communications with the homeworld emphasized how mineral-poor it was, and presented the local kzinti as a loyal garrison of Heroes holding it for the Patriarch in case of need.

"I'd say this planet, with its wide continents in the cool-temperate zone we like, became a kind of paradise of spoiled, land-rich kzinti. Plus one small city for those who liked business or recreation there, also supporting one spaceport. There are a number of such worlds in the Patriarchy.

"Then, as the First War with Men got under way, a lot enlisted in the Patriarch's Navy. Of course freebooters also took off in their own prides seeking Names and riches, and relatively few came back at the end of it all. It cut the breeding rate, too, because a lot of the survivors had their genes scrambled by radiation, but weren't about to give their kzinretti to anyone else to breed from. Fertile males tried to steal kzinretti when they saw the sterile males holding them, and that led to more fighting. I'd guess that Warrgh-Churrg expanded his lands by incorporating estates that had no heir powerful enough to hold them.

"Anyway, you understand that population pressure is not usually a problem on kzinti worlds. A good war is population control and fun at the same time. Did you know that the First War with Men was the first time in a long while that the kzinti population of most of the planets involved actually *increased*? They stopped fighting each other and stopped killing surplus kittens."

"That's a thought."

"It was a thought for many of us on Wunderland, when we worked through the implications. It was a thought that was present at the birth of kdaptism: Stop fighting, and life is longer and better."

"Well, obviously."

"Only in hindsight. Most kzinti don't grasp it even yet. I might remind you it's a fairly recent concept among men, too."

"Not all that recent."

"To be willing to die for peace? And not just in ancient legends?"

"Kdaptists will do that?"

"Did you get *any* training?" Ginger exclaimed.

"A little. But they said there wasn't the time or resources. With the probability of another war so high . . . They said to ask you."

"That's what they told me, too, when I protested about an inexperienced partner: 'Get them out while you can! Teach her on the job!' If it makes you feel better, however, it's been said that in this job, like any other sort of martyrdom, mere willingness is a very large part of the qualification."

"It doesn't make me feel a great deal better, actually. Martyrdom is not my first ambition."

"It's not invariably a volunteer job. Kdaptism first spread during the aftermath of the first human victory on Wunderland among those—computer nerds and telepaths, a lot of them—who suddenly realized they were sick of being barbarians. And a few officers and soldiers who'd listened to Chuut-Riit and had lived with human slaves, later led by at least one genius in the form of Vaemar. So you had kzinti on post-Liberation Wunderland who gave themselves names like Mister Robinson, and eventually kzinti like me, who probably talk too much even if we still have secret self-conferred kzinti Names that we cling to. It's less a religion than a set of attitudes and a long-term . . . well, perhaps 'dream' is as good a word as any. Whatever it is, it's all another reason I'm glad great-great-grandsire stayed on Wunderland after the First War."

"You don't envy Warrgh-Churrg, then?"

"I told you, he scares me. . . . I wonder what he'd think of a kzin who admitted fear to a monkey?"

"That's quite a thought. I think I'll have a drop of that bourbon myself. Any sign of kdaptism here?"

"None that I can see. The most visible signs are of vehement persecution, of course. The Blackfurs—priests—have always had the attitude of the Inquisition. With the ability to smell heretics."

"Well, if there are any here, I hope they don't have a nose for you either."

"Unlikely. We're rare, and very rare off Wunderland."

"They have Jotoki here. They're an exotic species."

"They have them pretty well everywhere in the kzinti worlds," said the kzin. "Useful creatures. Prey animals *and* mechanics in one! And the feral ones cunning and dangerous enough to give Heroes decent sport. A hint of what humans might have been if the wars had gone differently. I'm glad they didn't."

"I know that, Ginger."

"Anyway, it seems there is something in the reports. Despite Warrgh-Churrg's lack of specificity, there may be unrepatriated slaves here. What did you think about the ears? I didn't want to be seen looking too closely."

"They *might* be human. But it was hard to tell. The slaves we saw shuffling round *might* have been human too, under those sacks they wore—I didn't see that they weren't, anyway."

"I'll have to get on a hunt."

"Will that be possible?"

"I don't know, but I don't see why not. A part of hospitality, and it could be very beneficial for him. He likes gold. I could see that, all right. And his ears twitched when I mentioned that I trade in it."

"He certainly seemed to have plenty of it around."

"Which is an infallible sign that he wants more. Excuse me, Perpetua, I'd like to brush my fangs. That *vatach* stinks. As if his piss wasn't enough to put up with!"

"Won't they be offended?"

"Let them think it's an exotic offworld custom. They expect offworlders to smell funny. Mark you, this place smells odd to me itself."

"How do you mean?"

"It's hard to say. The closest I can come is, it's not pure kzinti. Or not any pure kzinti I know. The large windows are the most obviously strange thing. I've never seen that in a major kzinti dwelling before."

"Different worlds, different styles, I suppose."

"Even the Patriarch's palace wouldn't have them so close to the ground. He must be very confident."

"Aren't all kzinti confident? Or fearless?"

"They try to be. If they have fears, only Telepaths know about it, which is one reason Telepaths of the Patriarchy are hated and despised—and short-lived. But big windows are a definite cultural statement. . . . Our footprints in the snow as we came back—there was something odd there too, but I can't get my claws into it. . . . Apart from a few slaves, who did we see as we returned?"

"Other kzinti."

"Yes, and they took you for granted."

"I hadn't thought of that!"

"Human slaves are not rare. Well, that may be understandable. . . . But there was something else. By human standards kzinti culture is pretty uniform, with some local variations, but I get a feeling that there is something different here, something non-kzinti . . ." His voice trailed off.

"Can you be more precise?"

"I'm trying . . . gold . . . there's something . . . You don't really walk like a slave."

"I'm sorry."

"It could be fatal for you on some—probably most—kzinti worlds. But here you hardly rated a glance."

"I didn't realize you were watching like that."

"We must *always* watch like that! In this job the vigilant and the dead are the only kinds of operatives they are—though sometimes the vigilant are the dead all the same. Anyway, *we've* used fang paste for five generations and I'm not changing now."

"What if there is a telepath?"

"It would be dishonorable to use one on me unless he can be certain I've lied about something significant. And you may have noticed I've told as few direct lies as possible in case his *ziirgrah* picks them up. Even the occupation 'slave trader' can, with rationalization, be translated into something approximating the truth, since the Heroes' Tongue has no expression for our particular task."

"And does your own *ziirgrah* pick up anything?"

"This feeling of oddness, which, no, I can't be more precise about. And that he's keeping a lot back. When I mentioned 'honor'—which was a mistake, by the way; it's slightly bad form to talk about honor to a noble kzin—I felt an odd stiffening. As if he's doing something his own sense of honor is not entirely happy about. I must say that doesn't surprise me much. Any noble kzinti house tends to have plots and secrets, the more subtle and complex because kzinti hardly ever actually lie outright. It makes for certain tensions.

"But I can't see that any plots are remotely likely to be anything to do with us. I don't feel more suspicion emanating from him than kzintoshi usually feel in the presence of strangers like me. But if I feel anything I'll leap it back here and we'll be off. You'd better keep alert in case we have to move quickly."

"Don't you worry about that, I'll not be goofing off. A human doesn't on a kzinti world."

"It would be bad manners—and theft—for anyone else to eat you, unless I get into a duel and lose. Then my property becomes my conqueror's. But we may have to take off in a hurry. By the way, I take it you've noticed these." He pointed to dots of orange light circling the hologram of the planet.

"Orbiting spaceships."

"Yes, they still have a couple of battle wagons, though they look dead. My guess is they're either laid up or have small maintenance crews on board."

"Two ships aren't enough to do much."

"They're big enough to be carriers. And even if not, if they've got weapons systems functioning—and these are kzinti ships we're talking about, so they will have if they're alive at all—they could make any takeoff hairy. If you do have to lift on your own, keep well away from them."

"The alarms are set. All the cloaking devices are ready. And the missiles are armed."

"Good. But I don't think trespassers will be a problem. Now that I've been pissed on I'm formally Warrgh-Churrg's guest . . . though he might send agents to check if I'm telling the truth about the hyperdrive."

"That's a cheery thought. So I'm to wait here tonight listening for the pad of little cat feet while you're partying?"

"Yes. It goes with the territory. Keep your eyes on the sensors and lock yourself in the furthest possible cabin if anything gets in. At discretion, you are to take off. That is an order, by the way, and I'm formally recording it as such. You have your suicide pill if need be. It's unfortunate that buildings here are much closer together than they usually are on kzinti worlds, but you've got a clear field of vision round the ship. . . . I wonder why the architecture is different?"

"Yes, now that you mention it, it looks different even to me."

"But if you think I'm dead, or it seems I can't get back to you, take off fast. I gather they have too few deep-space ships left now to keep many simply sitting around on standby, but the fact we've seen none docked doesn't mean there aren't any—from what he said, they have a few at least—and there are aircraft that could pursue, not to mention beams and missiles, plus whatever war satellites they may have put up in the past. I'm nearly sure those ships they're got in parking orbit are empty, or have only maintenance crews at most." The kzin wrinkled his ears thoughtfully. "But if we do have to run, they will wonder why we affected so much interest in the *kz'zeerekti* here."

"But they won't know. The *kz'zeerekti* will be no worse off than they are already."

"That's probably plenty bad enough, Perpetua. I think he'll let me join a hunt. Don't talk to me in English anymore. From now on I've got to think in the Heroes' Tongue."

"Good luck, Ginger."

"A Hero does not need luck. *Snarr' grarrch.*"

"*Urr.*"

III

Sunset had deepened into night. The gravity vehicles halted near a small observation tower.

Ginger, known to these kzinti as Trader, disembarked from the car which Warrgh-Churrg had lent him, and joined Hunt Master, Estate Manager, and the other local gentry, including one with the accouterments of a full-Named noble, grim-eyed, his jaws set in a permanent snarl. A couple of eights of kzinti youngsters, proudly bedecked with the time-honored weapons of the hunt and with minor, kittenish trophies, frolicked around them. A small squad of guards with modern weapons deployed around the vehicles.

Hunt Master gestured to the others to follow him in single file to the crest of the slope. Trader spat a command in the slaves' patois to the human squatting in the shadow of his car. It prostrated itself and crept back into the vehicle.

Silently, the felinoids moved through the tall grass up the ridge. Three moons, small but with brilliant albedo, cast a bright light and confused patterns of shadow. From the crest there was a panoramic view across a wide valley and plain, to a distant slope dark with vegetation. Instinctively, they had gone down on all fours, crawling forward with bellies to the ground, tails twitching.

"*Kz'zeerekti* country," Hunt Master said. He touched a stud on his helmet and vision-enhancers slid over eyes already far better than those of any human. The other kzinti copied him. "See there!"

The beam of his laser, set to illuminate rather than burn, touched what the others recognized as a scatter of brown, weathered bones on the other side of the river that ran below. It jumped to light other such jumbled heaps nearby. Here and there round, small-toothed skulls stared back at them—convincingly human.

"You recognize the bones of *kz'zeerekti*? Indeed. But it is my duty to point out to you that not all the bones that lie under the sky were owned by monkeys." His laser touched upon what was plainly a kzinti skull, broken and weathered. There was a stir and growl among the youngsters who had been following his pointer. A respected warrior who died in battle might expect his bones to be recovered by his companions or sons for installation in an ancestral shrine. An unblooded kit who perished in his first action far from home often left his bones where they fell.

"*Kz'zeerekti* killed a Hero on Kzrral?" asked one kit, in a tone of outrage that provoked a ripple of amusement from some of the elder kzinti.

"*Kz'zeerekti* have killed many Heroes," Hunt Master replied. "And even more kits. And they have killed not only on Kzrral. Look and you will see. And at present we are but at the marches of one planet's Monkeydom. Look, cubs, and be wise. You too, offworlder. I do not know if the *kz'zeerekti* of this planet will make the slaves you desire."

"When do we see them, Respected Hunt Master?" asked a cub, jumping and rolling on the ground with excitement.

"Probably soon after we cross the valley and climb the next slope into the trees. Be sure, youngster, that they watch for us. You see how short the grass is on the slopes beyond the river? The monkeys burn it to deny approaching Heroes cover. Now arm and armor yourselves as I have shown you." The hunting kzinti's rifles were powerful and accurate repeaters, but antiques for all that: solid-bullet projectors with chemical propellants, *rifles* in the literal sense, not beam-weapons. The kits were given a few scraps of leather "armor."

"By the standards I am used to, these indeed seem fierce *kz'zeerekti*, Respected Hunt Master," Trader remarked. He passed Hunt Master a generous flask of shrimp-flavored bourbon, part of his stock. "But surely they are no match for modern weaponry," he continued. "I wonder you do not simply wipe them out."

"If we use modern science in the hunt—real body armor, overly enhanced heat and other sensors, beam-weapons—where is the sport in that, Trader?" Hunt Master replied, disposing of the bourbon in a single, gracious swig. "Where the training of kits? We might as well simply missile them from the air or from space. Besides, we have come to realize that exterminating a cunning and warlike species would deprive us permanently of both a valuable training asset and a rewarding game. The world would be duller with no *kz'zeerekti*."

"I have heard some of our ancestors regarded the Sol monkeys so. Until they deployed relativistic weapons and acquired the hyperdrive."

"These aren't like that. I have studied them. Indeed to conserve the species, I have often allowed young ones and pregnant females to live when, hunting alone, I came across them."

"Do they ever cross this valley?"

"They go as far as the river, but they never cross it in force. If they did, I suppose it would become a matter of exterminating them. They would be a menace to other game. Rogues or single scouts do cross though. I've found monkey droppings this side of the river a few times. I also found individuals, including that one." He pointed to a weathered skeleton scattered in the grass nearby. "Old villain! He got careless. But when they cross they don't usually attack or draw attention to themselves. I think they spy out the land, with a little thieving. As it is, they occupy only some fringe wooded country here and roam south into the hot savannah and deserts beyond.

"I do have some supplies of special body armor," Hunt Master continued. He could not ask Trader if he wished to avail himself of this without implying an insult to his courage. Kzinti had dueled to the death for saying less.

Trader replied with a casually polite ear twitch, as if Hunt Master's words had been a mildly interesting pleasantry about his collecting hobby, rather than a potentially dire test. Now that they were ready to move, Hunt Master glanced quickly over the kits' armor and weapons.

These were sprigs of landowners and various, mainly minor, nobility and he was tasked not only to train them but also to protect them to an elementary extent. However, any young kzintosh, once weaned, was expected basically to look after himself, and even the games and competitions of young kits were often and deliberately lethal. Apart from the sheer enjoyment, a large part of the purpose of hunting dangerous game on all kzinti worlds was to teach youngsters by experience the difference between the quick and the dead. It was never expected that all would survive their teaching, and a Hunt Master who trained kits without casualties would not be doing his job. Those who survived would be fit for proper warrior training.

"I leave the bones here on purpose," Hunt Master remarked to Trader. "They serve as a valuable reminder."

Weapons at the ready, the kzinti spread out and descended into the valley. Silent as they were, a few small animals scuttled away at their approach and some flying creatures burst noisily into the air out of the low ground cover. The kits, and one or two of the older hunters, leaped at these tantalizing things. They splashed through the wide, shallow river at the valley bottom. All kzinti hated getting wet, and across the deeper channel in the center there were crude fords and weirs of stones that they might have used for stepping, had not Hunt Master stopped them. He had a small rocket gun that fired lines tipped with articulated-tentacle grapnels.

"Fools!" he snarled. "Do you not think the monkeys know the paths? Did they not place the stones? May they not have fixed weapons sighted on each one?" He cuffed a kit marked with four white stripes on its side, who had been first to the river. Some of the kits looked thoughtful as he hurried them, clutching the lines he'd fired across, at points which he selected apparently at random. Once across the deeper channels he kept them on all fours until, wet and foul-tempered, they assembled in a concave bay of dead ground on the other side.

"There," said Hunt Master, "is a sign of *kz'zeerekti* territory. They scratch it on trees and rocks sometimes." He pointed.

"They seem to think in terms of a frontier," Trader remarked. He memorized a copy of the sign.

"Yes, very much so. As I have said, it is as well for them that they don't make excursions in force beyond it."

One kit, falling back with a flying creature clutched triumphantly in his claws, disappeared into the ground with a scream, abruptly cut off. Hunt Master strode to the spot with grim deliberation. The kit lay bleeding in a pitfall, already dying, the wooden spikes at the bottom driven through his body. The spikes were triangular in cross section, with what looked like grooves down each face: a wound couldn't clamp shut, but blood could get out freely. *One* could be lethal in the right spot. The pit held more than sixteen.

"I have already said the *kz'zeerekti* came as far as the river," Hunt Master told the other kits. "You see now that you hunt *real* game."

Krrar Landowner, the sire of the dead kit, furious and ashamed, dashed forward, then fell. A dozen arrows whistled at them. Kzinti reflexes preserved all except one Hero, younger brother of Krrar Landowner, who was struck in the forearm. Rifles blazed into the bushes from which the arrows had been fired. Hunt Master, crouching, ran to the fallen kzin and kicked the vegetation away from around him. A stout rope had been stretched a little way above the ground.

"Stop wasting ammunition," Hunt Master said. "There are no *kz'zeerekti* here. Remember the Fanged God gave you *ziirgrah* and be proud to use it!" *Ziirgrah* was the rudimentary telepathic sense all kzinti possessed which, properly used, allowed them to sense the presence and emotions of game—the terror of *Zianya* at table was an instance—and which in the case of certain rare kzinti could be developed with drugs and training into full telepathy. Since telepaths were not warriors but among the most despised and downtrodden of the kzinti castes—the condition had unpleasant side effects—many kzinti now felt *ziirgrah* was something very impolite to mention. Hunt-Master plainly had no such inhibitions.

"It was another trap, long-set," he told the kits, who were now standing round-eyed and silent, their earlier exuberance greatly modified. "There are many such. This place is well defended."

The arrow had been double-barbed, and was securely lodged in the forearm of the wounded kzintosh, who was dripping orange and purple blood copiously from severed veins and arteries—competent weaponcrafting again, as an ordinary wound would have squeezed down to a trickle. Hunt Master inspected the damage.

"I advise you solemnly to return to the cars for treatment," he said. "I cannot remove this. Tendons have already been cut. Further, I smell poison."

The wounded kzintosh snarled curses at his elder brother. Krrar Landowner, already furious, drew his *wtsai* and the two flew at each other. They rolled down the slope, slashing and screaming.

"We are doing well, as you see," said Hunt Master quietly to Trader. "Two or three casualties already and not a sniff of a *kz'zeerekti* yet, though that noise will certainly have alerted every monkey for miles around. See there!" He pointed to a hole in a jumble of rocks ahead.

"A cave. Should we investigate it, esteemed Hunt Master?"

"That cave, Trader, is one of the openings of a tunnel system the *kz'zeerekti* dug. We entered it when first we became aware of it.

"The main passages were quite spacious. Big enough for a warrior to pass through easily, even with weapons. We soon realized it was a labyrinth of tunnels below tunnels. What we did not realize was that it was threaded with other tunnels, too small for a Hero to crawl into but quite big enough for a monkey. Many Heroes died in that system."

The shiver of loathing Trader gave was completely genuine. The ends of his whiskers and the muscles of his flanks tingled at the thought of unyielding rock and earth pressing against them so on either side. Like most felinoids, kzinti loved exploring likely holes and caves but hated spaces which held and confined on any terms other than their own.

"Finally we mapped it, more or less, with ground-penetrating radar, then sealed up all the exits and pumped in nerve gas. There were some, I may tell you, including Noble Trrask-Rarr, who wished to simply turn the whole hill over with a nuclear strike. However the lands of Honored Warrgh-Churrg and others would have been in the path of the fallout. . . . There was talk of building ground-piercing conventional bombs but it was felt that it was not worth tooling up factories for such a one-off use. We turn multifrequency masers on it at irregular intervals and, we hope, cook any monkeys inside. Now and then they come running out, which can be amusing. We wait for them, but on occasion they have ambushed the waiting party. . . . What do you think of your monkeys now?"

"I thought they were tree-swingers."

"Only among other things. The *kz'zeerekti* have unblocked that entrance again recently. No, I do not think we will enter it on this occasion. I was in the tunnels before, and from now on I will allow some other Hunt Master the glory of discovering what surprises they may have installed in there, and how deep they may have dug. Further, our radar shows there are big natural caves further south. They might link up. I believe in hard training but there is no point in throwing kits away for nothing."

"What surprises did they have before?"

"Too many. Not just poisoned arrows and stakes in the darkness. Roof collapses, gases of their own—not as effective as ours, but worthy enough in a confined space—fire, those swords and knives they use, and, increasingly, guns they took from our own dead—or at least I *hope* they took them from our dead. There were feral Jotoki, too. They cooperated with the monkeys."

"Strange," said Trader. "I know of feral Jotoki on many worlds, in many hunting preserves. But unless they are trained young they are solitary and savage. I have never heard of them behaving cooperatively before, least of all with another species. Anyway, it seems these monkeys of yours are smart."

"I doubt you'll find them good slaves. At least, not without a lot of breaking in and culling. However I have not had the opportunity to travel to other worlds and I do not know what the fashions may be. Perhaps some like savage little animals for their own hunts."

"Kill them all!" snarled Trrask-Rarr. "Why tolerate a plague on our planet?" He glared at Trader and Hunt Master as if defying them to say differently. An insult or an aspersion cast by one kzin on another could explode into a death duel in an instant, but the full-named Noble knew both were under the protection of Warrgh-Churrg, and an attack on his people would be an attack on the magnate himself.

Trader, avoiding any overt gesture of either insolence or subservience to the snarling kzin, made a diplomatic answer: "It can be difficult to throw things away sometimes." It was about as far as he could go in exploiting Warrgh-Churrg's protective power; and the association of *kz'zeerekti* with inedible offals did seem to amuse Trrask-Rarr.

"You said, you *hoped* they had taken guns from your dead," Trader prompted Hunt Master.

"Yes. They certainly shot at us with guns; the alternative supposition is that they made their own. I like that idea less."

"Do they have any technology?"

"Some. They sometimes wear pieces of metal armor, so I suppose they have smelters somewhere." There was no interest in Hunt Master's voice or body language. Kzinti were as curious as any other cats when on the hunt, but sustained abstract curiosity was a fairly rare trait in them—their intelligences could be very high, but their culture militated against the survival of intellectuals.

"How good could their armor be?" Trader also betrayed no great interest. "You understand their level of competence may be of professional importance to me—and of benefit to this planet, if they are acute enough to be an exportable resource. I have spoken to Honored Warrgh-Churrg but you are the expert and on the spot. Would you say they could be as technologically capable—potentially—as trained Jotoki, for example?"

"I could not say. Their armor is metal alloys. But you may find pieces of it lying around if you wish to see it. There have been hunts here for a long time."

Hunt Master's keen eyes lit on something on the ground. He picked it up and handed it to Trader, bending the flattened, corroded metal back into its original shape with his powerful grip. "This looks as if it was one of their helmets once."

"Worthy Hunt Master, may I keep it to examine?"

"It is of no use to me."

"A Hero collects his enemies' ears for trophies," Trader agreed. His own eyes now recognizing what they sought, he too bent and collected a few more scraps of metal from the ground, stowing them in a belt pouch. He also, as Hunt Master turned away, gathered up a few scraps of weathered bone.

Estate Manager screamed and leapt to one side. There was the sudden unmistakable whistle of a flight of arrows and a sudden turmoil in the bushes on the crest above them. Kzinti screamed with rage and pain, kzinti rifles cracked. Dim shapes could just be made out high in trees too slender for full-grown kzintoshi to climb. A couple fell.

"After them, kits!" cried Hunt Master. "Win your first ears! Anticipate their counterattack and destroy it!"

The youngsters, ululating joyously again, raced for the trees through whose upper branches the shadows of *kz'zeerekti* were fast disappearing. Another flight of arrows made them pause for a moment, but a running kzin among the whipping branches was too fast to be any sort of target. Estate Manager, who had got into the spirit of the hunt by sporting a crossbow of antique design, fired several bolts in rapid succession. The solid thump of a bolt finding its home was followed by a dead *kz'zeerekt* plumping to the ground.

The *kz'zeerekti* screams were not meaningless animal noises, Trader realized. They were taunts and insults in the Hero's Tongue: "Come and get your Name! Come give your ears for my trophy belt! Piss-Licker! Arrow-Target! Coward!" Females too joined in, exploiting all the Hero's Tongue's truly remarkable resources of deadly insults: "Come watch me shit half-digested vegetable matter down on your ancestors' shrines!" At any rate they were effective, kits breaking away and rushing shrieking into battle. Trader saw the white-striped kit completely out of control, screaming meaninglessly. As they passed he found himself fighting down an atavistic impulse to join them.

A couple more adult kzintoshi had been wounded by the first volley: Rress Landowner, and a Senior-Fixer-of-Computers, here in honor for what must have been immense competence. Hunt Master sent them back to the cars with a peremptory voice that brooked no denial. When the hunt turned to battle his orders compelled even nobles of partial Name. Trader followed him to examine the fallen *kz'zeerekti*.

They were pale-skinned under the dirt on their bodies, and, for *kz'zeerekti*, who tended to be spindly and fragile, they were tough, wiry-looking specimens. A male and female. One was dead, killed either by the shots that had brought them down or by the fall. The other was thrashing feebly in terminal "shock," that mysterious alien condition. Hunt Master gave them a cursory glance.

"None of the old-men monkeys I'm after here," he said.

"You know them?" asked Trader.

"Most of the local old stagers, yes. I've even picked up a few words of their language over the years." He bent and placed the sucker of what looked like an electronic book on the mouths of each, holding the dying female still with his extended claws.

"DNA readouts," he explained.

"What do you need them for?" Trader asked with rather elaborate casualness.

"To see if these are part of a local troop or if they've moved here from somewhere else." He dropped the female onto the ground and bent his gaze to the readouts. "Yes, these are locals, related to others I've got recorded here. If a big new *kz'zeerekt* band moves into the area it's as well to know about it."

"You are very thorough, Skilled Hunt Master."

"Got to know your monkey. I pick up what I can about them when things are quiet. Not like Trrask-Rarr."

"The Full-Named one? How so?"

"He's a Noble coming down in the world. To add to his troubles, the monkeys have raided his lands and destroyed some of his hunt-beasts' pastures. Not a great thing, but he hates them. I mean *really* hates them."

"Have any in the hunt used telepaths?" That was a delicate question. No fighting kzin liked admitting association with telepaths. They had mainly military uses, and to suggest to a hunter that he accepted aid from such despised creatures might be taken as an insult. Hunt Master, tough, hulking, hard-bitten, and scarred, with a good collection of kzinti as well as simian ears on his belt ring, did not look like the sort of kzintosh one would duel lightly. However, perhaps because of his orders to cooperate with the trader, he evidently decided to take it as a mere professional question.

"No. One picks things up. They shout insults, sometimes the kits shout things back. One follows tracks, spoor, droppings, you pick up some knowledge of their ways. Where they'll hide, where they'll ambush, where they'll dodge and flee, whether they'll use poison or pitfalls, how they'll provoke the kits. Some of the rascals really have personalities of their own. You come to know which are likely to arrow you from behind, which to dig pitfalls, which may stand and fight. But it's *Marrrkusarrg-tuss* I'm really after."

"Who?"

"Their local leader."

"They have Names?"

In the Hero's Tongue the word "Name" had huge significance, something far beyond "Title" or "Honorific" or "Designation" or "Description." A partial Name signified Nobility, the highest Valor, and Heroism, a limited right to breed. Names had to be earned or won and not even the Patriarch's offspring were given them at birth. A Full Name signified these things with a quantum leap of intensity.

The idea of any non-kzin having a Name was, to a kzin of the old school, a contradiction in terms, though after two wars devastatingly lost to the humans some kzinti attitudes were changing, and not, Trader thought, only among the Wunderkzin—the kdaptist families of Wunderland, like his own. Kzinti had, for purposes of identification and communication, in their first major war against a spacefaring enemy since they overthrew the Jotoki millennia before, come to identify human warships by their own odd names: *Missouri, Graf Spee, Ark Royal, Yamato, Blue Baboon, Male Mandrill,* and so forth, and individual humans as well: simply to refer to "the monkeyship" or "the dominant monkey" had been unsatisfactory for military intelligence purposes. But on a backwater planet like Kzrral he had not expected the old ways to have altered so.

"They give themselves names. To tell one another apart, I suppose, since they cannot smell and their sight and hearing are poor," Hunt Master said. "It seems the easiest thing to do. Since they attach no honor to them there is no dishonor in us using them."

So even in these circumstances they are subverting your culture a little, Trader thought.

He left the bodies to the trophy-takers and they hurried on to follow the hunt on foot. In the dark trees ahead and above them was a confusion of cries. Another young kzin fell not far away, fangs and claws tearing at a monkey that in turn still slashed with a knife that looked the size of a *wtsai.* There was also a commotion on the ground under the dark bushes away to the left. Trader, night-eyed, saw three young kzinti struggling on the ground with the shapes of Jotoki. Hunt Master must have seen it too, but he affected not to notice. Young kzinti caught and killed—or were killed by—their own prey. Trrask-Rarr was dismembering another simian.

"They're certainly tool-users," said Trader.

"Oh yes, there's even a lot of standardization in their gear." They crossed to the combatants, who had fallen silent.

"I'd like to get one of those knives of theirs. I will gladly part with a piece of gold."

"Take that one, then." He gestured at the two still forms of kzin and simian on the ground, locked together in death. "Neither of them will be needing it again. Two pieces of gold."

"Indeed, it does not become me to offer a warrior such as yourself less than a fair price. Two pieces it shall be."

A crescendo of simian and kzinti screams filled the night. Again the whistle and thump of arrows came to the felinoids' ears. There was the roar of kzinti rifles.

"That sounds like their counterattack," Hunt Master said, "as I warned the kits."

"Counterattack? Is that common?"

"The monkeys often have a reserve waiting. They watch and see what they're up against. If it's seasoned warriors they pull back. If it's kits and youngsters they'll wait till they are engrossed in the chase and scattered, then come up. You see a kit who collects *kz'zeerekti* ears here can feel he's earned them."

"It sounds like a properly organized military culture."

"It is. Well, Trader, how does their potential strike you? Nice house slaves for Kzinhome? Decorous tenders of the Nobility's harems? Would this—" he turned the female over with his foot, its bloody head and slack, splayed limbs flopping and twitching. "—have made a groom for the Patriarch's favorite kzinrett?"

"I suppose it's a matter of catching and training them young, like Jotoki. . . ."

"There!" Hunt Master leapt vertically, claws slashing at something like a huge black starfish in the bushes above.

"Speaking of Jotoki," he remarked, disentangling himself from the pieces, "there was an old rogue. Ready to drop on us. Well, Jotok and monkey meat for all survivors tonight!"

IV

"Seven *kz'zeerekti* dead at least," said Ginger as he reentered the groundcar and closed the hatch, "and eleven kzinti—though eight were kits on their first hunt, and of course it's important to cull the unfit early. But from the kzinti point of view, not a very successful kill ratio. There might have been more *kz'zeerekti* dead that the others carried away. But a successful night for Warrgh-Churrg."

"How so?"

"One of the adult kzinti who died was a small landowner. He had an estate that borders on Warrgh-Churrg's and owed him money. Warrgh-Churrg will pick it up without trouble now. Plus the harem, of course, and the kits if he should happen to want them—and the deceased landowner's eldest kit was among the other dead. A fairly easy night's work for Warrgh-Churrg, letting the *kz'zeerekti* expand his estates for him."

"But a casualty ratio like that? There was nothing like it in the wars, even when human troops were well equipped. How do you account for it?" asked Perpetua. She had kept the car locked in Ginger's absence and herself crouched down inside it, well out of the sight and the attention of the guard—and especially of the furious wounded kzinti as they returned.

"The kzinti sought out the *kz'zeerekti* on their own ground, as usual, and the *kz'zeerekti* had well-prepared traps and ambushes—"

"As usual."

"Tactless, Pet. These *kz'zeerekti* were exceptionally tough with it. And the kits, also as usual, were overexcited, overeager and inexperienced."

"And nobody told them?"

"Hunt Master believes there's no teacher like experience. Between you and me—which is a rather silly phrase in these circumstances—I think Hunt Master had directions to get a few knocked off. With modern life most affluent kzinti households grow up with too many male kits unless they are thinned out one way or another—and this helps thin out the slow and stupid, as well as the overeager who might grow up to be a nuisance by challenging their fathers. It's a rough and ready system, though. Among the kits who survived tonight were some I'd marked down as not the brightest."

"It sounds a pretty unstable society."

"It is, once you come to see it a certain way. Why do you think you humans keep winning wars? One reason my great-grandsire and a few others threw in their lot with humans after the Liberation was because they could see kzinti technology and culture were so grossly out of sync. We're barbarians with high technology, and we're lucky we didn't exterminate ourselves before space travel gave us elbow room.

"Perhaps you understand now something of what I was trying to explain before, about me. We Wunderkzin families are called the ultimate traitors to our species by the Patriarchy, but *we* believe we carry the best ultimate hope of our species' survival, because we see that hope as encompassing a society where half the male children don't have to be killed in the process of growing up; and where there are other ends in life beyond war and hunting. But I'm getting off the point."

"I don't mind, it's all new to me still. I'm eating it up."

Ginger curled his ears at her briefly, then said, "You omnivores have some disturbing turns of phrase. Anyway, Hunt Master limited the technology they used—with modern weapons and detection equipment it would have been a different story and no hunt at all. The *kz'zeerekti* were tough for humans, and had resourcefulness and cooperation. And those Jotoki cooperating with them were very aggressive and well trained. They accounted for several of the young kzinti on their own. Also, they're good in trees; I think it was a Jotok that acted to create a diversion in the branches, to draw the hunt away from the human withdrawal. I've not known them to cooperate with another species before, apart from those specially trained by kzinti slave masters."

"*Kz'zeerekti* on Kzinhome don't speak, do they?"

"Not really. A variety of squeals and grunts. I guess if any evolved speech or intelligence in the past they would have been jumped on pretty quickly."

"And yet these talk?"

"Oh, yes, no doubt about it! Damned cheek, some of it! I heard one of them calling *me* a— Well, I won't go into that."

"Are they truly human?"

"That's for you to say. They certainly seemed to have the usual number of fingers and toes and nipples and things. I kept some tissue samples when they passed out the monkey meat afterwards, as well as some old bones. Here."

"Thanks. How delightful." Perpetua placed the fragments into an autodoc.

"Somebody's got to do the job. And this—" Ginger produced some different tissue—"is a sample of the local Jotoki. Better analyze that too.

"And there are these." Ginger's clawtip stirred the metal fragments spread on the table.

"Smelted, refined, tempered metal."

"Yes. Smart. I'd like to have seen the heads better, but the brain cases looked big. I did get a look at a female's pelvis during the feast, and the birth canal looked big enough for a big-brained head to pass. As far as I know human anatomy, it didn't look unusual. It tasted like ordinary monkey meat. It had a fetus but I couldn't get a good look at that in time."

"...I see."

"Are you unwell?"

"No. Excuse me; I forget sometimes. . . . This helmet: it ought to fit a human head. More than that . . . there's something about it I can't put my finger on. Anything else?"

"I think I've told you most of it, the tunnels and traps and so forth. There were only two *kz'zeerekti* females killed. Maybe that was just chance, but it suggests most of their fighters are male, which suggests moderate sexual dimorphism. What else . . . We passed a sign just after we crossed the river. I memorized it. Let me see—yes. It was like this." He copied some marks onto an old-fashioned pad. "Hunt Master said *kz'zeerekti* used it for marking their territory."

"Hmm, it looks like writing. . . . Why not just zap them from space, or nuke them?"

"If they were going to do that, they should have done it right at the beginning. As a race, we don't like admitting it when we've got a problem. You must have noticed. Further, if too many young males survived there would be a higher level of endemic civil war for territory, especially now without the space war to draw them off. Civil war and generational blood feuds are endemic at a fairly low level anyway, but without a high death rate from other causes—such as hunting—among the young it would escalate. It's an acceptable loss rate, especially without the space war. But I'll tell you something else: There's something odd about Hunt Master. It took me a while to work out what, because it's something you find only relatively rarely among kzinti, but now I'm sure of it: He's a crook."

"As you say, rare in kzinti. Or so all my reading tells me."

"All successful nonviolent crime depends on the manipulation of appearances. That's what he's doing. I think he got a couple of kzinti killed deliberately—adults and kits. No honorable trainer, no matter how lethal and ruthless *as a trainer*, would do that when leading them in the face of an enemy. You see the difference between the two situations?"

Perpetua nodded.

"My *ziirgrah* sense isn't comparable to telepathy, but it's pretty good."

"Then why don't the local kzinti see it?"

"Maybe they don't know what to look for. Weathered old kzintoshi like Hunt Master—tough and hard-bitten even by kzinti standards—tend to be limited in imagination, but almost icons of propriety."

"And another thing. Even if it's not a question of space-based

lasers, why not just push in with modern weapons and take the
kz'zeerekti territory?"

"You feel how hot it is, this far south? I imagine that's why
Warrgh-Churrg is content to let Estate Manager run this place
while he lives it up in his northern palace. As a marquis he
should be living on and dominating the borders personally—the
responsibility of guarding them goes with the title. But we're
really past the edge of the temperature range which kzinti like.
Not too much further south the trees give way to the savannah
and then hot desert and mountains. With this planet's small axial
tilt seasons hardly exist and south of here it's always hot. The
slow rotation accentuates the heat during the day. Further south
again and you're in unending tropic rain and steam. Conditions
as horrible for kzinti as you can get.

"Kzinti don't want the badlands when there's ample land in
the higher latitudes with a cooler climate. Besides, deserts don't
breed enough game or support big-bodied prey. Who wants to
eat rodents or telepath food?

"Also, we have here a fairly plainly defined frontier. Further west
the river broadens into swamps and deltas which kzinti also don't
like, and then on to the sea, which they have very little interest
in. With three moons you get hypertides often enough to make
building near the sea unattractive anyway, and at low tide there
are vast shallows, too shallow to navigate with a sea ship, right
out to the continental shelf. . . . Odd, that. The river should have
cut a very deep channel through the shallows by now. . . .

"Further east, where the aquifer that gives birth to the head-
waters of this river rises, the frontier peters out into mountains
and desert, of no use to anyone.

"Of course, the kzin *could* attack anywhere if they were fighting a war of extermination, whether on foot or with mechanized
forces, but that's not their purpose. But basically, as I said, it suits
them to keep the *kz'zeerekti* for sport and training. Hunt Master
said something to the effect that life would be boring without
them. . . . Apart from the fact that he'd be out of a job—hunting
and getting paid for it!—that any kzintosh would envy.

"The *kz'zeerekti* tunnels puzzle me, though. Hunt Master said a
nuclear strike would poison the surrounding land. But you could
smash them effectively enough in other ways. Drop heavy conventional bombs on them, for example, or scatter mines at the entrances.

You wouldn't even need smart munitions, let alone advanced weapons like disintegrators or walking doomsday dolls. Holding back like that doesn't fit in with kzinti ruthlessness toward an enemy.

"But it does fit in with the pattern of kzinti behavior toward game species on other worlds: We're not bad conservationists, actually, especially where good hunt-beasts are concerned. Better than you've been, as I read Earth history—but of course you can eat anything you find, so why would you bother?

"And it fits with what seems to be an immutable in hunting cultures: When you're dealing with a clever, hardy prey species in difficult hunts, a prey species capable of retaliation, a kind of empathy often develops between hunter and prey. Some of the terms Hunt Master was using for the *kz'zeerekti* have a color of affection about them, the kind a kzintosh in benign mood might use for his naughty kittens. You may have noticed Warrgh-Churrg had some stuffed *kz'zeerekti* specimens as well as heads mounted on his walls?"

"I could hardly help noticing. I didn't get a close look, though."

"Probably beasts considered noble—hard to kill, or somehow courageous *Ya nar Kzinti*. Further, I gather there's occasionally something like a tacit, informal truce between kzinti and *kz'zeerekti*. You'd probably die if you bet your life on it, but I gather from Hunt Master there are times when both species are a little less aggressive toward each other. That's the liver of what puzzles me: Toleration is not a kzinti trait. We conserve species, and we know dead slaves fetch no food and work no factories, but we don't stand any nonsense.

"The mechanics of it I don't understand. And I may be wrong anyway. It's hard to interpret the nuances of body language and ear twitches in a strange culture."

"You say the kzinti don't want a lot of Kzrral because it's got a lousy climate. Surely with modern engineering they could change a lot of the climate, or build large-scale habitats?"

"At this stage it's not worth the effort and expense, not with the present population, and land for all the nobility. Most of those on the hunt had only partial names, indicating there isn't much difficulty in becoming at least a modest landowner. Kzinti government and administration are pretty sketchy on any planet. We don't like paying taxes, and without a lot of slave labor we're not much good at large-scale cooperative projects except war—and you've shown us we could be a lot better at that.

"As a matter of fact," he went on, "since we've begun to study what Vaemar once described as 'those strange Human disciplines'— economics and economic history—we've come to realize many of our wars weren't for hunting territory, or perhaps even glory, but to acquire slaves to pay our taxes for us. Thanks to the Jotoki giving us the gravity drive, we got into space without ever realizing little things like the fact that slavery creates unemployment—and is inefficient to boot. Once we defeated the Jotoki, we nearly exterminated each other because we saw the universe as a glorious prey we could simply drag down and feast upon. If we'd understood economics and administration better, I don't know if you'd have beaten us, hyperdrive or not. . . . One of history's many ironies: None of our enemies came as close to destroying us as the Jotoki did, simply by giving us high technology and powerful weapons so we never had to develop an intellectual or scientific culture. . . . There, how's that for a human thought?"

"Human thought?"

"We Wunderkzin are taught to think like humans. We've had a tradition of good teachers, including Dimity Carmody herself. But there's something else: I'm a kdaptist and a Wunderkzin whose family have been in close contact with humans—and not as conquerors—for several generations. We are the least aggressive, least xenophobic, kzinti that there are: We know we are *not typical*. Perpetua . . . ?"

"Yes?"

"You understand, don't you, that I am not a telepath?"

"Of course! I would never dream of thinking of you as such a thing!"

"It is just that, although I am no telepath, my *ziirgrah* sense is a little more highly developed than that of an average kzintosh."

"My friend, I accept that you are no telepath. I am glad of all the senses the God gave you."

"It is an embarrassment to me. Nonetheless, I cannot ignore its input. There was more going on at the hunt than there seemed.

"It took me a little while to realize how these kzinti are not typical in several ways. I can see all the reasons they tolerate the presence of wild humans or *kz'zeerekti* or whatever they are on their planet—they all look good and sensible reasons to me, but when you remember this is a kzinti planet, with a kzinti culture, it smells odd somehow." He knotted his ears in thought. "Small things. Even the way Warrgh-Churrg lay on the *fooch*."

"The couch?"

"Yes. Kzintoshi normally rest on them after the hunt, when relaxing in hunting preserves, and in the company of members of their own pride, but not as a rule indoors and in front of strange kzintoshi. It makes it a little more difficult to leap up if one has to react to a sudden attack. It's a small thing, but it's part of that slight feeling of oddness. And another thing: The audience chamber was stone, wasn't it?"

"Yes."

"Red sandstone. The sort of re-creation of Old Kzin I've seen on a dozen kzinti worlds. The sort Sire and I have ourselves at home on Wunderland for that matter. But the floor was different somehow. . . . I know! You should have felt it with your bare hairless feet. The temperature changed! In the audience chamber it was warm." Ears knotted again. "But what can that mean?"

"He doesn't like cold feet?"

"But is it significant? Kzinti distrust too much comfort. We like luxury when we can take it, but are hostile to anything that might soften us. But as I was dodging arrows in the night out there I realized what one of the oddities at the spaceport was. The thing I was puzzling about immediately afterwards and couldn't quite get a fang into. We left footprints in the snow. . . ."

"I remember! I was worried I'd get frostbite! But a slave has to know her place."

"The point is, both when we went to the palace together and when I went to the banquet later, I saw human footprints *without* kzinti footprints beside them. Coming back to the ship after the banquet I saw one or two human slaves abroad, at night and unsupervised—and they didn't flee at the sight of me. Warrgh-Churrg has human house-slaves. We saw that. But he said almost nothing about it, despite the fact human slaves were the very subject of our conversation, and ostensibly the very point of my visit to this planet. I saw a couple at the banquet, too—they were carrying food and so forth, and I supposed they cleaned up afterwards—but none of the kzinti referred to them.

"Talk about humans as prey animals and sport, yes! Have human trophies on the walls. But to talk about humans as house slaves, as waiters, perhaps as errand-runners, as the cleaners of those trophies—a sort of tacit taboo. *That's* one of the oddities. Once or twice at the banquet human slaves came bearing meat to me and those near me, and what my *ziirgrah* picked up from my fellow guests was a faint suggestion of an emotion I've encountered in humans often enough but not with kzintoshi—embarrassment! That's something I've never encountered on a kzinti world before. Have *you* ever heard of an embarrassed kzin?"

"You're cats. I've never heard of an embarrassed cat of any kind. It's practically a contradiction in terms."

"It's something to bite at. I feel there's meat there."

"Uh-huh." Perpetua was absorbed in her examination of the inscription and the helmet. "I'm certain this was writing. What's more, these characters are derived from West European letters!"

"So they are from Wunderland. Not a convergent native species."

"That's right, but . . . this language isn't English, or Wunderlander."

"Let me see. If *these* marks had been linked when new, then the characters . . . 'Nihil . . . proficiat . . . inimicus . . .'" Ginger spelled out the words carefully. Human and kzin shook head and ears in puzzlement. Perpetua turned to the helmet.

"What's this?" She pried at the rusted metal. A flake of something fell into her hand. "It's . . . paint?"

"Yes. And look at this piece."

"What about it?"

"First of all, those are beads of glass. They have a sense of decoration. More than that, they have a technology for making glass. Glass is *difficult*. Oh, that's just the beginning. Look at this! Look closely now!"

"How did they do *that*? They have no smelters."

"Haven't they? Hunt Master took it for granted they have them somewhere."

"We're talking high-temperature metallurgy here, not a few molds in a charcoal fire to make bronze or something—though even that would be significant enough."

"Maybe the Jotoki made it," said Perpetua. "They had high technology. Their gravity motors got as close to the light-barrier as one can get without the hyperdrive shunt." Ginger knotted his ears down in a gesture of puzzlement.

"You've got to train Jotoki young, practically from the time they're tadpoles. Feral Jotoki are feral forever. But human or Jotoki, if they had smelters, even primitive ones, kzinti satellites would detect the smoke plumes—for that matter, since practically all kzinti satellites have military capabilities and military sense enhancers, the heat sources would stick out like the Patriarch's testicles after a battle!"

"You're a kzin. You're allowed to say that?"

"It implies no disrespect, quite the reverse. But setting our cultural differences aside, I have the idea reinforced that these particular monkeys have more to them than meets the eye."

"Did you get any idea how many there are?"

"Hunt Master says there are different troops, and he doesn't know how far south their territory extends. I doubt he's got the means to count them."

"Would someone lend him a satellite?"

"If they were a major threat the high-tech response would be quick enough. As it is, who cares?"

"Could the monkey lands reach the equator? Maybe even into the southern hemisphere?"

"I doubt it. Near the equator it's too hot. The seas nearly boil. But they might extend a long way toward it. You monkeys are adaptable and sometimes tougher than you look."

"This whole situation could pose us problems. We've got the bullion to buy individual unrepatriated slaves from individual owners and the ship to get them home. But this sounds like a much bigger business. It'll mean putting repatriation on an industrial basis."

The autodoc beeped. Colored blocks appeared on its screen.

"Human DNA," said Perpetua. "So these *are* runaway slaves, not a native species. In fact, I'm taking it closer . . . now this is odd, very odd."

"What?"

"Look at that profile. What was the principal source of human slaves?"

"Wunderland, of course. They were shipping them out in herds—sorry; wholesale—during the occupation. Very few from other planets. There aren't many prisoners from space battles."

"Exactly. And Wunderland was settled by a North European consortium with a few Japanese and South Africans. Of course the whole human race was getting pretty mixed up by that time, and racial profiling can be misleading in any case. But Wunderland DNA tends to be recognizable, simply as coming from a particular melting pot. Here, though, according to the templates a lot of this DNA profile is far *less* variegated. As if it's from a population that's been separate much longer than Wunderland. And I see Southern European—Iberian, Italian, a bit of North African; plus either Irish or very old Scots. And a surprisingly strong presence of something that the library shows looks close to old Welsh, but not quite.

"Certainly there are Celts and some Anglo-Saxons on Wunderland, but the rest are minority groups; and I doubt you'd ever find a DNA profile like this anywhere there. I've tested the fresh meat and the old bones—which are from several different individuals—and they're all about the same. This is a homogenous population, and it's significantly different from Wunderland's."

"They are not from Wunderland?"

"Impossible. There's no Goth strain at all. Even the isolated, backwoods communities there are descended from people who came in the original slowboats, and the only colonists with no Goth ancestry were Japanese—which isn't even hinted here."

"What about the slowboat that disappeared?"

Perpetua shook her head. "Lost Travelers' Day hasn't been observed rigorously since before the First War, but it's still marked on calendars—on the anniversary of the day Wunderland's telescopes *saw* the *Evita Peron* blow up."

"What if that was faked?"

"Its colonists were descendants of North European refugees. There'd be Goth."

"Oh. And what of the Jotoki?"

"The Jotoki do seem to be the same kind as on Wunderland, but you did say you find the same on practically every kzinti world."

"Urrr . . . This helmet," said Ginger. "You say there's something else about it?"

"Yes. Connect your notebook up to the ship's library. I want to ask it some questions."

"What do you think that helmet is?"

"I need to check our encyclopedia, but—" she called up a picture "—you see the attachment for a crest, the cheek guards, the lobster tail at the back?"

"Lobster! Don't torture me, you tree-swinging sadist! Where will we get lobsters on this damned world!"

"Not a real lobster, you stomach-ruled furball! See the armor of overlapping plates that protects the back of the neck?"

"Yes."

"We had to relearn military history when your ancestors jumped on us." She stabbed with one finger at the picture on the screen. "Do you see?"

"There is a resemblance, I agree . . . 'Roman'? . . . 'Ancient Roman'?"

"What do you think we should do, Ginger?"

"Explore further."

"How easy will that be?"

"I've already paid Hunt Master to let me make a private expedition. I don't know that he actually had the power to permit or prevent me—it's up to Warrgh-Churrg while we're on his land—but it's as well to keep on Hunt Master's good side."

"I know it's an insulting question, and forgive me, but isn't that dangerous?"

"They would call me—to put it politely—a strange kind of kzin if they knew all about me, but I am a kzin for all that, Perpetua. Danger doesn't enter into it. For that matter I'm looking forward to the hunt. You'll never breed that reflex out of us!"

"I'm not one who would want to. I've got to admit life on Wunderland would be duller if some of you furballs hadn't joined us and kept some of your little ways. But, it's partly my own fear I speak from. I don't want you dead on the end of a *kz'zeerekti* spear. Who wishes a friend to face danger alone?"

"Cheer up! Naturally I shall take my tame monkey with me, as bait and interpreter. I won't be facing it alone!"

"Thanks, furball!"

"Quiet your trembling heart, tree-swinger! This time we *will* be taking full body armor, sense enhancers and modern weapons. Even Hunt Master could hardly call me a coward for that, venturing deep into *kz'zeerekti* territory with only my own ape in tow! And we'll be flying, not walking."

"And as another ape once said, 'This is another fine mess you've gotten us into!' I'd be better off going in alone."

"Hunt Master would never stand for it. Nor would Warrgh-Churrg. If he found out, I'd probably be dueled for letting a monkey go loose without permission; and you'd find a very hungry reception committee when and if you returned."

"You won't tell Warrgh-Churrg you're going?"

"I think that is probably not necessary. We'll make it a quick look in and out."

"Won't he be offended?"

"Hard to see exactly why he should be. He's not the only landowner and the *kz'zeerekti* lands are unoccupied. And I did pay him gold for the hire of the car.

"Anyway, you can learn some of the language. I had Hunt Master teach me all the local *kz'zeerekti* words he's picked up, and you'll be learning them tonight."

"What's their word for 'sword'?"

Ginger's vocal cords did something difficult. Without microsurgery in his youth it would have been impossible.

"*Gladius,*" said Perpetua. "The Latin hasn't changed much. It's a useful language, though the numeration system is hopeless. It should be possible for us to improve on Hunt Master's vocabulary."

"You recognize it?"

"An old Earth language. English and Wunderlander are full of traces of it. You said that Hunt Master called one by a name?" Perpetua found herself suddenly a little shy of saying such a thing to a kzin. But another feeling was stronger than embarrassment.

"Yes, *Marrrkusarrg-tuss.*"

"Could it have been 'Marcus Augustus'?"

"I suppose so." He passed her a disk and sleeper's headset, standard equipment for absorbing a new language quickly. "But here's the dictionary. Learn."

"Thanks. And you'd better do the same. But I do know some of the words already. . . . I wonder what could have happened?"

V

Their car crossed on low power to the scrub woods on the southern side of the river.

Once out of sight of the kzinti on the northern bank they halted and reconnoitered. The land about seemed still and empty, and they picked no body-heat signatures from large live animals. They waited for a time without result at the scene of the recent fight.

Perpetua changed into the robes which the car's machine shop had made the previous night, worn over light formfitting body armor. Ginger, this time also in armor with modern sense enhancers, scanned the area ceaselessly. Insects buzzed and the air smelled strongly of recent death close by. The kzinti kits' bodies they found had been stripped of gear and lacked ears but were otherwise more or less whole. Now in daylight, they saw many bones old and new littering the area, making it look like the kzinti hunting preserve it was. They closed the car's hatch with relief.

"They haven't been too mutilated," said Perpetua.

"No, that would be too much of a provocation. Grounds for a war of extermination." They flew on over taller trees.

"Look there!" There was a stirring in the vegetation below. A heat sensor began flashing.

"Probably *kz'zeerekti*. What do you think we should do?"

"Ignore them for the time being. Let them see we're aware of them but not attacking."

"We could drop them food. Show them we're friendly?"

"They'd think it was poisoned. Kzinti *aren't* friendly."

They flew round the vegetation, seeing movement, slow to the kzin's eyes, fast and fleeting to the human's. Then the car headed south.

There was no obvious or sudden change in the landscape below, and an hour later they were still flying over green-looking country, quite well-grown with trees, even if these were more widely spread.

"I'm surprised the kzinti haven't taken this for themselves," said Perpetua. "It looks fertile enough."

"I'm not so sure," said Ginger. "Or rather I'm sure it isn't. According to the map the coastal hills south of the delta make a rain shadow, and even without them the rainfall would be poor anyway. Those plants that don't have spiny leaves have shiny ones, and they are keeping them turned edge-on to the sun. I'd say they'll have every kind of moisture-conservation mechanism you can imagine, and this is a green desert with perhaps an occasional cloudburst. Look there." He pointed to something Perpetua could barely see. "Dust devils blowing about. Land here and I'd say you'll find that grass is hard dry spines, growing out of dust. And have you seen any surface water since we left the river?"

"I can't say I have."

"Or large animals?"

"No. Blurred signs on the sensor that suggest burrowing life-forms. But the *kz'zeerekti* live here."

"The *kz'zeerekti* aren't native," said Ginger. "And, as my species found to our cost, they are the most adaptable creatures known in space. I'd say all the native animals in these parts are small, also highly adapted to moisture-conservation. In fact, they are quite plentiful and I've seen a few already, even if you haven't. But not much meat or sport for kzinti. But in any event, have you seen any *kz'zeerekti*?"

"No. Where are they anyway?"

"Hiding, I suppose. Hills coming up. Notice anything else about those dust devils?"

"Like what?"

"The color."

"They're red. So is the soil that I can see."

"Yes, red and dusty. Filled with iron, I'd guess. This is old country. The mountains are eroded here, though they're sharp enough further south, where the tectonic plates collided more recently."

"Is that significant?"

"Perhaps not in terms of our mission. But it does mean the country could be rich in minerals. Especially in the vicinity of the rivers. These are the roots of mountains we are flying over, exposed anticlines and synclines. I can see granite in those outcrops, quartz and limestone. Traces of other minerals, too—jasper, copper, and more than traces of gold. This planet is bigger than Earth but has a much smaller core. I speculate that core formation hasn't progressed as far, taking fewer heavy elements out of the crust.

"You might have kzinti mines here if the local moons weren't so mineral-rich," he went on. "In fact I'd say they *have* mined it sometime in the past—see those low mounds? They look to me like the spoil of mining dumps, but somebody's spread them out as if to hide them. I desire that we had our own ship, with its deep-radar."

They flew on. A cloud of dust below resolved itself into a group of fleeing animals, vaguely caninoid, certainly carnivorous.

"Pack raiders," said Ginger. "There must be prey for them."

"And there's a river," said Perpetua. "See that line of darker trees?"

"I saw it ten minutes ago. But as we get closer you'll see its bed is dry sand. Dig in it and you probably will find water eventually. I'd guess that, apart from the aftermath of the occasional cloudburst, the rivers in this country flow underground."

"There's a big hole."

"And there are others—see, they are in a line. I'd say it's a series of roof collapses in a big cave system. Mines and caves—they probably join up. . . . I would expect more vegetation. It seems to be concentrated around the riverbeds. Perhaps they divert water from outlying areas with underground tunnels, to grow heavier cover?"

"Maybe that's another reason we don't see *kz'zeerekti*. They'd use the cave lines for travel, too."

"How far would cave lines reach? I suppose that's like asking: How long is a river? But when you look there are a lot of sinkholes, and they do seem to follow lines. Still, collapsed tunnels would transport water."

"Yes. And the lines don't look entirely natural. There are a lot of odd things about this planet."

"Want to land and investigate?"

"Not yet, thanks! We'd better get the big picture first."

Ginger crouched forward, ears spreading and knotting, tail rigid. "Let's get a bit of height well before we reach those hills," he said after a time. "There's something about them . . ."

"What do you mean?"

"I'm getting something from my *ziirgrah* now. It's hard to define . . . but there's a lot more than one pair of eyes looking at us. They're in those hills."

"They can hardly hurt a car like this with bows and arrows."

"They are an unknown," said Ginger. "Don't you think unknown means danger, on a kzinti world to boot? We're going up."

"All right. And I have suspicions of my own." The horizon widened dramatically as the car climbed. Perpetua pointed. "See there!"

"By the Fanged God! Stone walls!"

"And see there! Real mining dumps!"

"Warrgh-Churrg hass been falsse with uss. Why did he not tell uss of thesse thingss? Urrrgh!"

"Careful, Ginger!" The hissing in her companion's accent was a danger sign to Perpetua. Outright lying between kzinti was a mortal insult, and, unlike some other mortal offenses, such as open taunts and mockery, the worse because it was rare. "If he has been economical with truth, so have we. . . . Calm, my friend."

"S-sorry. But he must have known. Satellitess would have shown. And these have been here long."

"There's no point in hanging about up here. We'll have to go down," said Perpetua after they had examined the scene for a while.

"They'll see it's a kzinti car."

"But if a human gets out of it? And a human female should look especially harmless."

"It's a risk for you."

"We're paid to take risks. Should we take her down slowly? Give them a chance to get out of the way?"

"Or a chance to prepare some really nasty surprise for us?"

"We've detected nothing on the instruments. But descending slowly might show we mean no harm."

"If you were fighting the kzinti on a kzinti planet," said Ginger, "and you saw a kzinti craft descending, fast or slow, would you think it meant no harm?"

"I take your point. But look at that!"

"A statue! Of a kzin!"

"Not just a kzin. See the length of the fangs?"

"Does that mean anything?"

"It might. The God has such fangs. I don't understand. . . . Perhaps we could broadcast an audio signal to them," said Ginger. "Tell them we come in peace. If the translator knows enough of the language yet."

"I think I know more of the language than the translator."

The car descended, its bullhorn shouting a message. Perpetua, in a white robe with narrow gold edging, which covered her body armor, alighted. The car rose and remained hovering above her, beyond the reach of primitive weapons. One hand upraised in a peculiar gesture, Perpetua walked toward the dark, rectangular apertures in the stone wall.

At first everything seemed deserted. Then, cautiously, a small group of men appeared. Ginger, watching from above, saw them exchange a complex pattern of arm movements, and, gathered round Perpetua, move back into the structure. He waited. In ancient reflex his fur rose and fell to compensate for the movement of his breathing. Then Perpetua's face appeared on the communicator.

"Come down," she said. "Their leaders are here, and I think

I've convinced them you're *foederati*—an ally. They seem prepared to give you the benefit of the doubt for the moment. Bring no weapons but your *wtsai*. They expect that. Keep your communicator on. Tread carefully. We are being met by none other than Marcus Augustus himself."

VI

They were led by two humans, one introduced as Marcus Augustus, in white robes bordered with purple strips. Others followed, carrying long knives, and other things, hidden under clothes, that were plainly weapons. "What is that?" Ginger asked Marcus Augustus, pointing at the statue.

"Why, your Feline god of course. We promised to give him worship in our Pantheon in return for certain favors."

"Fair enough," Ginger mused. "There are kdaptists who have become Christians. And did he actually grant those favors?"

"Obviously. We are here and alive."

"How did you know the Fanged God looked like that?"

"Some of our slaves make statues of him for kzinti nobles."

"I see. . . . I think," said Ginger, "that perhaps I am beginning to understand a little more."

Marcus Augustus nodded and moved ahead.

"I see at least three classes of humans here," said Ginger to Perpetua.

"Classes?"

"Yes. A concept we got to know fairly well on Wunderland. We haven't exactly been top dogs—top cats?—the whole time, you know. You get to recognize these things. The humans in white and purple are the bosses, of course. The ones with the checkered trousers and the funny hair seem an intermediate class. And there are slaves."

"Slaves?"

They were led out the far side of the building, which proved startlingly small. Now they were moving though a mass of closely spaced trees, the needle foliage obscuring the sky. It was a tight fit for Ginger in spots.

"Yes. Look at their clothes. More importantly, look at their gait. I may know more about some aspects of human society than you, and I would say this is not one of your democracies. And if they're fighting a war against modern kzinti with the odd patchwork of technology we've seen so far, I'm not surprised. You don't fight a species war with majority resolutions.

"But slave societies are always looking for more slaves," he continued. "They may see us in that category. Not me, perhaps. If they know anything about kzinti they'd know we don't make slaves. But you . . . who knows? And by human standards of beauty you are attractive. A good prize. Keep your weapon handy."

"By human standards of beauty? I suppose that's a compliment?"

"Personally I like long whiskers, and fur with a pleasing alternation of orange and yellow stripes, among other things. Four nicely shaped teats help, too, and muscular haunches, not to mention the right smell. But be alert."

Marcus Augustus halted them, glanced at the sky, took a step to the side, and disappeared.

Ginger's ears opened like Chinese parasols. The man had walked inside a tree.

No; a colony of trees, grown together.

It was a *really* tight fit getting in. Warrgh-Churrg very likely didn't know about this; an uninvited kzin entering here would not be seen again, except possibly as a rug.

"We kept records," Marcus Augustus said, "and the Jotoki gave us better books than scrolls and wooden boards for writing on. Our ancestors were the Ninth Legion, the Hispania. You don't seem surprised."

"I guessed it might be that," said Perpetua. "The legion that marched north into Scotland—ah, Caledonia—from Hadrian's Wall and was never seen again."

"You know that!" Marcus Augustus jumped forward, clasping Perpetua's arms with both hands. "But . . . with time-dilation effects . . . from Earth's point of view . . . I'm not sure, but it must have been thousands of years ago!"

"About two thousand five hundred years, almost."

"Then— Does Rome still stand? Our battles were not in vain? We led the felines away?"

"She is still a great city, but much has changed."

"Was Rome conquered?"

"Not by the kzinti. Only by other humans. And the Human Empire in space that defeated the kzinti is the heir of the empire of Rome. You see I know your language."

"I suppose Earth has got old."

"Old enough to build spaceships of her own. We come from a colony at Earth's nearest star."

"That is good to hear. And the felines?"

"We fought long wars. We won. Now some, like my companion here, are *foederati*. Didn't your people recruit Germans? But you spoke of time dilation. You know how time is related to the speed of light?"

"Of course. The Jotoki taught our ancestors. . . . How could you have traveled so far?"

"We travel faster than light."

"It cannot be done!"

"It is how we beat the kzinti. They were a great empire when the leading edge of their wave of conquest reached Earth and its colony worlds and attacked them. We almost perished. Then the hyperdrive came to us."

"I cannot think you are lying. If you were but a kzinti puppet you would not know so much about us."

"So what happened?"

"Do you wish to hear the story firsthand?"

"Firsthand?"

"I told you. We—and the Jotoki—have good records."

He led them to another room in the underground complex, inviting Perpetua to recline on a human-sized couch. Other couches were pushed together for Ginger. Somehow well-used libraries have something of the same atmosphere in every culture. He touched a panel and a screen came to life.

"Behold Maximus Gaius Pontus of senatorial rank, strategos of the Hispania."

A man with an aquiline nose, a peculiar mark burnt between his eyebrows, sat in a carved wooden chair, speaking into a camera.

VII

This record is for posterity. Wherever that may be. At least I need not fuss with scribe and scroll, or fear that mouse or termite shall devour this disk. I will begin when I traveled north with a bulla of authority to take over the Ninth Legion at Hadrian's Wall.

It was, I thought, a remote (Ha! *Remote!*) and desolate place, though I traveled north toward Caledonia in some comfort. I had campaigned in far worse conditions. There were towns at first, with stone buildings. Then villages, then straggling huts, and finally just the carven milestones and tombstones beside the road. A draft of replacements, specialists, and some civilians accompanied me and my escort.

Old Crassus was a hard taskmaster to the convoy. He had to be. The civilians and women traveling with us in creaking wains were a hindrance and a peril. We did not let the emptiness of the land deceive us into thinking that we were unobserved. We knew the land was alive though it seemed desolate, and we avoided or hastened through limestone country for we knew it meant caves.

With the legionaries not only singing their usual interminable marching songs about the venereal charms of Lalarge, but with women actually present, there were potential discipline problems. Crassus routed women out of their lines when we made camp at night, stuck to our predawn starts, and generally made himself exceptionally hated even for a ducenarius. He was as tough an old stick of gnarled vinewood as his own cudgel, and I had little to do but look impressive. I also began dictating an account for the old man to Publius, my secretary.

We saw nothing really strange, apart from moving lights in the northern sky: some like drifting stars, some larger and nearer, one huge like a second moon. Sometimes they formed patterns. No one, including the veterans and merchants who knew this country, had seen anything like them before, but at that time they did not trouble us. We were more concerned with robbers and broken men nipping at our heels, or even attacking in force if there were enough of them or if the Scots had landed to encourage them against us. But we reached the wall at Borcovicus with little trouble, apart from a few arrows fired into the camp one night.

Winter is the defining fact about the wall. The climate is even worse than the rest of Britain, with its cold drizzling rain so many days. On the wall you have wind-driven sleet month after month, and dream of walking in the sun under a purple sky in the olive-groves and vineyards of Tuscany, or quaffing the wine of Melita amid the bee-pastures of its flowers (though I have seen more than purple skies since then). Troops from Germany regard it as a soft billet after the winters they have there, but for Spaniards like the Ninth it was very much a hardship posting. They had done their best to modify it with baths and barbers and brothels, but they wore padded woolens under their armor and shivered.

Still, the bathhouses were a credit to several generations of military engineering, and the Principia was well lined with woven rugs. Further, the day after our arrival was actually fine, with blue skies and wide views. Those rolling hills of red and brown heather had a kind of beauty under the sun.

The prefect, Bassus Septimus, was the type I expected: weather-beaten and wind-bitten, eyes permanently narrowed from squinting across heather and into sleet, an old sandal-leather man. He had a keen eye for his own comfort but he was a competent veteran who knew the land. I had seen plenty of the type in Gaul. The officers and senior centurions I met were much the same. Some think our officers are fops and amateurs, but these of the frontiers were not, and those who think that way might find it difficult to explain how we have ruled an empire of four thousand cities and forty-four provinces with swords, spears, and animal power.

The men were legionaries, and when you have said that you have said all. They were the drilled, disciplined troops of an empire that was an island of civilization in a world that was a welter of barbarism. They were versatile soldiers and engineers, who could fight barbarians or other Romans by land or sea, build walls and siege engines which I then thought gigantic, drain marshes, drive roads and bridges through wilderness, calculate to a fraction what pay they were owed, fight fires in multistory tenements, plow the land to feed themselves in any climate or distribute food in a famine. Versatile.

I thought that then. How much more do I think it now!

Some said we ruled the world, but we senior officers knew better: We had silks from China and merchants' tales from further yet. The Greeks had measured the sphere that is the world and we knew the size of it. That helped me understand much later, but for the moment, if forty-four provinces sounded large, and it was, the Barbaricum, we knew, was larger.

I tried from the start, as they were presented to me, to remember as many names as I might but knew it would take some time to tell the centurions apart: they looked as if they had been hammered from the same metal in the same mold by the same smith; as indeed they had been. Our army was full of such. I knew that later they would become individuals to me. Sooner rather than later, if we saw action.

Bassus took me to the wall. He was worried, which was part of his job, but he was also more bewildered than I had often seen such a one.

"Patrols have disappeared before," he said. "They go too far and the Picts suddenly decide they would like the armor and weapons of the metal men. Or they run into a few boatloads of those cursed Gaels from Hibernia. But sooner or later we always hear from our spies what happened.

"Anyway, the local Picts are on their way to being civilized—we've sent enough punitive expeditions to teach them that attacking the metal men was not a good idea, and I can drink with the local chiefs without all of us keeping our hands on our swords or even needing a poison-taster. It's become not much more than a bit of sport for us to fire arrows at each other when they come to steal blades from the ditch.

"Now, nothing. No patrols returned, no spies, and no Picts. We have a frontier scout force beyond the wall and no word from that either, though of course it's sometimes gone for weeks at a time. That wolf pack hardly drills like Praetorians—I commanded an ordo of them a long time ago—but they know the country and they fear nothing in it. If it was an attack by the Caledoni they'd report it as such. That's what they're there for. This is something different.

"Also, the spymasters and political officers who work among the Northern tribesmen know their business. They don't last long otherwise.

"Look!"—he gestured across the vast sweep of heather—"not a wisp of smoke anywhere. There are Pictish villages beyond those hills. Normally on a day like this you can see the smoke of their fires. But they've cleared off. No word. I don't know why, unless the tribes are gathering in the highlands for some sort of mass descent."

"Would they be capable of such organization?"

"Did Varus ever wonder such a thing?"

I had spoken of Varus with the old man and I wondered now that his name still seemed to keep cropping up after more than a century. Perhaps it haunted every frontier commander. I wondered how often it was mentioned on the Rhine, or in those distant red deserts of sand where our legions wait for the Parthians or Persians.

"Anyway, they're gone without a word," he continued. "After the patrols we'd lost I wasn't taking any chances. I sent a strong force to investigate, with orders to turn back at the first suspicion of trouble and not to march north beyond sight of our beacons. They reported the Pictish villages deserted. Nothing else, except those lights in the sky."

"I thought you always saw them in these parts," I said.

"That's the aurora borealis, the northern glow. The further north you go in Caledonia the more you tend to see it, in winter anyway, but it's nothing like these. These moving stars are new."

"Pictish gods?"

"I've been a soldier a long time. I've never seen gods like that." He too had the brand of Mithras on his brow and knew the mysteries. "We have all sorts of religions here, even Jews and the fish-worshipping Christians. Gods from Spain and Syria and Melita and places only the gods themselves know. But no one has a god that is a light traveling in the sky. Some of them are frightened, I think, and they'd show it, if they weren't more frightened of me and their centurions."

I didn't like the idea of a legionary frightened by anything but his own superiors. It should be what the philosophers and logicians call a contradiction in terms. "So what do you think?"

"Since it's futile to speculate about gods, I speculate about men, which may be just as futile. I think what I told you: that the tribes are gathering for a massive attack southwards. If they breach the wall, there's nothing to stop them before Eboracum. And that's not much more than a shell, now that we've brought the Ninth here. They'd take it. Then they'd either straggle back to Caledonia with their booty or they'd go on. I think they'd go on."

"Why?"

"You don't fire siege ballistas at a hare in a field. An attack to punch through the wall isn't just to plunder the northern marches and return. They'd be aiming for Londinium and the channel—to chuck us right out of Britannia. It would be more than brigandage and piracy, it would be politics. If the Gauls cooperated with them, and the Germans . . ." He made an eloquent gesture.

"The Britons tried it themselves once," I reminded him. "It didn't do them any good. Two legions brought them to bay and wiped them out."

He had been in Britain longer than I and knew more of its history.

"They were disunited and had bad leaders," he said. "Another attack may be better led. And they know us now. They're not going to flee in panic at the sight of a Testudo, and they know better than to close against a legion with short swords in the field.

"Even if we could beat them in a pitched battle, that wouldn't solve it. If I commanded them, my tactic would be to dodge our field army, and wear down our supply trains with ceaseless harassment. They can live off the land better than we can. Nip off isolated forts and garrisons and ambush the relief forces. Then melt back into the forests and dare us to follow them. Only this time they would be taking cities, not mile castles. Harassment happens all the time in wild country, of course, but think of it on a far bigger scale. Then, when we're scattered and worn down and Londinium says the money's running out and we can't pay our auxiliaries, they launch a main-force attack."

He waved again to left and right, at the miles of wall marching across the hills and valleys to east and west and out of sight. Here and there the helmets of pacing sentries shone as they caught the sun, seeming to slide atop the stonework. It was new, almost unweathered, and majestic. A colossal statement of the might of Rome.

"Look at the wall itself. Our garrison is stretched from sea to sea, from Luguvallium in the west to Segedunum in the east. Our problem here is the problem of the Empire in miniature: they can attack when and where they choose. We have to try to be strong at all points at once and we can't be. Where is our central reserve?

"We have better tactics and discipline, but we have to spread the grease on the bread very thinly. This wall looks impressive but it's largely a bluff. See that sentry?" He pointed to the glittering bead of a helmet visible above the rampart of the next mile castle. "Twenty men and a decurion are sometimes all we've got in a castle, along with their women and camp followers. We rely on our spies and scouts to warn us when an attack is coming so we can concentrate our forces to meet it. But one real punch, delivered without warning, could go through a weakly garrisoned section like wet parchment. Especially if they had help from the other side—we can't watch all the coast to know what landings may take place beyond our lines. This wall is trying to do something too big for it."

"And once they were through?"

"We'd attack them from east and west, of course. Cut their communications. We can handle a big attack. But not an all-out attack by all the tribes, and not at too many points simultaneously. I'm not saying they would inevitably throw us out of Britannia if they tried—you know how good our boys are—but they could do a lot of damage, and leave us that much weaker when they've bred up enough to try again."

"So what do you recommend?"

"Find out whatever is happening and nip it in the bud. One thing on our side is the fact that these tribesmen take a long time to assemble. Not just their people. Even *some* barbarian chiefs know now that you've got to get a commissariat together for a serious war far from home. That puts a delay on them.

"We've wasted a lot of time already, but I'd say hit them now, at once, with everything we're got. You've got the Ninth Legion. And we're not Picts and Scots. We can march in strength at short notice. Break the back of the thing with one quick stroke. Kill and return.

"Whatever happens," he went on, "don't let the Caledonians make a massed charge from close by. A long-distance charge across the rocks and heather you can break up with javelins and artillery, perhaps—and we have put a lot of emphasis on making sure the scorpions and other light artillery can be worked *quickly*. But get a horde of the screaming red-haired devils leaping at you from a quarter-mile away—and they like to hide in ditches and wait for you—and you're in real trouble. More than one Roman formation has come to grief at the wrong end of a Caledonian charge. Men and women, shrieking, half-naked, foam on their mouths. Between you and me—" he lowered his voice, as though we might be overheard in that windy, empty place "—enough of them, and they might give a full legion a hard time."

"And the flying lights?"

"Maybe they've stuck swans' wings on chariots. I don't know. But I'm sure they're not ready to attack yet. Otherwise we'd see them now. They aren't good at patience. But if we find the tribes mustering and break up an attack before it's delivered, then it's a Triumph for you."

From the way he said "Triumph" I knew he meant it in the particular as well as the general sense. That could lead to other things. He probably thought that I, like so many of my rank, felt a bit more purple would look well on my cloak and toga; and perhaps he wasn't wrong.

"And if we don't find the tribes mustering?"

"We come home. We've given these loafers of ours a good exercise and we've shown the Picts the reach of civilization."

So we talked. I repeat this talk because I remembered its arguments many times in later days. I inspected the men as we prepared, and met some of the scouts as they came in. Gaunt, keen-eyed frontier wolves they were, battered and scarred by weather almost as much as by battle, they made me think uneasily on what the philosophers had written, of how luxury and soft living could corrupt, of how Rome was allegedly going soft at the heart. Still, we were its hard edge yet. I thought of the pleasant villas and smiling vales of the south, even here in Britain, of the farms of Tuscany, and reflected that civilized men must be guarded by less civilized ones.

Still, I felt no guilt about relaxing with my officers in the bath-house that night. We would not, we knew, enjoy them again for some time.

Normally, despite the prefect's bravado, it took a legion time to prepare for a march. Six thousand fighting men and their auxiliaries are not easily uprooted. But the Ninth had only just arrived. It was rested but not settled down, and anticipating any possible siege the granaries and warehouses behind the wall were kept filled (crucifixion was a deterrent to pilfering). It could be quickly resupplied from them.

So once again, a few days later, it was our usual predawn start. A whole legion this time, the aquilifer with the Eagle and the significers in their leopard skins bearing the legion's battle honors at the front of the column. (Though not quite at the front of the force—we had scouts ahead of us. Unlike Varus.)

The wall appeared even more imposing looking back at it from the north, without the straggle of civilian dwellings along its southern side: a grim, hard rampart of civilization. New as it was, it seemed to have been standing since time began. And Mithras knows, a legion marching with its Aquila and its standards going before was a sight to see!

The country looked superficially the same as the hills and heather moors to the south, but felt different. There was, if you allowed it to get to you, a feeling of nakedness, knowing that we were outside the wall, beyond the Roman World. Even that column of armored men looked small in the vast purple heather country, under that sky. It had been different in Gaul, where there was no such obvious rampart, though perhaps crossing the Rhine would have felt like this. For a moment the sight of the wall marching east and west to the distant hilltops and out of sight filled me with pride, as when, a boy on my first visit to Rome, I had seen the great buildings of the capitol. And again I felt, as I had then, a sudden stab of feeling like despair and death, a feeling the poetry of Virgil echoed for me: "Man can do no more!" The god of the Jews was gaining converts in Rome now, I had heard, and I thought I knew why. We had need of a god to save the world, more powerful than our little godlings of sanitation and so forth, our pantheon of deceased emperors. . . . I set my head to the north, and I think I betrayed nothing in my face.

We were in Britannia Barbara, part of the encircling, ever-threatening Barbaricum, where anything might happen.

But nothing did, for the rest of that day. We passed the Pictish villages, with their cold hearths, some dead livestock around and a few hungry dogs and wildcats scavenging. I was interested to see that the Caledonian wildcats, great fanged things, easily kept the dogs at bay. Crassus said it was odd the Picts had abandoned their livestock. Our scouts looked for tracks, but too much rain had fallen for anything to be made out apart from their general route further into the north and the hills. We had the scouts, both on foot and mounted, and the auxiliaries, spread out far and wide. We saw and heard nothing human.

We didn't have to entrench ourselves that night. There was hard-standing for a camp a long day's march north of the Wall. (Though calculating a day's march was fiendishly difficult in that country, where the sun seemed to shine almost all night in summer and was gone as soon as it had arisen in winter. As a worshipper of Sol Invictus I had wondered sometimes why that happened. Now I know!) There was a ditch and walls ready for our use if we supplied the stakes for the palisades and our soldiers used their entrenching tools to repair the erosion. There were a few sheep grazing inside it, and in that uncanny emptiness and silence we were glad to see them as tokens of the world we knew. The cooks soon had them on spits.

It grew dark. The night sentries were posted. A nearly full-strength legion and its auxiliaries, six thousand fighting men, plus a well-trained and armed servant for every four men and a straggle of camp followers who could also heft arms if necessary, need not normally fear attack—rather anything in the rest of the world should fear them—but if the Caledoni attacked in force, who knew? And I thought again of Varus.

With Crassus, the other senior officers, and the pilus primus I inspected the lines. Scouts from outlying pickets came and went. We had brought extra scorpions and set them up around the camp.

The Picts attacked at dusk. There was a shower of arrows and confused shouting and screaming from an outlying picket. The men were standing to and ready. Three cohorts went for them and drove them into a prepared killing ground. They charged—they always charge—straight into our scorpions and as they floundered in the ditch we poured bolts and arrows into them.

I did not, I thought, have Varus's problem. It was no overwhelming force that attacked us, but an ill-armed, ill-commanded rabble from several different tribes. When I had some of the survivors brought before me and questioned, they seemed confused and terrified. They claimed we had attacked them, and carried off their people. They had attacked an entrenched legion because they were desperate. They must, I thought, be desperate indeed. It made no sense. Still, a couple of crucifixions would do them no harm and the rest would earn something in the slave market. Then the prefect pointed.

For a moment I thought it was a fiery serpent. Then I realized it was but a line of torches carried by men: but a long line. The Caledoni had crept upon us in the dark in force while a few of their number created a diversion.

I gave thanks that we were prepared, and by no means taken by surprise. But no battle against a wolfish people like the Caledoni, fighting at a time and place of their choosing, is a certain thing.

And as a strategos should not, I fretted myself at that moment with fears about events I could no longer control. What if this was but a greater diversion, while other barbarians attacked the wall?

I looked impassive enough, as I rode forward through the camp with my staff officers and gallopers. Drums were rattling with the trumpets now, and as missiles and bolts began to fly I saw the shields going up as a testudo was formed. I gave thanks again for those centurions who needed no more than a word of command. The testudo would give protection from the arrows, spears, and the lighter missiles.

Then Roman and Caledoni stopped together.

The stars had changed again. Great lights moved in the sky, forming strange designs. Across a drifting cloud there appeared the picture of a Roman soldier in full armor. It was projected, I know now, by an ordinary sword-light, but the effect on all may be imagined. The gods themselves, both sides thought, had intervened. We Romans accepted this with pleasure and surprise, but also as something no more than our right, and certainly not as something to break discipline over. I knew Mithras was a good god for soldiers and was gratified. The Caledoni, as might be expected, too terror-stricken to run, stood wailing.

The testudo moved upon them, then dissolved into men with flickering swords. Rank upon rank, the legionaries advanced like the vast single-minded engine they were. They cheered and at the command surged forward. But it was a disciplined surge. The javelins of the front ranks flew in a dark mass, their swords flickered stabbing like the tongues of vipers. Crassus had not had them blacken the blades for night work, thinking the enemy ought to see the steel, and Crassus had been right.

As the Picts went down squealing, I thought: "This will buy peace south of the wall, peace for Eboracum and Londinium. I have vindicated Hadrian's decision to build the wall." Hadrian was reported dead but his successor might appreciate my contribution to the imperial numen.

Then the Jotoki ships began to descend. With their double torsion, scorpion bolts can penetrate iron armor, if not the molecularly bonded ceramics the Jotoki used. The Jotoki were forbearing. They burned the bolts in flight with sword-lights until we had no ammunition left, then began to talk to us. They fired a plasma jet to emphasize their words.

The Jotoki had done this, or something like this, before. They picked up a fair number of our womenfolk, and civilians, specialists, and other auxiliaries from the wall, and some Pictish villagers.

They say there are Roman soldiers garrisoning forts in China, who found their way there after their detachments were cut off by the Persians. It is easy to change masters when you have no choice in the matter.

Perpetua held up a hand. Marcus Augustus paused the film.

"This makes no sense," she said. "I have been searching the records in our ship's library. It's had all the major encyclopedias read into it. We know the Ninth Legion, the Hispania, marched north of the wall—it was newly built then—into Caledonia and was never seen again. But we know nothing of Jotoki raids along Hadrian's Wall."

"What should we expect a primitive Earth historian to say?" asked Ginger. "That giant starfish came from the sky and picked them up? He'd be kept in a little room at the top of the castle. House, I mean."

"True enough. Perhaps it does make a kind of sense. Hadrian's Wall was suddenly extended and fortified about the time the Ninth Legion is said to have marched north. Then, after quite a short time, it was abandoned, and another work, the Antonine Wall, was built further north again. That was abandoned, too, after quite a short time, and the Romans fell back on Hadrian's Wall.

"The Romans put a huge effort into fortifying it and manning it—for about three hundred years. I gather scholars still disagree as to why. Maybe somebody did say something. And what of all the magic surrounding Arthur? Merlin and the flying dragons? And the Celtic myths? Flying, enchantments, magic weapons? Chesterton wrote in his history: 'Suddenly the soldier of civilization is no longer fighting Goths but Goblins.' After wars and invasions and race migrations, centuries of near-illiteracy, changes of languages, in a couple of non-technological millennia, what else might you expect to remain by way of memory of a Jotoki recruitment effort?"

"Millennia," said Marcus to Perpetua. "Two and a half thousand Earth years, you said."

"Yes."

"About nine hundred have passed for us, as far as we can tell. We traveled fast."

"Then you didn't come directly here?" Ginger broke in. Marcus glanced at him but did not deign to reply.

"That is why your language has changed so little," said Perpetua quickly. "That and the fact you had no tongues of human invaders to overlay it. On Earth, six hundred years after your ancestors left, there were still fragments of the Western Empire extant in France. Latin was long the language of government and scholarship—where there was government and scholarship—and of the Church in Europe. The ruler in Ravenna still styled himself 'King of Rome, Emperor of the West,' and the Eastern Empire still had centuries of life ahead. You are almost contemporaries of Boethius."

"We are still Romans! However far we have traveled! In the Mithraeum the Mysteries are still enacted. We honor our various gods. There are Jews in our ranks still, and fish-worshippers, but we have kept faith with Rome."

The picture resumed.

You to whom I leave this story will know much of the ships that travel between worlds. I need not tell you of our awe and amazement, our initial disbelief, our wild thoughts that we were dead and in a Hades unlike any we had imagined, as we were taken aboard the great warship that the Jotoki named the *Hard Bargainer,* and its consort, the *Shrewd Merchant,* while about us flew as escort the *Five Arms of the Wise Trade Councillor.* These things you may imagine. But Roman or Caledonian, we were warriors, and we behaved as warriors. The centurions maintained discipline among our legionaries and civilians. The Caledonians wailed and howled in the manner of barbarians, but when they saw it availed them nothing they became tractable.

It was great good fortune that our political officers already knew the Caledonian chiefs and we could speak together. Thinking I had knowledge in the matter the Caledonian chiefs agreed, grudgingly enough, to place themselves under my direction. They, being barbarians, were of course far more overawed than we. But we saw that we were all human and that bound us together. The gold the Jotoki gave us helped, and the glass and beads and mirrors for the women, both Roman and Caledonian.

Meanwhile, we were heading away from Terra, our world, at a speed which the Jotoki told us was close to the speed of light itself, to do battle. The Jotoki had shown us representations of our enemies: great beasts like lions or Indian tigers, but armed as the Jotoki themselves were armed, with weapons of flame, and traveling like the Jotoki through the skies.

We had little love for the Jotoki then, though they fed us and clothed us and spoke to us in our own language (though at first only through images, not daring to confront us in the flesh). But then we realized that something the Jotoki told us many times was true:

Better we fight these felines far away than have them fall upon Terra.

The Jotoki told us first they were taking us to a new world to train us with new weapons and tactics to fight creatures which menaced them and which, if unchecked, would conquer our own world and Rome itself. After the campaign they would, if they were able, return us to our homes. We obviously had no choice but to believe them and obey.

Before we were placed in the chambers of deep sleep the Jotoki began to teach us of the heavens. They explained that they were traders and had taught other races before us. Once, said Jegarvindertsa, who talked to me most, they had tried to spread civilization among the stars.

"'Civilization is our business.' Those were the old governor's words, when we marched north to the wall," I recalled.

"You defend civilization now," said Jegarvindertsa. "This is but Rome writ large. It has been said there is only one civilization, and all civilized beings are a part of one another, almost as we Jotoki are compound entities. Are you afraid?"

"When I campaigned in Gaul and Caledonia we had short swords and javelins, and our armor was iron and leather. Now . . . why should I be afraid?" I had seen and tried some of the Jotoki weapons then, and certain of our centurions and other instructors had begun practicing with them.

"Yes, your weapons and armor are very different. But so are your enemies."

I knew those enemies now. The Jotoki had shown me holographic eidolons of them. We fought for the gold the Jotoki gave us, and we fought because they had really given us no choice. We could hardly march home! But we were also more than mercenaries and slaves. How small and provincial our skirmishes against Germans and Gauls and Picts seemed now!

"Let's get at them!"

"You and your people have learnt a lot in a short time," said Jegarvindertsa. "If we had found you earlier things might have been very different. As it is, we still might turn the tide. But we have a long way to go. We are close to the speed of light, but still you must pass time in sleep. As you sleep you will learn more."

I thought then, with my newly acquired way of looking at things, that the Jotoki use of the word "tide" showed they had once been wide-ranging sailors on their own world before they went into space. It was not long since we Romans had come to know of tides. Caesar himself had not understood, during the first Roman expedition to Britannia, the difficulties and opportunities a tidal beach on Oceanus Atlanticus presented. Well, that was not surprising.

Did we sleep long or short? There was a period of black nothingness, and then the chambers that enclosed us were opened, and the Jotoki assembled us on the great deck of the ship. As the men were mustered, Jegarvindertsa led me to the pilot's tower.

There was a jump and a flickering in the image. Centuries had corrupted some of the data.

"This is the story of our forebears' first great battle with the kzinti," Marcus said. "It is told to all our children. When the Jotoki awoke our fathers from sleep they told them that feline ships were closing upon them." The picture resumed.

"I think they will board us," he said.

"Then stop them."

"That will not be easy. If we were part of a proper fleet, and if we had not lost so many Jotoki in battles already, ship-to-ship battle would be right and proper. But there are too few of us to fight this ship properly. We might engage one or two enemy ships, but if we looked like winning the others would simply use missiles or beams against this ship and we should all perish."

"What do you intend to do, then?"

"Let them board. We shall not resist them in space with the heavy weapons. Jufadirvanlums might think differently, but they sleep still. We shall not waken them."

"And then? You would surrender to these monsters?" For a moment I thought it strange that I should be calling other creatures monsters to a Jotok, but I had become used to Jotoki appearance now.

"No. You and we will fight them. We do not like it but we see no other choice. Their numbers are not great and their discipline is not good. We will fire but a few weapons at first, lest they suspect a trap. All, we think, will board, eager for loot."

"Yes! The new weapons! The plasma jets and beam-rifles!"

"A few. But used inside a spaceship at maximum power they would do too much damage. I know a couple of squads have begun training with them and we will use them on low power, but most of your men must fight them as they know how to fight."

The sketchy Jotoki resistance at the airlocks was hardly heard as we deployed the troops. I heard one legionary complaining to a centurion: "I thought only condemned criminals fought lions and tigers in the arena."

And the centurion's answer: "These are not lions or tigers, this is not the arena, and we are not criminals. Now stand firm or feel the weight of my cudgel!"

The ship we traveled in was vast. I thought that the felines who attacked it did not lack courage. It dwarfed their own vessels. They did not know how few Jotoki it contained.

But they did not know it contained the Ninth Legion, either.

Beside me Jegarvindertsa pointed to a screen that monitored their progress.

"See now why I made the resistance so light! They think the few Jotoki that died at the airlock or fled before them were all the armed Jotoki aboard."

"Explain."

"They are slinging their weapons. They look forward to slaying the rest of us with fangs and claws alone."

"They can unsling them again."

"Yes. And they will do it quickly. But perhaps not quickly enough. This is no open plain where they can watch an enemy approach."

I had seen many images of the ferocious ones and liked them no better as I watched them on the screen now, marking their approach through the ship's corridors. Like tigers, but larger, heavier, with strange pink tails and mouths full of long fangs. Our trumpets began to sound, and the standards went up. Forward went the aquilifer, bearing the Eagle of the Ninth.

They burst into the troop deck. Trained to count enemy in battle, I saw there were not many more than a hundred, but as they poured in their sheer size and hideous appearance made their numbers seem more than they were.

The sight of our legion, drawn up in armor, halted them. Our trumpets screamed, and a shower of javelins hurtled through the air at them. They moved fast, but not a few of the javelins found their marks. But there was no time for conventional battle tactics. Even as the javelins were still in the air, the legionaries were rushing them.

Few had begun to train with the Jotoki fire-weapons and these, set to the lowest possible charge, they plied manfully against the creatures, filling the ship with black choking fumes and the smell of burnt feline flesh. A full charge of those plasmajets would have destroyed man, Jotok, feline, and probably ship alike.

The battle was terrible. The first rank of legionaries died to a man. I have seen men fight beasts, even lions and tigers, once or twice in the arena, but it was never like this, heads and limbs torn from torsos and flung into the air like rubbish by demons twice the height of men, whose claws flashed like lightning, rending and unstoppable! But the legion and whatever gods they worshipped had taught them to die aright, and they took some felines with them. They stopped the rest from drawing their weapons before the second rank struck. The men of the third rank threw their second javelins into the feline ranks and advanced at the rush. Orders were futile, lost in the screams and roars of men and felines. I thought, even at that moment, that we must have the Jotoki build amplifiers so orders might be given in the chaotic din of battle with such creatures.

Some javelins struck the felines and rebounded broken from their armor and garments. Others, not armored, were pierced by them but came on as unmindful of their wounds as Assyrian lions or German savages. But the javelins bent as they were meant to, and their trailing butts impeded the enemy even as the points tore about within their wounds and made the purple and orange blood spurt. The sheer horror of their appearance and their deafening screams and roars might have made the bravest quail, had they not been legionaries who faced them. I have heard wounded lions snarl and roar to shake the very air but nothing like this.

Then, screaming their battle cries, blood-maddened, the Caledonians poured in. If the kzinti had been beginning to get the measure of Roman tactics, this savage onslaught caught them off-balance. Their claws slashed, sending red human blood up in fountains as they went down, but go down they did.

Oh! the felines proved hard to kill. And oh! the Caledonians died, but what a way to die! How I wished the effete fools who pay to see criminals torn to pieces by beasts had been here! Better still, if they had been thrown into the first rank of the front line!

I saw a knot of legionaries about the aquilifer with the Eagle that swayed above the mass. The kzinti must have sensed it for what it was, for a group of them leapt upon it. The Eagle fell. As commander I knew it was not yet my place to fight hand-to-hand—my job was to direct the battle and to die well if all was lost—but it was hard to hold myself back at that moment. Legionaries in plenty rushed into the slashing claws, their own swords slashing, and a great shout went up from all the ranks as we saw the Eagle of Rome rise above the press again!

The legionaries lacked nothing in death-defying courage, but the Caledonian charge simply passed through them. The felines had their own beam-weapons out now, and one beam-weapon, wielded by a ferocious beast at close quarters, is the equal of many swords and axes. But on the human sides there was ferocity too, and those of our own who had the new weapons flinched no more than did those who had the ancient steel of our fathers.

In the way of all fights, I do not know how long it lasted, but end at last it did. The deck ran deep in blood. Humans, even armored legionaries, had been torn limb from limb. Legionaries lay dead in dozens, Caledonians in hundreds—more than half their men were gone. But all the felines were dead or dying, and their purple and orange blood mixed with the red of the humans. I have always had one weakness: I weep and shake a little after a battle, I know not why. But I wiped the tears away.

The Jotoki mechanisms whined and roared as they strove to clear the air. Our legionary doctors hurried forward to tend the wounded, and so did certain Jotoki.

Other Jotoki hurried to secure the kzinti craft.

"Twenty times five kzinti dead," said Jegarvindertsa. The Jotoki counted strangely, but any might see that our human dead out-numbered the kzinti several times. "Also we have captured four kzinti spacecraft. There are tadpoles in this fleet's few breeding ponds who will live to join together and grow sentient because of this victory today. Strong and valiant are the legions. Yes, and your barbarians, too."

"We lost too many. It was a Pyrrhic victory," I said. The one saving grace, I thought, was that the Caledoni had lost far more than the legions, partly because they had charged into battle without armor. There would be a supply of red-polled widows to keep our men happy.

"You will not have to fight again without modern weapons and armor," Jegarvindertsa said. "That was the misfortune of war. Be proud that you conquered at all."

There was no more time for talk then. As always after a battle, my duty was among the wounded, raising their spirits (and indeed with the medicines and physicians of the Jotoki, much more could be done for them than I would ever have believed possible), cheering the surviving legionaries with promises of promotion and decorations, inventorying the stores with the quartermasters, and consoling widows and orphans. We had had a shortage of women previously. Now we had a surplus. I suspected that with our next battle the surplus would grow larger. I also noticed that some of the Caledonian women, now that they had been washed and decently dressed, some in the Romano-British style, were by no means uncomely, with their red hair and their muscles and bodies hardened in their hard country. The first mothers of Rome must have been women like these. The Caledonian chiefs had, sensibly, taken the comeliest women for themselves. A number of these were now among the widows.

I had much to do and learn, and it was some time before I had a chance to talk at leisure with Jegarvindertsa again.

"Next time they board, use gravity traps," I told him. "Direct them into spaces on the ship where you have previously hidden gravity engines, then activate them and crush them. It will save us men and Jotoki."

"Did you think of that by yourselves?"

"By myself, yes."

"We are astonished. We did not think of that. We sorrow we found you so late. We hope we have not found you too late.

"You are warriors yet administrators too. And for primitives you have a remarkable capacity for abstract thought. Who else in a culture with your technological level would have a god of excrement disposal? And a military system with NCOs as its hinge, specialized engineering corps, and books of strategy? To say nothing of the systematized disaster-relief that first interested us in you."

"We are the heirs of Troy, so Virgil tells us. The Hero Aeneas founded Rome."

"Yes, that is odd, too. Your art. Something gave your kind more brain than you had any obvious need for. That is true of all spacefaring races, of course. It is one of the Great Mysteries. But you are mystery beyond mystery. In shape and physiology, you are like the kzinti. But in some aspects of mind you are more like us. Our kinds have both tried to be bearers of civilization in a Barbaricum. We are an old race, but we have found traces of other civilizations that rose and perished long ago, across a waste of time which you could not conceive. We did not intend to follow them into oblivion. We had poets and thinkers, once, who wrote of the Jotoki Mission, and celebrated the Jotoki who died to bring civilization to barbaric planets. We thought well of ourselves. We brought happiness and prosperity to many worlds."

"Where are those worlds now? Will they not come to our help?"

"The kzinti have them for hunting territories and their inhabitants as slaves or prey. We unleashed huge evil on the galaxy. It would be better if we had never been."

"You did not know."

"We should have. We had the science, the civilization. We should have had the foresight. There is a great virtue for traders: strict attention to business. And there is a great vice of traders: too little attention to anything else. We learned too late that in our way we were as unbalanced as the kzinti."

"But now you know better?"

"Yes. Too late. We have lost too many. We fight a rearguard action without hope as the kzinti devour all we created. . . . We did not do it all for ourselves, you know, though profit was the engine that drove us. Yes, we wanted wealthy and prosperous customers and trading partners—was that evil? Prosperous customers rather than slaves? We lifted species from savagery and barbarism, added a cumulative total of countless billions of years to the lives of individuals alien to us, created security and happiness . . . our mistake was to assume that given knowledge and instruction, the kzinti would be the same as other species."

"What can one legion and the people of a few Pictish villages do against such an enemy?"

"You are an . . . experiment. Some of us wanted no more alien mercenaries. If you are good enough soldiers to beat the kzinti, and faithful, we may recruit more of you."

"Raid Earth again, you mean? To enslave more?"

"No. We are not slavers, however we may seem to you. We recruited you as we did because we had little choice in the matter. When we return to your Earth we will release you from our service with fair pay—enough to make you more than rich for life—and trust you to recruit for us. We know that enslaved conscripts do not fight as well as freely enlisted men."

That was true enough. It was one of the principles on which Rome had built her Empire.

"Besides the gold, you will have the products of our science and medicine. And I think I can promise that you will be rich in stories to tell your children."

That was worth pondering too. Rome with Jotoki weapons would be invincible indeed! Providing—and here a thought came to chill the heart—providing its enemies were no more than men! But I thought of another matter.

"By the time we see Earth again, we will be too old to make sense," I said.

"We trust not. First, you will spend time in deep sleep if needs be, and will not age. Second, we travel at near the speed of light. There is an effect at such speeds so that time seems to change. You will find when you set your feet on Terra again that less time has passed for you than might seem. . . . Now, we must leave this region before kzinti reconnaissance returns."

But when we spoke again things had changed. There was news of other battles, more feline victories. It seemed that we would not be going home yet. When I spoke with Jegarvindertsa a few weeks later there was a change in their manner. There was less talk of possibilities of victories, or even of prolonging the war, now, more talk of fleeing. "We found you too late," they said. "There is nothing left on the ledger but to try to save some last poor remnant of our kind. We do not know if we can keep faith with you."

I showed no feeling or emotion. I had my sword by my side, and it occurred to me that the best policy would to plunge it into them then and there. Some of us had learnt something of spaceflight by then, and I thought that with a scratch crew we might still be able to get the ship back to Earth. Take the consorts by surprise and destroy them without warning.

Men had achieved such things before. I remembered the Greek story of Xenophon's march to the sea, of Odysseus and his wanderings, fighting perils and monsters. Better to die trying to get home than be lost in the stars forever. But I would try to learn a little more before I struck.

"Where will you go?" I asked.

"The universe is big."

"So I have learned. Would they follow?"

"We can accelerate to near light-speed. But so can the kzinti. The longer start we have the better."

"Where will you go ultimately? Would you head for another star cluster? Another galaxy?" I talked of these things easily now.

"It would take too long. Even if we put ourselves into hibernation, as we usually do, the air would gradually leak out through the hulls, atom by atom. Our automatics would fail, micrometeorites and free hydrogen atoms would erode hull material at last. In any event, our life systems would eventually disintegrate. So would our bodies, in hibernation or not. And so, at last, would the hulls of our ships. We can travel far, but there is a limit."

"Where will you go?" I pressed them.

"Our friend, if we do not tell you, you cannot reveal it under torture."

"I am a Roman still. I do not fear torture."

"Forgive us, but you have not experienced kzinti torture. In a matter as important as that they would not hesitate a moment. Also you know they have telepaths—think what it means to be tortured by a telepathic race, and pardon us if we do not entrust you with our most priceless secret. But perhaps we are not clear yet ourselves. We must seek among the stars for the furthest that it is practical for us or our tadpoles' tadpoles to reach."

"You will go and leave us here? To fight the kzinti alone and without hope?"

"No. Only a few of us will go. Enough, just, to crew the ships and care for the tadpoles. The rest remain to delay the kzinti."

"I see. Like Horatius."

"Who?"

"A hero of our people."

"If we defeat the kzinti, we buy not only the survival of our kind, but also the survival of your kind, perhaps. Conquer them, and you will have the ships to go where you will. Back to your own planet, perhaps. The kzinti will strike your kind sooner or later, but if it is late enough, perhaps your kind will have science enough to fight them."

"You really believe that?" I thought of the onagers and javelins of the legions and of Rome attacked by kzinti weaponry. Hannibal and his elephants had been hard enough to subdue. And the cold hand that had touched my heart at a certain vision touched it again—kzinti falling upon Earth, upon the towns and cities of the Empire, of legions marching out with eagles and trumpets and small swords and javelins to fight sword-lights and plasma cannon. All the Empire, all Terra, turned into a vast arena for humans to be hunted by beasts. Forever. Delay them, he said. But could we delay them or divert them long enough?

"All things are possible," Jegarvindertsa said. "You have barely begun to discover metal alloys, but your military and civil organization are amazingly advanced—we traded with many primitive races and we know potential when we see it."

Their strange eyes with their pupils like crosses looked deep into my eyes. Somehow—perhaps Mithras Himself spoke to me—I knew that I stood at one of those moments when the decision of a soldier may change all the world. Mithras had been a soldier.

"You have seen the star maps and you know we speak truth." Jegarvindertsa said. "Your world, your Terra, lies that way. We intend to flee. We think the kzinti will pursue us. We will draw them away from your Terra, a sector of space which they would otherwise reach within a few generations real-time."

"But you have shown us how the kzinti advance everywhere."

"In some directions faster than others. But the longer the kzinti are delayed, the better the chance we will have of escape. Which means leading their empire away from your Earth. That is also buying time for your kind to develop defenses of your own."

"Spaceships? Beam-weapons?"

"One day, perhaps. Why not? Your kind have the brain for arches and aqueducts, maps and mathematics and even a bureaucracy. That means, we think, you have the brain to build spaceships. We do not know why the gods gave your kind—plains-dwelling apes—so much brain, though they also gave it to us, colonial amphibians, and to the cursed cats. There is more brain in each of us than you—or we, or they—ever needed for mere survival. But if it happened once, if can happen again. Perhaps it is a condition of amphibianism."

"But we are not amphibians! We are not frogs or sea creatures!"

"You have poetry, art, philosophy, as well as arches and aqueducts and armies. You have religion. *That* makes you amphibians. That is why we argued against Jufadirvanlums that you be recruited."

"The felines appear to have all those things too."

"Yes. That is a part of the mystery. Those barbarians have a glimmering of something else as well. We have tried to civilize them and failed. Now nothing remains for us but to fight to ward off our final destruction by them. We, and the species we brought forward into the light, are doomed to be but their slaves and prey. And yet, perhaps, one day far beyond our vision, you may be the agent that . . ." They stopped, and their strange eyes took on a yet stranger cast, as though they were focused upon some faraway light.

"Yes?"

"Perhaps, perhaps . . . one day . . . *you* will civilize them. We cannot."

"We have civilized Greeks, and Gauls, and Britons. A few Caledonians. Even a few Germans. But for how long? I do not know."

"You are physically more like the kzinti than we are."

"I am surprised you recruited us, then."

The strange mood was broken. Jegarvindertsa laughed.

"My dear Maximus, that was precisely the reason we did recruit you. That and the fact we were desperately short of mass for our fighting units anyway. But it was the argument we—that is, this five-unit of the Jotoki, comprising the group-individual that is Jegarvindertsa—put before the poor makeshift that has replaced our trade council."

The strange mood was broken. But I left my sword sheathed. I knew now what the Ninth Legion had to do. The old man had often spoken to me when I was a child, of the ultimate duty of dying for civilization. I wished my task had been so simple and easy.

Again the picture jumped.

A strategos does not lead a Legion on foot. Nor did I now. For all that had changed, and for all the Jotoki learning machines had taught us, our legionaries still remembered something of Roman tactics: scrupulous preparation, and then a thrust in the right place—use the sword for the thrust into the belly, don't waste time slashing at the armored head and chest. We dealt with the felines in the same way. The vanguard of their ships rushed at us, and we passed between them to attack from behind.

The kzinti gravity polarizers were as good as ours, as were their beam-weapons, but when the legions had fought barbarians it had been feet and hooves against feet and hooves, and swords and spears against swords and spears. When, with their scout ships and fighters smashed, we closed on their line of capital ships, it reminded me of tales of fighting in the arena.

We had learnt not to attack the heavily armored weapons turrets, or the strengthened prows, but to burn into the sides. Damage in the vacuum of space multiplies itself. The first felines I saw then were bodies flying into space when my beams tore into the semi-globular belly of a great feline warship.

We cut their line at two points, using their own speed against them and allowing their van to fly on until it could return and join the battle. By the time they did, the line was in chaos.

Human barbarians often keep attacking though it is plain they have lost the tactical upper hand, and have no concept of a fighting, strategic withdrawal, fighting instead as a furious disorganized mass, each unable to support the other. The kzinti were much the same.

There were gaps in our ranks—there always are after a battle—when we flew back to the carrier, but there was wine and women and feasting too. The Jotoki poured freshly minted gold on us, still valuable even though they had a technology for transmuting metals. I had read Caesar's *Commentaries* and imagined how he would have relished being here, lecturing the Jotoki on how to improve their space tactics and quietly plotting to take them over. It was then that I began to write this commentary of my own.

And we fought. Many times, crossing distances I cannot grasp even now, to strike in unexpected new places. And we won, many times.

Not always.

We must have missed a survivor once, who told the tale.

Finally we found kzinti who were ready for us.

Then, with our fleet slashed by kzinti claws, it was ground fighting again. We of the Ninth—the Caledonian cales were mostly expended by then—and what Jotoki could be spared.

A couple of the Jotoki ships, almost empty, with only the barest shadows of Jotoki crews, escaped. We bought them that chance of escape at the cost of our own. I do not know where they went. But perhaps they led the kzinti away from Terra as they promised. Perhaps they escaped and bred their little swimmers again.

We were left behind to divert and delay the kzinti like Horatius on the ground, defending the abandoned hulks of most of the Jotoki ships. Jegarvindertsa were one of the Jotoki who remained with us. The kzinti had withdrawn at last, but we knew they would soon be back, with fresh legions of their own.

Again the picture flickered and jumped.

"We have lost everything and there is no hope. We die here on a strange, cruel world. Well, we can still die like Romans. We are not strangers to hardness. I suppose we had better kill the women and children first. We will not give them to the beasts as if they were criminals in the arena."

"It may not be necessary to die at all," said Jegarvindertsa. "We still have other weapons."

"I see none. Can we fight the felines with short swords?"

"No. With gold."

"I do not understand."

"We will hide. Human and Jotok together. There is gold on this world, and we know the kzinti like gold as do so many species."

I did not understand.

"This world has underground rivers." I did not then know how he knew that, but I accepted that he did. "Many could hide in the wilderness, where kzinti believe nothing could live, for a long time."

"The felines would hunt us out. I do not want to die like criminals I have seen, fleeing and hunted by lions in pits and cellars under the arena."

"There are caves. We Jotoki might even breed there. It is unfortunate we are unlikely to have more than a little time to deepen them further."

That gave me a thought. I have seen the mines on my Sardinian estates. "Use your gravity engines, then. With them and Jotoki weapons you can break and move great masses of rock very quickly. You can enlarge the caves, join them up, and you can dump the spoil in the sea where it will not alert the enemy."

The kzinti returned in strength. We hid and fled. The kzinti hunted and captured and killed as they might. And then they began to see this world had much rich land that supported the game and hunting they craved. Perhaps they thought us all dead.

Another gap. Then a new speaker took up the story. He looked enough like Maximus Gaius Pontus to be his son—Perpetua realized he almost certainly *was* his son—but, like a number she had just seen, with red in his hair, that suggested something other than Latin in his parentage.

Gold was left out for the kzinti. It came to be seen that when and where gold was left out, the kzinti would take it and not attack. That was the first real victory.

There were other things we left—platinum, precious gems, carvings... slowly, the kzinti began to take it for granted that these would be left for them in certain places. A human bringing them would be unmolested, and allowed to depart in peace. It took decades. It was the first modification of total war....

"Total peace was too much to expect," said Marcus Augustus. "We settled for the best that could be hoped for: low-intensity, contained conflict along defined borders while we bought peace elsewhere.

"But there were two things to note: We brought the kzinti gold and other tribute on our terms. We were not slaves but, tacitly at least, trading partners as well as game. And slowly, slowly, as they became used to luxury, they became dependent on us, used to the luxuries we could provide, even as they hunted us. At last, it was our artisans—brave ones, those—who offered themselves as slaves and who installed hypocausts to warm their floors in the long nights. Over the centuries, we have got as far as you have seen. A fragile, unspoken, imperfect *modus vivendi* far too fragile ever to put to a real test."

VIII

Marcus Augustus looked steadily at Perpetua. "And now men make *allies* of the kzinti?" His expression did not indicate that he considered this probable—nor particularly desirable.

It seemed like a very good time for Ginger to switch on their translator's active function. "Not all kzinti," he said, the speaker startling Marcus for a moment. "I am what the humans sometimes call a kdaptist. Kdapt-Pilot was a Hero of noble birth who had the radical inspiration that peace was better than war. He found followers after the First Defeat. Some fought on the human side in the Second War with Men, simply because Men were the only ones who were trying to establish peace."

"Indeed." The translator carried overtones well; which was not to say agreeably.

Ginger said, "I don't know it all, but there's a poem. About the siege of a base on an asteroid orbiting Proxima Centauri. A *human* wrote it." He half-closed his eyes and ears, and began to recite:

> *We served the deep-space radar guiding the*
> *   giant laser guns:*
> *We'd hold for fifteen days, or twenty at the most.*
> *Hold! Manteufel told us, in that dark Hell past*
> *   the suns!*
> *Hold! His dying words: Let every Man die at*
> *   his post!*
>
> *We fought with desperate makeshifts, caught*
> *   unprepared for war*
> *Found death as we manned our weapons, death*
> *   as we burned the dead.*
> *Death at gunport and conduit, death at each*
> *   airlock door,*
> *Death from the Vengeful Slashers in the sky of*
> *   black and red.*
>
> *Handful that we were, we were Man in heart*
> *   and limb*
> *Strong with the strength of Men, to obey,*
> *   command, endure!*
> *Each of us fought as if hope for the garrison*
> *   hung on only him,*
> *Though the siege went on forever and it seemed*
> *   our doom was sure.*
>
> *But honor our kdaptist allies, and give the*
> *   kdaptists their due!*
> *Remember the valiant kdaptists, who fought by*
> *   us, faithful and few,*

*Fought as the bravest among us, and slashed
and burned and slew,
Where blood flowed under the blood-red sun,
kdaptist blood flowed too!*

Ginger trailed off, and said, "I don't remember everything, but
I do know the end."

*Saved by kdaptists, sing their praise,
Saved by the blessing of Heaven!
We couldn't have held for twenty days.
We held for ninety-seven.*

Marcus Augustus cleared his throat. Then he cleared it again.
"I must speak with you sometime soon, of Horatius," he said at
last. "Excuse me a moment." He left the chamber, not wishing to
show his face just now.

The translator had carried overtones very well indeed.

Ginger switched it off as Perpetua said, "Quick thinking."

"I got up and read some of their literature last night. Learning sets cost me sleep. How are we going to get them out of
here?"

"The slaves, you mean?"

"The ones here too."

"The slaves?"

"All of them."

"What, *every human on the planet*?"

"It's the only way to free *all* the slaves," Ginger said reasonably. "Otherwise the kzinti and the patricians will just make
more slaves."

"You're certifiable. There must be thousands."

"Probably about fifty thousand," Ginger estimated. "Certifiable
as what?"

"Demented. Any psychist would recommend you for treatment
at public expense. We might get one percent out on our ship if
we packed them in in stasis, if we *had* a stasis field, which we
don't."

"We'll need more ships, certainly," Ginger agreed.

"Stop agreeing with me when I'm arguing with you! *Even*," she
said, breathing hard, "even if we had the ships, we've got *no* pilots,

no fuel, *no* weapons, and no destination we could reach before we were caught! And we don't have the ships, and we don't have the money to get the ships!"

"It is possible these problems may be overcome," said a synthesized voice.

They both looked up. A Jotok was settled in the web of branches overhead, two tentacles holding an oblong metallic device that had clearly been repaired many times.

Marcus Augustus hadn't been surprised by their translator for very long, Ginger recalled. "What are you doing here?" he exclaimed, beginning to be offended.

"We live here," said the Jotok.

"I mean in this room!"

"So do we. We are Jinvaretsimok, senior archivist." The Jotok swung down by one tentacle and landed on the two free ones. "Tradition tells us that most problems are the result of insufficient money. This should not be the case here. If there are aspects of the problem that money cannot solve, perhaps something else will prove applicable. May we hear more about the circumstances?"

IX

Once they were back in the car, the first thing Perpetua said was, "Incredible."

"Having never spoken with Jotoki who have been free for the past nine centuries, I am in no position to judge," Ginger remarked. "At least now we know why they've never been found. I hope my sense of smell comes back. I wonder what those trees are?"

"Cedar," she said absently. "From Earth. Must have intended the wood as trade goods. . . . I meant all that gold is incredible!"

"I suppose the Jotoki had to find something to keep themselves busy for nine hundred years," Ginger said.

"They certainly haven't been sitting on their hands," Perpetua said.

Ginger thought about it. "Yes they have," he finally said. "Where else could they?"

"It's a metaphor," she said.

"Oh." Ginger, like most Wunderkzin, understood metaphors, though many other kzinti simply found them annoying—a race which occasionally resorts to disembowelment in the course of reasoned debate has little motivation to search for subtle means of expression. "Would that be why Marcus Augustus warned me against garlic? An unusually obscure metaphor?"

"Garlic? When was this?"

"When you and Jinvaretsimok were talking about how to get hold of phase initiators."

"Garlic," she said, puzzled. "I have no idea. Maybe they've bred poisonous insects that attack anything that smells like it? They certainly had plenty of other schemes in the works!"

"Not that one," Ginger said positively. "The *kz'zeerekti* on the hunt had been eating it, and so had the Jotoki. The local kzinti have actually developed a taste for the stuff." He blew out air through his mouth to expel the memory of the taste of a particularly concentrated mouthful.

"You never mentioned that."

"I noticed the details were troubling you. Arm yourself. The car is not going where I'm telling it to."

Perpetua leaped up to look out the windscreen, then got down and opened an access panel. Then she said, "There's something that's probably an autopilot override, and a transceiver, and a booby trap in case I try to remove them. I think somebody can hear us."

"Let me in there." Ginger got down and looked it over. It was a good booby trap. It wouldn't blow up the car; just the control circuitry, crashing them. "Well, this is hopeless," he said, picking up a pad to write her a note.

The car landed in the courtyard of Trrask-Rarr's castle—an almost traditional structure—and shut down. The troops standing by kept it covered, and Trrask-Rarr went to the hatch himself and opened it.

Trader was on the deck, using his *wtsai* to hack frantically though a mass of seat restraints he'd evidently tried to make into a net. He seemed pretty well immobilized. Trrask-Rarr stepped in, amused, and the monkey appeared overhead, head down, and dropped a bomb on him.

It was a can of emergency patching foam, rigged to burst open; and, as it was designed to do, the foam stuck to everything it touched. Trrask-Rarr tried to take a swing at the monkey before the stuff could set, but Trader turned out not to be tangled, naturally, and whipped the webwork around Trrask-Rarr's arm and jerked it off course.

Trrask-Rarr inhaled deeply and held his breath until the foam went rigid—not long—then exhaled, disdaining to notice the yanks on his fur as he breathed.

The monkey dropped down, landing on its feet as they always seemed to do, and said, "Please excuse the poor hospitality." In formal Kzin. Not a bad accent, either. "We are still recovering from the interruption in our efforts to arrange the removal of all *kz'zeerekti* from Kzrral."

It took Trrask-Rarr a moment to absorb this. He stopped planning the details of their vivisection and said, "I'm listening."

"May I offer our guest some solvent?" said Trader, putting Trrask-Rarr on the spot.

Soon, bound by hospitality and his honor, instead of the less-definitely-confining hull-repair material, Trrask-Rarr was brushing conditioner through his fur and taking in the most amazing scheme he'd ever heard. The monkey kept speaking without permission, but as Trrask-Rarr was now in the role of guest, and Trader didn't object, he treated this as if it were normal. A Jotok was brought in to remove the monitor and override, and worked as they discussed the plan.

The two of them were engaged in an effort to collect humans from wherever they were being kept as slaves, for some reason—it might be a religious ritual, if it mattered—and, working to that end, were practicing subtlety and deceit on Warrgh-Churrg. Successfully, so far. Still, they had never encountered such a large human population, and were unprepared to deal with it. The feral Jotoki, however, sneaking little beasts, had worked out plans for all kinds of situations, and had one that could be adapted now. Once he heard it, Trrask-Rarr immediately pointed out, "Warrgh-Churrg doesn't own the ships in orbit outright. He'll need to buy out the other partners before he'll agree—he wouldn't do anything that he thinks benefits them."

"The Jotoki can provide the gold," Trader said.

"Not without a reason he'll believe. But if you give me the gold, I can claim I captured it on a raid, and use it to buy land from him."

"You'd need to do a real raid," said the monkey—their many faults didn't include stupidity.

"Of course," Trrask-Rarr said tolerantly. "Have them collect it somewhere and flee at our approach. I buy land, Warrgh-Churrg buys out the ships and starts refitting them, and you take his gold and go off to wherever you go, and bring back what you need to."

"Aren't you concerned about the possible consequences to the Patriarchy?" said the monkey, then leapt back when he grinned at it. (Not stupid at all.)

"If the Patriarch desires my assistance," Trrask-Rarr rumbled, "let the Patriarch send an investigator to find how Warrgh-Churrg's Hunt Master managed to get my two best sons killed but bring the foolish ones back alive. Warrgh-Churrg is using *kz'zeerekti* to weaken every clan but his own, which means he's acting against the Patriarchy himself. Anything that keeps him from doing that helps the Patriarch."

They discussed money. It was going to be expensive to buy back the land that should be his—more than the ships cost. Trrask-Rarr didn't like the idea of Warrgh-Churrg having the surplus, but the monkey said, "If we get you more gold than that, you can spend it on other things after you buy the land, and prices will go up."

"Why should they do that?" said Trrask-Rarr.

"Inflation. More money in circulation," said the monkey unhelpfully. Trrask-Rarr puzzled over the images this called up.

"Everybody will want some," Trader explained.

That was reasonable. "So the ships will cost more," Trrask-Rarr said, to be certain.

Both agreed. "Parts shouldn't. Refitting will, though," said the monkey.

"I doubt the slaves will be getting higher pay," he said ironically. "Supplies."

Trrask-Rarr ran the brush along his leg, then turned to the

Jotok that had been waiting nearby for a little while and said, "Report."

"Potent Trrask-Rarr, the adjuncts are removed. Shall we do engine maintenance, so as to provide evidence of why a landing here was necessary?"

"Yes. Good thinking." As the Jotok left, Trrask-Rarr said, "*Marrrkusarrg-tuss* was very probably warning you not to go on another hunt when he warned about garlic, Trader. They eat it constantly, and no doubt another group of assassinations is planned."

"I . . . don't *think* Warrgh-Churrg makes direct arrangements with the *kz'zeerekti*," said Trader doubtfully.

"Of course not. I don't make them either. And yet, arrangements seem to have been made," Trrask-Rarr said dryly.

"Urr. I see what you mean. I believe the press of business will be too heavy for me to join another hunt in any case."

"Of course. So: First you propose the plan to Warrgh-Churrg, then I get the gold and buy land. He buys out the ships and sends you for what he needs, and the refit begins . . . ?"

"While we're gone," the monkey said.

."Urr. Good." He was beginning to understand how Trader could put up with it: The monkey tended to be interesting. "When will you get back with the key parts?"

Trader and the monkey looked at one another. "Two hundred days?" Trader hazarded.

"Two hundred!"

"We'll have to go to more than one place," the monkey said, misunderstanding.

Trader got it. "Trrask-Rarr was expecting it to be *longer*," he explained. "It's hard to get used to how fast hyperdrive is."

"Oh."

"It occurs to me that the fastest way for the Patriarch to learn of Warrgh-Churrg's folly would be through you," Trrask-Rarr said. "Have you some means of contacting someone who can reach him?"

"Somebody will have it," the monkey said confidently.

X

In the circumstances, it was reasonable not to discuss anything in the car on the way back, and Ginger was too busy flying to hold a written conversation. Likewise there was no sense in talking in Warrgh-Churrg's car hangar, nor in the open; so by the time they were back in the ship, there was a certain amount of pressure built up.

As soon as the airlock had cycled, Perpetua burst out, "That Jotok mechanic was a spy for the Romans!"

Ginger, who had his own revelations to make, stopped. "How do you know?"

"It spoke with the same accent as Jinvaretsimok's translator."

"Are you sure?"

"Ginger, have I ever disputed your sense of smell?"

"Urr." He thought about it, then added, "No offense was intended."

"Thank you," she replied, a little startled. "So now we know how the car got bugged."

It took Ginger a second. "They *all* work together!"

"Sure. Trrask-Rarr's Jotoki talked to Warrgh-Churrg's."

"That'll save us some time," Ginger said thoughtfully. "The gold-theft ruse is probably being arranged already."

"Hadn't thought of that. . . . You know, the male population of the original colonists must have been almost completely wiped out."

"They all smelled about the same on the hunt," he agreed. "Hunt Master had to use instruments to check for outsiders." Then he said, "How did *you* know?"

"They pronounce the 's' at the end of a name. That was out of fashion by the time of Julius Caesar. Most of the first generation must have learned Latin in written form, so that means the

Caledonians—and *their* men had an even higher casualty rate than the Romans."

"They did, didn't they?" Ginger was a pacifist, but still a kzin. Somebody else's casualty rate had not particularly commended itself to his attention. "Did you notice the floor was warm there, too?"

"Well, it *is* the tropics—hey," Perpetua said, frowning.

"'Hey' indeed. We were in a *tree*. Trees are cool."

"A hypocaust in a forest?"

"If that was a forest, a farm is a meadow. Those trees were planted just where they wanted them," Ginger said, "and now I know why their industries have never been detected. The foundries are underground, and they use the water from that dam—"

"*What* dam?"

"The one we walked through," he said, surprised.

"That was a dam? Where was the water?"

"Underground," Ginger said. "Where most of the dam was. They must have been a couple of centuries diverting the entire aquifer into that channel. It'd be why there's no offshore trench—the runoff must be spread out to blur the heat signature."

"You just *happened* to *notice* that?" Perpetua said incredulously.

"No, of course not, I was paying very close attention," he said. "The way you were to the language and culture. It's called perspective. It's why we're a team, Pet. And why it works . . . their industrial exhaust gases must be cooled and filtered with water, and they probably use slag and ashes to neutralize the acids that makes . . . Remember what I said about humans and conservation? I was right but I was wrong. Omnivores aren't much motivated to limit their effect on their environment, but humans do turn out to be awfully good at *concealing* it. If they want to. These do, and they're making more effective use of their resources than any culture I've seen, human or kzinti. Hunt Master couldn't very well say much, but the idea that the humans he was hunting might be making their own firearms worried him. I think they do, and I think they could do a great deal more if they wanted. I think these hunts are used to cull out weak and stupid humans, too—except that the humans are really doing it, not corrupting the system." His tail lashed once.

"I wonder if that was Warrgh-Churrg's own idea," Perpetua said.

"I'm off the scent."

"Well, if the Jotoki are all working together, what about the humans? During the Occupation there were some Wunderland-ers who managed to talk their masters into some *amazingly* bad plans. And that was after just a few years' acquaintance."

Ginger's tail lashed again. "I now find myself less enthused about rescuing them. Some kzinti's *only* virtues are courage and honor. It's consistent with what I've read of Roman history, too."

"Huh?"

"They raised the children of potential rebels in the homes of Roman nobles. Disgraceful. No respect for heritage."

Every so often Perpetua was forcibly reminded that her partner was an *alien*. His regarding Rome's most brilliant peacekeeping innovation as a betrayal of family values accomplished this now. "Oh. I didn't know where, but I knew they had to have decent industrial technology."

"The lamps?"

"No, M— what about the lamps?"

"They gave white light. That takes superior refining techniques. The thorium that goes into lamp mantles is found with other things that are hard to remove, and those would have made the light yellow."

"How come you know so much about thorium?"

"It can be bred into fissionable material. I got interested in its other uses when I was a student."

"Why did you want to know about fissionable material?" she said, a little alarmed.

"I didn't, particularly. It's just used in making weapons." See-ing her expression, he said, "I'm a kzin! Do I get all suspicious because you know how to cook things? I mean, you might be planning to boil me up, right?"

"Meat isn't usually boiled," she said, her expression one of distaste.

"Aha," he said archly. "You've been thinking about this, then?"

Perpetua made a strangling noise in her throat, then said, "Behave."

Having made his point, and enjoyed it, he recalled what he'd been saying. "So if it wasn't the lamps, what?"

"Marcus Augustus didn't talk down to me, and the female slaves we saw were treated about the same as the males. You surely know that humans die easily. Well, pregnant female humans, in a society without high technology, die *really* easily. Women tend to be regarded as property unless they're aristocrats, and even then they're not included in serious discussions. Nothing that'll endanger them, see?"

"Not really."

"I guess you'll have to take my word for it. He didn't treat me like I was helpless, so he's used to women who aren't."

"Oh, now I see. —I think that purple dye was synthetic, too."

"You can see purple?" she said.

"Of course," he said, surprised. "Why not?"

"Well, Kzin's sun is a lot redder than Sol. I'd have thought it was outside your range."

"How are we supposed to tell if a kill is diseased?" he said. "Liver color is everything."

"Oh."

Ginger reflected for a moment. "I never thought about it before, but now that I do, purple tends to look brighter than other colors. I suppose it doesn't show up well on Kzinhome. We should make a note of that; it could be useful to someone."

"How?"

"Well, say if someone is trying to hide from kzinti aerial surveillance in a garden, he'll want to look for violets. They'll blot out what's around them."

Perpetua frowned, but plugged in a pad and began writing. She was far from the first, of either species, to find such things counterintuitive. (During the Second War, when there was real combat rather than conquest, it had taken considerable time for the combatants to realize that human eyes identify shapes, while kzinti eyes detect motion—so that, at first, both had used camouflage gear that was *guaranteed to stand out* to the enemy's vision.) When she finished, she said, "It occurs to me to wonder what the Romans are planning that they haven't told us."

It had evidently just crossed her mind for the first time. Every so often Ginger was forcibly reminded that his partner was an alien. "We just have to present them with nothing but specific courses of action and explain it as force of circumstance," he said, as if he had thought it up on the spot.

"I suppose," she said, looking something up. "I hope things go quickly. It's going to be summer soon on We Made It."

Ginger thought about it. "How does that affect us?"

"It's hard to land in a wind traveling twice the speed of sound."

"Why would we want to?"

"Aren't we going there for hyperdrive parts?"

"What? No. Earth," said Ginger, confused.

"*Earth*? How are we supposed to keep the ARM from finding out?"

"But that's who we have to get them from," Ginger said. "They're the only ones who would keep it a secret. If anybody else found out about the Romans, they'd never be left alone again. The ARMs will keep it a secret, because they keep *everything* a secret."

"I don't . . . If . . . But . . . Give me a minute here."

"Certainly."

Perpetua sat and thought it through. Finally she said, "Why would they help us?"

"To reduce the Patriarchy's capabilities, which is one of their constant goals, without having to go through channels. I know some of the flatlander veterans who settled on Wunderland, and more than one has joked that the UN bureaucracy was a kzinti plot. I'll give you an example—and I had to see records of this before I believed this fellow wasn't making fun of me, so I know it's true: Chemical firearms, delivered in response to a properly logged requisition, arrive without ammunition. There's a different requisition to be completed, for ammunition without which the firearm is useless. This procedure is still in use. My Name as my Word."

Perpetua, who had lived with human government all her life and didn't see what was so odd about the story, said, "I'm convinced that's true," which was meant to please him, and did. "Maybe it will be enough to get them to agree. We can try."

Warrgh-Churrg summoned Trader the next day, and when the offworlder arrived (without the monkey) demanded, without formalities, "You went for a look at the *kz'zeerekti*, and had to land at Trrask-Rarr's castle with a breakdown. Did you say anything that might have let him know where they kept their gold?"

Trader froze, his ears cupped and swinging slowly from side to side: genuine surprise. "Feared Warrgh-Churrg, I don't *know* where they keep their gold," he replied.

"They don't," the satrap snarled. "Trrask-Rarr has it. Made a sudden raid this morning on a cavern deep in the wasteland, and when a wall caved in his troops found a stockpile."

Trader settled himself slightly and said, "Dominant One, did he take any slaves?"

"Not one. They'd cleared out, almost as if they were warned. . . ." Warrgh-Churrg glared at one of his own slaves, standing in an alcove, ready to fetch on command. The *kz'zeerekti* very properly stayed in its place, but began to smell panicky.

"The reason I ask, Fully-Named, is that there are far more *kz'zeerekti* out there than I had even speculated, and with that quantity of gold I thought he might be interested in taking part in a major shipment."

Warrgh-Churrg abruptly looked at the eyes of Trader, who ducked. "Why would *he* need gold to do that?"

"There isn't enough room on my ship for that many slaves. It would be necessary to obtain one or two large ships, possibly equipping them with hyperdrive if the price was right."

"You had implied that you couldn't get ships with hyperdrive," Warrgh-Churrg said, growing dangerous.

"I cannot. But most of the parts for a hyperdrive can be fabricated, and the key parts are available as spares. I never had enough money to do it, but if Trrask-Rarr has that much gold—"

"He's spending it," Warrgh-Churrg cut him off. "Buying land his sires once held. Suppose someone already had a large ship. Or two," he added offhandedly. "What would hyperdrive parts cost?"

Ginger was pleased to see that Perpetua had a shattergun aimed at the airlock door as he came through. When she saw it was him, she safetied it, set it down carefully, and ran up and grabbed him around the middle, to his great astonishment. She held him very hard, as human strength went, and after a few seconds he began having the strangest urge to wash her head like a kitten's. This gave him a hint about what she was doing, though, and after a little thought he patted her head, a gesture much used in entertainments. It appeared to help. She let go and looked up and said, "You're okay."

"I'm okay," he agreed. It seemed better than *I know.* "I have been cleverly talked around into going to purchase hyperdrive parts."

Perpetua began laughing. It took her a while to get it under control.

The gold began arriving two days later.

XI

The trip to Earth took almost ten weeks. As usual, they spent a lot of time playing games; as usual, Ginger almost always won.

The dangerous part of the trip, at least in Ginger's estimation, had been right at the start, when they were depending on pursuit countermeasures to stay intact. Perpetua, however, grew more uneasy the closer they got to Earth. She didn't say anything about it, but she was at least partly conscious of it: She bathed more often, sometimes twice in a day. (He in turn was not conscious of the fact that his tail began lashing when she smelled upset; but she was. She was trying to keep at least one of them calm.)

He would never have asked why. Such an assumption of authority over her mental state would have been treating her as a subordinate, and she was a friend; more, she was a *Hthnar*—something humans translated as Battle Companion, a term which did express the concept if given sufficient thought.

However, she was also a human, and therefore weird, so one day she suddenly decided to explain. "I don't trust the ARM," she said when he showed up for his watch on the mass detector.

"Good," he said agreeably, steering them around a fuzzy patch that was probably nothing much. (The thing worked better for him than for her. Its manual spoke of psionic aptitude and something called the Copenhagen Interpretation, but to him the matter was simple: It was a hunting device.)

"That's why I've been so worried. They were the ones who got Wunderland conquered, you know."

Ginger cupped an ear at her. "I'm pretty sure the Patriarchy was involved too."

She snorted. "They suppressed weapon technology and rewrote

history books as propaganda, so everybody believed that no civilized being was capable of making war. When the first reports of contact with the kzinti came in they suppressed those too, as disruptive."

"I didn't know *that!*" he exclaimed.

"It's not something humans are proud to discuss," she said.

He had no idea what to say—before confiding something that potentially demeaning, a Hero would want hostages. However, she continued almost at once.

"They're perfectly capable of suppressing knowledge of the Romans and keeping them all for study somewhere," she said.

"They'd want them off Kzrral first, though, right?" Ginger said.

"I would think so," Perpetua said, sounding puzzled.

"Then we'll be fine. I won't make a final plan until we've left Earth, so they won't be able to get it out of us."

"You haven't decided what to do after we have the Romans?"

"What would be the point? We *don't* have them," he said, honestly puzzled. "We don't even know if we can get the hyperdrives here."

"What? You acted so confident!"

"I'm a kzin. I am confident. I may also be wrong."

"I'm starting to get a glimmering of why we won," she muttered, walking out.

Ginger thought about that for a while, but couldn't see the connection.

They'd dropped out of hyperspace and were moving into Sol System, and Perpetua was trying to ease her own tension. " . . . and the Herrenmann says, 'Never mind the thanks—*repeat the instructions!*' "

Ginger was just starting to laugh when the hyperwave spoke up: "Incoming ship, identify yourselves."

Ginger tapped the mike. "We're the *Jubilee*, out of Wunderland," he said in quite good Flatlander. "Who are you?"

"Triton Relay Customs Station. Are you carrying any fissionables or bioactives?"

"No, but if you make a list we could come back," Ginger said cheerfully. Perpetua's eyes went wide and she clapped her hands over her mouth as he continued, "We'd like to talk to an ARM."

The Belter Customs officer said, "Why?" He sounded honestly perplexed.

"To engage in commerce."

"With the ARM? You'll walk out smiling and holding two coat hangers."

Ginger looked at Perpetua, who was no more enlightened than he. "Nevertheless."

"Well, I'll pass the word. —I advise against joking with them," the voice added. "There's a flatlander law against ARMs laughing at any jokes but their own."

"Thanks," Ginger said, and cut the mike.

"You don't *ever* joke with Customs, have you taken leave of your senses?" Perpetua exploded.

"No, but hopefully you won't be the last to think of that," Ginger said. "It may help. The idea came to me when I heard that silly question—as if a smuggler of murder supplies would be surprised into blurting out a truthful answer." His ears waved, once. "Suddenly I thought of a way to cope with human bureaucracy."

"*I'll* talk to the next one!" she said.

A com laser found them about an hour later. "Attention *Jubilee*, this is T.C. Smith, senior agent, ARM ident RM35M4419. I am the ARM officer at earliest available rendezvous, presently at Juno, coordinates follow. Be seeing you." A datastream beeped in and was recorded.

As Ginger altered course, Perpetua sent, "Senior Agent Smith, this is *Jubilee*, we will arrive your location—" Ginger showed the figures "—in about twenty-nine hours." She set that to repeat, then said, "He sounded positively friendly."

"I've heard that ARMs are all supposed to be kept insane," Ginger said. "Perhaps he welcomes the company. I wonder what he's doing at Juno?"

"Why, where's Juno?"

"According to these figures, it's an asteroid. Not under ARM jurisdiction."

Perpetua looked for herself, because she had to—if a kzin had done so it would have been insulting—and said, "That's weird."

Juno Traffic Control had them lie off two thousand kilometers, and at that the region seemed pretty busy. "There must be five hundred ships here!" Perpetua said wonderingly.

"About half with their drives aimed at us," Ginger commented. When she stared at him, he said, "We are of largely kzinti design, after all. And Belters who trusted strange ships in either war probably didn't survive long enough to teach the habit to anyone."

A tanker began signaling them. Perpetua acknowledged, and the speaker said, "Smith here. You need any fuel?"

"No, our planer is rigged to scoop up ambient hydrogen constantly," she replied, and Ginger stuck his finger in her mouth. She spit it out, cut the mike, and said, "What *are* you doing?"

"Not revealing capabilities," he said. "How did you people last long enough to get to space?"

She glared, then switched back on. "Are you in the tanker, or relaying?"

"In. Permission to come aboard?"

"Granted."

The tanker moved alongside and extended a travel tube, and presently Smith came through the lock with a parcel bigger than he was. "Great, gravity," he said, taking his helmet off.

He was one-gee short, and blond as a Herrenmann, but his skin was quite black, at least on his head. Also, his pressure suit was decorated with the head and shoulders of a pale-skinned man in an odd-looking cap, with a bill in back as well as in front; the man was smoking a curly pipe and holding a magnifying glass before one eye. Perpetua, who had spent the past day learning something about Sol Belter culture, said, "Just how long have you been at Juno?"

"Open curiosity, that's refreshing! Just over eleven years now. Well done. Junior assistant to the second deputy secretary of the consul."

"What does that mean?" Ginger said, stepping into view.

"I thought you sounded like a kzin. It means by the time I'd accumulated enough procedural complaints to be retired, my pension would have come to more than I get in salary, so they sent me where I couldn't annoy anybody worse than they normally are."

"What does T.C. stand for?" Perpetua said.

"The name of a classical author. I come from a long line of subversives, and I joined the ARM to stop being inundated with the material. So what do they do but put me in Propaganda. Where can I put this?" He indicated his parcel.

"What is it?" said Ginger.

"My official weaponry. If you want to search it, don't press any switches. Can I use your shower? I've spent the past day suited up and reading the manuals on all this junk."

"Why'd you do that in a pressure suit?" Perpetua said.

"The display's in the helmet." He grimaced.

"Through there," she said.

As he departed, she murmured, "Wonder what the complaints were for?"

"Throoping!" he called back up the passageway.

"Good ears," said Ginger. After the refresher had opened and closed, he added, "What's 'throoping'?"

"No idea."

The ship's database defined it as *Intra-bureaucratic use of sarcasm and absurdity to point out, refute, and if possible punish extreme foolishness. Context invariably implies the sole voice of reason speaking with total lack of concern for consequences. Origin artificial, circa 1950.* "Interesting concept," Ginger said, opening the parcel. "But does it work?"

"They must have had some reason for sending him here," she said. Then she fell silent.

There was a slug gun, a folding multibladed hullmetal knife, a hullwelding laser with a huge battery, a variable stunner, small grenades of assorted types both lethal and nonlethal, interrogation drugs, flare goggles, and impact armor; then there were the *concealed* weapons, like the dartgun rings, and the watch with its loop of Sinclair filament. "Interesting," Ginger said.

"A man arrives equipped for piracy and you call it 'interesting'?"

"No, what's interesting is that it's all newly opened. Still smells of packing foam. Never been used."

"And he must have brought it all with him eleven years ago," Perpetua realized.

"Oh?"

"The Belters wouldn't have allowed the ARM to establish an arsenal. They're as touchy about independence as Wunderlanders, and they've actually *got* it."

"Urr. Good for them."

They sorted things out into weapons, probable weapons, probable nonweapons, and who-knows-what. The last category included an elaborately sealed box of what was labeled as ordinary candy, three packages Perpetua thought looked like inflatable boats, a first-aid kit that included a small electric drill, and a sculpting rig that included an amazingly elaborate set of vibratory controls for one standard cutting bit, plus a headband with a heavy cable attaching it to the controls.

They were still puzzling over that one when Smith came out and said, "That's a touch-sculpting rig. You got some odd controls on your dispenser. What's with the sorting arrangement?" He was wearing clothes he certainly hadn't had under his suit.

"Weapons, possible, likely not, unknown," said Ginger, pointing.

"Oh, put everything in weapons," he said. "The Outfit makes a big deal over being able to kill anybody with anything. Except the candy; I got that from a woman when I said I was leaving . . . maybe you should just put that out the lock."

Perpetua and Ginger exchanged a glance, and Perpetua said, "Um, are you a paranoid?"

"No. But she is."

"Wish we had a stasis box," Ginger muttered in Wunderlander.

"Three right there," Smith replied, with a horrible accent. He pointed at the "boats" and said, in Flatlander again, "So what did you want to talk to an ARM for?"

"Ah," said Perpetua. "We're engaged in rescuing humans in kzinti custody. A couple of thousand years ago, the Jotoki recruited some Romans as mercenaries, north of Hadrian's Wall—"

"*The Ninth Legion was abducted by aliens*?" Smith exclaimed, then burst out laughing.

It took him some time to calm down. While he was wiping his eyes, Perpetua said, "You just happen to know all about the Ninth Legion?"

"Well, I guess I do now," he said, chuckling.

"Why is that funny?" Ginger said.

"Kind of a personal joke. Fission Era mythology was full of stories of people being abducted by aliens, and I got exposed to a lot of it as a kid. I gather you've found their descendants?"

"Yes . . . this seems like a funny coincidence. It's kind of obscure," Perpetua said warily.

"No coincidence at all. I told you, I'm in Propaganda. Most of it's historical work. You have to know what you're lying *about*."

"Oh."

"So where do I come in?"

"Well, there's thousands of them, and the planet they're on has two old kzinti troop carriers in orbit, so we've put together a plan to steal those, load up the humans and Jotoki, and escape. The thing is, they're slow ships. We needed an excuse to get to them, though, so we've gotten the owner to hire us to install hyperdrives in them. So we need phase initiators—everything else can be made there."

"It takes about a thousand man-hours to shake down a new phase initiator," Smith said, "and that's in a drive whose other parts are known to work together. You need two complete hyperdrives. No way I can make those just disappear; what have you got to trade?"

"Gold. You'll do it?" Perpetua said, astonished.

"Oh, absolutely, I love the idea. Gold, huh? Not many people . . . hm. I may know somebody on Mars."

"Mars?"

"Mars. Fourth planet. It's on the other side of the sun just now, so it'll be, oh, three days to get there with this rig."

"More like two," Ginger said, getting up.

"Not unless you plan to skim the sun."

"Three," Ginger agreed.

"How did you decide to believe us so quickly?" Perpetua said at their first meal.

"VSA implant," Smith replied. "Voice stress analysis. Lie detector. I don't have the kind of brain chemistry that can be tweaked into continuous heavy-duty intuition, which is what most ARMs rely on."

"I thought they were paranoid," she said.

"That's the term for public consumption," he agreed. "Keeps 'em nervous. The ARM doesn't have the omnipotence it had before the wars, so we take any advantage we can get. Untrained, unchanneled paranoids did a lot of damage in the past. People remember that." He grinned. "We remind them regularly."

"Oh," she said uneasily. "What's Mars like?"

"Cold," he said. "Dry. Less of both with each generation, though. The residents are gradually terraforming it. Before the wars it was a real hole. We used it as a dumping ground for troublemakers—writers, roleplayers, history buffs."

"Who lives there now?"

"Same people. Just not brainwashed. They like it. Don't ask me why. Part of the whole fantasist culture." He took a bite, chewed, swallowed, and added, "Not brainwashed by us, anyway."

He grew gloomy and avoided conversation for a day or so.

◇   ◇   ◇

In the middle of the third day he suddenly told Ginger, "There's people on Earth who think the ARM made the wars up."

This was apropos of nothing whatsoever, and ridiculous to boot; Ginger said, "*What?*"

"There are people who earnestly believe the whole interstellar war story is just a huge juice job. That is, all the death on Wunderland was something we caused ourselves, and we're blaming you to discredit you so you can't expose us."

Ginger thought about that, then said, "That's crazy."

"True. With eighteen billion people on Earth you get *all* kinds. At the other end of the spectrum of insanity you get the tweeties—that is, people who think the kzinti are responsible for everything that goes wrong, and this literally includes poor weather."

"What do you *do* with people like that?" Perpetua wondered, and Ginger realized it was a good question—they wouldn't simply get killed in the course of their daily affairs.

"Unless they're really deranged, ignore them. They're not that numerous."

"And the extreme cases?" she said.

"We recruit them into Technology Restriction."

Her initial laughter died down as she realized he wasn't smiling.

"There's a placement test after you qualify for the ARMs," he said. "They give you a little sliver of soap and a sheet of paper, and you're supposed to write down five fundamentally different ways to kill someone with the soap. There are only four. You can poison him, lubricate something to cause an accident, use it as fuel for combustion or explosive, or stuff it down his throat to strangle him."

"Bludgeon," said Ginger.

"It's too small. If you think of a fifth method, you're qualified for Technology Restriction. Usually." He half-smiled. "I wrote down a fifth: 'Force him to concentrate on the thing until his head explodes.' They put me in Propaganda."

Amused, Ginger said, "So what's the fifth?"

"Oh, they never tell anyone outside TR Division *that.*" He put on an expression of grim, heroic concern: " 'There's an awful lot of soap out there.' " He laughed at their incredulity, and nodded vigorously.

"I'm surprised you still have *fire,*" Ginger said.

"They're more or less resigned to fire," Smith said thoughtfully. "But I'm fairly sure they'd like to crack down on bronze."

XII

As they made the approach to Mars, Smith told Perpetua, "We want that white spot on the equator."

"Right," she said nervously—she hadn't made many landings. Then she said, "Are those *clouds*?"

"Yeah. Set down outside the northern edge, there's water under the clouds."

"A *lake*?"

"Actually the locals call it 'the Sea of Issus.' Literary reference. The ARMs call it 'O'Donnell's Surprise.' Bartholomew O'Donnell got his degree in exotic physics right at the start of the First War and came up with a proposal for more effective bombs. In those days they were desperate for something they could make quickly, so they gave him research facilities and plenty of room."

"What happened?" Perpetua said.

"All his notes and designs were in his lab, so nobody really knows, but the general consensus is that he succeeded. He had this wild notion that he could cause natural thorium to spontaneously fission—"

"Uh-oh," said Ginger.

"Well said. Fission into iron and nickel and a whole lot of beta rays. The prospectus called for never having more than a nanogram of thorium in his field generator at a time. My guess is the generator produced a somewhat larger field than he expected."

They were descending toward the settlement by then. It was on higher ground than the cloud layer, which looked thinner up close. That seemed to be about ten times the diameter of the lake, which radar said was about four kilometers across. "Some blast," said Ginger admiringly.

"There was an automated monitor on Phobos—that's the nearer moon, it was passing almost overhead—that was able to relay a picture of a big circle around the base turning X-ray blue before it melted."

"The orbital monitor *melted*?" said Perpetua.

"*Phobos* melted. A lot of it, anyway. The monitor evaporated along with that side of Phobos's surface. Recoil kicked Phobos into a less eccentric orbit, as a matter of fact."

Ginger said, "At a planet's surface, thorium can be easier to find than lead. You're lucky he didn't sterilize the system."

"I know. The affected area was a bit over half a kilometer across—pretty sharply defined, in the pictures. The blast was later calculated at something like thirty thousand megatons. Popped every dome on the planet. Land by that big one, it's the Customs shack."

Perpetua was settling *Jubilee* when Smith abruptly said, "Damn, come back up and move us to the other side of the dome."

She took them up smoothly and shifted position, then said, "People?"

"No, some kind of plants. This whole region is in a depression, not just the lake and clouds. Pictures taken right after it happened show this hemisphere looking like somebody put a bullet through a sheet of glass. This area was scooped out, and even up here it has ten times the atmospheric pressure you'd find at the antipodes. Still not much, but they've been trying to breed grass that'll survive it. Either they've succeeded, or they dumped in another ice asteroid when I wasn't paying attention. Here's good."

They suited up and went outside. There were smaller domes clustered about the Customs station, and various people had already come out of these, holding guns in a conspicuous fashion, not quite pointed at them. They paid a lot of attention to Ginger.

Smith held up an ARM ident and triggered its flasher, then said over the common channel, "If it's your intention to start fighting the next war now, by all means let me know so I can start conscripting troops." People began to disperse.

"What do you expect people to do when they see a kzinti ship landing?" somebody said defensively.

"Around here? Raise meat prices."

There was some grumbling, and another voice said in amused tones, "There's still time, Kate."

"Aw, shut up," said somebody else.

Smith signaled for the private channel and said, "Don't say anything you don't want heard. Sooner or later someone will break the encryption."

"ARMs?" Perpetua said.

"Hobbyists. These people are all obsessives. This place is still a dumping ground for lunatics—it's just that now they're self-diagnosed."

"You grew up here," Ginger guessed suddenly.

"Yes, didn't I say? I didn't. Yeah. I started working out very young." The gravity was about two-thirds that of Wunderland; he must have started wearing a weight suit well before puberty.

As they went through the airlock—the biggest they'd ever seen—Perpetua said, "You wanted to join the ARMs that young?"

"I wanted to *leave* that young. The ARMs had the best deal."

"Were there any survivors of the blast?" Ginger said.

"Everybody except the ARMs survived," Smith said. "The exiles lived on the other side of the planet, but they heard about the project and started wearing pressure suits all the time, and keeping their kids near them with bubbles handy. The ARMs made fun of them, until Blowout Day. Then they stopped." The inner door opened, and he and Perpetua took off their helmets, while Ginger folded his back.

"Any fissionables or bioactives?" said a bored-looking man with beige skin and a green-and-yellow suit. The suits outside had just been green.

"Okay. How much?" Smith said.

The man frowned, then saw the ARM ident and grunted. "Get your own," he said, and waved them by. As they passed, he said, "Hey, why is he wearing a military suit?"

"What do you mean?" Smith said.

"No tail."

Ginger had never thought about it before, but it made sense; the convenience of being able to stretch his tail for balance would make the suit more vulnerable. This was simply the only design anyone on Wunderland had ever seen.

"So nobody will suspect he's a spy," said Smith.

Ginger and Perpetua both stared at him, but the Customs inspector just snorted and waved them back into motion.

They went through another pressure door, but before either of them could say anything to Smith, somebody said, "Hey, *Waldo,* what's the password?"

Smith, in the lead, stopped, and slowly turned to the group of five men to the left of the doorway. "There's a new one," he said, in a low voice. "It's, 'I'm not an unarmed child anymore.'"

He had been a mild, affable companion for the past three days. Now Ginger smelled murder.

Since humans who fight for trivial reasons are typically of inferior intelligence, it was a common error to suppose that kzinti were rather dim. In fact, they averaged somewhat brighter than humans, due to intense competition for mates; but for the same reason, they just didn't *care*.

But Ginger had a responsibility to see to. "Excuse me, sir," he said to Smith, "but you did say back at the embassy you wouldn't kill anyone else until you found me another job."

Smith turned sharply, staring. "*What*?"

Ginger moved, quickly and smoothly, out of Smith's reach. "I realize these aren't kzinti, Mr. Smith, but you did say *anyone*, sir."

The five men had already dwindled to two, the others having worked out the implications at once. Smith blinked a few times, looked back at the remaining two, looked at Ginger again, and nodded. "Fair enough." He turned to face the pair again, and said in a declamatory tone, "'Would you buy it for a quarter?'"

Both of the men had the smoothness of motion that indicated a human past 100, but Smith must have been nearly that old himself; and while he was no Hero, compared to a low-gee build he looked like a Jinxian. One was whispering frantically in the other's ear; Ginger was able to catch the phrase "ARM Commando," this being one of the first terms he'd learned in Flatlander. The one being spoken to was shorter and solider, but not in Smith's shape.

That human looked at Ginger, then at his own companion; then he said, "Uh, pass, friend."

As they went by, Ginger thought to hear a suit's recycler start up. He didn't look—he was pretty certain whose it was, anyway.

They were in a broad inner space, like a courtyard, only with no gun turrets. Smith led them through it, past unlabeled pressure doors, to a door just like the others, and started it opening. Perpetua, who was just getting the idea that she'd come very close to being held by the UN as principal witness, started up an innocuous subject: "How did this settlement get started?"

"After the Blowout one of the old lifers talked people into

gathering everything up and bringing it here. More air and water. They stayed up here because it wasn't stable down lower. Still isn't. Once a habitat was set up, they formed a government and petitioned the UN for membership before the ARM thought of jamming them. The ARMs try to keep people from hearing more than absolutely necessary about this place, but it's really popular with smugglers since the ARM moved in on Luna," he said.

"What was this lifer's name?" Ginger said, impressed—he was picturing what the weather must have been like for the migration.

"He didn't know. He dated to brainwipe days," said Smith. They entered the door, and he closed it; abruptly the floor began to descend. "There are stories that he was actually Raymond Sinclair, but I checked ARM records, and Sinclair was murdered years before the Founder arrived. He seems to have been something of an invisible man—the Founder, that is. Have you ever heard of the Tehuantepec Canal?" They hadn't. "Okay. On Earth there's an ocean bordered by two continents, and one of the two is kept from freezing solid by an ocean current from the other. Now, the sun has been abnormally cool for thousands of years, and keeps getting worse by stages. The warm current started to give up most of its heat in hurricanes as a result. Sharper gradient, see? What the Founder appears to have done, to get arrested and brainwiped, was make secret arrangements with local officials and investors to blast open a sea-level trench at a place called Tehuantepec, where two oceans weren't separated very far. The ocean to the east was the one with the current, and the one to the west was cooler, with a higher sea level. Water washed out the trench, and mixed with the warm water, so it got stirred up and wouldn't stay put long enough to let hurricanes form. They need still, saturated air. The ocean current wound up transporting more heat than it had in a thousand years, so everybody was saved. But the man responsible had already been brainwiped, so the ARM made his records vanish and claimed it was their own project. The Founder turned out to be one of those people who does really well in low gravity, so he was still here a couple of centuries later for the Blowout." The elevator stopped. Another door was now visible.

Perpetua began, "That is the filthiest—"

"Who goes there?" said a speaker over the door.

"A true believer," said Smith.

"What do you want?" said the speaker.

"To do one thing."

The door began opening. "Surely they didn't call him Founder all the time," Ginger said, and stopped to gape.

The cavern before them had to be artificial, its lining fused dust; but it looked like an enormous natural cave, bigger than the dome they'd landed by. There were gardens, with *trees*, and light sources in the roof that made it about twice as bright as on the surface. In the center of the cavity floor, hundreds of meters away, was what looked like a big rock formation with its own cave opening; a waterfall trickled down one side over a couple of pretty good bonsai. There was a sign above the cave opening:

ODD JOHN'S TOXIC DUMP

"No," said Smith. "They called him John Smith."

"Your ancestor?" Ginger said.

"Who knows? Lots of people on Mars took the name Smith after the Blowout. Classical allusion. In his case, though, it was just a standard label for someone whose name was unknown." He led them toward the rocks.

"'Toxic dump'?" Perpetua said, alarmed at the unfamiliar term.

"Another ancient reference. People didn't use to reduce sewage and garbage to simple organics with superheated steam. They just left things in pits."

"How did they make plastics?" wondered Ginger.

"The raw materials originally came from underground." Smith paused to look at Ginger. "Your homeworld hasn't had petroleum for about ten thousand years, has it?"

"Wunderland has petroleum," Ginger said, surprised.

"He means Kzinhome," Perpetua said. "Like his is Earth."

Smith scowled, and Ginger snorted amusement. "I see. Probably not. What did people do about the smell?"

"Lived somewhere else," Smith said.

"The fellow who first began mining those pits must have gotten awfully rich," Ginger speculated as they got to the entrance. There was a door a little ways in.

"No, on Earth it's a branch of government. There's still some garbage fortunes in the Belt, though," said Smith, lifting a sign that said SCOPPY FEVER and tapping the keypad underneath. The door opened, and he went in first.

They heard, "What the hell do you— *Waldo!*"

"*Hilda!*" Smith replied as they moved into better lighting than the entryway's.

After a short silence the woman said, "Theo. Good to see you. What do— Theo, there's a kzin behind you."

"Yes, he keeps me out of trouble. I gather Larch is still mooching off his mother."

The shop was something out of Davidson, with counters and racks and display cases crammed with unrelated oddities. There was actually a stuffed crocodile up by the ceiling; it must have been ruinously expensive. The woman behind the sales counter was very tall, like most other locals, and beige, but with hair going gray and lines at the corners of her eyes. "Yes," she said, watching Ginger. Then she pointed at him and said, "Don't think you can try your telepathy for a better price. I'm a junk dealer, the only thing that works on me is money."

Smith held up a hand in front of Ginger—unnecessarily, as Ginger was too astonished and offended to speak—and stepped forward to tell her in a very low voice, "Mom, first of all, it was the Slavers who used telepathy to control minds; second, damn few kzinti are telepaths; third, none of those have Names, which he does, indicating high social value; and fourth, telepaths are all addicted to a drug that enhances the facility and destroys their health, so you've just done the equivalent of greeting a total stranger by calling him a wirehead."

She opened her eyes wide, then closed them and kept them shut for a bit. She hunched down about a handspan—human handspan—and her face changed color, getting lighter in some places and darker in others. She took a deep breath, opened her eyes, and said in a low voice, "Sir, I apologize. Please feel welcome."

"Thank you," said Ginger.

There was a moment of awkward silence. Perpetua broke it by saying, "Was Larch the short one?"

Smith gave her a stare, then apparently realized that she was shorter than every person they'd met except one, and said, "Yeah. Hey Mom, you should have heard Ginger. Managed to convey the idea that I was some kind of trained killer."

"You *are* a trained killer," said his mother.

"I don't go around single-handedly massacring groups of kzinti when I get offended, which is what he implied."

"Of course, you couldn't talk about it if you did," she observed with a straight face.

Smith sighed heavily, then said, "How quickly I recall why I don't drop by more often. We need two hyperdrives."

His mother gave an incredulous chuckle—a little late, Ginger thought. "You want inertialess drives along with those?"

"It's Marley Foundation business."

Her manner changed utterly. She leaned back, her face grew still, and her eyes narrowed. She said, "What have you done for it?"

"I got transferred to the Belt eleven years ago. Check funding and dates for the Outback Restoration Project."

She nodded once and went through a door. Ginger heard tiny clicks from different parts of the room they were in, and held quite still. Perpetua said, "T.C., what's going on?"

"The Marley Foundation is a private charity dedicated to saving people from foolish planning, often their own. Very old. I was assigned to investigate them and wound up joining, about fifty years back. Twelve years ago there was a big ARM project to clear out the Australian Outback—a large desert—so it could be preserved in its natural condition, without a lot of tourists coming in. I was in charge of selling the idea to the voters. The thing is, there were people who'd been living there for thousands of years, and they couldn't be expelled—they were arguably part of the natural condition. I went and talked to a lot of them, and we cooked up a plan. I sold the ARM on the idea of making them official caretakers of the region, and I arranged to supply them with plans and equipment, and as soon as they were put in charge of the region they cut a channel from the sea to the middle of the desert. Logarithmic spiral, uniform grade, so Coriolis force caused air to move up the channel of its own accord. Water condensed out as the air rose, and a little stream formed. In another century it'll be a pretty decent river. They didn't particularly *like* the desert, you see. They were just the descendants of people who knew how to survive there."

Perpetua was openmouthed and shaking with silent laughter. "How did they mask the explosions?" she finally got out.

"Oh, I gave them a couple of disintegrators."

"*That's* the shape!" Ginger exclaimed, making them both jump. "This cavern was carved with a disintegrator, wasn't it?"

Smith recovered and said, "Yeah, they didn't have too much intact dome material. Bored down, ran an air tube in to blow the dust out, and had another disintegrator up on the surface aimed at the falling dust. Opposite charge, so when it came down it fused to the ground."

"And the current fused the wall of the chamber," Ginger said, as pleased as if he'd done it himself. "There are caverns back home that humans carved that way during the Second War, with openings a kzin couldn't get a leg into. A lot of invaders died after passing by one of those."

"Oh, yeah," said Perpetua.

"How come it took you so long?" Smith wondered.

"This one's a lot bigger," Ginger said.

"Never saw one with *trees* in it, either," said Perpetua.

"True."

The proprietor returned. "Excuse me; what's your name?" said Perpetua.

"Joanna." She seemed a little startled, but went on with what she had come back for: "This way."

"Perpetua, and Ginger."

"How do."

They followed her into a back corridor, then into a cramped chamber which looked like a storeroom for things too odd to keep out front—which was saying something. Ginger just had time to notice that while things sat on the floor or hung on the walls, nothing on the floor leaned against a wall. Then the floor descended.

The elevator was slower than the one before. "I keep meaning to study tap dancing," Joanna said after a while, for no discernible reason.

T.C. seemed to find it funny. "Another archaic reference," he told them. "One reason the ARM presence here is so thin on the ground. They have to do constant data searches to find out what people are saying. Usually just conversation—drives them nuts."

The light was from overhead, and grew fainter as they went down. The walls ended, leaving blackness at the edge of the floor. They were in a big volume, and still descending. Ginger's tail tried to lash.

When they stopped, Joanna said, "Basement dungeon, everybody out."

"As I said," T.C. remarked, but didn't go on.

When they were off the platform, lights began to go on.

This took a while.

Eventually Ginger said, "Why don't you all live down here? There's more room than all the domes."

"We do. Different families have their own caverns, but they all connect up—how do you think we got this stuff down here?"

The equipment could have made up a well-equipped multifunction carrier—troopship, fighter station, hospital, and kzinforming—though the assembled hull sections would have given it an awfully odd profile. And extra nacelles would have had to be custom-made for all the weaponry. Possibly a tertiary power plant to supply them, too.

"This way," Joanna said, interrupting Ginger's reverie. They stepped onto a slidewalk, one of many, and began moving through what might have been the toy box of a precocious infant Titan. "What do you need *two* hyperdrives for?" she said.

"Equipping a couple of transport ships to evacuate a lot of humans from a kzinti world," T.C. said.

"And Jotoki," said Perpetua.

"What's that?" Joanna said.

Ginger and Perpetua stared at her, speechless with astonishment.

"They look sort of like starfish," T.C. said. "They don't come to Sol System much," he explained to the Wunderlanders. "The ARM harasses them about what they can sell."

"They're aquatic?" Joanna said.

"Amphibious, if I remember right," T.C. said.

"They have an immature aquatic stage, and five sexes," Ginger said. "Each limb starts as a separate nonsentient creature. They meet and join at maturity. They develop intelligence just before they breed."

"Oh," said Joanna. "Just the opposite of us, then."

They had to get off to go back and get Perpetua; she was laughing so hard she fell off the slidewalk.

Once they were going again, Joanna asked T.C., "You two up to something?"

"*Mother*," he said.

"Well, I just don't like surprises."

"Neither do I, so keep the next one to yourself. . . . Great Ghu, where did all these *come* from?"

There were five complete hyperdrive systems, and parts to make up perhaps a dozen more. Two of the complete hyperdrives would need extensive rework before use—there is something distinctive and disquieting about a functional hyperdrive, at least to most organic intelligences, and those two systems didn't have it. Of the working ones, one was immense—about the right size for the hypothetical ship made from everything in the cavern. The other two were about of a size, but not much alike in appearance. One was clearly human design. The other . . . "Who made *that*?" said T.C.

"Beats the free ions out of me," said Joanna. "Came off a smuggler that piled in about nine years back. Notice how all the parts are linked to a central armature, so you can disconnect them without them floating away?"

"Pierin," said Ginger. "I've never met one, but they're supposed to do things like that. Incredibly fussy about details. Very good at war, the Patriarchy still isn't making much progress against them."

"They're warlike?" Joanna said. She sounded surprised.

"Did you think we were the only ones?" Ginger said, and he definitely was surprised.

"Well, yes. I thought you were found by some peaceful species and got to space by conquering them."

Ginger snorted. "We were found by the Jotoki, but what they wanted us for was to be mercenaries. If there's a 'peaceful' race advanced enough for star travel, I've never heard of them."

"There's the puppeteers," said Joanna. "They never attack anybody."

"Funny how you never hear about anyone attacking them, either," Ginger said. "How much for these two?"

"How much would you like to pay?"

"Nothing. Thanks, where can we hire a lifter?"

Perpetua and T.C. merely stood by and watched the two traders at work. Due to his combination of predatory shrewdness and disconcerting honesty, Ginger was even more effective at bargaining with humans than with kzinti. It threw off human merchants to have their claims taken with apparent seriousness; it slowed them down, forcing them to think about what they were actually saying.

There was another consideration. "Mom," T.C. interrupted after about ten minutes' chaffering, "has it occurred to you that he *literally* has a nose for just how low you'll go?"

Joanna stared at her son, then looked at Ginger.

Cats always look like they're smiling.

Joanna grumbled something inarticulate and named a price.

"Done," said Ginger.

"I can rent you a lifter," Joanna began.

T.C. sighed loudly—and theatrically—and then told the Wunderlanders, "My treat." He opened one of his suit pockets and undid a sealed container. Inside was a tiny vial of yellow powder, resembling pollen.

Joanna said, "Is . . ." and trailed off.

"A gift from Aunt Sophronia," her son said.

"Where did it *come* from?" she exclaimed.

"Jinx," he said, as if to a small and unclever child.

"I know *that*," she snapped.

"T.C., no," Perpetua said. "We can't let you give up your booster-spice."

He looked blank. Then he dug out four more vials. "Where do you think confiscated contraband ends *up*?" he said.

The quickest way to effect the trade turned out to be bringing *Jubilee* into the cavern. Perpetua didn't even think of doing the piloting for this. Ginger brought the ship through the series of hatchways and chambers not only safely, but symmetrically—that is, with almost identical clearance on all sides. (Locals in pressure suits stood around clapping after some of the narrower turns.) After he set the ship down and the cavern door began to shut, he turned to T.C. and said, "Breathe. It's very distracting when you stop."

Joanna ran the cargo lifter herself. She paused to stare at the gold. "I've never seen so much," she said softly.

"Sol System uses a power standard, don't they?" Ginger said.

"What?" she said, startled out of reverie. "Yes, of course, what else has a value that can't change?"

"Nothing I know of. I was just wondering why gold is still so prized."

"Eighteen billion flatlanders watch a lot of television," she replied. "The only stuff that makes better connections is superconductor, and that can't be laid down only one atom thick." She started the lifter loading. "This planet with the refugees—" (she hadn't been told they were Romans) "—does it have a lot of volcanoes?"

"I don't believe it has any," Ginger realized.

"That's weird," she said.

"Why? Jinx has no volcanoes."

"And no gold. I was wondering where this stuff came from. Quartz is out."

"There's quartz," he said.

"Must be old, if there's no geological activity."

"There's hot springs," he recalled.

She paused the lifter and said, "It's going to bug me." She did some searching on its control screen, then said, "Calaverite and sylvanite. Gold ores found in upwelling deposits from springs. Huh, no wonder the humans haven't been rooted out!"

"What do you mean?"

"They're tellurium compounds. Any refining process would produce huge amounts of tellurium residues, and that'd definitely keep away anyone with a nose like yours!" She started up the lifter again and got back to work.

"Why?" he said to her back.

"They reek. Smell just like garlic," she called over her shoulder.

Once *Jubilee* was back outside, T.C. wandered around while they spent some of their gold on extra supplies. They were just coming in for another load when he showed up and said, "You guys have to go now. The ARM has figured out you're buying starship parts, and they'll have a ship here in five hours or so."

Ginger just nodded, but Perpetua said, "You're doing this without permission?"

They both looked at her, and T.C. told Ginger, "Look out for her, will you?"

"She doesn't need it, she's just surprised sometimes," Ginger said. "Before we go, tell me: Where did Joanna locate a tank of lobsters for sale?"

Smith just spread his hands. "She does that."

"Yes, but *how*?"

"I've always assumed some sort of pact. Look, no fooling, you need all the head start you can get. I'll stay here and get a ride from somebody."

"Will you be in much trouble?" Perpetua said.

"You kidding? If they fire me my income goes up eight and a half percent. Go, shoo." He made brushing motions away from himself.

On a sudden impulse Perpetua stepped forward and kissed him. She took her time about it. When she let him go, Smith said faintly, "Cogswell."

"What?"

"My middle name. You better go."

Jubilee had a fusion drive along with the planer, and using the two together gave an acceleration of just under thirty-one gees. They left atmosphere on planer alone, then boosted straight down from the ecliptic until they could get into hyperdrive. The planer couldn't be used to compensate for all the fusion thrust, so they put up with as much as they could stand—about two gees. It was worse for Ginger; Perpetua had a tank of water she could float in.

The transition to hyperdrive was blissful relief.

"What was that kiss about?" was the first thing Ginger said when conversation was worth trying. "You weren't interested in mating with him. I'd have noticed."

She smiled. "No. But I thought he'd enjoy thinking so."

Ginger thought about that. He suspected there was an insight to be had into human thinking.

"Hey, he left us his stuff!" she exclaimed.

"Well, don't open anything."

"Of course not. But he could have got it out in about a minute. I must have done a better job than I thought."

Definitely called for more thought. He'd have a few days before they got to Wunderland.

Finding a spy to inform to shouldn't be difficult. There were markhams everywhere, it seemed sometimes.

XIII

Old Conalus Leophagus, whose scars were mute testimony to the standard that had won his family their surname, walked with a marked limp until he was near his commander's workroom; then he straightened and strode as befit a herald. Outside the groveroom he coughed for attention; then he coughed a lot more.

Marcus Augustus came out and guided him in, bent over and gasping, to a seat with a back, and put him in it. The Jotoki leader, Kaluseritash, who had been coordinating plans with Marcus, opened a medical kit and got out a patch, which they slapped onto Conalus's neck. "You should not be performing extra duties," they said sternly.

"I wanted to be the one," Conalus wheezed, the adrenaline opening his lungs already, "to give the news. Caesar, the *hyperdrives*"—he pronounced the foreign word carefully—"are being installed even now. The crews will be ready to steal the ships as soon as we can start our diversion."

"Well done," said Marcus. "Ask each legionary if he is certain, then tell them: the morning after tomorrow. And Conalus . . . are *you* certain?" he said, a little sadly.

"I am, Caesar. I am too weakened to hold a shield on the line, but I can kill one more kzin this way." He grinned abruptly. "Maybe two or three. I'm a big man."

"So say the women, too," Marcus replied, and they laughed together for a moment before Marcus Augustus sent the man who taught him swordsmanship out to die.

"Trader, your resourcefulness is truly astonishing," Warrgh-Churrg said, admiring his reflection in the stasis box. "I accept your opening offer."

"Thank you, Potent One," Ginger said, astounded and not a little concerned that he'd underpriced the thing—oh, well, they had two more. "It might be best not to deploy it before opening of outright hostilities."

"Deploy?"

"On your flagship?"

"Ftah. This thing guarantees fresh meat whenever I want! What is it?" Warrgh-Churrg snarled at the human messenger who had just crept in.

"Warrgh-Churrg, there is an attack by ferals on your hunting estate," the messenger quavered from the floor, emphasizing his entire Name, as was wisest when delivering *really* bad news.

"Fools. What part of the border?"

"All, Warrgh-Churrg."

"*WHAT*?" he screamed. "*How many*?"

"The immediate report was more than five sixty-fours, Warrgh-Churrg."

Warrgh-Churrg howled red wrath. *"Trader, do you wish to go on a hunt?"*

"I wasn't expecting to leave my monkey alone that long," Ginger said. "It gets into things. . . ."

"Fine, go to your ship! You, tell my bursar to pay for this! . . . I'll be using this at once," Warrgh-Churrg said with some satisfaction. He switched off the field, then folded the container and left with it.

The messenger peeked after him when he was gone. Then he looked at Ginger.

And winked.

Slave Instructor was overseeing circuit tests of the new installation when the emergency call came in. He listened to his helmet speaker in growing amazement, then announced to his gang, "Down tools, we're stopping work to go planetside."

A human slave with a welding laser raised his visor. "Master, I've got the gravity planer working well enough to take the ship there directly."

"That hardly matters to *me*," Slave Instructor said haughtily.

"True," said the human, lowering his visor again.

Slave Instructor just had time to notice the other humans and the Jotoki covering their eyes before the laser flared.

They were in zero gee. Slave Instructor's last sight was an inverted view, of a kzin, in space armor, arms flailing, looking very foolish without a head.

The loading might have been practiced every day. In a sense, it had been; a legionary's life was one of constant drills and exercises, almost all of them (up to now) for things that never did happen.

The Jotoki had maintained piloting skills with tenderly preserved simulators.

The noncombatants—meaning the very young and the crippled, for *everyone* else fought—had centuries they were attached to, and if some became confused and didn't form up with the troops, they were found. A number of children were found in favorite places they didn't want to leave; but they were all *found.*

There were others who were normally noncombatants. . . .

Warrgh-Churrg had commanded that he be uninterrupted in the hunt.

The ferals didn't provide much sport, but they displayed astounding destructive capabilities. A favorite tactic was setting a grass fire upwind of a herd of *zianya*. This had the added effect of overloading the *ziirgrah* sense, making the humans harder to pay attention to.

The hunt took eleven days. Messengers for him—all kzinti—had been sent back to his palace to await his pleasure.

When Warrgh-Churrg's cargo carrier, bearing tons of fresh meat in stasis, landed in his courtyard, the first thing the Marquis saw on emerging was Trrask-Rarr. The lordling appeared to be sunning himself. Warrgh-Churrg—who had been getting a little twitchy just lately—was too startled to be angry. He ambled over to where his rival lay and said, "What are you doing here?"

"Being courteous," Trrask-Rarr literally purred. "I was certain you wouldn't want to hear this from someone you *liked*. The humans and Jotoki are gone."

"Have someone round them up," Warrgh-Churrg told Hunt Master.

"They're *gone*, Warrgh-Churrg," chuckled Trrask-Rarr. "They took the ships you rebuilt for them, and they left. The only ones left on the planet are in your meat locker there."

He was far too pleased for Warrgh-Churrg not to take offense. He took a deep breath and began to crouch, and a voice from the donjon gate called, "Warrgh-Churrg, I have come to guide you on a journey."

He froze, and slowly turned.

Great golden eyes in a face of deepest black confronted him. More golden eyes were tattooed on the ears and the tail.

His tail drooped and lay on the ground. "Holy One, your Name?"

"I am Nabichi," said the Blackfur. "You are called upon to share your wisdom and be instructed in turn."

The Question, and death by torture. "But why?"

"Your plans were revealed earlier, though not in time to prevent the theft of the slaves. We will learn where you have had them taken, be assured."

Warrgh-Churrg sagged all over, and followed the Inquisitor of the Fanged God out the castle gate, to his doom. There was really nothing else he could do.

Trrask-Rarr bounced to his feet and said, "Show me those supplies." When the stasis box was opened, he took a long sniff and said, "Already seasoned. How very thoughtful. Invite the other lords to a feast tonight. I am celebrating the ownership of my new castle."

The ships had to break out of hyperspace periodically to communicate for course adjustments, as *Jubilee* had the only hyperwave. There were meetings of leaders at those times. During the fifth such stop, Ginger found time to tell Marcus Augustus, "I figured out about the garlic."

"I am impressed."

"Not as impressed as I am. You've had it planned for how long?"

Marcus looked surprised and said, "I don't know." He looked at Kaluseritash.

"About three hundred years," said the Jotoki leader.

"What *about* the garlic?" Perpetua said.

"They've been eating garlic before going out to fight kzinti," said Ginger, "to get their enemies accustomed to the smell. Their gold ore was combined with tellurium. It's a poisonous metal. One of the symptoms of tellurium poisoning is 'garlic breath,' according to *Jubilee*'s database."

Marcus took over. "It tends to accumulate in the liver. A man can build up a tolerance for it, but it makes his lungs collect fluid." He looked distracted for a moment, then went on. "We had hundreds of volunteers—men and women too old or injured to fight very well or for long, but who wanted to strike one last blow."

"As did we," said Kaluseritash. "Anyone who eats them will suffer massive neural degeneration and circulatory disorders, and if lucky will die."

Perpetua was very wide-eyed. "You had that *planned* for *three hundred years?*"

"'Use any weapon you can make, and make any weapon you can use.' Brutus Leophagus," said Marcus. "I hope it isn't much further to Wunderland. Metal walls disturb me. Are there caverns? It will be some time before we have trees growing properly."

"There are," Ginger said dubiously, "but there are dangerous native creatures in them. We thought we had killed them all, but the caverns stretched further and deeper than we knew. You might want to dig your own with disintegrators."

"Disintegrators? Are these weapons?" Marcus said, interested.

"Not very good ones. Too slow. They're used for digging and large sculpture," said Ginger. "They work by decreasing the charge of atomic particles, positive or negative depending on how they're set."

"What happens when you have one of each kind side by side?" said Marcus.

Ginger looked at Perpetua. Perpetua looked at Ginger.

"I think you'll be very welcome when the next war starts," said Perpetua.

SPQR

THE TROOPER AND THE TRIANGLE

◆　◆　◆

Hal Colebatch

Wunderland, 2382 AD

Although Trooper Number Eight knew how to lie up in ambush, he also knew that he was not a very good soldier. He knew this with special force at the most terrible moment of his life, as he stared down at the furry white creatures spurting digestive acid over long-dead kzin and human tissue, and knew that his world had ended.

Perhaps his somewhat ambiguous heritage and upbringing had been to blame for his lack of military prowess. His Sire had been a soldier in his day, but had been regarded as a mediocre one until he had saved a senior officer's life, receiving honorably incapacitating wounds in the process. He had been rewarded with a set of battle drums and also with the gift of a mate who had grown too old to be sufficiently attractive or fertile to remain in the senior officer's harem, though not quite beyond breeding, and had settled down to a life of trade, selling medicines which healers recommended. He had had a small shop in the town near the governor's palace and indeed had numbered some kzinti from the palace among his customers. Trooper Number Eight had been his only son.

Despite his spurt of valor, there had been a streak of mildness in Sire, and he had treated his kitten kindly. His mother, too, had been, for a kzinrett, of gentle disposition. Trooper Number Eight's earliest days had been sunny. Indeed, he had been somewhat indulged and, by kzin standards, spoilt.

Had he been a scion of the aristocracy, such spoiling would have been taken for granted. Further, he would have had the best

of combat and physical trainers and a rich diet. As it was, he
was sprung from what might possibly be called the lower middle
class of kzin society, though with a military heritage which should
have given him something to live up to. His Sire's wounds had
prevented him giving him personal combat training.

For a time as he grew up he had been very happy. After the
normal young male kitten's pursuits of chasing small game, he
had come to enjoy playing his Sire's drums and even reading
books, a pastime generally thought more suitable for the honorably retired than for a future Hero. Unfortunately, there were
other young kzinti, and in the way of kzinti society, with most
females the property of the aristocracy, they tended to be broth-
ers and cousins. As an only male kitten he had not been well-
equipped for socializing with them, and he had had no relatives
with whom to ally.

The odds had been that he would not survive adolescence.
Other young kzinti had a keen instinct for spotting and ganging
up on such natural victims. The nickname they had given him
then, "Thinker," had definite connotations of insult about it which
could very, very easily have proven fatal.

He would have enjoyed having a friend, and this would also
have made his position safer, but after some observation he had
decided that it was not worth the risk of making overtures to
anyone and being rejected. He continued his precarious position on the edge of the group of youngsters, camouflaging his
constant fear. He worked desperately to stalk the delicate path
between over-self-effacement and an overprominence that might
be equally fatal without sufficient swinging claw to back it up.
Eccentric activities like reading he learned to keep strictly to
himself. Sometimes the others enjoyed his drumming, which was
a good thing.

However, and fortunately for him, among his contemporaries
there had been another, even more of a nonconformist, whose fate
he had watched and learned from. He had become fairly adept at
joining in the persecution of this one in order to deflect it from
himself. By the time this other was dead and his contemporaries
were casting about for a replacement, the Patriarch's army had
claimed them all.

His juvenile experiences of self-protection had been good
preparation for staying alive as a recruit. He had survived military

training, and the army disapproved of death duels entered into lightly between troopers upon whose training resources had been expended. He had been, at different times, a toady, a clown, a butt of jokes (very dangerous), and not yet quite a victim, but it had been a near-run thing.

In any case, on the completion of his training period he had been drafted to a new unit where, he reasoned, he might make a fresh start. "You will win glory for the Patriarch!" he and his fellows had been told upon completion of training and the granting of their new rank-titles. They had been marched aboard a heavy transport, placed in hibernation tanks, and shipped to the newly conquered *kz'zeerekti* world of *Ka'ashi*.

Most of the talks by senior officers emphasized the value not so much of surviving with victory, rewards and honor, but of a Noble Death. The ancient Lord Dragga-Skrull's famous signal before leading his fleet to death and glory against the Jotok in the ancient days of the Glorious Insurrection was frequently quoted: "The Patriarch knows each Hero will kill eights of times before Dying Heroically!" That had been the one-eyed, one-armed, one-eared, noseless Lord High Admiral's final signal to the fleet as he flashed in upon the enemy.

But when they had disembarked on *Ka'ashi* and had been given their new quarters it appeared that they were not going to be made into new Admiral Dragga-Skrulls just yet. They had a special Hunt on the anniversary of Lord Dragga-Skrull's last battle, but there was plenty of humbler work to be done. They were replacements, and the draft was soon broken up and sent out piecemeal to other units. Trooper Number Eight did not mind this particularly. Further, his new rank-title was much safer than "Thinker."

Unfortunately for Trooper Number Eight he had made a bad start with his new platoon. On his first day he had failed to recognize and salute the sergeant. In other ways, too, he had soon shown that he was less than a perfect soldier. He had lost or spoiled pieces of his issued equipment. He had endured punishments and learned to dread the prospect of worse punishments. The sergeant was a tough veteran, scarred from battles and with a number of kzinti and human ears on his earring. Of course no one in the new draft had been so suicidally tactless as to ask him what had happened, that he should have found himself put in charge of a second-line unit in a humdrum post. It soon became obvious to all that Sergeant was not one to cross.

After a time the new troopers came to understand that *Ka'ashi* was not quite as conquered as they had been told. Bands of feral *kz'zeerekti* were still resisting the Patriarchy, and, unlike the *kz'zeerekti* on Kzinhome and elsewhere, they had weapons. The other troopers, when they learned this, had been exhilarated by prospects of battle and glory. Some spoke of promotion, estates, mates—*names* even!—of their own. Trooper Number Eight joined cautiously in this talk because he had learned that staying alive depended upon joining in, but his liver had no enthusiasm of its own.

They had seen no fighting while they formed part of the general garrison pool held in one of the big infantry bases near the human city of Munchen, areas of which had now been rebuilt as kzinti government and administrative headquarters. He had not been branded a coward, but neither had he distinguished himself by heroic blood-lust and savagery.

The *kz'zeerekti*—or as he gradually came to think of them, the *human*—slaves assigned to the platoon at the base had taken to approaching Trooper Number Eight for their orders.

In two ways this had been a bad sign—the others in the platoon might pick up that the humans sensed he was a less ferocious warrior, and this would help to fatally mark him out. It also confirmed his status as the lowliest of them. But on the other hand, it gave him a confirmed position of a sort, a stable one below which it would be difficult to sink.

Further, it was a job none of the other kzin would have deigned to accept, and were glad to leave to him, provided, or course, that he did it so as to leave them no cause for complaint. He had a chance to make himself useful, if not publicly appreciated.

The consequences of doing the job badly would be disastrous, and it had become plain to him that to be effective he would have to learn the slaves' patois "language." He had set out to do so.

All kzinti had a rudimentary ability to feel something of their prey's state of mind, should they care to exercise it. It had evolved, presumably, as an aid in hunting in caves, tall grass, or other places where, for prey, hiding was easy. However, because in a few cases it could be developed into the despised gift of the telepaths (and also because in some cases it was reported to have led to a contemptible empathy for members of various prey and slave races), normal kzinti were ashamed of it and disdained to use it. Trooper Number Eight, who knew he needed all the advantages he could acquire to survive, had not only used it, but had exerted himself, furtively, to develop it. In his dealings with slaves it had stood him in good stead. It had also made learning the language much easier.

Indeed it had been true that the slaves apparently realized that he was not like Sergeant or the other troops. He had never killed any of them. Once when a clumsy, white-haired slave had spilled food over him just before he had been due to go on parade, he had not punished it.

A few nights after that incident, Corporal and some of the other troopers who had drawn irksome duties had decided to work off their bad temper with monkey meat following a group hunt for a few slaves. Slaves, or at least trained ones, had some value of course, and they would have to provoke an incident, even an runaway attempt, but that would not be at all difficult. Trooper Number Eight had heard their talk. It would, he had thought then, be a waste of his action in deciding to let the white-haired slave live intact if it was included among the hunted. He had sought out the white-haired slave and quietly told it to make itself scarce for a while. He had suggested it and its mate clean and check the inside cabins of the officers' cars, a duty in which they would be out of sight.

A few days later, he and Trooper Number Seven had had the job of checking the slave camp for any forbidden technology or weapons. Much technology for heating and other power for the humans of Munchen had been reduced to steam, sometimes produced by heating water with wood-fired boilers. There were old heaps of ash from some of these about the camp (the ash itself being kept for eventual use in soap making and other surviving low-tech human industries), and to make sure there was nothing hidden in them the kzinti had kicked the larger of these heaps apart. The white-haired human had been there and warned him that one of these was in fact fresh and glowing red and white-hot beneath the surface. Trooper Number Eight had appreciated the warning (which somehow did not reach his companion) and had seen to it after that that the white-haired one received lighter duties.

Later again, in the wait for assignment to combat duty, this slave had nervously presented him with a monkey musical instrument. It was called a "triangle" and this described it well. It was a piece of metal in triangular shape which gave off a musical note when struck.

Trooper Number Eight did not know what a philharmonic orchestra was, or that this slave had once been a musician in the Munchen Philharmonic, but he had kept the triangle and the small mace with which it was struck. He had known it would annoy Sergeant, so had only struck it when he was alone. Striking the triangle and hearing and meditating upon its solitary note was better than thinking about either the past, about the Sire and mother and the home on another world that he knew he would never see again, or about the future.

Eventually a movement order had come. They were going south, they were told, to a rioting jungle where feral humans hid.

It turned out that it was not quite a jungle, but not far off one. They had been added to the garrison of a small post on the edge of a large area of hilly rainforest under a single officer.

Their new assignment—disappointingly unimportant, and without the compensations of servants or amenities and generally inglorious—had increased the ill-temper of the other kzinti, who had expectations of great battles and conquests. There were rumors that the planetary governor was holding back his best troops and weapons for his own purposes. A double-star system with its mineral-rich asteroid belt and what the humans called the Proxima System not far away could add up to a fertile hunting territory in which one of high nobility might nurture ambitions and plans. Earth and its rich belt, as well as other minable planets and the satellites of its gas giants, were but little more than four light-years away—a distance that fell very far short of daunting the heroic race. The governor might plan much.

All this talk had been exciting enough for the Patriarch's army and navy in general but had brought the sidelined kzinti of Trooper Number Eight's unit little prospect of glory. It seemed that the prizes would go to others. Further, the kzin had evolved on a cooler planet than *Ka'ashi* and this area was hotter even than the Munchen area or the forests and mountains to the north and east. There were none of the diversions of the cities, and though it had been described to them as a combat posting, the kzinti troopers soon saw their role there, rather than a posting to the areas of real fighting, as a plain indication that their superiors did not consider them a first-class unit, an impression which was strengthened by the tired-looking, unimpressive pawful of kzinti they reinforced.

Trooper Number Eight had discovered that his role as the unit's driver-of-slaves seemed to cling about him even though, on active service, there were no slaves to drive. Somehow all had agreed that he should carry on the duties which slaves under his command had carried out previously—he would be responsible for keeping the unit's quarters clean, though at least each trooper cleaned and maintained his own weapons and equipment. He also found that he had become Sergeant's personal servant for certain tasks.

They had learned that the feral humans in the area were actually few in number, and that the campaign on both sides was mainly a matter of small-scale ambushes. To give it a little excitement—some sauce to a tasteless dish—the kzinti tended to use *wtsais* where possible, rather than their modern weapons. The heat and the low quality of the enemy also gave them motives not to wear the heavy and constricting battle armor. The humans themselves seemed poorly armed with an assortment of projectile weapons and from the parsimonious way they used ammunition it appeared that they were not well supplied with it. Those humans they killed appeared ill fed and in poor health.

The human strategy was, it seemed, to infuriate the kzin garrison by pinprick attacks against patrols or to launch a few bombs and missiles at the kzin base and then disperse. This meant that the kzinti, who could not let the area be turned into a privileged sanctuary for the human resistance forces, had to commit more assets to pacifying the area than it would otherwise have warranted. The heavy vegetation cover and abundance of life-forms with heat signatures meant that satellite surveillance showed little of tactical use. Further, the feral humans in space made a point of destroying kzinti satellites whenever they could, or editing their transmissions so the pictures that they sent were false—they had even caused kzinti to attack their own positions at times.

Nuclear, chemical, biological, oscillation, or a number of other weapons in the kzin armory could have made short work of the forest and everything in it, but the higher command wished to keep the place as a future hunting territory. Whether or not the feral humans knew this, they had kept their activities several rungs below the threshold where such massive retaliation would be warranted and never assembled in large concentrations. So the campaigning consisted largely of lurking in ambush or patrolling, either stalking on foot or on a gravity sled, though the thick vegetation limited the use of the latter. Though kzinti loved hunting for its own sake, this particular hunt was accompanied by a great deal of frustration. Tempers had frayed. The only compensation the posting had offered for most of the kzinti had been that there was a large amount of game, but even so solitary expeditions far into the forest were forbidden.

Trooper Number Eight had been at first less unhappy than previously. Indeed he was probably the least unhappy kzin in the garrison. He had no expectation or hope of achieving the only things which, given any wishes, he would have wished for: to return to his homeworld and family and to escape from Sergeant and the others. But campaigning, even such feeble and unheroic campaigning as this, did tend to create a sense of camaraderie of some kind, and when they were so few of them, death duels between kzinti rankers were plainly and strictly forbidden.

He had got away by himself occasionally, and sometimes, when alone, enjoyed striking the triangle. Further, there was a small collection of human books on the post, taken from a ruined human dwelling nearby—actually the remnants of one attempt to put together a military library and technology base in the first days of the kzin invasion—written by a human named Braddon and others. Sometimes in the long, eventless days, he had read them and tried to understand them, and that had also helped pass the time. He had taken the precaution of first getting Officer's permission to do this, explaining that it would make him a more effective slave master when they had slaves again. Officer had not cared one way or the other, but had agreed.

However, the climate and the exotic life-forms had not made his duties lighter—cleaning barracks and equipment had been never-ending. A constant problem had been the small, white, blue-eyed things which humans at Munchen had called "Beam's Beasts." Despite their harmless appearance they had poisonous fangs and secreted a powerful acid which dissolved not only the body tissues of their prey but a variety of other things. They bred in large numbers in the forest and were constantly invading the base, giving him a great deal of work. He had kept out of Sergeant's way as much as he could. Sergeant, as time went on without the chance of glory, grew increasingly ill-tempered and Corporal followed him. One day, there had been disaster.

Trooper Number Eight had been in charge of the unit's trophy-maintenance-and-cleaning engine. The ears, kzinti and human, which successful duelists and warriors carried in rings on their belts as trophies and signs of status, could be a problem. Though freeze-dried in small units developed for the purpose, they still had a tendency to get knocked around and eventually fall apart, as well as becoming ill-smelling, unless specially preserved in clear envelopes of strong material. Further, in this warmer environment it was discovered that there were species of fungi which had a lik-ing for the ears, causing them to turn black and eventually crumble unless they were cleaned at intervals. Several of the other troopers had a few human ears, but only Sergeant and Corporal had kzinti ears as well, and kzinti ears were what really mattered.

Sergeant had given Trooper Number Eight his earring and told him to clean the ears and renew the protective envelopes. In his nervousness, Trooper Number Eight had spoilt one of the kzinti ears—the oldest and most precious—causing it to break up into a handful of membrane and cartilage.

Trooper Number Eight tried to persuade himself that Sergeant would not punish him in such a way as to make him physically useless. Nor, he thought, would Sergeant sully his trophy ring with ears as unworthy as his own. Nor, he thought, would he scar him, since scars could be taken as a badge of honorable combat. He was correct.

He was punished with the Hot Needle of Discipline. The kzinti had refined and specialized their instruments of torture over thousands of years, and this one had been developed specially for stupid or inept soldiery. He was allowed an eight of days to recover, a time period specified in the Patriarch's Regulations, not out of mercy, but because it had been found that a lesser period left the soldiers so punished still unfit for battle.

He was noticed by no one during this period, being regarded as unfit to be noticed. No one cared when, one night late at the end of this period of "invisibility," when he could once again walk, or at least shuffle, he left the post and climbed a winding game path to a small, solitary hill. He sat and played the triangle there in the night.

Far above there were moving lights in the sky, shifting and winking stars, a soundless battle fought on the edge of space.

He was still recovering, though considered fit for duty, when Officer called them together for a briefing.

A transport vessel carrying military equipment to one of the outpost garrisons in the Serpent Swarm Asteroids had been attacked by feral human spacecraft as it climbed through the upper fringes of *Kaashi's* atmosphere, Officer told them. Its gravity motors had been badly damaged. It had been able to make a soft landing in the forest not far away but could not take off again.

The pilot was defending it, but plainly its cargo would be a great prize for the local ferals. The Heroes of Sergeant's platoon were to secure the area and assist the pilot until a heavy-lift unit arrived to retrieve it.

With the favor of the Fanged God, Officer pointed out, this unfortunate incident could be made into a positive opportunity—the downed transport could serve as a trap to draw the local ferals to their doom under the teeth and claws of Sergeant's Heroes. Sergeant, Corporal, and their eight of troopers were being given a chance for a battle of significance. They would travel on foot, stalking, because of the nature of the terrain, and they would travel fast and light. Given the puny and contemptible nature of the enemy, the question of armor was not raised. Officer suggested in his briefing that the destruction of the feral human troop might be the key to transfers to more glorious assignments for all. He did not dwell on the consequences of failure and did not need to.

They checked their weapons and gear, were inspected by Sergeant and Officer himself, drew rations and additional ammunition, and set off.

There were dark, jungle-grown ravines and gullies where humans might wait with weapons. These they avoided. Kzinti have far better night vision than humans, even when it is not artificially enhanced, but even so they would be disadvantaged coming out of bright sunlight. They lay up in ambush for several hours during the earlier part of the first night, but heard and saw no humans. The forest creatures with sensitive smell also gave them a wide berth. After a few futile hours they pressed on.

By daybreak, they had covered much of the distance to the crash site. The pilot's radio messages were unsatisfactory. He thought he had glimpsed humans and his movement sensors had detected large life-forms. He wished to leave the transport and hunt on foot. Sergeant tersely forbade him to leave his post. As the sun rose they saw the downed transport, its metal body gleaming in the sun on the next hill.

Morning inspection brought an explosion of rage from Sergeant. While they had lain in ambush his earring had picked up a swarm of small parasites which were burrowing into the tried tissue of the trophies and hastening their destruction. Of course, this could not divert him from his responsibilities to secure the area. He dispersed his Heroes, ordering them to approach the transport with stealth from different directions and lie up in the closest possible cover to it. Then he gave Trooper Number Eight the earring and told him to clean it. He also pointed out the route Trooper Number Eight should take and the place where he should lurk until further orders.

Trooper Number Eight, when he reached his position on the edge of a small clearing, found it quiet. Several hours passed while he waited motionless as he had been trained, in the light that filtered reddish through the vegetation. A few small creatures became used to his unmoving presence and returned. When the sun was high in the sky and nothing had happened, he remembered Sergeant's earring and turned his attention to it.

Two small Beam's Beasts had crept upon it as it lay on the ground beside him. They had eaten most of the trophies.

For a moment he felt merely numb, his mind too stunned and dazed to take the horror in. He had lost Sergeant's trophies. He gave a cry of despair. A good soldier would, of course, have made no unnecessary noise. But Trooper Number Eight had found that, after the Hot Needle of Discipline, being a good soldier mattered even less to him than it had done before. Anyway, no one had said anything about the fact that Trooper Number Seven, who now had partially prosthetic feet, could no longer move in perfect silence. Panic-stricken notions chased one another through his head. To desert? To flee into the forest? He had forgotten he was lying in ambush. He rose and paced distractedly about. To desert was futile, he knew. Elsewhere on this planet it might be remotely feasible, but here there was nowhere to go. He was a city-dweller and the son of a city-dweller from another world, and knew he would not survive. He did not even know the geography of the continent they were on.

Finally he sat on a fallen tree near the edge of the clearing. To distract his mind, he took the triangle and the mallet from his belt pouch and struck it, holding it close against the ear which he knew he would not possess for much longer. Again he struck it, letting the single, silvery note drift away. Some of the local creatures resumed making their own sounds. Again. His thoughts drifted away, following the notes.

A sudden shocking, tearing pain pierced him from behind. An indescribable sensation of bursting and breaking within him. He looked down to see something protruding from his chest, his blood spurting and pumping around it in orange and purple. Then he fell forward, throwing up his hands, with an involuntary, undignified and inarticulate cry.

All feeling was suddenly gone below the wound. His lower limbs and tail disobeyed his brain's command that they should propel him upward, and then its command to at least kick and slash. But he was still able to feel and move above it. He turned his head. A human was standing over him, holding a bloody metal spear. The human was raising the spear to stab him again. Yet he detected something more than rage and bloodlust there. Something to do with the fact he had been engrossed in the notes of the triangle? Trooper Number Eight did not want to be stabbed again, and he did not think he would be quick enough any longer to slash at the human.

He remembered a useful phrase from his reading. He moved his hands in a gesture, and added words in the slaves' patois: "No need. I am dying anyway."

As he said this, a wonderful thought came to him. Because he was going to die, he would be beyond Sergeant's reach and beyond the Hot Needle forever. The Fanged God might disapprove of him letting Sergeant's earring be spoiled, and, for that matter, of him having a monkey take him by surprise, but his terror of the Fanged God was less than his terror of Sergeant had been. He might, it came to him, see his Sire and his mother.

He realized that the human had not stabbed him again. It had backed away, and while it continued watching him, it was also glancing down at the triangle, which he had dropped. He called to it, and it moved cautiously toward him, holding the spear ready to stab or slash. He stared up into the eyes of the human, sensing clearly the creature's confusion, even its regret.

"Thank you," he said, in the slaves' patois. His voice was faint.

It was as if the creature did not understand. It made a sound of puzzlement and interrogation. Trooper Number Eight made an effort.

"Thank you," he said again, more loudly and clearly.

Orange moving in the bushes at the edge of the clearing, silent. Trooper Number Eight realized that here was a way he could repay his benefactor with more than words. Gathering his strength he cried:

"Look out! Behind you!"

The human moved quickly for one of its kind. Sergeant leapt into the clearing, *wtsai* flashing. There was an explosion, then another. The monkey's spear was evidently combined with a bullet-projector. Spent bullets fountained from it in a pretty, golden spray. Kzinti were far quicker than humans, as well as far stronger. But they were not quicker than bullets. Trooper's sight was dimming at the edges now, but he saw the eruptions in Sergeant's flesh as the bullets struck him. He should, Trooper thought, have used his own powerful sidearm, not charged with *wtsai* alone. So Sergeant was not as good a soldier as Trooper had thought, either. Then Sergeant was on the human, and his *wtsai* flashed. Trooper Number Eight found he could still move his arms. Though feeling below the wound was gone, he groped for the sidearm attached to his belt and worked it free. He wondered if he should let Sergeant live—he would be blamed and punished. But no, there was too great a risk that he might retrieve the situation and emerge a true Hero. Victory in a skirmish against a single monkey would not earn Sergeant a Name, but it would a good entry on his report. For the first time since he knew he was dying horror returned as he realized that he had become too weak to aim and fire the heavy weapon.

Another orange movement in the vegetation. There was Corporal, bounding in, also brandishing *wtsai* alone. These kzinti, with their limited combat experience, had not learned that humans often called guns "equalizers." The human jumped back, firing as it turned. Its bullets struck Corporal on the helmet. He went down then, shaking his head, was back on his feet again, roaring. No use for the *wtsai* now. His sidearm seemed to flash into his hand.

Trooper had his own sidearm clear. Its bullets were kzin-sized, cored with osmium backed by Teflon needles. He fired.

Sergeant and Corporal fell together. The human stood looking at them for a moment, then dropped its weapon, stood for a moment clutching at itself, and then collapsed too. As it fell, Trooper saw that Sergeant's *wtsai* had slashed it deeply. Its own blood was spurting out now in rhythmic gushes, and white things, that he took to be the severed ends of the creature's oddly arranged bones, stood out along the wound in its chest. Then it began to crawl toward him. Somewhere, far off, there were explosions, human cries, the roars and screams of kzin.

Trooper's vision was contracting now, and a great cold was descending upon him. The journey to the Fanged God was not unwelcome, but it would be lonely. The human was quite near now, reaching toward him.

"Thank you."

Over Sergeant's fallen comlink the pilot's voice hissed and snarled, calling for support.

The surviving human guerrillas entered the clearing. They were guiding two gravity sleds from the transport, piled with kzinti arms, equipment, and supplies. They halted at the sight of three dead kzin and a dead human.

"Well, Boyd certainly did all right," said the leader.

"I didn't know he had it in him," said the second-in-command. "Not bad going to take out three! I've never heard of such a thing. And look at his bayonet!" The weapon was dripping with purple and orange kzin blood. "That's some use of cold steel! Three! I didn't think it was possible."

The leader pointed to the badges on the bodies. "More than that! Two of them are NCOs. I'd say that biggest one must been have been in charge of the section. No wonder they weren't coordinated!"

"And I thought he was too soft for this. I wish I'd treated him better now."

"We owe him big time," said the leader, bending to close the dead man's eyes. And then: "There can't be many of them left at the base."

"With these," he said, patting some prize booty—the smart mortars that were sometimes misnamed plasma guns but which though they did not actually fire plasma were quite deadly enough in their own right, "and these,"—the high-tech beam-weapons—"we can take out the whole base. And be a long way away before any other ratcats realize it."

Then he saw something else that made no sense. The human and the smallest of the kzin were lying together in a pool of mingled blood, and, bizarrely, the right hands of the two were clasped together. Between them lay a triangular piece of metal which none of the humans recognized.

But there was no time to stay and wonder. The guerrillas knew more enemy might arrive at any time. They moved quickly to add the dead kzinti's ears and weapons to those they already possessed. The intelligence specialist stripped the bodies of comlinks, recorders, and other electronics.

The next lot of kzin, when they arrived, should see the earless bodies of the dead kzin NCOs, that was obvious and elementary psychological warfare, but they would have no monkey meat.

The humans and the sleds were already laden with as much booty as they could carry, and Boyd's body could not be added to the load. The leader waved the beam of a newly acquired handgun over it, cremating it instantly. Then, moved by an odd impulse, waved it again, cremating the smallest kzin with him. The smoke from the two bodies drifted away, its dispersing particles to mingle above the treetops with the smoke of the burning transport.

STRING

◆　◆　◆

Hal Colebatch and
Matthew Joseph Harrington

2895 CE

"This will be a change from your last assignment for us," the puppeteer said. The grizzled ARM general apparently standing beside it nodded agreement. Given modern medical techniques, not even counting whatever the ARM kept for themselves, the gray had to be pure theater, to establish dominance via human respect for elders. It wasn't that effective—there were too many elders these days.

"It had better be," said Richard Guthlac. "The last was not something we'd like to repeat."

"You did well enough then, though your companion did better," it replied. "A great menace was destroyed. That is one reason you have been chosen again. That and the fact Charrgh-Captain asked for you."

Richard and Gay exchanged eloquent looks. Charrgh-Captain had been the Patriarchy observer assigned to accompany their small human-Wunderkzin team to the last stasis box to be found.

"He evidently appreciates your resourcefulness," the puppeteer went on. "More, by the terms of the treaty they are only obliged to accept one observer, but he said you were a mated team. Unasked concessions like that from a kzin of the Patriarchy, an officer very much of the old school, are too rare to be lightly set aside."

Richard and Gay nodded. They and Charrgh-Captain had been through a memorable time together.

"This time," the general said, "it's been the kzinti's turn to find a stasis box. You will be the human observers attached to a kzinti expedition.

"Of course you don't have to go," he went on. "But the pay will be good."

151

"For sharing a ship with a crew of kzinti of the Patriarchy? It had better be!" Richard exclaimed.

"For sharing a ship with a crew of kzinti, and for facing a possibly very dangerous unknown at the end of it. But you know that better than I can tell you.

"Anyway," said the general, "it appears the kzinti are abiding by the treaty like good little kitties. They have informed us of the discovery, have given you time to join them, and, of course, have agreed that you will have diplomatic status and immunity. Your reserve ranks will also be respected, so you will be entitled to fighters' privileges, though I hope it won't be necessary for you to invoke them.

"The box will be opened where it is, not taken to Kzin-aga. In some ways that has problems, but both sides insisted on it, neither trusting the other, and it's written in. High Admiral Zzarrk-Skrull has given his Name as his Word that the box has not been surreptitiously opened already and then closed again for our benefit. I don't need to tell you to try *discreetly* to confirm that if you can," he said, telling them anyway. ARMs. "But I think the kzinti are genuinely wary about bringing home stasis boxes to open, and in this case I think their paranoia is justified—pretty much everybody's had problems in that direction in the past, as you probably know. There's no reason why it shouldn't all go according to the protocols."

"Charrgh-Captain," said the puppeteer—its pronunciation of the kzinti Name was as perfect as its contralto Interworld—"has assured us that he is aware of human requirements and comforts. You will have your own cabin and kitchen."

"I don't suppose the job includes having bombs implanted in us in case the box turns out to hold something really danger-ous?" asked Richard.

"Good heavens! How do you get such terrible ideas?" said the puppeteer convincingly.

"Working with ARMs. They'll be doing a full scan on us, huh?" he asked the general.

The puppeteer looked itself in the eyes. The general said noth-ing, and pointedly looked at Gay.

"How big is this stasis box?" asked Gay, very politely.

"Large, but much smaller than the last one you investigated. Too small for there to be anything, ah, comparable inside.—I don't think the kzinti really mind that either.—It's quite a long trip, but not so long that you'll have to go into coldsleep again. Twenty-five light-years. A matter of about eighty days each way, counting in STL acceleration and deceleration time. The actual retrieval and opening of the box shouldn't take long."

"And the pay will be?"

The general named a figure.

"That's hard to refuse," said Richard. "We could always do with more capital."

"Yes, I'd heard you'd taken up farming. But land's still cheap on Wunderland, isn't it?"

"Yes, but machines aren't. Farming needs sophisticated robotics to be competitive. Well, we'll think about it."

"Don't think too long," said the general. "Others would jump at the chance—making a name for themselves, a big hatful of stars in the bank."

"Do tell. How many others *are* there in this unruly mob of volunteers? Within a factor of two, say?"

"Humans are brave," said the puppeteer. "And curious. Many would jump at the opportunity."

"But you wouldn't? You don't feel like going yourself, by any chance?" Richard asked innocently. If he had not known the puppeteer's heads contained no brains, its brain—an extremely large one—being located under a reinforced bony hump between its shoulders, he might have sworn a look of horror crossed the vapid faces. Certainly the creature flinched, and seemed to stop itself going into a crouch only with a great effort of will.

Richard felt a faint stab of guilt. Teasing a puppeteer about danger was too easy to be any achievement. Still, if the puppeteers were extremely averse to risking their own necks, they seemed to have few qualms about having others risk theirs. He waved a hand in apology and reassurance. This puppeteer had, by the standards of its kind, done a very brave thing by walking abroad on Wunderland at all, even if this was only a hologram of it. It would have to be barking mad, of course, which would make so much courage easier for it. All sane puppeteers had fled Known Space long before.

"There weren't many qualified volunteers," the general said, oblivious to the exchange; an ARM's usual ration of empathy would be deemed a shortage if the same amount were detected in a brick.

"It does seem like a pretty narrow window of qualification," Richard observed. "Smart enough to do a good job, but dumb enough to agree to it?"

The puppeteer looked itself in the eyes again, and the general said brusquely, "The expedition leaves from Kzin-aga. There's a commercial flight there leaving in three days."

The puppeteer added hopefully, "You may also expect salvage fees for anything our distribution network may safely market."

"As I said, we'll think about it."

When they had privacy again, Gay shoved him in the shoulder. "How come I had to be the respectable one?" she said, laughing.

"Because I'm no good at it?" Richard suggested.

"Standard procedure will be followed," said Charrgh-Captain. "There is a telepath with us. The instant the box is opened he must probe it. Should it contain live Slavers, experience suggests it will take them at least a few moments to orient themselves. In those moments Telepath must detect them and we must destroy them.

"Your cabin!" he announced, flinging open a kzin-scale door with a grand gesture. "Spacious enough, I take it? It is of course Hero-sized!"

"Thank you," said Gay. Charrgh-Captain had obviously devoted some thought to making it not uncomfortable. Even the light was brighter and bluer than the kzinti used for themselves, and the cabin somewhat warmer than kzinti liked. Kzinti, though masters of gravity control, officially eschewed the decadent human luxury of sleeping plates, but a Hero-sized bunk made more than a double bed for humans. The monsters which Heroes battled and bloodily slew in the bulkhead pictures were not human or even simian—quite a rare piece of cultural sensitivity for kzinti interior decor. Marks on the bulkhead, however, suggested some less-tactful decorations might have been recently removed. There was also a versatile human-type kitchen/recycler and a library, part of the basic-maintenance human autodoc.

"The kzin is a generous host," said Richard.

"I had some of your personnel from the embassy to advise." Charrgh-Captain's ears twitched, corresponding to a slightly mischievous smile. "Apart from my previous experiences of you and other humans. You will note I am returning you the compliment of providing a lockable door. Unfortunately, in preparing your comfort there was no time to alter the sanitary facilities to human scale. You will have to sit and balance carefully, I think, if you do not want to fall backwards and down into the waste turbines. And here is a facility for water to immerse yourself—a *sho-urr*."

"You have done us proud." *And had your little joke. But things could be a lot worse.*

"We are companions," said Charrgh-Captain. "In a companion-ship sealed by bonds that will not be broken lightly. In any case, this is a large ship, with a small crew. We all like what you call elbow room, and here we can be generous with living space."

Yes, thought Richard, *you kzinti always build ships larger than you need—as though you just might want them for something else one day. I'm sure this one is a lot more intricately subdivided than a simple trader needs to be, too. And lots of mountings and installations for very high-energy signaling devices, just in case your message laser fails, of course.* Aloud he said: "How small a crew, Honored Charrgh-Captain?"

"Myself, a weapons officer who is second-in-command, two flyer/watchkeepers, a Slaverexpert, two engineers, four troopers, and the telepath."

Twelve kzinti. If it comes to a fight over the stasis box, we wouldn't stand much chance against that lot. I don't suppose we're here to fight for the stasis box, though. We're really only here taking the role of canaries in ancient submarines or coal mines. As long as we live, things are okay. If the kzinti don't let us return to make a full report, humanity will assume the box contained a major weapon of the Slavers, and will hit the kzinti worlds with everything it's got.

"Leave your things here for the moment," said Charrgh-Captain. The commonplace, domestic phrases of hospitality sounded strange from a nine-foot-tall felinoid with dagger fangs. "You are officially part of the crew and should familiarize yourselves with the ship."

He escorted them through it from end to end. It turned out to be a refitted warship—most kzinti vessels were, not too surprisingly; a ship built entirely out of hardpoints doesn't tend to wear out very soon. The puppeteers were still running a few General Products outlets, to help with moving expenses, but aside from a yacht for the Patriarch, for the publicity, they weren't providing the kzinti with invulnerable hulls. (Which was a pity; one would have been nice now, under the circumstances.) Still, there were a lot of awfully tough merchant ships out there lately.

Slowly, the kzinti were becoming integrated into the great web of interstellar trade and commerce. Slowly, some kzinti were taking to the business and mercantile life and coming to appreciate the rewards it brought. At first they put a good face on it by saying to one another that it was a temporary expedient, until more Heroic times returned; but as time went on, and sons grew up in family businesses, this claim was made less often.

Humans (with puppeteer advice, when that wasn't absurdly naïve) had gradually initiated them into a system of rewards, rituals, stories, respect, and honors for successful merchants. There was a Kzinti Chamber of Commerce now, with the Patriarch's ninth son as Honorary President, and several wholly or partially kzinti chapters of Rotary Interstellar—though the Rotarians' cherished ritual of the Sergeant-at-Arms levying small fines upon members before dinner, for charitable purposes, had been dropped in the kzinti chapters, as it had occasionally led to death duels.

This ship, *Cunning Stalker*, was officially a merchant vessel, seconded to the science-and-research branch of the new Kzinti Mercantile College. (Kzinti of the old school, who had not read Adam Smith's writing on trade's mutual advantages for both parties, still called it "House-to-Learn-Plundering-from-Animals-by-Stealth.") *Cunning Stalker* was built in the classical kzinti hemisphere-and-cone pattern, though with three drives—a traditional kzinti gravity-planer, a human-derived hydrogen-fusion reaction drive, and of course a hyperdrive. The first two had long been obsolete for interstellar travel, but were still essential within a star's singularity, and had other uses. The hugely oversized power plants of the Red Age were now banned by treaty, so that gravity effects were no longer used for casual convenience—like, as an alternative to reaching for things—but lesser motors throughout the ship did allow for a variety of useful effects, including whatever was comfortable at the moment.

The aft part of the ship contained several cargo holds, whose partitioning could be altered. Richard wondered briefly if it might have been a slave transport; it was just barely old enough. There was a control center well forward. The engineers had sleeping cabins near the engine spaces, the rest of the personnel about the control center. There were many empty cabins and other spaces, some of these suggestive to a trained eye. As Charrgh-Captain had said, there was plenty of room.

Sometimes in the wars, humans, who, one way or another, found themselves sharing ships with kzinti, had managed to elude or ambush those kzinti by climbing through ducting too narrow for the great felinoids to enter. Richard noticed, not without wry amusement, that *Cunning Stalker* appeared to have been refitted with memories of this in mind. Any ducting too small to admit a kzin was either also too small to admit a human, or else covered with very tough gratings.

Overall, it contained few surprises for the humans, though much of the machinery and instrumentation was quite alien to them. Both Richard and Gay had long ago absorbed the standard layout of various classes of kzinti ships through imprinting, as part of their reserve officer training, but those designs were from the Red Age, pre-hyperdrive, when transit times were measured in decades; back then, any innovation meant newly arrived personnel would require complete retraining. Nowadays changes could be implemented Empire-wide in months, with the result that the Guthlacs found the latest kzinti designs just short of baffling. The control center was downright intimidating, with three kzinti busy at instrument consoles whose combined complexity was worthy of a hospital doc. The ports had not yet been opaqued for the transition to hyperspace, and Kzinhome's primary was a vast red ball filling the sky to one side as they skimmed it. (Slingshot maneuvers were thrifty if there was no hurry, and of course kzinti were up on all the gravity business.)

There too was Telepath, smaller, bowed, skittering nervously about, not daring yet to sleep. Beside the tigerish magnificence of Charrgh-Captain, and after the tall, strong, normal-looking Wunderkzin telepaths Richard and Gay knew at home on Wunderland, the twitchy, doomed, neurotic creature was an awful sight. Looking at him, they understood afresh why so many telepath POWs had aided humanity; and why so many other telepaths, stranded in the Centauri System after its liberation in the first great war, had been so eager to throw in their lot with humanity, with its milder, less-destructive drugs, and to take human names and loyalties.

Richard and Gay were used to non-humans, particularly

kzinti—on Wunderland there were Wunderkzin they thought of as companions and friends. But these were not Wunderkzin. The Guthlacs' nerves were on edge in the ruddy orange light, hulking tigerish forms around them.

The last time they had flown with Charrgh-Captain, he had been the attached observer, and their crew had been two other humans and a Wunderkzin. Now they felt their minority status with painful nervous tension. It was not improved by the knowledge that even nontelepathic kzinti could sense emotions, so that their companions were certainly aware of how the humans felt. Even Earth canines could smell fear, and to kzinti it could be an intoxicant. It was a relief to thank Charrgh-Captain for the tour and close their cabin door behind them.

"This bed is something!" Gay commented, bouncing on it. "And the covers are real fabric! I was half-afraid they'd be human skin or something."

Richard bounced onto the bed beside her. Was the gravity here less? It was something the kzinti could arrange easily enough, but he had not anticipated such thoughtfulness. Gay grabbed him and wound her arms around him.

"I do feel a bit nervous here," she said, "and I think I need some comforting."

"You want to make love *now*?"

"Yes. Don't you? I think we'd better give this bed a test flight." She grabbed him and pulled him down.

I feel sorry for those who need new partners all the time, Richard thought afterward as they lay in each other's arms, dreamy and contented, thoughts drifting. They had been married nearly twenty years, and the more they knew one another's bodies the better they became, even as—something they had once thought impossible—their love for one another seemed to continue to deepen. *This is perfection*, he thought, kissing his wife's skin. Most twenty-ninth-century human bodies were perfect, but beyond that their minds, spirits, and desires were in a radiant union. Lying together there, his arms about her, it was as if each basked in an aura of the other's comfort, happiness, and contentment. He murmured something below speech, running his knuckles along her spine.

She turned away from him, her curves of shoulder and back

and buttocks making her seem rather more surrendered and giving than when she faced him.

"You know, eighty days of this each way shouldn't be too hard to bear," Richard mused.

"And we're getting paid to do it!"

"Hah! True. Not sure how I'd phrase it on a resumé, though. Of course the kzinti aren't what they were, not quite. Even with a full shipyard doing nothing else it would take several hours, at least, to convert this ship back for Navy use in another war. . . . I'm still digesting the idea of kzinti Rotarians."

"I remember hearing somewhere there's been attempts to set up kzinti Lions Clubs. The fines officer's known as the Tail-Twister, you know! The mind boggles."

They both laughed, rather nervously, and Richard reached for her again.

The door beeped. Someone desired entrance. Gay kicked herself over and pulled the cover up to her chin, then let it fall. "What the hell, kzinti aren't going to be shocked by monkeys."

"Shall we let them in?"

"Why not?"

"Admit," said Richard. Unless specially locked, the door was voice-keyed.

"May I join you?" It was Telepath. Like Charrgh-Captain, he spoke Interworld, the largely Jinxian-based common human tongue which, despite its name, was difficult for nonhumans to pronounce.

"We speak some kzinti tongues," said Richard, experimentally. Even on Wunderland, some kzinti strongly disliked simians "defiling" the Heroes' Tongue—and this, as he was all too well aware, was not Wunderland. Still, his accent was good; and a certain amount of the hostility was due to frequent mangled pronunciation.

"I would be grateful," said the telepath, "if I could spend some time here with you. The minds of the Heroes leak at me endlessly. I can shield, but it is not enough. Humans are so different that when I am not drugged I need to concentrate to understand you at all. The noise drowns out the others. This cabin, your minds, give me a refuge."

Richard felt uncomfortable. Telepath was obviously trying to control his neurotic behavior. Good manners toward the humans were clamped about him like a coat of mail. Yet this timid, wistful, depressed, and undersized kzin was so hideously unnatural. *It's just the instinctive revulsion one feels towards a sick animal,* he thought. *Don't let him sense it! How do I stop him sensing it? No headaches yet. He's not trying to read my mind. But I'll bet he gets the vibes.*

Gay nodded. "Stay awhile," she said, sitting up. "We can offer you bourbon if you like."

"A small one, thank you. So that is what you really look like, without your clothing."

They had forgotten for a moment that they were naked. Richard and Gay came from a culture where nudity, if not everyday, was less uncommon for everyone than it had been in the past—after the wars, Wunderland had needed a lot of work to clean up its climate, and there had been no reason to stop short of comfort. In any case Telepath himself, like most kzinti, wore very minimal garments consisting chiefly of utility belts and pouches for tools (including, they presumed, his drugs). "What you see is what you get," said Richard, a laugh covering a momentary stab of embarrassment. He swung his feet to the deck and crossed to the drinks cabinet.

"It is fascinating," said Telepath, looking them both up and down. "I knew you were tailless, but I have never actually seen tailless beings like you before. How do you balance? And would you not need them when you are swinging through trees?"

"We don't actually swing through trees very much," Richard said. "Not now."

"And only two teats. You must have small litters."

"Yes, usually one, sometimes two. More are rare."

"A lot of your cubs must survive, then. This is the first time I have left Kzin-aga. You are the first aliens I have met. Such spindly limbs, no muscles at all." He reached out and touched. "Such soft skins. Yet you have fought Heroes. And won. I am glad you are not like Heroes."

His voice changed.

"But so many similarities," he said. "Spinal column, skull, ribs, two forelimbs, two hindlimbs. Same number of eyes and ears, similar mouth, same arrangement of alimentary canal, same division of functions by organ. Both mammalian. It is extraordinary."

"Well, it's a good design," said Richard. "Crops up all over. The ancestors of humans evolved on a world in the Galactic Core, while I understand that kzinti evolution can be traced back in a nearly unbroken chain to an incredible distance."

"I hadn't known that myself," Telepath said.

"It was in an article in Jinx *Goshographic*," Richard said. "Something about geological stability—or, no, continuity of processes," he said, trying to remember. "What's the word—gradualism! Changes were very standard, and laid down fossils pretty reliably up to two or three million years ago."

"What happened then?" Telepath wondered.

"Asteroid impact. After that the geology wasn't as stable. Anyway, it's not that big a coincidence."

"But our brains have functional similarities, too, I think. I have read minds of Pierin, of Jotoki. More strange. They don't understand about the need to fight." Telepath's voice was becoming slurred. His eyelids were beginning to droop. "I think I am going to sleep now," he said. "Let me sleep here. They will not come and kick me here." He curled on the deck like a house cat after a large meal. After a minute he began to purr faintly, his claws extending and retracting rhythmically, though irregular twitches also ran over his muscles. He was runtish for a kzin, under eight feet tall, but it was still fortunate that their cabin was roomy. *I think the poor creature is actually happy at this moment,* Richard realized with a shock. With some memory of their own old cat in mind, he moved to scratch him under the chin, a gesture which with old Shebee had never failed to produce an ecstatic purring. Gay reached out quickly to halt him, and he stopped, shaking his head at himself. Telepath was, after all, still a kzin, small and weak by kzinti standards, but still with teeth and claws and speed capable of dismembering a buffalo. The rules for a human touching kzinti were very strict, and the rule for touching a sleeping one was NEVER.

It was a long time later that Telepath awoke.

"I have never slept so well that I remember," he said. "But I should not have trespassed on you."

"Perhaps you will come and talk with us again," said Gay.

"We don't want him as a permanent guest!" said Richard after Telepath left.

"I think he knows that. Well, he would, wouldn't he? But I'm sorry for him."

"I'd rather have him for a friend than an enemy," said Richard. "I hate to think what a telepath enemy might do! But you're right as usual. And I guess I'm sorry for him, too."

"I know you are. I've known you a long time, remember?"

The voyage proceeded. Neither Richard nor Gay could feel very comfortable in the main body of the ship, with its dim light, lower temperatures, and the hulking kzinti here and there—not all of them, they suspected, as sophisticated as Charrgh-Captain about the company of humans, or with the pathetic friendliness of Telepath. Their orange fur, camouflage in this light, and their capacity for perfect stillness, often made them hard to see, for all their size, until the humans came startlingly close. Their eyes, glowing in the dimness, were not friendly, and both Richard and Gay knew enough of kzinti body language to be under no illusions about that.

Things were peaceful enough—the kzinti had a gym to work off their energy and aggression, Charrgh-Captain forbade death duels among the relatively small crew, and foodmakers in private quarters avoided the most common source of fights—but it was still like walking through a cage of tigers.

They spent some time with Charrgh-Captain on the bridge, familiarizing themselves further with the ship—it was the instinct of any spacer to do that, though they couldn't really hope to know more than the rudiments of the systems. Especially since they were wary of touching meters or control panels or interrupting kzinti watchstanders. Both made as sure as they could that the other kzinti were reminded as often as possible, by the sight of the three of them together, that they were under Charrgh-Captain's protection—the Patriarch's protection, if it came to that.

Sometimes—not very often—Charrgh-Captain was in the mood to talk; sometimes, when he wished to relax, even to joke and share a drink and reminiscences, or game with them in his suite; but the other kzinti were not companions from a past adventure, and it soon became abundantly clear that, for some reason, they had no particular inclination to socialize with representatives of the most terrible enemy their race had ever known.

As far as Richard could tell, none of the other kzinti spoke Interworld. He thought it unwise to try to press conversation upon them in either his insulting, monkey-mangled attempt at the

Heroes' Tongue, or in what was still known in the Patriarchy (of which this ship was a part) as the slaves' patois. The windows were opaqued and there was nothing to be gained by looking through them anyway, except possibly madness—the blind-spot effect of looking upon hyperspace affected kzinti every bit as badly as it did humans. In their cabin there were entertainments.

Telepath, however, visited them; as often, they surmised, as he thought they could tolerate him. They played chess and card games with him sometimes, never developing the violent headache which would have warned them he was cheating. He won routinely at chess, but card games that involved bluffing were something of a kzinti handicap. He could easily sense their emotions when one of them had a good hand; it was the idea of folding—surrendering—that so often threw him.

They had brought some old-fashioned jigsaw puzzles. He enjoyed them hugely, and could assemble them with blur-quick movements—except for the one that was all-white. That kept him poring over the pieces for hours at a time. They gathered he had no possessions or pastimes of his own. Anything a telepath had that another kzin fancied, the other kzin would take as a matter of course. Once he surprised them by bringing them a model of a kitten he had carved from some kind of wood—surprised them doubly, as they hadn't realized that sculpture was so strongly nonvisual. (Kzinti paintings could be incomprehensible to human perceptions.) Sometimes he told them about his life, including the fact, which also surprised them, that he had kits. Both Richard and Gay, as reserve officers, filed his information away, though they felt slightly uncomfortable about doing so. Mostly he took their company, games, and talk as a preliminary and aid to relaxation and sleep, and their cabin as a refuge from the other kzinti.

There came the indescribable moment, the discontinuity as the ship dropped out of hyperspace. The ports became transparent again, and stars reappeared. Strange stars. Then there were planets. They swung past two ringed gas giants, with the families of moons and Trojan-point asteroids that had first attracted kzinti miners to this system. They fell toward the system's heart, and toward a small inner planet.

It was not unlike Mars. A red surface suggested oxygen locked in iron. There were eroded stumps of mountains and what might have been seas a billion years previously. There was a tenuous atmosphere, mainly nitrogen and carbon dioxide, which for breathing purposes might as well have been a vacuum, but which sufficed to stir winds and dust clouds, and slowly traveling processions of crescent dunes. Kzinti instruments had detected no life but microbes. There were small icecaps. A small but bright sun gave good light.

With hyperdrive, this was not far beyond the existing borders of kzin-settled space. If the kzinti ran out of better planets, and humans let them, they could probably kzinform it one day. Despite the broad streaks of anarchy in their government, and a bureaucracy which depended largely on inefficient and unreliable slaves, they were capable of great constructive feats when they put their minds to it.

At present they had an application before the human worlds to mine the gas giants' moons: on probation after four major and several minor wars launched against humans, the Patriarchy was now under close observation in any effort to expand its territories. The kzinti had lost all the wars, of course. If they had won one, there would have been no more after it.

The stasis box, its general position already known, was easy to locate with deep-radar, and easy to uncover. *Cunning Stalker* simply hovered over it, holding position with a gravity generator, and ran its reaction drive on very low power so as to blow the dust away.

The mirror surface of the stasis box was revealed about fifty feet down. Magnification brought the image of the exposed section into the control center. Whether it had been deliberately buried there, or it and the planet had collided in the remote past, or it had once been housed in some installation whose metal was now coloring the sand, there was no way of telling. There were curves of vitrified rock that might be the last traces of the rimwall of an ancient impact crater—not necessarily related. Anyway, unanswerable speculations as to how it got there were of no importance at all, beside the question of what it might contain.

Deep-radar showed it was spherical—unusual—and about twenty feet in diameter. Far smaller than the last one, but still huge for a stasis box. All aboard *Cunning Stalker* knew it was quite big enough to contain live Slavers.

The box was now uncovered. A "mining robot" (which bore a remarkable resemblance to a Third War automated sapper) was landed next to it; it burrowed beneath the box with a disintegrator, emerged a few minutes later, and rose to be picked up. *Cunning Stalker* moved aside, and a fusion charge blew the stasis box off the planet.

They had to catch it before it fell back; it didn't reach escape speed. The charge had been meant to accomplish that, so the box was significantly more massive than expected. This might be good or bad: it could mean the box was packed solid, with no room for inhabitants, or it could mean that there was extremely heavy equipment inside, which suggested weapons—and someone to use them.

The box was towed to high orbit, and the ship's fusion drive was aimed at it and kept hot. Charrgh-Captain, Slaverexpert, Telepath, two troopers, and the humans took the gig over to it. (The "gig" had oversized gravity compensators and a remarkably heavy layer of hullmetal lining its nose, almost as if it was meant to be used to ram a hole in something.) Slaverexpert fired a parcel of fine black material at it: superconductor. The fabric wrapped around the box, formed a closed surface, turned silver briefly, and rolled itself back up into the parcel. "Clever," Gay murmured.

"The dropcloth is Pierin emergency firefighting equipment," Charrgh-Captain remarked. "I don't think they had this in mind."

The container's surface was still seamless, but had acquired a creamy hue. Richard had been watching the views from the scanners around the box, and he said, "Where's the cutoff switch?"

Slaverexpert, who had never previously spoken unless directly addressed, startled Richard by saying, "True." In Interworld.

"Explain," commanded Charrgh-Captain.

"These were designed to be opened easily, Charrgh-Captain. A panel would be spring-loaded, to break the conductive surface when the field was interrupted. The stasis has ended, but the surface is still seamless."

Gay, who had gotten curious and was having a look, said, "It isn't. It's split in half. Look, there." She pointed at one of the screens. The seam was at an inconvenient angle, so nobody else had noticed it.

And it hadn't been as big. The split was getting wider.

"Battle stations," Charrgh-Captain said. Still in Interworld, addressing the two humans—kzinti routine *was* Battle Stations. The Guthlacs got to their couches and strapped in.

"Sir," Telepath said dopily, drugged with *sthondat*-lymph extract, "I detect no life."

"You can't read Slaverexpert, either," Charrgh-Captain replied.

"No, sir, but I can tell where he is."

"Noted. Slaverexpert, report."

"The only energy I detect is heat, in amounts consistent with being present before stasis began, plus the separation of the shell. Shall I deep-radar?"

"Yes. Display the results."

The image on the humans' screens was divided into wedge-shaped compartments, almost all full of materials slightly denser than water. One held even denser material, probably metallic, in boxes. "It looks like an orange designed by ARMs," Richard said.

Charrgh-Captain, relieved of tension, snorted amusement. "An orange? The *fruit*?"

"Sure. Armor-plated for safety, big so it's easy to find, opens automatically when ripe."

"So what's all the metal?" Gay chuckled, pointing at the last wedge.

Slaverexpert spoke up. "Emergency escape pods for the seeds?" After a moment of utter silence, he looked up to find everyone else staring at him—even Telepath. "Sorry, sir," he said faintly to Charrgh-Captain, and looked back down at his instruments in a marked manner.

"We'll examine that section before taking the box in tow," Charrgh-Captain said.

Probably the best thing about working in space with kzinti was that they had been doing it for so long. Lighting, for instance. Humans, even those in the mining industries, tended to put up one or two bright lights, and wear one or two smaller lights on their helmets, producing sharp-edged shadows and a nagging conviction that something was hiding just out of sight. Here, though, Second Trooper strewed fistfuls of little spheres toward the partitions: where they hit, they stuck, and presently began to glow gently. They had frosted surfaces, so the light was diffuse. The kzinti suits also had multiple lights: a couple at each wrist, and two rows of three each down the torso, where things would be held to work on them. A light under the chin illuminated things directly ahead.

The Guthlacs were given clusters of faint blue lights to strap onto their suits, which in conjunction with standard kzinti lighting gave them a spectrum they could use easily. The amount of thought and preparation this implied was extremely flattering: They were being extended enormous courtesy. Richard found himself wondering if Charrgh-Captain had known all along that human-model food dispensers included a toilet.

There wasn't much time to dwell on this. The parcels were full of gadgets.

Most of them were pretty straightforward power tools: drills, saws, hammers, trimmers, shapers, diggers, a couple of amazingly elaborate grippies, and something that Gay and Slaverexpert tentatively labeled, after much consultation, as a handheld turret lathe. "These must have been for the use of a slave race," said Slaverexpert. "They are too large for Tnuctipun hands, and Thrintun would rather starve than toil." He sounded troubled.

"What's wrong?" said Richard.

"There is something familiar about the workmanship. Disturbing."

"What would this be?" Charrgh-Captain said, holding up a thing that included a short spike, a knife, a crank, and little spring-loaded rollers. "It hardly seems useful as a weapon."

Slaverexpert took it and turned it over a few times. "I am open to any suggestion," he said, baffled.

"It looks . . ." Richard began, then said, "Nah, crazy."

"So?" said Charrgh-Captain.

"Good point. Well, it looks like an apple peeler. A good one, too."

"It does, doesn't it?" Gay agreed.

Slaverexpert worked the crank a little. "It seems articulated to follow a complex surface."

"Potato peeler, then?" Gay said.

Slaverexpert looked at her, then at Richard. His ears were distinctly cupped, as if he were expecting ambush. He said, "Charrgh-Captain, it may be prudent to inspect the other sections as well."

"Very well, once we're done with this one."

Other devices were more complex. Several were lasers, or included lasers, but would have required great modification of focus for use as weapons. Another seemed intended to take in some kind of powder and extrude solid material in any desired shape. The purpose of a few remained unclear. All the tools that required power had to be plugged in; they had no power supplies of their own.

And it was Telepath, whose drugs were wearing off, who said, "Are there two of anything?"

Charrgh-Captain gave a startled grunt. "He's right," he said. "There are no duplications. Or spare parts," he realized. He picked up an object that had been mysterious a moment before. "This could be used to wind wire around a rotor." He added in Hero, "Everyone pick up an object and examine it for signs of usage."

His tone of command was such that the Guthlacs did so along with the rest. Richard inspected the peeler and found the blade and spike unstained. "Clean, no wear," he said. Similar remarks were made by others.

"These may be models," Charrgh-Captain declared. "Meant only to be copied. Were not the Slavers highly mercantile?"

"Charrgh-Captain, they were," said Slaverexpert. "These may indeed be articles of commerce. Shall I see what organic goods they stocked?"

"Certainly."

Slaverexpert had gone from being taciturn to interested, and had now gone from interested to stiffly formal. If Richard understood kzinti reactions (and he had some reason to think he might), Slaverexpert was experiencing immense stress, about something he didn't want to discuss.

Slaverexpert's conduct while inspecting the other segments verged on bizarre. One held thirty-one bacterial-containment canisters, and he barely glanced at them. The next three held clear plastic shells, each containing seeds of different sizes and shapes, which were also virtually ignored. The fifth held larger bins, that fitted into the shell segment; he shone a light on one, then said, "Charrgh-Captain, I have a security problem."

"From *plants*?"

"Tree-of-life," said Slaverexpert. There was a moment's silence.

Then, "Discuss it with the humans. The rest of you withdraw and switch to a music channel. Telepath, take your sedative."

"Thank you, sir."

"Tree-of-life" was a term coined over seven centuries earlier by a man who had eaten some. It had been brought by a Pak protector, a sort-of-alien from the Galactic Core, and it had turned the man into an asexual killing machine with vastly increased intelligence and the single goal of ensuring his descendants' propagation—just the effect it had on the Pak. An ill-conceived attempt by the ARM to do the same thing deliberately during the First War had misfired, and had things gone even a little worse all other intelligent life in Known Space would have been methodically exterminated.

Richard was beginning to recover from the shock, but only in stages. "This can't be tree-of-life," he protested. "The time is off by a factor of, of *eight hundred*. How the tanj do *you* know about tree-of-life, anyway?"

"It's in my area," said Slaverexpert. "The Pak were a Tnuctip bioweapon."

Richard stared for a moment, then said, "Impossible. In two billion years they would have evolved beyond recognition."

"They ate their mutations," said Slaverexpert. "They could distinguish variation of a single codon by smell."

"Richard, I read a monograph on that once," Gay said. "The author made a good case."

"Where was this?" he exclaimed.

"*Fractal Edge* netzine."

Richard sighed. "Gay, the only people who contribute to that are conspiracy theorists."

"You mean, like the people who used to believe in alien abductions?"

Gay was one of a large proportion of modern Wunderlanders descended from kidnapped humans that the Jotoki had engaged as mercenaries; Richard's ancestral kin had been aboard so many kzinti warships that it was practically a Guthlac family tradition. Richard opened and closed his mouth once, scowled, and stuck out his tongue.

"Don't change the subject," Gay said primly.

As Richard was sputtering, Second Trooper, who had been idly watching him from a distance, touched helmets with First Trooper and said, "Why would he expose his tongue?"

"From what I've read on them, humans spend most of their spare time either mating or making plans to mate. That's why there are so many of them."

"What does that have to do with what I said?"

"Human mating rituals include grooming each other's genitals," First Trooper replied.

Second Trooper, who like all kzinti had a tongue not unlike a wood rasp, looked at the Guthlacs with new respect. No wonder human fighters were so tough.

Richard got back on track: "Look, two and a half million years ago the Pak colonized Earth, the root didn't grow right, the breeders stopped turning into protectors, and they wound up evolving into us. If the Pak had been around for two billion years, wouldn't that have happened somewhere else by now?"

"It likely did," said Slaverexpert. "Repeatedly. It may have come to your attention that humans are warlike. Certainly it has not escaped ours. It would have been easy for them to exterminate one another."

Richard was still finding it too incredible. "Look, the plants needed thallium to work right. Where's the thallium supply?"

"Richard Guthlac," Slaverexpert said gently, "did you see any tools suitable for Tnuctip use? This is a cache prepared for rebellion *against the Tnuctipun*. The proto-Pak would have tailored a root for themselves that was not limited by the availability of a rare-earth element, which was doubtless a feature designed by the Tnuctipun to restrict their spread."

It was chillingly plausible.

Gay made it a little more so: "I just realized there are no fabricators, to copy those model tools," she said. "A protector would build one on the spot after the stasis box was opened, rather than waste storage space that could be used for more models."

It accounted for the potato peeler.

—Except that *nothing* accounted for the potato peeler: "Why is there a potato peeler?" Richard exclaimed. "They ate the whole things, didn't they?"

Slaverexpert thought. Then he looked at the roots and thought some more. Finally he said, "All I can think of is flavor, which is illogical; they could surely have tailored for that as well. I shall have to analyze one for better information."

As Slaverexpert signaled to Charrgh-Captain, Gay murmured to Richard, "Do you think he'd have destroyed them without testing otherwise?"

"If they're tree-of-life, I'd help," he replied in equally low tones.

"Protectors are asexual and all look ancient. I prefer to be young and dumb and . . . keep my hair."

"I like your hair too." She smiled.

Cunning Stalker's lab was a thorough one, and its safety features were appallingly practical: In an emergency, the entire lab would be ejected from the ship and into the path of the message laser, which would keep firing until the beam was unobstructed. "No need for the calcium notch," said Richard weakly. He had won the toss, and Gay was back in their compartment, watching by screen.

"Urr?" said Slaverexpert, as he put the sample case into the lab manipulator with one hand and began undoing his suit with the other.

"On the spectroscope next to the laser."

"Why a spectroscope?" The kzin's Interworld was excellent.

Surprised, Richard said, "I thought it was standard equipment. When something is blown up, the spectroscope scans the cloud, and if there's no band at the calcium frequency it was a miss or a decoy."

"Because a real target would include something with a skeleton," Slaverexpert said. "I see. Richard Guthlac, I find I enjoy working with you, so I hope you will take this suggestion: Do not say things like that very often around kzinti. There is something deeply disturbing in the didacticism that humans bring to the business of battle."

Richard could think of nothing to say—it probably *had* been thought up by someone sitting at a desk somewhere, who might never have so much as seen a live kzin.

Slaverexpert opened a cabinet next to the manipulator controls and put on a set of goggles from it. He looked through various compartments in the cabinet, growled very deep in his throat, and took off his goggles. "There is no human-version viewer," he said, putting them away, "so we will have to use window displays. I would prefer something that stayed in view when I turned my head, but leaving you out would violate the agreement."

Richard was about to ask why he couldn't use kzinti goggles, when the displays appeared on the window before them. The one in front of him was familiar in style, with different kinds of information displayed in different colors of high chroma, arranged in rows and columns with any useful diagrams at the top. The one in front of Slaverexpert had kzinti script in deep purple written right across light gray diagrams, whose shapes were constantly shifting, just slightly. The writing moved around slowly within the diagrams. The positions of the diagrams underwent abrupt changes every few seconds, too. Just looking at it was disturbing; trying to get information out of it would have given him a bad headache very quickly. "Telepath should see this," Richard murmured.

He'd forgotten kzinti hearing. "Why?" said Slaverexpert.

"Oh, a while back he was talking to us about the similarities in human and kzinti thinking. There's some fundamental differences in brain structure suggested here, and it might be of interest."

"Oh. Good, I thought I was going to have to wake him up. He doesn't sleep enough." Before Richard could absorb the concept of a healthy kzin showing concern for a telepath, Slaverexpert went on, "He's right, though. The fact that your readout looks like something I'd watch to get to sleep merely reflects a difference in hunting style." His ears curled up for a moment as the readouts changed several times. Then they uncurled, the readouts steadied, and he said, "Unfamiliar equipment. I've got it now."

Behind the window, waldoes opened the bin of roots and removed one. Richard had controls at his own station, and directed a sniffer to sample the air that had been in the container. "I did read somewhere that humans and kzinti are the only races to use fissionables to make bombs," he remarked.

"Odd. It seems such an obvious idea," said Slaverexpert. "No thallium, but I didn't expect it. Air interesting?"

"Nitrogen, oxygen, a little argon. Pretty standard habitable-planet issue," Richard said, and heard the kzin snort in amusement. "Traces of medium-sized hydrocarbons."

"Urr?" Slaverexpert brought some new instruments into play, then said, "The root is rich in terpenes. And there is no taurine."

"Taurine?"

"An amino acid human metabolism uses in dendrite connections. You do not synthesize it, so tree-of-life should be crammed with it to facilitate the change. . . . Though you may have lost the ability to synthesize it due to the supply available in Earth prey—no, Jack Brennan had no difficulty. . . . I am unable to detect any trace of steroid compounds. The roots from the Pak ship that came to

Sol System were found to contain a hormone for rapid muscle and bone development. This does not appear to be tree-of-life," Slaverexpert concluded.

"Good!" Richard said. "So what is it?"

"Let me try something." A waldo took up the uncut half of the root, then tossed it at a wall. It bounced back. "It's rubber."

"What?"

"Rubber. Rather, a long-chain molecule assembled from terpene monomers, suitable for insulation, seals, and padding. Hardenable and readily cast into nonconductive parts."

"Rubber," said Richard, amused.

"A valuable industrial material. I speculate that many of the life-forms we have found here will be tailored to produce such. Shall we investigate?'

"Let's." Now that fear was going, avarice had come out of hiding to put in a few words.

Unreasonably many hours later, Richard said, "Is that the last?" and wiped his brow with a hand that, he noticed, was developing a twitch from operating waldo gloves for so long.

"It is," said Slaverexpert. "I marvel at your endurance."

"I'm ready to fall down," Richard protested. "You're in much better shape."

"I possess medical enhancements added long ago to repair lethal injuries, and can produce my own natural stimulants at will. Nevertheless I am losing image persistence. I need exercise and sleep."

"Me too, not in that order."

"Urr. I can't remember whether you said there were any microorganisms present in anything."

"Just the handmade stuff in the cans."

"Good." Slaverexpert cycled a sample box through the containment lock, put a few roots into it, and brought it out, saying, "These should be amus— What's wrong?"

Richard had backed across the lab and was squinting. "I'm not that fond of mint." Even the traces on the outside of the closed box were disagreeably strong.

"You'll want to avoid the relaxroom, then, because I'll be bouncing one of these around. You don't like this? It seems quite pleasant to me."

Richard's throat was trying to close up. "Have to go," he choked out, and fled.

Telepath was in their quarters, looking like he just woke up, which was likely. Gay, off monitor duty, was already in the shower. Richard said to Telepath, "Excuse me please," and began peeling off his suit.

"Certainly. What smells so good?"

"That's right, you slept through the analysis. Well, I've got time"—a pressure suit should not come off quickly—"so: there was a root that looked a lot like Pak protector root, but it turned out to be something that produced a useful organic polymer. You're smelling the monomer. There were roots that produced other polymers, bacteria that made enzymes that chelated trace elements from iodine to uranium, seeds for trees that collected other elements in their bark, other this and that. We're all going to be rich. You look better," Richard realized.

"Possibly the good news. I feel better. I'll return to my own quarters now, in case you two wish to get in some more breeding practice." Telepath left.

Richard, almost stripped, stared at the closed door for a moment. That had sounded like humor.

Even in the shower, Gay was bleary with fatigue. She'd been watching everything, and hadn't had the stimulation of doing the actual work to keep her going. "You smell like a Vurguuz bottle," she said, frowning.

"I knew there was a reason I don't like the stuff. That monomer in the roots. Kzinti apparently enjoy it."

"What did you do, roll in them?"

"This is just what wafted over and stuck to my face when Slaverexpert got a closed box out of the containment. They're elastic, he's going to bat them around to wind down."

"Phew." She used a squirter and began shampooing his hair.

They'd gone straight to sleep. Richard had bad dreams, and awoke suddenly, remembering an obscure reference in chemistry. "*Fuck*," he exclaimed.

"Brush'r teeth," Gay murmured, not awake.

He was already headed for their library.

He worked fast. Once he excluded cooking, most references to any sort of mint were in folk medicine, where their analgesic effects produced the illusion of recovery. He added a search for references to terpenes, and got *false mint*: nepetalactone. It was not a salicylate as mints were, but scent receptors et cetera, right, composed of two isoprene groups, aha! there's your monomer. Found in various Earth plants never successfully raised on other worlds, chiefly *nepeta cataria*.

More commonly known as catnip.

He wasn't aware of making any kind of sound, and Gay was later unable to describe the noise clearly, but she came running out and said, "Richard, what's wrong?"

"The roots are made of catnip extract," he said.

She burst out laughing. Abruptly she stopped and covered her mouth, then uncovered it and said, "Oh my *god*."

"Uh-huh. It's in the relaxroom, thousands of times any sane concentration, and it's hours late to warn Charrgh-Captain. Any ideas?"

She was paralyzed for a long moment, then sat at the other screen and began hunting. Soon she said, "Says here the effect only lasts a few minutes, and is followed by temporary immunity."

"Sounds like someone working from theory. Shebee used to get blitzed for about an hour, sleep it off for four, and repeat until the catnip was used up," Richard said. He found the page she was on. "Also claims it has to be smelled, 'eating it has no effect.' What is this atad doing in our library?"

"*I* don't know!" Gay said, frazzled. "Richard, I think we'd better get the stuff off the ship. Suit up and go out really carefully."

The door beeped.

They both looked at it.

Gay had the wit to turn on the intercom and say, "Is it important? We're a little busy," putting a chuckle into her voice.

"You aren't either," said a voice much like Telepath's. "The crew are stalking one another, Charrgh-Captain is running on the walls, Weapons Officer is chasing his tail, and I cannot awaken Slaverexpert for more than a few seconds at a time. We need to make plans."

They looked at each other. "Admit," they said in unison.

Telepath came in, closed the door, and said, "Better lock."

They did. Richard might have hit his switch first.

Telepath was neatly groomed, relaxed, and clear-eyed. "I heard you wake up all the way from my quarters," he said, and settled on the deck. "You should eat. I already have."

He smelled of mint. "Are you okay?" Gay said.

"Depends what you mean. Like everyone else but you two, I'm dead drunk. It's just that in my case it happens to be an improvement."

"You *heard* us?" Richard repeated.

"You only. I seem to have the . . . hang of it? Is that a fabric-working term? You make your language do such funny things. That's part of it. I'll use a metaphor. Think of thought as hunting. A kzin sees his prey and pounces. Humans follow it wherever it wanders until it tires and stops moving. Right now I seem to be chasing mice all over a crowded warehouse." He took a deep breath, sat up, and brought his tail around his feet. "I'm able to follow your train of thought," he clarified.

"This stuff has improved your filters?" Gay guessed.

Telepath shook his head. "If anything they're weaker. It's just destroyed my sense of criticism. Everything's great."

"What do we do now?" Richard said.

"I already said. Eat."

"I meant about our situation."

"So do I. You'll think better."

That was undoubtedly true. They got meals from the dispenser. Gay said, "This doesn't bother you?"

"Right now I can hear three Heroes trying to eat *textiles*. Reconstituted vegetables are a decided improvement."

While they ate Telepath sat quietly, aside from an occasional soft rumble. His eyes narrowed briefly each time he exhaled, which when Shebee had done it indicated great comfort. It was something only done at home.

When Richard realized this, Telepath focused on him, leaned forward a bit, and gave a sleepy-looking blink: a gesture of abiding fondness. "This room and your company have been a good time in my life," Telepath said. "And no, pity does not offend me. It is many steps up from fear and contempt." The comment made Richard acutely self-conscious, and Telepath added, "There is truly no need to reply to everything I say. I spoke to clarify: I feel good. Eat."

As he finished, Richard realized who Telepath was making him think of. "Gay, remember Steve Rhee?"

"Richard," she reproved.

"I am not offended," Telepath said. "But thank you for your concern."

Steve Rhee was a Jinxian immigrant who had settled outside Aus-
landburg and started a farm, a café, a bakery, a music shop, and a
furrier's, in that order. The fur business was successful. Through all
his business failures he had never lost his cheerful attitude, due to
his intrinsic good nature, his enjoyment of living under a third of
the gravity he was accustomed to, and his careful selective breeding
of a staggeringly powerful strain of hemp on his homestead plot.
The fact that smoking hemp never caught on with Wunderlanders
was not a problem; his own consumption of the stuff was vast, and
what he didn't smoke, stray Morlocks, living in deep woods now that
there were no uncollapsed caves in the region, came out and ate all
night. He would go out among the stupefied creatures in the morning and snap their necks, which was where he got so many pelts.

"So he brought the hemp with him?" Telepath remarked.

"No, Wunderlanders have grown it for cheap cordage for a
long time," Gay said. "It's pretty strong, for a natural fiber. And
it makes wonderful toys." She looked at Richard suddenly.

"Shebee," he agreed, not catching on yet. Gay stood and started
to examine the dispenser settings. Telepath began chuckling.
"What have I missed?" Richard said, and got it. "Oh." Then he
began laughing too.

"This may just get us into the control room," she said, and
tapped switches.

After the dispenser had worked for a minute or so, Telepath
said, "First Engineer is sneaking up the corridor outside."

"Do tell," said Gay. She stopped the dispenser, took out what
it had made so far, and handed it to Richard before restarting.
"Care to do the honors?"

"Sure." Richard unlocked, opened the door manually, tossed out
the fist-sized fuzzy ball of twine, and sealed the door again.

They waited.

Shortly there was a thump from the wall.

It was followed, after a pause, by several more in quick succession. An intermittent series of further thumps moved off down
the corridor over the next couple of minutes. All three listeners
kept as quiet as possible. At one point Gay shifted her head as
if to speak, but Telepath softly placed a fingertip against her lips.
Then he took it away, gave her a sidelong look, and, while Gay
tried desperately to keep her helpless laughter silent, wiped his
perfectly dry finger repeatedly on his fur.

By and by Telepath said, "He's out of earshot."

"What was that about?" Richard said, pointing at Telepath's hand.

Gay was still shaking, and made as if to grab something with her mouth. Telepath said, "She had a sudden urge to nibble on my finger. I believe the term is *contact high*. I think I had better block you two out for the duration; there appears to be feedback."

Richard finally figured out something that had been bothering him on a subliminal level, and found he couldn't think of a courteous way to bring it up: Telepath was talking a lot more clearly.

"I'm less self-conscious," Telepath said. "And I can detect the way you use your own vocal apparatus. I think perhaps *sthondat* lymph may not be an amplifier at all, but a tranquilizer—my mind is wandering. We will need Slaverexpert."

"We will?" Richard said.

"I cannot fly a ship."

"He can?" said Richard, just as Gay said, "Can't you read the others?"

"He can. I can read the others readily, if all I want to do is chase my tuft. First Engineer is currently the most rational of them."

"Oh *great*," Richard said. "Telepath, Slaverexpert must have gotten the biggest dose of all!"

"He can control his biological responses."

"I thought you couldn't read his mind."

"I can't. But nobody will duel with him."

That was indicative, all right. Modern kzinti wouldn't fight unless they had a chance of winning. "Okay, how do we get to him?"

"We need to isolate the others. Charrgh-Captain first, so I only have to change the security codes once." Telepath stopped talking, and suddenly his ears waggled as he turned to look at Gay. "I think that could work," he said.

The procession started with a short figure in a pressure suit, followed by a larger figure in a similar suit, followed by a small-ish kzin whose tail was generously decorated with silver ribbons tied into bows. A bell was tied to the tuft. In one hand the lead figure carried an object like a drumhead, with miniature cymbals set into the rim. This was shaken continuously except when it was struck with the other hand.

The procession set out from the observers' quarters. Progress was slow, as there were evidently rules concerning the length and rhythm of the paces taken: They were short, and often a step or two went backward. A good deal of noisemaking was clearly required as well. No fewer than five kzinti gave the group immediate and undivided attention on the trip to the bridge. Fourth Trooper seemed to consider joining in as they passed, but was distracted by a fragment falling off his chunk of vegetable.

Telepath buzzed for entrance, and they paraded in a little circle while awaiting a reply. It was not prompt. "I do not *believe* we're going through a shipful of Heroes in a conga line," Richard said over the suit radio.

"Then where do you believe you are?" Telepath said interestedly.

Ignoring Gay's sudden laughter, Richard mused, "I suppose I could be in a tank with that ARM general doing synthetic-perception experiments on me."

Gay said, still laughing, "Why would the ARM do that?"

"Why not?"

The hatch opened before Gay could think of a reply, and she banged her tambourine and marched through.

They stopped performing once the hatch was shut again, but Charrgh-Captain looked at them for a long time before speaking. Finally he said, "Why were you doing that?"

"To avoid attention, sir," Richard said through the suit speaker.

One of the advantages of dealing with almost anyone of any intelligent species is that when you say something that makes no sense to him, he comes up with his own explanation. As expected, Charrgh-Captain thought this over, gave a brief snort of what he supposed to be comprehension, and said, "What do you want? I'm very busy."

This was manifestly true. Charrgh-Captain had apparently been alone on the bridge. That is, there did not appear to be room for another kzin underneath the incredible quantity of shredded packing foam covering every available surface there, said surfaces including the top of the kzin's head.

"Noble Sir," Telepath said, "we came seeking your wisdom to counsel us in a matter of grave importance to the security of this vessel and success of the mission."

Charrgh-Captain's manner underwent a shift, and he said formally, "What is the trouble?"

"What is the proper procedure for addressing a very superior officer said to be severely intoxicated?" Telepath asked humbly.

Charrgh-Captain thought for a moment. Then he suddenly bristled all over and roared at an astonishing volume, "*Who says I'm drunk?*"

"He went in there," Gay said quickly, pointing to the Captain's Battle Quarters.

The senior kzin's scream was not transliterable. He leapt through the hatchway without touching sides or deck, and Telepath hit the wall next to it an instant later and tapped out a security override on the keypad. "Nine to go," he said.

"I cannot begin to imagine what he's going to say about this," Richard said.

"I can hear him. Would you like me to tell you?" said Telepath.

"*No,*" Richard and Gay said in unison.

The next target was supposed to be Weapons Officer, but Fourth Trooper wasn't far from the bridge when they came out, so they formed up again and circled him until he joined in. They congaed down to his quarters, went in, Richard said, "Oops!" and dropped a ball of twine, and the three of them congaed back out and sealed the door.

Weapons Officer was in his quarters already, inspecting the dispenser. Telepath reported, "He's checking the tattoo settings."

"Fine," said Gay. "Lock up."

"I feel I should interrupt him. He's not so bad as some."

"If he wants a tattoo that's his decision," Richard said.

"He's looking at pictures of butterflies," Telepath said.

The two humans thought about what life would be like for a kzin with butterflies on his ears or tail or both. They looked at each other.

"No," said Telepath.

"I'll go, I'm smaller and female and not a threat," said Gay.

Telepath curled his ears partway and said, "You must not improvise anything. Just once through, doing one thing. Please."

"All right."

Weapons Officer was contemplating images of the monarch and viceroy butterflies. The viceroy was decidedly more refined, less baroque. On the other hand, the monarch was no good to eat, which was a matter of personal dignity.

He was somewhat distracted by the sudden opening of the door of his quarters. He had stunner and *wtsai* out at once, but the human—the smaller one—who ran in never came near him; she just ran around the entryway twice, shouting, "Bats! Bats! Bats!" and waving her hands overhead until she ran out again.

Well, this was the kind of thing you had to expect from hunters who cremate their prey. He went over to the door, made sure it was locked, and went back to his screen, shaking his head. Bats. What were bats?

He looked them up.

In the corridor, Richard and Telepath were about equally worried. They tried to pass the time with talk, but it was no distraction:

"I have sometimes wondered what having a sapient mate would be like," Telepath remarked. "Traveling with you I have learned a great deal."

"Good or bad?"

"I am not sure I can answer that yet."

Gay came out and flung her hands about as if chasing something away from her, then stopped and looked at the door in some surprise.

"Weapons Officer just locked his door," Telepath said as Gay was entering the security code.

Richard had to be given a little shake to keep him from hysterics. There had to be a better way.

There was.

Somewhat, anyway.

Second Flyer was amusing himself, tying knots in his pressure suit and watching them untie themselves, when he was distracted by the sound of a tiny bell. He looked around to see a little fuzzy knot of something bouncing along, jingling as it moved. He turned his body slowly, and pounced—and it jumped out of reach! This did not deter him, nor even slow him: He kept after it, bounding off walls at corners, until he had cornered it in his quarters.

Then he ate it.

One by one, Second Engineer, First Trooper, Third Trooper, and First Engineer had much the same experience.

After the first couple of times, Richard had gotten the knack of switching off the camera in a twine-wrapped medical-exploration robot before it disappeared down a kzin's *incredibly* toothy maw, but he was still pretty ragged. "You want to bathe?" said Telepath. "Or eat a potato? That calms humans."

"It does?" Richard said.

"Well, humans who have run out of potatoes are supposed to be very excitable, so I'm assuming the complement."

"I can do the next one," Gay offered again, and again Richard shook his head.

"It won't work on the others anyway," Telepath said. "First Flyer likes Intelligence novels and would assume a trick, and Second Trooper has adopted concealment."

"I keep thinking of that old joke about the Herrenmann who decided to import some tigers," Richard said weakly. "A zoologist who'd just come from Plateau wanted to be paid for advising him about the habits of big cats."

"What do mountaineers know about big cats?" Telepath wondered.

"I guess he'd read a lot. He advised the Herrenmann to have his people wear little bells on their clothing when dealing with any big cat, so it would hear them approach and not be startled into attacking, and to carry pepper spray in case the cat became hostile. All cats should react pretty much the same way. A few weeks later the Herrenmann sent him back a message that said they'd tried the advice, and the zoologist's information on big cats was incomplete: The droppings of tigers, for example, smelled like ammonia and were smooth, while the droppings of kzinti smelled like pepper and had little bells in them."

The question of whether they were being routinely read was settled at once: Telepath literally fell down laughing.

After they'd watched him roll around for a while, Richard said, "It's all very well for you. You haven't been getting the bell's-eye view."

"We should be able to get the smell out of the ship now," Gay said encouragingly.

That turned out not to be the case.

Not entirely, anyway. The ship's design considered the possibility of boarding, and gas, so the walls were highly resistant to adsorption of volatiles; but a single molecule can be enough to trigger a conditioned response without actually being perceived on a conscious level.

All of which went a long way to explain why, even after all detectable roots had been spaced and the corridors had been through basic decontamination, Telepath kept having sudden fits of the earwiggles.

At least Richard didn't need to wear a pressure suit to keep from getting ill.

And Telepath *could* function.

First Flyer was gradually getting the idea that something was wrong. The bridge was empty—aside from what looked like a kzintosh's first unsupervised experience with packing foam—and the controls were locked, and nobody else seemed to be around. He was headed blearily back to his quarters to do a remote systems check when he saw Telepath rolling down the corridor.

Telepath was hanging on to a huge hairy sphere, about a third his own volume, and acting like he was trying to gut it.

Aliens!

First Flyer screamed and leapt, *wtsai* plunging into the sphere in sure, swift strokes.

After fifteen stabs there was still no blood.

Telepath was staring at him over the edge of the sphere. His ears were spread very wide, in a position of astonishment.

The sphere appeared to be wound from some kind of stiff cellulose-based cord.

Incensed, First Flyer knotted his ears.

Telepath immediately leapt to his feet and came to attention.

First Flyer stood, looked at Telepath, looked at the huge *toy* Telepath had made for himself, and growled, "Go to your quarters."

"Sir!" said Telepath, and leapt away down the corridor.

The hairy thing had loose strands sticking out all over it now.

It did look like fun.

When he got near his own quarters with it he noticed the humans leaning against a wall. Their bodies were together, faces touching. Probably checking one another for parasites or something. They took no notice as he dragged the thing in and sealed the door.

Richard got to the keypad first. "Just one now," he said.

"We can ignore Second Trooper," said Telepath from three feet away, causing them both to leap into the air. He stared at them for a moment, then reached up and actually held onto his ears as he continued, "He'll be staying out of the way."

"Slaverexpert, then," Gay said, breathing hard.

"Are you tired?" said Telepath.

"No."

"Oh." He thought. "Good diversion."

As they got to Slaverexpert's quarters, Richard said, "We shouldn't stand close to him."

"Good idea," said Telepath. "We can move all his stuff onto lower shelves, too."

Richard stopped in his tracks as he tried to figure that out. "How would that make it safer to wake him up?" he finally asked.

"Oh. I thought you wanted him to think the drug had made him taller."

Richard shook his head, said nothing, and walked on.

As he passed, Telepath said mildly, "That wasn't called for."

Slaverexpert heard movement and opened his eyes to see Telepath. "You again," he said in Hero. "I told you to let me sleep."

"That was three days ago," said Telepath.

"Oh." Slaverexpert considered. "Then I really am this hungry." He established a coherent pattern of behavior, rolled off his *fooch*, scooped the fabric into the recycler, and punched for something not too drippy and a gallon of lager. Then he noticed the humans. "Good day, Richard and Gay Guthlac," he said in Interworld. "On reflection I believe the polymer roots we found should not be admitted into general use."

After perhaps half a minute watching two humans lean against one another laughing insanely, Slaverexpert turned to Telepath and said, "I gather there have been developments."

"Oh yes."

"Describe—are you hungry?"

"In fact, I am."

"Will those two be safe in the corridor?"

"Yes."

"Push them out the door and key something for yourself."

"Thank you," said Telepath, surprised. He got the Guthlacs out, and turned back just as Slaverexpert's haunch and mug came out. "I wonder why humans call it a dial," he said as he made his selection. "Like an instrument dial."

"Some historical reference involving mating, religion, or money," Slaverexpert said, and took a healthy bite.

"Involving how?"

"Who knows? But practically every odd thing humans do does. Tell me what's been happening."

Telepath began to do so, pausing only to get his own meat and hot milk when they came out, and to say, "This is better than Charrgh-Captain's dispenser makes!"

Obviously he'd monitored others at meals, and who could blame him? "Yes, it was custom-made," Slaverexpert said. "I've kept it with me ever since. How did you know I could fly a ship? Oh, of course, Charrgh-Captain knows it. Tell me the rest after you've eaten."

Telepath devoured his food gratefully. As they were cleaning their faces he said quietly, "My thanks for the honor."

"My regrets for its lateness. My duties kept me from doing anything that might draw undue attention, such as treating a telepath with respect for a difficult job reliably done."

"You're a Patriarch's Eye?" Telepath blurted, then said, embarrassed, "I did not speak."

Slaverexpert spread his ears amiably and said, "A traditionalist, I see. Rather than 'I heard nothing,' the proper reply in this case would be, 'There is no shame.' I was never an Eye. I used to train them for the Speakers-to-Animals, but I gave it up because my better students could never tell me what they did. The best one simply disappeared. Maddening. I began studying Slavers instead. I was very disappointed not to be on the *Wallaby* expedition, but at the time I had obligations-of-duty." The term he used indicated a significant degree of responsibility to underlings who trusted him with their future prosperity, and a kzin who would neglect that would eat grass. "If we are done, we should join the humans and see to the ship. You may then tell—ftah. At your earliest convenience I would like to hear the rest of what has happened."

Telepath was gazing at him with a kitten's wonder. He realized it and looked down. "I meant no intrusion."

"I do not duel."

Telepath's ears extended back against his head in the position of utmost curiosity, but he said merely, "Urr. I believe we are done . . . Commander."

"Well, that wasn't too dignified," Richard said after they'd gotten themselves under control and had been waiting a while.

"In the circumstances I doubt they'll hold it against us," Gay said.

"Mm, no," he agreed. "And there is the formal excuse that we wouldn't want to watch them eat." Kzinti courtesy was decidedly not human courtesy, but one of the points in common was occasionally pretending not to notice something.

The door opened, and Telepath said in Interworld, "Good, you're still clothed. We should go to the bridge now."

Richard opened his mouth, realized that Telepath had never dropped in on them while they were making love or immediately after and therefore knew their habits, and closed his mouth again, attempting to keep some dignity.

It didn't help that Gay giggled all the way to the bridge.

Slaverexpert looked around and said, "I had hoped you were exaggerating. Start a cleaning robot."

"Sir," said Telepath, and obeyed.

"I cannot use a mass detector," said Slaverexpert, "so we will need a kzin and a human here at all times. Watches will be . . ." He thought, and found the word. "Staggered. Four hours. Which of you is currently less fatigued?"

Richard and Gay looked at each other.

"They need much rest before they can proceed, sir," Telepath said.

Slaverexpert growled wordlessly, then caught himself. Old habits came back unexpectedly. "There will be a few days before we enter hyperspace. After that we will all have to make do with solitary . . ." He found the word. "Naps."

The humans left without a word, their postures dismayed.

"They're not getting paid enough," Telepath said after they had left. "Each of them thought that." His ears were twitching just a bit.

"Given that my own household will still be six light-years away once we get back to Kzin-aga, my sympathy is all that it should be. You seem well; how are you able to read them without drugs or pain?"

"The euphoria the roots produce has a remarkable stabilizing effect, sir."

"But the ship has been decontaminated," Slaverexpert said.

Telepath stood very still for a long moment. Then he looked

toward the door of the Captain's Battle Quarters. Then he said—almost a question—"I still feel good."

Without hesitation Slaverexpert firmly said, "Good. What has been done with the rest of the roots?" They represented a tremendously powerful weapon against the Patriarchy.

"Spaced, sir."

Slaverexpert stared in shock. "How did you get them to agree to *that*?"

"It was their idea, sir. They were concerned about the effect on our civilization, sir."

Slaverexpert contemplated that, and came to the same conclusion he had shortly after he had awakened as a cyborg: Humans were *weird*. Then he said, "Telepath, in the circumstances I think it reasonable to regard military discipline as held in abeyance. You don't have to be formal in your address."

"Thank you. I think I should stay in practice, though."

Slaverexpert said mildly, "As executive officer the ship's records are in your keeping, including those of the last three days and those of the events in private cabins. I imagine henceforth you may *never* have to be formal in your address."

Telepath looked at him in puzzlement, then visibly realized the implications. His ears stood out, but his voice was controlled as he said, "I will need instruction in guiding the ship."

"Of course." Slaverexpert stepped over the cleaning robot to indicate controls, politely ignoring the faint purring Telepath produced as he contemplated a voyage under the command of a flagrant subversive.

Gay knew that Slaverexpert was being considerate. She also knew that the kzin would never understand that to a human—at least, to a civilized human—there are few things likelier to diminish arousal than a deadline. A kzin would probably be trying to establish a record.

Both the Guthlacs were frustrated and irritable by the time the *Cunning Stalker* left the system's singularity.

Weeks of watch-and-watch routine did nothing to improve this.

Second Trooper's intermittent brief appearances and immediately disappearances were provoking in the extreme. He still had a chunk of the root, too, so they persisted.

Returning from her second watch of the fifty-first day in hyperspace, having steered the ship around a record *four* suspicious fuzzy red lines, Gay was passing the door to Second Trooper's quarters when it suddenly opened. She jumped and stared at him.

In response to this perceived aggression, equally surprised, Second Trooper bared his teeth and claws.

Lacking both weapons and patience, Gay stuck her tongue out at him.

Second Trooper's pupils grew huge, his ears curled, and with a faint squeak he leapt back into his quarters and sealed the door.

Astounded, Gay stared at the door for a moment. The kzin had reacted like he was scared to death.

She shook off the momentary paralysis and quickly entered the door's security override, then turned, thinking to go back to the bridge and report the last straggler caught. She refrained. It could wait.

She continued back to their cabin for what sleep she could get.

She was always tired now, though, and never did think to ask what could have prompted the reaction.

Toward the end of hyperspace transit, even Slaverexpert's fatigue override system was under some strain. It manifested as garrulity.

At least he was interesting.

On the seventy-fifth day he was on watch with Richard when he looked up from his screen and said, "Most of the design changes in this ship are based on human ideas, you know."

"They are?" Richard said, looking around incredulously. Past the row of little blue globes the humans used to avoid eyestrain, the kzin-scale mechanisms with their deep orange lighting looked not unlike the foundry of the Cyclopes.

"Very much so. Crew posts not facing a common center, for instance, so everyone can see the same view. Far less distracting than my old command."

"You commanded a ship before?" Richard exclaimed.

"At the start of the Fourth War," Slaverexpert said, which made him something over three hundred years old—unheard of! "I had a partial Name then. I gave it up after my injuries were repaired. Having a Name is grounds for killing if it is not used properly, and I had lost the desire to kill."

"What was it?" Richard had never heard of any kzin giving up a Name, and hadn't known it was possible.

"Richard, I told you: I no longer use it," he said patiently. "Twice since then I have been offered one for my competence. Normally the degree of ability adhering to being an Expert carries such an honor. However, one of my crew had been an Expert, so I knew it was done."

"Why didn't he have one?"

"His behavior was too exotic," said Slaverexpert. "I learned much later that he had been raised in an obscure sect which worships death. He had left the faith, though."

"I may have heard of it," Richard said, taking another look at the mass detector. "There were a few incidents after the First War. When kdaptism got started there was a form that adopted crucifixion of humans as a means of prayer. Rare events, but memorable."

"Indeed. It does sound like the same sect as his. Some time after we parted I understand he resumed a worship of death."

"I wonder what happened," Richard said absently, noticing something at the edge of the globe.

Slaverexpert was silent for a moment, then said, "I suppose you could call it an epiphany—"

"I think we're there," said Richard. He pointed, then remembered and said, "Sorry."

"As long as you're correct," said Slaverexpert. "Take us to the edge and we'll drop out and look."

Richard was no daredevil, but he was very intent on getting home. He let the line get almost to the shell before shutting down the motor, then lit the viewscreens.

Slaverexpert studied the dome, altered the perspective twice, then pointed. "That's the Axe, and that's the Puffball," he said, indicating stars which suggested nothing to Richard, but were presumably grouped into constellations to the eye of a native of Kzin. "Well done, Richard Guthlac. Turn the Returning Vessel beacon to the fifth setting and pull twice."

"I remember." That was for Medical Assistance, Nonlethal. "What happened to the rest of your crew?"

"All but one are dead now," Slaverexpert said, starting deceleration. "The last is a Patriarch's Counselor."

"Wow."

"What? Where?"

"No no, sorry, 'wow' is a human expression of admiration. I'm sorry." *Wow* was also a kzinti exclamation, usually used when something was broken or lost.

Slaverexpert waved a hand in a very human gesture. "I'll live." He began preparing a message giving details of their situation.

After far too many unpleasant surprises, only the latest of which had been the *Wallaby* incident, the kzinti were taking no chances. The lead team of the boarding party was four telepaths in powered armor, each with a fusion bomb and his own gravity generator. They flew through the *Cunning Stalker*'s corridors on a swift initial survey and found them apparently clear. Three then stood guard while the fourth took out rescue bubbles, enclosed the four acting crew one by one, and linked them to retrieval lines that drew them to the intercept ship.

A judicious mixture of friendly persuasion and stunners got the other ten kzinti bagged and delivered. The telepaths packaged the items from the stasis box, followed by personal keepsakes, and sent those after the personnel. Then they flooded the *Cunning Stalker* with ozone, set off radiation flash bombs, let the atmosphere out, and did another inspection in vacuum. No green-scaled corpses were found, and they returned to the *Excessive Force*, which took the exploration vessel in tow.

The ARM general was keeping his voice and hands under control, but his body language would have started a fight in any bar on Kzin-aga. Probably on Earth, for that matter. "Our legal position is unassailable," he insisted. "The Guthlacs were working as employees of the UN, and any bonuses due for their performance belong to the ARM."

Charrgh-Uft replied cheerfully, "After five centuries of dealing with humans, the kzinti are well-qualified to state that *no* position is unassailable. You, personally, insisted on their military rank being officially acknowledged in all particulars for this mission. That makes them crew. They get prize shares."

"If these things are as good as they look it's going to leave two people owning half a dozen of the biggest industries in human space!"

Charrgh-Uft was growing tired of the argument, and he played the trump the Patriarch had told him he could if necessary: "This is a matter of the Patriarch's honor."

The gray-bristled human froze in place. The First War had dragged on well after it was lost, killing over a million kzinti, before a way was found for the then-Patriarch to surrender with honor. Weakly, he said, "All they wanted was enough money to start a farm."

"They'll be able to afford quite a large one, I should think," said Charrgh-Uft. "If I recall the invasion analysis correctly, there is an equatorial highland on Wunderland's second continent which could benefit from irrigation."

"It's the size of *France*! A bubble asteroid would cost less to make!"

"Good idea. Every landowner should have a vacation home as well," Charrgh-Uft said reasonably.

The Guthlacs had been given all the privacy they wanted, and had made enthusiastic use of it. After a week or so the pace slowed, and they began wearing clothing now and then, for meals and such.

"Slaverexpert must have some real pull to get us left alone like this," Richard said at the end of one meal. "I'd have thought someone would have been giving us a very thorough debriefing." He saw Gay's grin, and laughed, "Besides each other."

The computer's message light came on, for the first time since they were given their quarters. Gay was closer, and lit the screen. It said:

"Lord Krosp requests the honor of your company at the receiving platform of his landing shuttle, sometime prior to sunset of the day after tomorrow, when he will be departing for his estate on Kzrral."

"Who's Lord Krosp?" Richard said.

"He must be awfully important to get through to us," Gay said. "And you did say you were getting a little sore."

"Aren't you?"

"Yes, but you admitted it first."

They got there the morning of the second day, after spending some time in a fruitless search for the whereabouts of Slaver-expert. Charrgh-Uft had contacted them briefly to let them know he would be fully occupied socially (translation: looking over the daughters that various nobles were offering him), but thanked them for their help and assured them of fair treatment. He signed off before explaining that last.

The attitude of the kzin they'd asked for directions had altered from barely-tolerant to deeply impressed when the Name Krosp was mentioned: "You know *him*? I will tell my sons that I met you!"

Gay murmured, "Who *is* this 'tosh?"—Wunderkzin equivalent of "guy."

Lord Krosp's shuttle was a converted troop lander, and it had a place all to itself on the landing field. When their groundcar stopped, four kzinti formed an honor guard beside their path, and drew claws before their faces in salute as the Guthlacs got out.

Slaverstudent, in steel-studded harness with equipment pouches attached, marched out and said, "Welcome, Richard Guthlac and Gay Guthlac!"

"*You're* Lord Krosp?" Gay exclaimed.

"Hardly. I am his aide-de-camp. Hospitality!" he called out to the ship, and a dozen elegantly decorated Jotoki wearing Freed insignia deployed seats, table, dispensers, canopy, and windscreens.

Lord Krosp, resplendent in weapons belt and governor's sash, stepped out and declared, "My friends, and authors of my good fortune, be welcome!"

It was Telepath.

Naturally they were eaten *alive* by curiosity, but the manners they were raised with required him to bring it up first. Krosp knew it, and cheerfully tormented them by seating them and plying them with food and drink before sitting down himself. "I trust you have not been disturbed since we got back? I was most specific."

"That was you? Thanks!" Richard said.

"I hope you made good use of the time—" Krosp jumped a trifle, then went on, "I see. It is well my family is in the shuttle and not the main ship." He turned his head as a human would to ease a stiff neck, then said, "I wanted to thank you for your kindness, and inform you that should you ever visit Kzrral the governor's hospitality is open to you."

"How did you get appointed governor?" Gay burst out, finally unable to restrain her curiosity.

"It was entirely due to the vivid and enthusiastic praise of my accomplishments, given me by my crewmates from the *Cunning Stalker*— Ah, this will be Weapons Officer," he said, indicating a groundcar that was just approaching.

There was no honor guard for Weapons Officer, and Krosp did not get up. Ears mostly folded (and bats tattooed on his tail), Weapons Officer came up with a parcel and stood at attention.

"Relax. It is good to see you," Telepath said in Hero. "I was just discussing our trip with the Guthlacs, who like the rest of us are going to be very rich from the salvage we brought back. Is that a gift?"

"Yes, sir," said Weapons Officer, and held out the parcel. "It was my grandsire's."

"I am certain it does us both honor. I hope for your part you will find this small item gratifying," Telepath said, and took something from one of his belt pouches.

It looked remarkably like a recording crystal for a kzinti ship's log.

Weapons Officer accepted it, took a deep breath, let it out, and looked a lot less uncomfortable. His ears spread, and he said, "I am certain I will always be glad to have this. I have no doubt that you will fulfill the duties of your new post most capably," he added in a decidedly dry tone.

"A generous parting wish," Krosp said.

Weapons Officer saluted, and turned to the Guthlacs. "I hope you will enjoy your well deserved prosperity on Wunderland for many years to come," he said in Interworld.

Richard, staring at the ear tattoos, couldn't think of a thing to say. Gay got the context, and recovered sufficiently to say, "I'm sure we will, though sadly our responsibilities will prevent us from returning here to visit you."

With a distinct sigh of relief, Weapons Officer said, "We all do what we must," and departed.

Richard was still getting over the tattoos. The right ear had been decorated with tiny stylized bats, but the left displayed a human face: Herrenmann white, but with long black hair and a heavy jawline. The eyes were faintly outlined in black, and their wild stare was an excellent complement to a deeply disturbing grin. "Who was *that*?" he finally got out.

"An Earth musician from the post-classical period, I believe,"

Krosp said, opening the parcel. "Weapons Officer's family has considerable interest in the arts." A Jotok picked up the wrapping as the gift was revealed: a fan of cords attached to a long frame, with a hollow box at one end. He plucked a string with a claw, and a pleasant tone came out. It was a musical instrument.

Richard suddenly laughed, getting it under control just as quickly.

Krosp didn't seem offended, just puzzled: "What's funny?"

"I was just thinking: all you need to join the Gasperik Society is a motorcycle."

"What's that?"

"An outfit established a long time ago, even before space habitats, with the stated intention of being prepared for alien invasion. It was sort of a literary club, really. Every member was theoretically supposed to own, and keep in good order, a motorcycle, a guitar, a spacesuit, and an elephant gun. A kzinti sidearm could surely stop an elephant, we've seen your suit, and that ought to qualify as a guitar."

"Yes, I know about the Gasperik Division," said Krosp. "It was part of the Hellflare Corps. What's a motorcycle?"

"Oops. It's a vehicle with two wheels in a line, with a seat in between. Very popular in rough country. *Blackmail*?" Richard exclaimed.

"Oh, no," Krosp assured him. "Blackmail is an insult that warrants death, being a threat to publicly claim that the victim is dishonorable. However, when the question is one of looking like a fool for the rest of one's life, solicitation of bribery is another matter entirely. I am pleased that you were here when he arrived, as it saved considerable explanation."

Gay began to laugh. Richard, thinking of the abuse they had been unable to stop, joined in. Slaverexpert came over and said, "Lord Krosp, do you want to mention the plan?"

"Oh yes. Slaverexpert has—you have a question," he said to Richard.

"I never heard the kzinti Name Krosp before," Richard said, still laughing.

"It's not a kzinti Name. It was a character from human literature, a brilliant leader who provided calm insight and perspective when no one around him could see a solution."

"What's it from?"

"I don't know. The Patriarch suggested it. Did you want to hear Slaverexpert's plan?"

"Sure."

"Most of Kzrral is disagreeably hot. We plan to put gravity-planers on its moon, after which we will gradually drag it further from its primary over the course of the next few centuries—that is, Slaverexpert and my heirs will."

The two humans goggled at him. Gay said, "That'll cost a fortune!"

"We have two. We expect to get another, as we will be able to improve the health and reliability of telepaths all over the Patriarchy."

"How?"

"We're going to raise catnip."

For Frank and Peggy,
but especially for Jim.

PEACE AND FREEDOM

◆　◆　◆

Matthew Joseph Harrington

One of the less appreciated points of being the smartest organic intelligence in the known universe is that, when you find out you've screwed up, you get to feel much stupider than anyone else can.

Peace Corben switched the hyperwave to the Project Supervision channel and said, "Ling."

"Problem?" said Jennifer Ling.

"You need to divert resources and build a couple more Quantum II ships. The Outsiders have just informed me that someone's mining the Hot Spot, and I need to take *Cordelia* back to Known Space."

"The *Outsiders* called *you*?" The Outsiders were a life-form whose metabolism was based on the quantum effects that cropped up at superconductive temperatures. (Probably. If anyone ever tried to dissect one, he hadn't gotten back with details. Or at all.) They made their living all through the Galaxy by selling information to the races they encountered as they cruised past inhabited systems; the idea of them volunteering information was weirdness on the order of a Protector trusting a stranger's good intentions.

"They still owe me money for mass conversion and a new form of math. They're very scrupulous. Unfulfilled obligations give them bubbles in the liquid helium or something."

"Can I give you backup?"

"Wouldn't help. I've got a zip, if necessary." She could keep breeders in the zip, the Sinclair accelerator field. She could spend several years talking human breeders into becoming protectors, while a few days passed outside the field. Instant allies.

"We're on it," Jennifer said.

Peace signed off and moved *Cordelia* out of the main site on thrusters, to avoid dragging anything along. Of a population of almost two hundred thousand Protectors, more than half were working on the primary disintegrator array. (The region wasn't what you could call crowded, since they were spread through an area that would not quite have fitted into the orbit of Pluto, but alignment was important, and courtesy counts. Especially between people who do things like vaporizing planets for raw materials.) She paused to note that the work was going well—arrangements to disperse the oncoming particle blast from the Core explosion could be complete in a matter of decades—then went to hyperdrive.

She knew of two races that could be mining antimatter from Gregory Pelton's rogue solar system. One, human, had actually visited the Hot Spot briefly. The other species might have noticed, at closest approach to their home system, the inordinate neutrino production, from annihilation of interstellar matter, that had given it its nickname among Protectors. Both races qualified as very bad news, especially since the only way for either race to be doing it would be as a result of a massive cultural shift—greater than what a human Protector had arranged three and a half centuries back.

Therefore, somebody had done something unusually stupid. Peace never even wondered who would have to fix it.

Shleer couldn't take another minute of the horror in the harem, not one, so he went up the wall to the loops in the ceiling and used them to get across to the exhaust vent. The plastic wrapper was still in its crevice, and he put it on and squirmed out through a passage that shouldn't have held a kzintosh—was specifically designed not to, in fact; that was the whole point. It had been widened at key spots by Felix, of course.

Shleer missed Felix Buckminster. The ancient, fully-Named cyborg kzin might not have known what to do, but at least he would have been someone to talk to. Shleer was as alone as any kzin could be on his own planet.

He got to the death trap—stasis-wire mesh—and got out a grippy to work the maintenance controls, which were designed for Jotok use. The access panel slid back, Shleer checked for observers and emerged, and the panel shut again. Shleer opened the outside of the maintenance duct with a panel which wasn't supposed to be movable, swung out over empty air, and closed the panel, clinging to handholds invisible from below. He hung upside down by a foot while he removed the wrapper—if a human could do it, he could do it!—then hauled himself back up, took a better hold, and put it into another crevice.

Then he turned and leapt toward the God of the Jotok as an arm went past.

The souvenir of conquest of the Jotoki homeworld was immense, but there was no way to see the thing while settled firmly enough to leap the full distance, and as it was silent in its rotation Shleer simply had no choice but to remember the timing after seeing it upside down. If he ever got it wrong, there was going to be considerable puzzlement after they found his body; it was about a two-hundred-foot drop, from nowhere anybody knew about.

Getting back was always a lot easier, though. He faced his target then.

He got to the end of the arm just as it passed the floor, and gave himself a light, military-looking brushing once he was down. A front-and-back medallion went over his head, labeling him a Patriarch's Guest—well, he *was*—and he padded comfortably into the more modern areas of Rrit's Past.

It was a bad habit to get into a routine, but this was something nobody knew about anyway, so the first place he always went was to see the Patriarch's Peer.

Harvey Mossbauer stood in the exact spot he had been in when the bomb decapitated him. They'd had to pretty much build a new harem anyway, so that was done in a more secure location and the House of the Patriarch's Past was expanded to include this area. Reassembling him must have been awfully difficult, and there had been some dispute about whether to include both arms—one having been lost a couple of floors up. Patriarch Hrocht-Ao-Rritt had said all of him, though, and nobody had altered that since.

He had his gear these days. Some Patriarchs had thought he looked more fierce all by himself, but he looked more *right* with his weapons. He stood poised to spin and kick, flechette launcher strapped to the extended forearm, anemone in the hand drawn back to thrust. Five empty slots were left in the anemone bandolier, a nice historical touch; he'd left four in Companions who had decided to engage in claw-and-fang combat.

They were the only kzinti he'd killed before reaching the harem. He'd disabled more than sixty-four—

The bandolier, Shleer was annoyed to see, was now filled, by the new and unhistoried Tender-of-Legends no doubt. Shleer took four and put a fifth into the Peer's hand.

He wished the Peer was alive. The Peer had clearly known how to manage his priorities, and wouldn't attack kzinti until the real problem was solved.

Shleer realized someone was coming, and began moving to remain continuously out of sight. He was extremely annoyed at the interruption, which was the first of its kind.

A Tnuctip scurried in, through, and out the far side without so much as looking at the Peer. Shleer was doubly offended. They'd never come in here before; the least the little monster could have done was appreciate the display.

Though it might not have had a choice.

Come to that, what could it be doing? The only things down that way were still older history (which he doubted was its goal) or the servant quarters, with their laboratories—and the lifeboat they'd come from.

Shleer considered. What would the Peer have done in this situation?

Harvey Mossbauer (he deserved three Names, but no other was ever discovered, and it would have been disrespectful to assign him one) had come, after many years, to inflict justice. He had infallibly turned toward the harem wherever there was a choice; he had used ammunition that disabled without being immediately fatal, causing pursuit to be obstructed by autodoc remotes; he had blasted walls to open shortcuts, or to block reinforcements, but the only antipersonnel charge he'd set off was in the harem itself. The Patriarch had killed his family; he killed the Patriarch's family; now they were even.

The Peer would have gathered information. And he would have made plans.

Shleer followed the Tnuctip.

Larry Greenberg stepped into the stasis capsule and the door closed.

Suddenly the gravity was different—but *lighter*? This wasn't Jinx!

The door opened. There was an alien standing there, resembling nothing so much as the mummy of a patient dead of terminal arthritis. With a head like a deformed basketball. It wore a white sleeveless singlet from neck to knees, apparently made out of filled pockets.

A really *smart* alien, too. Mind too fast to read. "Speak English?" he said helplessly.

"Yes, but I still have to point at the menus," it replied.

"What?"

"Come out, will you?"

He came out, feeling foolish, and stopped. The *Lazy Eight III*, colony ship to Jinx, was *gone*. His stasis capsule had been brought inside another, bigger(!) ship— "What the hell happened?"

"From the damage I'd say the ramscoop field missed a good-sized speck of dust. Opened the crew module without disabling the ram, just as they were preparing for turnover. That was about eight and a half centuries ago. Nobody could afford to rescue you. It's now 2965 CE. Read this, it'll give you a general overview of the basics." It handed him what seemed to be a sheet of white cardboard—with touchpads on the margin. When he reached, it clasped a cuff on his left wrist and watched it for a moment. "Medical," it said. "—Hungry? Of course, a meal would have been extra weight. Read while you eat." She led him to another room, where he had the novel and dubious experience of seeing food dispensed by a machine. It was good, though.

The first part was just after his time—Lucas Garner was involved again. A Pak Protector—an alien, sort of—had arrived from the Galactic Core, with a supply of roots that would turn hominids of the right age into asexual fighting machines with superhuman intelligence. Larry got as far the description of what happened to Jack Brennan, and looked up and said, "You're a *human being*?"

"Yah. I know your name already; mine's Peace Corben." It was done eating—from a vessel the size of a punchbowl—and added, "It gets worse. I've got stuff to do, keep reading." It stood.

"How do you eat that fast with no teeth?" (Teeth fell out during the change, and Peace Corben's lips and gums were fused into a bony beak.)

"I've got a tongue that could shell oysters." It ran out. (Fast, too.)

He kept reading.

It got worse.

Brennan had exterminated the Martians, expanded the power of the ARM to the rewriting of history and brainwashing of all of Sol System. His successor/apprentice had released a virus on the colony world Home that killed about 90 percent of the population, turning the rest into an army of childless Protectors. (Protectors who had descendants recognized them by smell, and methodically slaughtered anything that looked like it might interfere with their populating the universe. Protectors whose instincts were not triggered by the smell of descendants either quit caring and starved, or worked to protect their entire species.) The Protectors of Home had killed off some incoming Pak scouts, then headed toward the Core to exterminate the rest of the species.

They did this because the Pak were *all* coming out in the direction of Earth. Earth was known to be habitable, and their own world wasn't going to be.

This was because the Galaxy was exploding.

Greenberg's head was exploding. He took a smoke break before he read on—

This was known hereabouts because it had been seen: The puppeteers had developed an improved hyperdrive, from mathematical hints dropped by Peace Corben after she'd become a protector. (The puppeteers had fled the Galaxy as soon as they saw the films.)

She'd become a Protector when she'd gone to Home fleeing a kzinti invasion of her home planet. (She had subsequently won that war single-handedly by walking into the Patriarchy's Central Command inside an accelerator field, walking out with their entire order of battle, and arranging for every kzinti attack after the first to be met with overwhelming force.)

The kzinti were now mining antimatter, from a stray solar cloud that was passing through the Galaxy at about point eight C. And that meant that her arrangements to alter kzinti civilization had been changed by someone capable of mental control.

The protector came back while he was reading her speculations about what was happening on Kzin. He looked up and said, "You did all this to collect *me*?"

"Right. The records don't say where the device was put."

Back in 2107, Larry Greenberg had been Earth's top telepath. Greenberg had been put into contact with an alien, Kzanol, who'd been in stasis for, it turned out, two billion years. Kzanol had been a much more powerful telepath—a Slaver of the Slaver Empire, with the Power to control dozens of ordinary minds—and his transferred memories had overwhelmed Greenberg's personality for weeks. There had ensued a hunt for something which would have made Kzanol, essentially, God:

"You mean the stasis field with the Slaver amplifier in it?"

"No, Lucas Garner's hoverchair, I always wanted it for my weapon collection." Given that Garner had then been a 169-year-old paranoid, that was almost reasonable; his travel chair probably violated all kinds of safety laws, and possibly one or two disarmament treaties.

Greenberg flushed a little and said, "It was dropped into Jupiter."

"Good. I was afraid Garner would have talked them into the sun. That'd be difficult."

"You can retrieve it?"

"What do you think I've been working on while you read, a better mousetrap?"

"Oh. . . . Still mice around, huh?"

"Yeah, but changed some. All that radiation during the Kzinti Wars. We've signed a treaty, though."

"You're kidding."

"Yes."

" . . . You *are* kidding."

"Yes."

He blinked a few times, shook his head violently, and said, "Where's everybody else?"

"Still in stasis. I wanted you apprised of the situation before I extended the accelerator field around them. I mean to spend about fifteen subjective years in this ship, in part to get them adapted before I release them, and I need you to look after their sanity."

"I thought you had an emergency."

"To the rest of the universe it'll be about eleven days. Stasis won't work inside any kind of time-distortion field, so I had to tell you separately."

"Wait a minute, what about my wife?"

"She's here. I got everybody."

"I mean, we wanted children."

Peace nodded. "This vessel was built to house up to half a million Protectors and their fighter craft. You won't find it crowded in fifteen years, I don't care *how* enthusiastic you are."

◇   ◇   ◇

The Tnuctip walked right past a group of older kzintosh, who were following a Pierin tutor. (Paid regular staff were a recent innovation, but one that seemed to work. All it took was regarding a contract as an oath.) There were six to avoid, not counting the Pierin, who wasn't being paid to notice Shleer. The group fell silent as the Tnuctip scurried by.

"Here we have the tablets of Great Sire Chof-Yff-Rrit, who, in amongst his personal tastes, specified the penalties for willfully ignoring a known gesture of surrender, which act was a great contribution to all kzinti cultures, and may be argued to have led to unification thereof under the Patriarchy. Who knows how humans signal surrender?" the Pierin asked. It would take more than the end of civilization to shut a Pierin up. Shleer crept along the wall behind his siblings—far behind.

K'nar-Rritt, who was likely to be the next Patriarch, said dryly, "Their hearts stop beating. It's not always a sure sign, though."

"Wittily phrased, though possibly misleading. Humans do not have a surrender gesture. They are descended from the Pak, a species that knew nothing but war, and are as a consequence the least reasonable or tractable intelligent race presently known. They are never satisfied until things are entirely the way they want them, and genuinely expect everyone else to cooperate."

One of his siblings was turning toward Shleer. Shleer froze, turned only his head, and made eye contact as soon as he was seen. The kzintosh flexed his ears a little and turned back to the Pierin. Shleer continued out of the hall, head pounding terribly.

The Tnuctip was out of his sight, but passed through somebody else's. Shleer took the correct exit from the next chamber, doing military respiration exercises to get the headache under control. It got a little easier each time.

He evaded the guards who'd seen the thing, which was indeed heading for the Jotoki labs. Shleer shortened the distance between them to get through the (manifestly useless) containment doors on the same activation, then let it get ahead. It went into the lifeboat, out of sight.

Then it vanished from his perception.

Shleer immediately took cover. The Tnuctip came out of the lifeboat wearing a cap of metal mesh, then went over to where the Jotoki traditionally worked on weapons they fondly imagined the kzinti didn't know about, entered, and was invisible again.

The Tnuctip was wearing a shield against telepathy. The *sthondat-nuzzling* imbeciles had had a mental shield, but hadn't been using it when they went into stasis! Shleer noticed his claws were out, and retracted them with an effort. A phrase he'd picked up from Felix crossed his mind: "unusually stupid." It certainly seemed to apply.

What would the Peer do now? Examine his options.

Shleer could sneak in on just nose and ears.

He could wait and follow the Tnuctip further.

He could wait and look inside after the Tnuctip left.

Or he could leave now—at least in theory; he only listed it to be thorough.

Shleer waited.

Eventually the Tnuctip came out—looking directly toward him. Pure chance, but bad. Shleer hoped really hard their brains were arranged like modern ones, and maintained eye contact. The Tnuctip sniffed a few times, then turned and went to put the shield back in the lifeboat.

After it had scurried away, Shleer moved for the first time in over an hour, stretching slowly. The only place for the Tnuctip to go was the Residence; it could therefore be ignored now. Shleer entered the Jotoki secret weapon shop for a look.

Nothing was lying out, but compartments had been handled. He sniffed them out, then checked for traps. One had a hair across the opening, another hair hanging from the hinge, and a dead-fall of a canister of dry lubricant powder inside. Intended only to reveal Jotoki interference—so kzinti reflexes kept the powder from spilling a grain.

The Tnuctip had been working on another mental shield. Cruder-looking, but with an active power source. Jamming? Would that work?

He looked it over carefully, Felix having taught him a great deal. It most certainly would not work. There were conductors that would melt if full power were applied for more than a few seconds. The Tnuctip had been Programmed to waste its time here.

Shleer almost pitied the evil little creature. Almost. He replaced the deadfall and the hairs, and began trying to remember, as he headed back toward the harem, where he'd last seen a camera.

The design seemed worth copying—and *Shleer* hadn't been Told to use flawed components.

◇   ◇   ◇

The Slaver Gnix watched a movie and sucked a gnal, or at least the best approximation his slaves had produced so far. He had nobody to tell it to—yet—but he was mostly pleased. He'd been lucky beyond belief.

He'd manifested full Power later than usual for a Thrint. This had led to his being employed at a food developer's, which was where he'd discovered the spy among the Tnuctipun. Darfoor, the spy, had had a generator for one of the new stasis fields, which had been developed in the course of his last spying job. All Tnuctipun innovations turned out to be part of a long-term plan to disrupt Thrintun commerce. Gnix had taken over Darfoor and his contacts, and they had been working on ways for Gnix to profit from the disruptions when a competing food company had attacked the development habitat.

By then Darfoor had installed the stasis field in the escape boat, and Gnix had Told him to forget to put on his Power shield.

The stasis had held while the galaxy rotated several times.

Amusingly, the creatures that had opened the field had been looking for a weapon to use to escape from slavery. They had built Gnix an amplifier, and he had taken over the rest of the creatures here and set his Tnuctipun to growing some females from his genetic material. There was some problem, not too clear—Tnuctipun minds *wandered* so—with getting the chemistry right in the host females, but there were plenty of them. His new chief slave had apparently been collecting females.

There were plenty of potential slave races, too, but the fighting slaves' records said some of them knew how to shield against the Power, so Gnix had sent some of the fighting slaves to gather antimatter from a source that had passed by a while back. (For some reason they hadn't done so before.) He was the only Thrint alive—stasis didn't count—and ruler of a small interstellar empire, soon to be a large interstellar empire.

Not bad for a foreman in a food workshop.

The only thing he really disliked was the slave telepaths. All the fighting slaves had a touch of it—his sire Gelku would have been terribly upset by that, as he'd been deeply religious—but some had so much that they'd developed mental shielding techniques to stop the noise. He'd finally ordered those removed from the palace. Not killed, since they were useful; but he didn't like running into them. It was too startling. The amplifier could get through a shield to detect them, of course, but that tended to paralyze anyone in range who didn't have one, which in this case meant most of the planet.

TOO MUCH OIL, he Told the slave burnishing his scales.

The Patriarch of Kzin wiped off the excess.

It was almost two years before Greenberg saw the protector again. Judy was expecting a daughter, according to the autodoc, and he was edgy: "Hey! Where've you been?"

"Working" was the reply. "What the hell did you think?"

"How should I know? There're discrepancies in the history you gave us."

"This is your idea of news? How are the rest getting along?"

That diverted him briefly. "They're afraid of you. They doubt the explanation of why they can't look outside the ship." *Cordelia* was in hyperdrive. "—And the history doesn't add up!"

"Okay, name some problems."

"How many wars were there with these 'kzinti'?"

"Depends who you ask. Flatlanders say six, because they got involved in all of them. Kzinti and Pleasanters say four because there have been that many peace treaties: Kzinti needed some kind of conceptual dividing line to get a handle on the idea of peace, and Pleasanters are almost all descended from lawyers. Old Wunderland vets say one, because there are still kzinti alive, so the war's still running." She spread her hands, momentarily resembling a cottonwood tree. "Take your pick. Next?"

"How many do *you* say?"

The look she gave him produced, in him, the exact feeling other people got when they first learned he was a telepath. After a moment she said, "Two. The first began with the invasion of Wunderland, and ended when I arranged for the subordination of the kzinti religion to secular authority. The second was an act of personal retaliation by one man, Harvey Mossbauer, whose family was killed at the end of the first, against the Patriarch; he killed the Patriarch's family in return. Since then the Patriarch of Kzin has understood that humans are, by kzinti terms, people, and has treated them as such in law. They can't be held as slaves or raised for meat, for example—though if a kzin from one of the cannibal cultures kills a human in a dispute, eating him is deemed fair. The cannibals are dying out, though. They get in too many fights. Next?"

"How come humans are related to primates that have been on Earth since long before the Pak supposedly brought us?"

"Obviously there must have been previous visits, with much smaller breeder populations. Lots more drift that way. The first was probably just a few million years after the Dinosaur Killer."

"Ah. Yucatán," he said wisely.

"Oh, were the ARMs still flogging 'nuclear winter' in your time? I thought that was just when they were getting set up."

"Excuse me?"

"Guess not, must have been residual. 'Nuclear winter' was the notion that throwing a lot of dust and soot into the atmosphere would cause an Ice Age in spite of halving the planet's albedo. It was one of those political hypotheses, meant to frighten people into accepting the need for restricting technology. The ARMs spread a lot of those in the early days. Anyway, the Yucatán crater has K-T iridium in it and is therefore older. Only an ocean strike will produce an Ice Age, and only if it's big enough to punch through the crust and boil a few cubic miles of ocean with magma. In this case it obviously was, as it also produced Iceland.

"As I was saying, the protectors in that migration saw a world with no big predators and settled in. Obviously they sent back word of what a nice place it was, and just as obviously the expedition that brought our ancestors destroyed the records before they left home, to keep from being followed."

"But Brennan and Truesdale never mention any earlier expeditions."

"Truesdale had other things to deal with. Brennan didn't *care*. He was a Belter, and Belters who lived long enough to establish their society were not the ones who let their minds wander or indulged casual curiosity. Next?"

"There's an implausible coincidence between the departure of human Protectors and first contact with the kzinti—"

"Coincidence my ossified ass!" she snapped, startling him badly. "The puppeteers first brought us to the kzinti's attention about *two months* after the Fleet left for the Core."

"That's the part I have trouble with. Puppeteers are herbivores. Peaceful."

"I should have cloned a bull."

"Huh?"

"In case it has escaped your attention, the class of herbivores includes cattle, horses, elephants, the Roman legionaries who conquered Gaul, and Pak Protectors. Herbivores casually obliterate anything that encroaches on their territory—or that looks like it might. Carnivores come in all types of personality, but dedicated herbivores are merciless killers. Anything else?"

"Um. I need to think some—yah, hey, what the hell did you mean by putting that big warning in the movie archive: 'DO NOT WATCH *FOR A BREATH I TARRY* AND *FIREBIRD* IN ONE SITTING!'?" He brimmed with outrage.

"It's a bad idea," she said ingenuously. "I take it you did?"

"*Everybody* did!" he bellowed. "And guess who got it all secondhand, as well?"

"Didn't like them?"

He shook all over, very abruptly, but forced himself back under control. "Don't you make fun, goddamn it," he said softly.

"I'm sorry," she said at once, and brushed fingertips on his shoulder; those, at least, weren't rocklike.

"There's only so much of anything we can stand. Even beauty."

"I know. That's why I did it."

He stared at her. "What?"

"Now everyone knows I don't give warnings without a good reason. Would you rather I'd set a trap that blew somebody's hand off?"

He glared, but she was right—no one would *ever* ignore one of her warnings after that shattering experience. Finally he nodded. Then he said, "We could only find the author for one—glad we looked, though, this guy Zelazny is incredible! Was *Firebird* published under some different title? The only other reference I could find was a piece of classical animation with the same music."

She nodded. "The one where the Firebird is the bad guy? This one was done in rebuttal, I believe. Later it was suppressed by the ARM because of its accurate depiction of the history of industrial development. I've never found the credits, but clearly somebody couldn't bring himself to destroy the last copy. The other one I made myself. I don't think anybody else ever trusted themselves to be able to convey Zelazny's imagery adequately. The old woman and the cube, for instance."

"'Go crush ore!'" he murmured, and his voice caught.

"It wasn't easy to get the timing on that pause right," she remarked. "Look, if there's nothing else right now I've got an errand. I'll be gone a couple of months your time." And she was off again.

Shleer had to spend six days out of sight while the Thrint wandered through the harem, nagging the Tnuctipun and their Jotoki assistants. Gnix had been an immensely powerful telepath even before he had the amplifier, but he was too stupid to follow his slaves' thoughts very far when they did something as simple as free-associating. The Tnuctipun had delayed the adaptation of the kzinretti as long as they could, simply to put off the day when they had another Thrint to cope with; still, Gnix's constant pestering—Pestering, rather—forced them to maintain *some* kind of progress, however slow.

About one surviving kzinrett in four was hairless and developing skin flakes—the biological modifications seemed to be trying to produce scales. The survivors weren't going toxic, so it appeared the Tnuctipun had stalled as long as they could.

Then, while Gnix was doing another nag-through, a kzinrett began screaming and thrashing. The thrashing continued after the screaming stopped; though her arms and legs gradually fell still, her torso kept jerking. Then a greenish larval thing tore a hole into the open air from inside her, shuddered, and died.

CLEAN THAT UP, Gnix commanded irritably. AND FIX THE PROBLEM. Then he left.

The Tnuctipun had not been surprised. That was what made Shleer risk detection and go searching for a camera that night. They hadn't been surprised.

Shleer's own birthing tunnel gave him a private place to work; his mother had been one of the first to die.

Peace shut down *Cordelia*'s accelerator as soon as she was in range.

Larry had living quarters set up outside the control area, so he could work on the door every day. Being able to draw on the expertise of dozens of colonists had actually gotten him through the first lock. He'd been working on the second long enough not only to grow a beard, but to start grooming it during the times when he couldn't think of what to try. He'd quit smoking and resumed, too, probably twice.

"I apologize," she said as soon as he saw her. "I should have set the field to shut down. Please come in, so I can show you how to run things in case I'm killed or trapped."

He said nothing as he entered.

"One of the things I was looking for was any residue of an ARM agent named Hamilton," she said, leading him to a workshop. "He was a telekinetic esper who lost an arm and an eye, and the shadow organs his brain produced in compensation let him feel inside things and see in the dark, and like that. I figured the proper training would allow a clone to develop an entire remote presence, very handy. Unfortunately the woman running the ARMs now really hates Protectors, and they wasted a lot of my time before I could meet her and frighten her into cooperation. There's a lot less margin now for what I need to do before we get to Kzin."

"So we'll just go out and have fun while you sit at home, alone, in the dark, and go blind," he said as they reached the shop.

She stared at him a little longer than necessary; it was no mean feat to surprise a Protector, and he was entitled to something for it. He kept his gratification off his face, but it had grown to be considerable by the time she said, "Sorry. I'll watch that." She opened the door and led him to where a crumpled perfect mirror lay. "I'll need to study your telepathy to develop some myself," she said as she got out the control for the accelerator field and switched it back on.

"Um," he said as the suit went from perfect reflection to merely shiny.

She looked at him, and saw that he was horribly embarrassed all of a sudden.

Something inside the suit moved.

She drew and aimed, realized what had to have happened, and was putting the gun away when he said, "It's a slave! Kzanol found a planet and brought one back with him."

"Yes. Let's get him out." She removed the helmet and opened up the suit, and a head the size of a breeder's fist poked warily out. Two eyes; those refractive nodes would serve as ears; a generally humanoid shape aside from thumb displacement; traces of something more like feathers than hair; and some pretty fine clothes and jewelry. Of course Kzanol had taken their leader.

"Oh my God, he was their High Judge," Greenberg said.

"Figures. And it never mattered to the Slaver, so you never realized it before. Talk to him while I rummage."

There was a baroquely embroidered cloth bundle, and as she got it out the trace of scent on it made her want to kill something. Hardwired response; the Pak were survivors of the Slaver era, and the Protectors had been created as a Tnuctipun weapon. (They hadn't evolved in two billion years because they ate mutated descendants; there wasn't really a tactful way to mention that to Greenberg.) She had to spend several seconds learning how to override it, then unwrapped the bundle to reveal a remarkably prosaic watch—with a casing of niobium chromide, so that it would survive events that would vaporize the wearer. Absurd: Anybody who could afford a watch like this didn't have to be on time. Two more bundles held figurines of extraordinary repulsiveness: Thrintun females. Next was the amplifier helmet.

She'd been listening and building up vocabulary, not without amusement. Greenberg had the unusual combination of perfect comprehension coupled with no ear at all. The alien was of a race called chukting, and of his names and titles the important one was Tinchamank. He was having a lot of trouble figuring out what Greenberg was saying. Admittedly there was a trick to the accent: the language was fourth-stage. (Much vocabulary is onomatopoetic. Tribal gatherers hear and repeat the sounds made by sticks and rocks. Hunters, herders, and farmers pick up animal sounds. Civilized people add metallic noises, and advanced peoples include sounds made by complex machinery. Names of things tend to change last as a language alters, so the chuktings must have been civilized for thousands of years.)

"There's a map in the sleeve," Greenberg said.

"Thanks." She got it out. The Milky Way had been a little sloppier in shape two billion years ago; of course the spiral arms bore no relationship to present arrangements. The sapphire pin would be Tinchamank's home system—well outside the main galactic lens. Might be worth looking at later. She spoke to him: "A long time has passed. Your home is gone. I will learn what you need to eat. Come."

Greenberg gasped suddenly, then recovered as he put up his shield. Tinchamank curled into what must be his fetal posture. Doubled wrist joints, looked useful. Peace picked him up and took him to the analytical doc. She limited the stunner effects to local anesthesia, since the hearing nodes looked very efficient and thus vulnerable, and waited while the microprobes sampled organs.

"Get any samples of that agent? Hamilton?" Greenberg said.

"Obviously not," she replied. "I'd have set up a culture tank at once. You should have figured that out without asking."

"Big talk from someone who can't walk and chew gum," he retorted, nettled.

A beak was no good for chewing gum. She gave him another stare. "You've been saving these up."

"I find you inspiring. How did you manage to scare the director of the ARM?"

"Threatened to build a giant robot and destroy Tokyo."

"Holy cow. Why Tokyo?"

"Traditional."

Simultaneously exasperated and amused, he said, "Goddamn it, I can never tell when you're kidding!"

"True," she said sadly. She looked at the doc readout and said, "Odd. His ribosomes are just like ours."

"Aren't everybody's? I mean, they're how DNA gets implemented, right?" He'd been a colonist back in the days when it took a city's annual income to send a ship to another star, and he'd studied everything that might be useful to qualify. And it wasn't like some Ivy League education—he'd had to understand the material.

She nodded, pleased with him. "Yes. But our Pak ancestors, and bandersnatchi, and the photosynthetic yeast everybody else is evolved from, all came from Tnuctipun design labs. The chukting were never anywhere near them, and they have the same ribosomes."

"The what?"

"The chukting. Tinchamank here."

"Oh. Kzanol called them 'racarliwun.'"

"Why?"

The question seemed to startle him. "Well, he named the planet after his grandfather Racarliw, who built the family stage-tree farm up into a major industrial enterprise."

"So this would be someone who used all his income to recapitalize the business, and didn't set anything aside for his descendants, which would be why Kzanol was out prospecting and ended up on Earth to cause the deaths of hundreds of human beings?"

"Um. Yeah."

"So the hell with him. As I said, the chukting have ribosomes just like ours, but are of completely unconnected origin. Which is weird."

"Panspermia?" Theorists had often speculated that life had only needed to evolve once per galaxy, then spread offplanet due to meteor impacts, and to other stars via light pressure.

"Their home system is far enough outside the then-explored Galaxy for any spores to die en route."

"Carried on something else?"

"The only things," she began, and blinked as everything finally fitted together. "Of course. Good thinking."

"Thanks," he said, not really understanding.

Tinchamank adjusted to circumstances better than Peace did. His had been the most adaptable mind of an advanced industrial society, chosen from among many thousands of trained experts to sit in judgment on any matter that arose, and he was able to serve in this capacity for the colonists as well. He actually settled some feuds that had been developing.

Peace, on the other hand, had no knack for direct mind contact at all. Seeing what breeders were thinking was something any Protector could do, but it wasn't telepathy; it was on the order of a breeder seeing a dog snarl and bare its fangs and guessing what would happen next. Monitoring and feedback devices were invaluable for telling her what, in her brain, was simply not happening.

They kept working at it for almost three years.

One day Larry stopped in the middle of another adjustment and said miserably, "I have to go in."

"You'd just die," she said.

He sighed. Then he said, "You're not that obtuse."

"I'm not that cold, either. I sure as hell wouldn't have given up sex if I'd had a choice."

He blinked. "I had an image of you as kind of a spinster."

She chuckled audibly. "I know. If I'd told you stories about my sex life your brain would have cooked in its own juices. Now, though—Larry, I want you to imagine being employed at the most enjoyable activity—sustainable activity, that is—you can think of."

"Hitting baseballs through the windows of ARM headquarters?" he said with a straight face.

"Damnation," she said earnestly.

"Sorry, I'll be serious."

"No, it's just I don't know when I'll get back there again, and I never once thought to do that." She enjoyed his astonishment for a moment, then added, "The top of that dome would be an ideal place to stand, too."

Hesitantly, he said, "Kidding?"

She waggled a hand. "Not entirely. Larry, imagine feeling like that *all the time.*"

"Look, I'm volunteering, right?"

"I wonder. This is what I originally planned, and I worked on you to push you in that direction, at least at first. I decided a few years back to learn telepathy myself instead."

"Well, you can't." He was as terrified as she'd ever seen anyone, not excepting kzinti who had supposed her to be the Wrath of God Incarnate; and he was going to go through with it. He had courage she'd never dreamed of as a breeder, and she loved him for it more than she'd loved any other human who'd ever lived.

"I know. Come on," she said, removing the contact helmet: "I'll buy you lunch."

Shleer had the disruption helmet finished in two days. He tried it out the only way he could, as befit a Hero: on himself. He put it on and hit the switch.

Everyone went away. The quiet was unbelievable.

He immediately switched it off and got moving out of the harem, in case the effect had been noticed.

It hadn't. In the Residence they had other things on their minds.

HOW CAN THEY MOVE THAT FAST? Gnix Screamed at the Patriarch, who staggered.

"Speed field," slurred Rrao-Chrun-Rrit. "Reduced inertia, almost five hundred and twelve times as fast as normal."

Aircraft had dropped into the atmosphere all over the planet, swarms of them, moving at something like two million miles an hour in all directions.

Suddenly they were in a ring, converging on the Patriarch's Palace.

DO SOMETHING!

The Patriarch opened the master panel of his *fooch* and tapped a switch.

The incoming craft slowed to about Mach 6 on the monitor system, and the palace defenses began shooting them down.

WELL DONE. . . . WHAT DID YOU DO?

"I accelerated us as well. The system was installed three hundred years ago, after we found signs that someone had gotten in undetected."

IF THEY WERE "UNDETECTED," HOW DID YOU FIND SIGNS?

"Things worked better, like food dispensers and data retrieval."

One of the craft hit the palace, not far from Rritt's Past.

A pilot hurtled out in a suit of powered armor, and began charging in through automatic defensive fire. Pieces of armor were jettisoned as lasers heated them intolerably—which was possibly their principal reason for existing. The pilot got a long way before the armor was down to a single flexible suit. That was black, coated with superconductor, and appeared to be venting coolant whenever lasers touched it.

The lasers made contact less often with each passing minute. The pilot was fast, almost invisibly so on the security screens. A funny-looking human.

Gnix detected recognition in two nearby minds. One was the Patriarch, whose perplexing and repetitive thought was *Peace*. The other was Darfoor.

Darfoor was terrified out of his mind, and he was thinking *assassin, assassin*! Gnix Told him, COME HERE. TELL ME WHAT YOU KNOW ABOUT THIS THING.

"I made them," whimpered the Tnuctip. "The tarkodun were too stupid to follow instructions, and we were told to make them smarter. We gave them a third stage of life. They have brains Thrintun can't control all at once. They're smarter than anything else, and they live forever, and we made them to kill you. They gave us the hyperjump and disintegrator and stasis field when we asked for ways to disrupt your lives. We're all going to die."

SHUT UP. STAY PUT AND ATTEND UNTIL I TELL YOU OTHERWISE. FIGHTING SLAVES, STOP THAT THING! —NOT YOU, CHIEF SLAVE.

On the screen, the assassin came into Rrit's Past at high speed, faster than a Hero's charge. Companions were still assembling in its path, and it produced a needlegun and shot them all. There was respectable return fire, but there was impact armor under the superconductor, and the assassin was either immune to stunners or shielded somehow. The needles got through all the armor the Companions had, but apparently didn't tumble—none of them began vomiting blood, anyway; they just fell asleep at once.

A Companion in powered armor was beyond the next archway. He fired a staggered laser array—and none of it hit. The assassin had turned sideways and bent backward and tilted its head, and all the beams passed it by. Then the assassin fired the needlegun into the wrist control of the armor, and the armor fell off. The Companion drew his *wtsai* and leapt even as the armor was hitting the ground, and the assassin dodged the blade and hit him with both hands, one on either side of the rib cage. The Companion fell, gasping. He wasn't dead or dying, but he wasn't going to be getting up until someone came with a medikit and pulled back his dislocated rib joints, where the assassin had caved them into his lungs.

The assassin got to where the stuffed alien stood on a pedestal and hesitated for an instant. That was enough for the lasers to slice up the needlegun. The assassin ran on.

A section of the monitoring system went dead, just as the assassin was getting to it.

HOW DID IT DO THAT? Gnix demanded.

"It couldn't have," the chief slave replied. "It could be damage from the crash."

FIND THAT THING!

"There are Heroes massing in its only path."

The statue looked like a six-legged Jotok. Given its imposing size, it was a religious image, probably based on a real individual; each Jotoki limb had its own brain lobe, so a six-legged Jotok would have been far smarter than usual, and probably also a holy cripple. Certainly a legend.

From above came a voice, speaking Flatlander: "Hey. Protector. Up here."

There was a half-grown kzintosh hanging by one foot. "I know a shortcut," he said.

An army could be heard ahead—could be *smelled* ahead.

After the youngster had been hauled into the duct and the hatch closed, he said, "There's one Thrint and four Tnuctipun.

Rrao-Chrun-Rrit is obeying as slowly as feasible. And," he said, "and he *is* my father, so—"

"Alive if any chance exists," the Protector said, and sniffed. "Harem? Right. Stay someplace safe."

"Felix said Protectors liked jokes."

"Felix?"

"Felix Buckminster. Former technology officer on the *Fury*. I'm a Patriarch's Son."

"Okay, but be inconspicuous."

The kzintosh wrapped a piece of metal mesh around his head and touched a switch. "The Thrint won't notice me. Felix taught me a lot."

"Good for him." The Protector wriggled down the duct, came out the access hatch, and pretty well ran along the ceiling loops to the wall handholds. It went down the wall and was working out the door mechanism before Shleer was all the way out of the hatch, and was gone well before he reached the ground.

It hadn't been patronizing him, though: It had scratched the combination into the wall before it left. Shleer followed as quickly as he could.

I CAN'T FIND IT! Gnix Shrieked, and slaves howled and fell.

"It may have a shield," Darfoor said.

MY AMPLIFIER CAN GET THROUGH A SHIELD, FOOL! UNLESS YOU MEAN THE KIND YOU WERE MAKING.

Despair added flavor to the spy's thoughts. "I do."

CAN YOU DO SOMETHING ABOUT THAT? Darfoor seemed much too pleased at this question, so Gnix learned why and said, CAN YOU DO IT WITHOUT SHUTTING DOWN THE AMPLIFIER?

"No," Darfoor said miserably.

THEN WAIT A MOMENT. Gnix paused to exclude his immediate group of slaves, then Told the rest of the palace:

GO TO SLEEP.

Then he Told Darfoor, *NOW* SHUT IT DOWN.

Shleer staggered a bit as his jammer quit, but it wasn't bad—almost everyone in range had gone to sleep.

He got to the Place of Contemplation, which the Thrint had had redone as a TV room, just as Rrao-Chrun-Rrit was stunned asleep by the Protector.

The Thrint had three of the Tnuctipun in front of him in a pyramid, and said something that the Tnuctipun understood to mean, "Drop your weapons." There was a strong Push behind it. It didn't work, and the Thrint raised a variable knife—the Patriarch's, Shleer noted, offended—and pushed the switch.

The glowing red ball fell off the end and rolled away. The Thrint stared after it. Then he looked up.

The Protector shot his eye out with a plain old slug pistol. "Apparently a knife doesn't always work," it said as Gnix fell backward.

Then it blew the three Tnuctipun's brains out too.

It turned to the fourth, Darfoor, who screeched desperately, "Fa la be me en lu ki da so mu nu e ti fa di om sa ti po ka et ri fu . . ." and more of that general nature.

The Protector said, "Glossolalia? . . . Machine code? . . . Hard . . . wire . . . ta . . . lo . . ."

Shleer pulled out one of the Peer's anemones, leapt into the room, and thrust its disk against the Tnuctip's side. As designed, the disk stayed put against the target's skin, while the ultrafine hullmetal wires it bound together passed through it, resuming their original shapes: curves, varying from slight to semicircular. In combination they made up a rather fluffy blossom: an anemone.

They had to pass through the Tnuctip to do it. It fell into two pieces and a good deal of goo.

The Protector shook its immense head in relief and said, "Kid, I owe you a big one."

"You don't either," said Shleer.

"I do. The Tnuctipun created my ancestors, and they clearly hardwired our brains to respond to a programming language this one knew. I was about to become his adoring slave. I owe you big."

"You gave me my father back."

"I wanted him healthy anyway. Give me a minute here." It went to the control panel and looked it over. "Wow, good traps you guys make. Got it." It shut down the acceleration field. Then it opened a belt pouch and got out a disk about the size of a decent snack, pulled a switch, and set it down to inflate into a globe.

"How did you do that with the variable knife?" Shleer said.

"One time-alteration field won't work inside another. The wire was too thin to support the weight of the ball when it wasn't in stasis. Sorry, I'm being rude. I'm Judy Greenberg."

"Who?" said Shleer, utterly surprised.

When he'd come out of it, Larry had abruptly sat up in his rinse tank and said, "Why the hell do kzinti dislike eye contact?"

They were felines, after all. "Good question," said Peace. "That's Judy there. She insisted. She'll be out tomorrow."

"What about the girls?" They had four daughters, Gail, Leslie, Joy, and Carolyn. Carolyn was four. (All had blond hair the young Peace Corben would have given up three fingers for.)

"Old Granny Corben explained everything, and they're all proud of you two." The colonists' children, at least, trusted her, not least because kids usually know a pushover when they see one. (It is a protector's duty to spoil children absolutely rotten.)

Larry had then said, "Oh god damn. Telepath in orbit to be sure the situation is resolved." So Judy had to be the one going in with the amplifier.

"At least she's a precog." So she'd duck before being shot at.

"Thanks." That had helped. Larry picked up a pack of cigarettes, left thoughtfully nearby, and lit one. "*Gaahhh!*" he bellowed, and threw it into the rinse tank he'd just left. "What did you *put* in that?"

"Tobacco," Peace said.

He looked her over. "They've always smelled like that to you?"

"Yes, but you seemed to enjoy them."

He spent almost a full second thinking this over. Then he said, "Thanks."

When the globe had inflated, it split open, and another Protector came out. Shleer goggled for a moment, then realized the globe had been a portable transfer booth.

The new Protector looked at the red ball, then at Judy Greenberg, and said, "Aristocrat." Judy snorted.

"What?" said Shleer.

"Sorry, ancient Earth joke," said the new one. "At a gunfight, how do you recognize an aristocrat—that is, a noble who inherited his rank? He's the one with the sword."

Shleer began laughing and found it hard to stop. He'd been

through a lot lately. The new arrival got out a brush and did Shleer's back a little, which calmed him down. "Thanks," he said.

"You would have done this yourself if we hadn't shown up, wouldn't you?"

"Not as fast."

"Details. I'm Peace Corben."

"Felix Buckminster told me about you."

"*Felix*? Hm! He did love gadgets. What's your Name?"

Shleer got self-conscious. "It's a milkname. I'm only four. Shleer." He took a deep breath, and said, "Can you help the harem?"

It was interesting to see that Protectors had claws that came out when they were upset too. Peace looked at Judy and said, "Doc."

"Larry's on it," said Judy, who had begun inflating a bigger receiver.

Peace was shaking her head. "The thing that gets me," she said, "is *why the hell someone who can do this didn't just tailor a disease to exterminate the Thrintun?*"

"Against their religion," Shleer said.

Peace looked at him. "You're a telepath."

"Uh—"

"You have to have gotten that from a Tnuctip, because no kzin who ever lived could *possibly* have come up with a reason that stupid."

They were making eye contact. Shleer gave it a try.

Peace shook her head. "I realize you're distressed," she said, "but if you ever give me another headache this bad, the slap you get is gonna give you an ear like a grapefruit. You're looking at it from the wrong end. This doesn't discredit you; it makes telepaths respectable. Are you aware that you've single-handedly saved civilization? *Everybody's* civilization? I intend to make damn sure everyone else is."

Judy was loading kzinretti into the autodoc that had arrived, and Peace joined in.

Notwithstanding their removal of the Thrintun—and Tnuctipun—embryos, and restoration of the kzinretti to health, the Patriarch had clearly been glad to see the Protectors go. While the Greenbergs had been tailoring plagues for kzinti ships to spread, to kill off any Thrint or Tnuctip that got loose in Known Space thereafter, Peace had spent some time interviewing survivors about the chain of events, and it had evidently upset her. Nobody really welcomes a cranky Protector.

She piloted *Cordelia* out to the local Oort cloud, then got on the hyperwave and said, "We need to talk."

Such was the seriousness in which she was held that the Outsider came via hyperdrive, which they normally didn't use. "It is good to see you were successful."

"Yeah, you don't have to blow up their sun or whatever. You're in contact with the puppeteer migration."

"That information is not available for sale."

"It wasn't a question. I have a message for you to relay to them, to be paid for out of my credit balance."

"Proceed."

"Keep going."

There was a pause. "Is that all?"

"If they don't seem to respond appropriately, add this:

"The kzinti found a stasis box you had neither opened nor destroyed, in the debris you abandoned in your system when you left Known Space. It held a Slaver and several Tnuctipun genetic engineers. They were found by the kzinti. The Slaver had the Tnuctipun growing Slaver females by the time they were stopped, and had the kzinti fleet preparing antimatter weapons. All you had to do was drop the thing into a quantum black hole. Your interference is offensive, but your irresponsibility is toxic. In the event that you inflict either upon humans, or their associates, ever again, you will be rendered extinct. Message ends."

"Peace Corben, you should be aware that we have contractual agreements with the puppeteers for their well-being. Whatever you have planned, we would have to stop it."

"*Planned*? What am I, Ming the Merciless?" she exclaimed. "I'm not going to warn someone about something I haven't done yet! I set up my arrangements over three hundred years ago."

"What arrangements?"

"It's the bald head, isn't it? *I don't know*. I expected to have this conversation someday, and I knew you could do a brain readout, so I erased it from my memory. If you're bound by an obligation to look out for their safety, the best help you can give is to have them get out of our lives and stay out.

"And as regards debts and contracts, diffidently I point out that I have just taken action to clean up the leftover results of your big mistake. Nobody will hear about that but Protectors, by the way."

"Thank you." And the Outsider was gone.

"Damn, I didn't mean to humiliate them," she said.

"Hm?" said Larry.

She glanced at him. "They— What *are* you doing?"

He took the tennis ball he'd been chewing out of his beak. "I just ate. Flossing."

The true tragedy of the Pak had been their utter lack of humor. Conversely, every human Protector was an Olympic-class smartass.

"Hm!" she said, and shook her head. "We got the name 'starseed' from the Outsiders, and nobody ever questioned it in spite of the fact that the damn things never sprout. The Outsiders made them. Starseeds go around sowing planets with microorganisms that are meant to evolve into customers. Outsiders keep track of what worlds are seeded and monitor development to make sure nothing really horrible happens. Three billion years ago they were lax in this, and two billion years ago a species they'd missed exterminated all organic intelligence in the Galaxy. They charge high for questions about starseeds because they're ashamed. So what's the verdict?"

"The kids all wanted to name whatever planet we settle everybody on *Peace*. I persuaded them it was against your religion."

"Thank you."

"Everybody else wants to call it *For a Breath I Tarry*. Including Judy and me."

Pleased, she said, "What about Tinchamank?"

"We thought we'd clone him some mates and find them their own planet. After that it's up to them. Can we go look at Altair One?"

"The Altairians didn't have time travel," she said.

He didn't read her mind. (He'd tried it once after the change. She was still a lot smarter than he was, so it had been much like peeking through a keyhole and seeing a really *big* eye looking back.) After a second he said, "You already looked." At her self-conscious nod he said, "So how did they vanish?"

"Kind of an immaterial stasis field is the best I can describe it.

The math's on record if you care. They'll reappear in a couple of thousand years, probably shooting. I left the kzinti a note."

He nodded. "I'm still a little sore about our kids smelling wrong. Judy's not."

"I did the same with my own."

"I didn't say I didn't understand it. We won't restart the Pak wars, fine. They just seem like strangers."

She nodded. "Yah."

Rrao-Chrun-Rrit signed the edict. Anyone using slaves would henceforth have no trade or tax advantages over anyone using paid free employees, and would face a choice of slowly going broke or changing over to workers who had a motive to do their work well. He had recently acquired some strong views on the subject of slavery.

He turned to his son, who had saved everything that mattered to anyone. Before the assembled clan of Rrit he declared, "Felix Buckminster taught you as well as I had hoped. Yes, I assigned him to you," he said, amused at Shleer's astonishment. "I'd have arranged for you to be brought out of the harem if he hadn't been sterile! You really thought I wouldn't know that a kzinrett came from a lineage of telepaths? My own mother did! But it's recessive. My son, you are not merely a telepath, you are a *full* telepath, with the ability humans call Plateau eyes. You can vanish, yes—but you can also charm disputants out of fighting.

"And you make plans.

"Good plans.

"You followed an enemy to gain information, you acted on what you learned to gain more, you built a mechanism to enable you to fight an unbeatable enemy, and when that enemy was dead you acted instantly and correctly to destroy another that proved even worse.

"My son of all sons:

"Choose your Name."

"Harvey," said the next Patriarch of Kzin.

INDEPENDENT

◆ ◆ ◆

Paul Chafe

I woke up disoriented in milky grey light. I got my eyes open and saw digits floating in front of my face, 1201. I was in a cube, a sleep cube, on a shelf of a bed barely big enough for the thin, firm mattress pressed gently against my back. The cube itself held the bed, a small desk/table and chair, room to stand up and get dressed, and no more. I pushed the stiff and cheap spinfiber blanket down around my waist. I was awake because the lights were on, the lights were on because I must have set them to come on at twelve. The digits blinked to 1202 and I tried to remember how I had gotten here, but there was just a big blank where last night should have been. Why wasn't I on *Elektra*?

"News," I said. The numerals vanished, replaced by a program list. Ceres local was one of the news options. That squared with the barely perceptible gravity that held me against the mattress. I was on Ceres. So far so good. I pointed that channel up and was rewarded with a holo of some net flak on the business beat talking about the current crisis. The rockjacks were still striking against the Consortium, and the Belt economy was spiraling downhill fast. I didn't care about that, what drew my eye was the market ticker running at the bottom. It featured the time and date, twelve oh two, April fifteenth.

April. It was suppose to be March. What was going on? I stumbled to my feet and through the door. I found myself in a nondescript cube dorm in my underwear. Most of the other cubes were marked vacant. Everyone else had already got up and left, and it was too early for the incoming crowd. I felt bleary; however long I had slept it hadn't been enough. I went back in

229

and hauled the blanket off the mattress and dumped it into the recycler by the door of the cube. The drawers beneath the narrow bed opened to my thumb and I hauled out my clothes. I went through the pockets for a clue as to what I had done last night, but there was nothing. I thumbed my beltcomp alive and checked it. It agreed the date was April 15th, but the entries since March 20th were blank. It wasn't just last night missing, it was better than three weeks. What was going on?

Nothing came to mind, the anonymous, identical cube doors looked back at me blankly. It was accomplishing nothing, and I could ponder the question in the shower. I resealed the drawers and padded down the hall, grabbing a towel on my way past the dispenser. My body knew where the shower was, so I'd been here before. I had a vague memory of checking in the previous night, but it was strangely hazy. I've gone on a few benders in my life, maybe a few more than normal recently, with little else to do but down cheap whiskey and skim for contracts at a booth in the Constellation. *But three weeks?*

The shower room wasn't overly clean, but the water was steaming hot and I let it stream over me, cascading off my body in lazy parabolas to slide down the walls to the pump-assisted drain. The dispenser spilled depilatory in my hand and I noticed words scrawled on my palm—OPAL STONE in big red block letters. I looked at them for long moment through the translucent depilatory gel. The writing looked like mine, and I have a habit of jotting things down on my palm when I want to remember them. This time the trick wasn't helpful. I couldn't imagine what they referred to, I'm not into jewelry, and opals come from Mars, not something I'd likely be carrying, even as a smuggled cargo. What did that have to do with me? I smeared the gel over my face. The hairs that came away were four or five days' growth. What on earth had I been doing?

I came out of the shower and dried off, feeling better if not less confused. The letters were washed off my palm, but the words were burned into my brain. OPAL STONE. I'd go back to *Elektra* and ask her what was going on. *Elektra* is my ship, a singleship officially, although that's more due to me bribing the registrar than any virtue of her design; her class is built for a crew of three. I'd put in a lot of modifications to make her manageable on my own. We've come to know each other well, and she looks after me. I remembered docking at Ceres, some three months ago now. I hadn't had a contract in that long. Docking fees were eating my savings alive, while the rockjacks and the Consortium fought their dirty little war over the concession split. I'm an independent, like all singleship pilots, and sometimes that has its downsides. I went back to my tube to dress, then went out the front desk and thumbed out, nodding to the attendant. There was a Goldskin cop by the door, and he came up to me.

"Dylan Thurmond?" He had his official voice on.

I nodded, not wanting to admit I was me, but if I denied it his next step would be to demand my thumbprint. No point in making him work for it. *What had I done?* My record isn't exactly spotless. I'm a singleship pilot, and it's a tribute to my skill that I have far fewer than the average number of smuggling convictions. Unfortunately that isn't the same as zero.

"I'd like you to come with me." His voice brooked no argument.

"What's this about?"

"They'll tell you at headquarters." He led me down to the tube station and invited me to share a tube car with him. He sat in stoic silence while I sweated out the twenty minute tube ride, trying to rack my brain for details, any details, but what I remembered wasn't going to help my case any. At headquarters he spoke briefly to the desk cop, and I heard a word that made my blood run cold. Murder. I told myself I had to be a witness, killing isn't in my nature, but my persistent amnesia wasn't reassuring. He took me into a small, unadorned room and turned me over to a tough-looking officer, Lieutenant Neels. Neels' voice was calm, inviting cooperation, but his manner was rock hard beneath the soft exterior. He didn't need to emphasize what would happen if I chose to be difficult.

"I'm not trying to be evasive, Lieutenant," I told him. "I woke up this morning with no idea where I was."

He nodded. "Just think back, and go over what you do remember."

Police stations look the same on any world. I looked up at the grey ceiling and worn sprayfoam walls and as I cast my mind back I suddenly understood where my memory had gone. It all started in the Constellation, I remembered that much. I told him what I knew.

It was an average night, March 20th, though if you'd asked me on the day I would have had to guess at the date. On the vid wall Reston Jameson was being interviewed about the violence between the Consortium and the rockjacks, and the economic disaster the strike was for the whole Belt. The sound was down, but I knew what he was talking about because it was all anyone was talking about. To an underemployed singleship pilot the resulting slump had a very personal impact. Maybe I should have sold out and gone to fly for Canexco or Nakamura Lines, but I'm an independent and flying for someone else would be one step above life in a cage for me. Jameson ran the Consortium, though you'd find other names over his on the directorship list, everyone knew the difference between the figureheads and the controlling mind. He had been quoted as saying he'd break the rockjacks and the Belt with them if that's what it took to keep the Consortium in control of metal mining, and of course he'd denied ever saying it. I was interested in hearing what he *was* saying, and was about to ask Joe to private me the audio when they came in.

I noticed the kzin first, two meters of orange fur and fangs. He walked in like he owned the bar, and hardened rockjacks made way for him. Beyond getting the space he wanted his presence didn't cause too much of a stir. There aren't that many kzinti on Ceres, but if you're going to see one, you're going to see him in the Constellation. The woman with him was striking, tall and slender as only a Belter can be. More than that she was beautiful, heartbreakingly beautiful, and I couldn't take my eyes off her, like a predator locked on a prey animal.

Prey animal. I'd been spending too much time with the kzinti out in Alpha Centauri's Serpent Swarm. There's a lot more of them there, and a lot of them run with the smugglers. She was my own species, homo sapiens sapiens, and we don't go in for cannibalism—at least not much, in recent history. I kept watching her with hunger of a different sort, my responses entirely in line with those of a human male presented with a fertile female. Her dress was stunning, concealing everything but designed to show off her figure, so I kept right on not taking my eyes off her until her companion got in my way. He was a lot less beautiful and he carried himself in a way that said *dangerous,* even more than simply being a quarter-ton carnivore said *dangerous.* His eyes scanned the crowd until they intercepted mine, and then he started in my direction. I felt a rush of adrenaline, though I knew he wasn't about to call me out for looking at his woman. He was looking for me before he knew I was looking at her, and now he'd found me. He had some business with me, and I might as well wait and find out what it was. He took the bar stool next to mine, overwhelming it with his bulk.

"You are Dylan Thurmond?" he asked.

Like when the Goldskin collared me, there's always that split-second decision to be made at a moment like this. Was it a good thing to be me right now, or a bad thing, and if it was a bad thing, would denying it make my situation better or worse? He couldn't thumb me like a Goldskin, but he might be a bounty hunter. Singleship pilots are by nature cautious, because the bold ones don't live long, and the good ones carry a lot of skills with them, just in case. Situational awareness is the same skill in a bar as it is on board ship, it's only the situation that's different.

But he clearly knew who I was so I gave up on denying it. Whether that would turn out to be bad or good remained to be seen.

I nodded. "I am."

He offered his hand and I shook it. So far so good.

"You're the pilot of the singleship *Elektra*?"

"Yes."

The woman slipped past me and sat on the other side of me; she wore a stylish slingback and she slipped it off and put it on the bar. The Constellation was a good place for her. The lighting is kept low to so you can see through the dome to the stars spinning overhead. Ceres goes around once every nine hours, and the Constellation is right on its equator, which means you can see every star in the sky if you stay there long enough. The view is breathtaking. You can see the ships coming in to the main hangar ship locks, because the Constellation is under the main approach funnel, and if you look carefully just off the zenith you can see Watchbird Alpha in its Ceres-synchronous orbit, a single bright star that stays fixed while the rest of the starfield spins, relaying signals, listening for distress calls, watching the barren surface with its unblinking high-resolution eye. Joe Retroni runs the Constellation and he'd gambled a lot of money getting the

dome put in. His bet was that tunnel-happy rockjacks would
pay high for the view. He was wrong about that, rockjacks won't
pay high for anything, but given that he charged what everyone
else charged they definitely preferred to drink at his place. That
was enough to pay for the dome. The decor was a little lacking
otherwise, laser-cut stone, glossy and cheap. No one cared about
that. It only made the woman more eye-catching, like a diamond
ring glinting in a dirty back alley.

"And you are?" I invited the kzin.

"You may call me Bodyguard, Dylan Thurmond. May I buy
you a drink?"

Bodyguard. I looked at the woman, and she certainly had a lot
of body to guard. Her manner was monofilm smooth, not giving
the players an opening to game her up on. "Anyone can buy me a
drink," I said, and beckoned Joe over. "Whiskey, straight up." He
nodded and squirted me a bulb. His house brand is Glencannon,
which tastes exactly like fine Glenlivet would taste if instead of
being made of pure barley and Highland spring water, carefully
fermented and aged thirty years in charred oak casks according
to a time-honored recipe, it was made yesterday out of raw ethyl
alcohol and the thousand-times-recycled blood, sweat, and tears
of Ceres' close-crowded millions, mixed with a healthy dose of
bioengineered flavoring agents.

I say blood, sweat, and tears as a poetic euphemism. Most of
the fluids that get processed through the asteroid's ecocycle are,
well, you know . . . They say the water is safe to drink. I say add-
ing alcohol kills the aftertaste. I'm used to recycling systems, and
Ceres has the worst I've ever experienced. Glencannon is pretty
rough going down, but then the original distillers of the Scot-
tish Highlands were more interested in producing cheap alcohol
and avoiding English taxation than maturing a fine whiskey, so
I claim the experience is still authentic.

I drained my bulb and turned to Bodyguard. "So what can I
do for you, other than drink on your tab?"

"I may have a contract for you."

"A contract?" That got my interest, though I had suspected that
was what he was after, once it became clear he didn't intend to
arrest me or kill me. "I'll listen to that."

"It's simple enough. I have a package that needs delivering."

I nodded and took his meaning. I'd sworn off smuggling, but at the moment I was desperate enough to take any cargo anywhere. "Where is it going?"

"You find out after you take the contract, when and if you take the contract."

I raised my eyebrows. There was more going on here than met the eye, but one of the prerequisites for getting a job like this is not asking too many questions. I asked the important one. "What's the pay?"

"Half a million stars."

I raised my eyebrows. "For a destination in Known Space?"

He nodded. "Jinx."

"That seems high."

"The cargo is secret. That pays for you, your ship, and a hole in your memory when you come back." He held up a paw and made a motion like he was triggering a sprayjector.

My eyebrows went higher. There were a bunch of drugs that would prevent short-term memory from getting stored to long-term memory. The new ones don't cause brain damage, or so they claim. "Why me?"

"Because you need the money and you have a ship of the required performance."

Bodyguard had been doing his homework. I squeezed the last drops of Glencannon down my throat, then spun the bulb into the disposal behind the bar. "Okay, I'll do it." It didn't sound like a healthy job to take on, but anything beat hanging around the Constellation watching my bank account swirl down the drain. Every singleship pilot smuggles when he thinks he can get away with it. *Elektra* and I hadn't had a contract in months, and the bank was going to call the mortgage on her. When the Consortium went to war with the rockjacks the demand for pilots went through the floor. No prospecting, no shipping, nobody could afford to go anywhere. I wasn't the only one in trouble. Even Nakamura Lines was running in the red, though they denied it officially.

He nodded. "We will talk in privacy." He gestured to Joe, who in turn motioned to another bartender. The bartender came around counter and led us into the back. Joe has some private tables there with privacy fields. They're available to anyone who asks, but it seemed my new friend had his space prearranged. The woman came with us, and the busy background noise of the bar suddenly vanished as we came under the sound damper. We sat down to business. She unsealed her slingback and reached inside. Suddenly even the sounds at our table became muted, the way everything sounds faraway when your ears can't equalize to a pressure change. She had a portable damper in the bag and she'd switched that on too. I took it in stride. If they were willing to drop half a million stars to convince me to take a brain blank then doubling up on the privacy field only made sense.

Bodyguard nodded to her and she pulled out a sprayjector. She held it up. Her eyes asked the question. *Ready?*

My eyes widened involuntarily. Those drugs are restricted, not easy to come by, and I somehow hadn't expected them quite this soon in the game. It was the moment of truth. "I'd like to see the money first." They could have had anything in that sprayjector, the whole thing could be a setup. Making them flash the cash wasn't a guarantee of safety, but at least it would ensure I wouldn't fall for some small-time scam.

Wordlessly the woman pulled a credit chip out of her pocket, thumbed it and handed it over. *Why is she the one carrying everything?* So she could run while he fought, if it came to that. This pair knew what they were doing. I verified the numbers on the front of the chip, thumbed it myself, and then slid it into my beltcomp. I tapped the keys like I was dumping the funds to my account, but I miskeyed the entry on purpose. When I put the comp down I slid the chip out with my thumb and palmed it. Another quick sleight of hand and it was in the little hidden pocket cut into the back side of my belt. That would make it a little harder for them to get their money back, just in case it was a scam after all. Singleship pilots need a lot of odd skills to survive. I can key a com laser in Morse code when the modulation fails, I can rig a fuel coolant system to scrub CO_2 out of the air, and I can spot a dirty setup nine times out of ten on body language alone.

I met the girl's eyes, read them and saw nothing dangerous. "Okay," I said, and held out my arm with my sleeve pulled back, hoping that this wasn't the tenth time. She pressed the sprayjector against my skin and triggered it. I felt the quick burn as the drugs went in, and the deal was done. I didn't feel any different, but the macromolecular labels from the sprayjector were now busy hooking up to binding sites in my synapses. The anticatalyst mixed with them would keep them from metabolizing for as long as it held out. My synapses would adapt to form memories normally during that time, but once the anticatalyst ran out the labels would attack the adaptations and undo any changes that had occurred since they were bound in the first place. A big chunk of experience would simply cease to exist for me.

You'd have to be desperate to take a deal like that. I was desperate.

I took my eyes off the patterned tile ceiling to look at Lieutenant Neels, brought back to the here-and-now. "And that's all I remember. I guess it worked."

He just looked at me for a long, painful time, his expression hard and unreadable. I'd sold three weeks for half a million stars and now I was a witness with no memory in a murder investigation. I told all that to the cop. He dropped a holoprint in front of me.

"Is that the woman?"

I nodded. It would take more than a brain blank to make me forget her. "That's her." I had a bad feeling about the way he asked the question, but I didn't know enough to start lying.

His lips compressed to a thin line. "Did you kill her?"

I looked at him in shock. I wasn't a witness, I was a suspect. *The* suspect, said a little voice at the back of my brain. I'd known the deal had something deep behind it, but Bodyguard had told me the job was a package delivery, straight up and simple. Kzinti don't lie, it's beneath their honor, and I wouldn't have taken anything dirtier anyway. A brain blank doesn't change the way you act, and I'm not a killer. I shook my head. "I didn't even know she was dead."

"You wouldn't under the circumstances, would you?" His eyes bored in to mine. "There's about a gallon of her blood in your airlock." He held my gaze for a long, uncomfortable time. "Anything you'd like to add to your statement?"

"Who is she?"

"Opal Stone."

Opal Stone. I felt a sudden urge to look at my palm, to the place the red inked words had been. Instead I just looked at him, not knowing what to say. I didn't remember anything. . . . *Opal Stone.*

He kept his eyes locked on mine for a long, long time, while I sat there feeling like a prey animal myself. Finally he turned away. "We don't have a body, yet. The UNSN has a ship scanning your

last recorded course, and we're talking to Jinx." He looked back at
me and his voice hardened. "If you spaced her, we'll find her."

"I don't . . ."

"Remember," he finished for me. "I know. You can go. Your
ship is under seal. Don't leave the asteroid."

I left with my head spinning and cursing myself for taking
the deal in the first place. I thought I was desperate before, but
now . . . I thought back again, trying to glean some missed detail
from my mind, but the brain blank was complete. My first memory
after the meeting was of staring up at the time display. She'd
died—nobody loses a gallon of blood and lives. It was supposed
to be a simple delivery trip. What had gone wrong? I pulled out
my beltcomp and tabbed my last transactions, another attempt to
fill in the blanks. There was a half-million-star deposit a week ago,
and then today there was the rental bill for the cube dorm on
horizontal sixteen—I hadn't thought to check the location when
I'd left with the cop. Now I knew the timeframe, but what was I
doing staying in a place like that with half a million stars to my
name? The answer came too easily. *Hiding.* That didn't help me
believe in my own innocence. I took a drop shaft to level sixteen
and found the place again. It was residential space awkwardly
converted to daily rental cubes, the kind of place that takes cash
and doesn't ask names. I had to ask the proprietor which cube
was mine. He sent me to number twenty-three. The lock opened
when I thumbed it, and I went inside.

Something slammed into me from behind, and suddenly my
face was jammed into a corner. Something soft and strong had
me by the neck, and three sharp needles pressed delicately against
my jugular vein. A kzin. I made a mental note to complain to
the management about their security.

"Where is my client, Dylan Thurmond?" he snarled.

"What client?" My life was getting progressively more confusing.

He spun me around to face him, and I found myself staring
into bared fangs. "Opal Stone." The kzin was Bodyguard. "She
is missing from your ship. I will have an answer." The needles
pressed harder.

I shook my head as well as I could. "You were there when she
brain-blanked me. I don't have any answers."

"Then I will have your life." His eyes got big and his ears
swiveled up.

"I didn't kill her. I know that much." I didn't know that much, but I said it. I hoped it was true.

"I watched her board your ship. Now her blood is all over your airlock." His grip tightened again and I began to have trouble breathing.

"It wasn't me," I gasped.

"Prove it."

"It's too obvious, I've been set up." His eyes bored in to mine, his fangs inches from my face. "With a brain blank I can't even defend myself." The kzin's grip didn't slacken. "Whoever framed me did it." I was grasping at straws, making it up on the fly. "If you kill me you lose your only link to them."

He let go and I slumped to the floor, rubbing my neck. "Thanks for your restraint."

Bodyguard snarled. "My honor has been insulted with the death of my client. That has earned quick death for those responsible." His eyes were still locked on me. "Except if I find that it is you after all. Deception added to insult will make your death slow and painful."

I nodded slowly, and fervently hoped I wasn't deceiving him. Kzinti earn high as bodyguards because they make the consequences of even a successful attack too severe for the most determined assassin. Any smuggler who gets to Centauri System knows better than to cross a kzin. Their honor code demands vengeance regardless of cost, and they're all too enthusiastic about following it.

I went over to the bed and sat down. The tiny space was barely big enough for me. With me and a hostile kzin it was decidedly claustrophobic. "What happened after the Constellation?"

"Hrrr. Opal boarded the ship with you."

"What was in the package?"

"She was the package."

I tried to control my surprise. "Did you see her get on?"

"Yes. I watched until the ship left. Her safety was my responsibility."

"Tell me what you know, about Opal, about anything that might be important."

He turned over a paw and studied his extended talons. "Dr. Stone is senior vice president for finance at the Consortium."

"Dr. Stone?" My eyebrows went up. I had assumed she had a bodyguard because she was a holo actress. Now I knew better, and the news wasn't good. I was in way over my head. It occurred to me that she hadn't said a word to me in the entire encounter in the Constellation. Had she said anything on board *Elektra?*

"Where was she going?"

"Jinx."

"And when she got to Jinx?"

"I do not know that."

"Do you usually go with her on trips?"

"Sometimes. At other times not. I am not privy to the details of her business arrangements."

Another advantage of kzinti bodyguards is their lack of insight into the subtleties of human interaction. *Opal Stone, what were you doing that you needed some desperate singleship pilot to take a brain blank?* I might have refused to take her if I knew who she was. Relations between the Consortium and us independents are hardly smooth. *And why didn't she take a Consortium ship?*

I needed the money badly, but if I'd thought a little more carefully I never would have taken the job. A brain blank is just too serious. I'd counted on myself to be smart enough to not get into exactly this kind of trouble. Obviously I'd been wrong. Whoever framed me had done a good job.

Whoever had framed me. When I put it that way there was only one answer. Opal Stone worked for the Consortium, at war with the rockjacks and controlled by Reston Jameson. The room had a vidwall and on a hunch I pointed up Reston's last interview. It was dated yesterday, and his image filled the screen.

". . . very upset about this. This man already has a record for smuggling. I have being saying all along that the cost of allowing these fly-by-night singleship operators . . ."

I muted the audio and pointed texttrans along the bottom of the image so I didn't have to listen to his voice. He mentioned me by name and the thrust of his argument was the same as it always been. The major lines could handle cargo and passengers, the major exploration companies could handle prospecting and mining, and the murder of Opal wouldn't have happened if only . . .

I switched it off in disgust, unable even to read the text. He was going to use me as an excuse to shut down the singleships. I couldn't believe he was holding my smuggling record as a strike against me. Every pilot smuggled, it was practically expected.

"I smell your tension, Dylan Thurmond." Bodyguard wrinkled his nose in way that suggested my tension didn't smell very good.

Would Reston Jameson kill one of his own senior directors? It didn't seem likely, but the only other explanation was that I had killed Opal myself and I wasn't willing to accept that one. "I think I know what's going on." *Who else could have sent her to Jinx?*

"Enlighten me."

"Reston Jameson kills Opal and get me blamed. He uses the public outcry to shut down the independent operators. The immediate target is singleships, but it's the rockjacks he's after, of course." I shrugged. "Simple." *Simple to say, probably impossible to prove.*

Bodyguard laid one ear flat. "I am unconvinced."

"Grant for a second I didn't do it. Can you think of a better motive?"

"Yes." He wasn't believing me.

"What if she was challenging him for power in the Consortium?"

"Irrelevant. I now have two suspects. Convince me that Reston Jameson is guilty and I will kill him instead of you."

I watched him for the rippling ears that would show he was joking, but he was dead serious. He wouldn't care that an attempt on Reston Jameson's life would almost certainly end his own. Kzinti were like that. Nor would he hesitate to kill me if he decided he wanted to.

"Help me find the truth and you can act with confidence and honor."

Bodyguard's lips twitched. "What do monkeys know of honor?" His claws edged out reflexively. "It seems our interests are aligned, Dylan Thurmond."

I took that as agreement. "Something went badly wrong. I must have anticipated problems when I got back. I would have made some kind of record to protect myself from exactly this circumstance."

"What sort of record?"

"*Elektra's* log is the most obvious answer, but perhaps that's too obvious. There are wheels within wheels here. Somewhere only I would look for it." I thought for moment. "I wrote her name on my palm. There're a few places on the ship I could think of."

"Then we should get on the ship, Dylan Thurmond."

We tubed over to the hangar bay. I could get on my own ship without disturbing the police seals over the airlocks, but when we got there we found not just seals but guards. That was a setback

I probably should have expected, the Goldskins were taking no chances. Instead of crawling on board through the drive inspection ports we went up to the Constellation and got a table with a sound damper, and I tapped into the ship on my beltcomp. I wasn't really surprised to see the log empty for the last three weeks, that was expected for this kind of mission. I was slightly more surprised to see the automatically recorded navigation journal also blanked. The same was true of the engine logs. As I tabbed through *Elektra*'s records more and more information was missing. There was only one person who had the access codes to do that. Me.

I tabbed over to Ceres flight control to check their records. They had logged *Elektra* departing and returning, and had her course plotted by transponder tracking to the edge of the singularity into hyperspace and then back again three weeks later. I was a little surprised at that, with all the secrecy I would've expected to have flown with the transponder off. That would be the course the Goldskins were having the Navy search. They had the radar and computing power required to track a pebble if they knew its start vector. If Opal's body was out there, they would find it sooner or later. They'd be in communication with the authorities on Jinx to get a similar search done there. Neels' promise to find her had teeth in it.

Which wasn't a very warming thought. *Why are you worried? You didn't kill her.* I wasn't sure I believed that anymore. Her blood was on *Elektra*, that was proof she'd been there. If someone is on a ship when it leaves and isn't there when it comes back the odds that they will be found alive are zero. A frame by Reston Jameson was enough of a theory to keep Bodyguard from killing me immediately, but it really didn't seem to fit the evidence. He was certainly seizing on the incident to press his agenda, but that wasn't enough of a motive for murder.

I went back to *Elektra*'s systems and systematically went through every log file. Internal and external video, audio, communications log, they were all blank except one, engineering systems. *Elektra* monitors her own vital signs automatically, and for some reason that data was still intact. Unfortunately it was unlikely to hold any relevant information. I scanned the entries anyway, and saw only the activity you'd expect to see for a three-week round-trip, air pressure nominal, cabin temperature, fuel flow, power flow, gravity levels, coolant temperature and pressure; there was nothing unusual there. Evidence perhaps that the trip had been made, but little else.

Except one thing. There was a small blip upward in cabin pressure right before departure. That was normal, because once I had the locks sealed I valved liquid oxygen inboard to pressurize the cabin and make sure it held steady against any possible leaks. There were the normal slow waverings in pressure as the cabin temperature and other variables changed, and finally there was another blip downward at the end of the three weeks. That was when the ship was back in the bay and I vented the cabin to equalize pressure inside and out. If Opal Stone had gotten out at Jinx, or anywhere, that pattern would have cycled twice, once for each leg of the trip. And if she'd left through the airlock in space there would have been the small but distinctive up/down pressure blip caused by the airlock cycling.

So if she hadn't gotten out at Jinx, and she hadn't gone through the airlock, where had she gone? And how did her blood get all over *Elektra*? I went over the rest of the life-support data and found another anomaly. The CO_2 scrubbers had been working half again as hard as I would have expected them to for two people. Had someone else been aboard, stowed away perhaps? Had that person killed Opal and then vanished along with her body? That made no sense.

"What are you learning?" Bodyguard was growing impatient.

"Nothing." I pushed the beltcomp away. "The log is blank. There are some question marks in the system records, but nothing that will lead us anywhere here." I briefly outlined my findings.

"Hrrr. We need progress, human."

I leaned back and looked up through the dome at the eternal and indifferent stars. "We have to speak to Reston Jameson."

"I remain unconvinced of his involvement."

"We have to talk to him to find out."

"Hrrr. This will be difficult."

I nodded. We sat in silence for a while. The more I thought of it the less likely it seemed Reston Jameson was even involved. Tying him in had been the first half-plausible thing that leapt to mind under threat of having my throat ripped out. The vidwall started showing the news and I watched the moving heads and read the texttrans scrolling beneath them. It was the usual fluff, a flood down on Earth, some struldbrug trapped in a tube capsule for twelve hours, a rockjack killed in a fight with another rockjack. They did the shipping news and then the business section came up. I was bored by then and ready to leave, and then suddenly I was paying attention to the words scrolling across the screen. The Consortium was under investigation for gross financial misconduct. Reston Jameson was under indictment. The information had been provided by his missing chief financial officer, Opal Stone. Suddenly she had a motive to hire a singleship to fly to Jinx and brainblank the pilot. Suddenly Reston Jameson had a motive for murder. On the face of it, it looked like Opal believed he would act on the motivation. My doubts vanished; unfortunately that didn't help my case any. *And now she's gone and There Ain't No Justice.*

Bodyguard had picked up on the significance of the information as well. "Let us waste no time. If it is Reston Jameson we need to speak to, we need to lay our plans. It will not be easy."

"We could just make an appointment."

Bodyguard rippled his years. "I will watch while you try."

I took out my beltcomp and referenced his office. His secretary answered, a woman as striking as Opal. Evidently Reston liked to surround himself with beauty. It took me under a minute to learn that Reston Jameson was not only not currently available but would remain unavailable to me for the foreseeable future. She managed to convey the message in a manner that combined impeccable style and grace with the warmth and slickness of an iceberg. She was so perfect in her role that I suspected her of being a digital construct, even though I knew a man like Reston Jameson would use a live secretary for the prestige if nothing else.

I snapped the cover shut on my beltcomp. "Now what?"

Bodyguard showed his teeth. "Now we attack." I got the feeling it was the answer he'd been waiting for.

Now we attack. He made it sound simple, logical, inevitable, but I was not a military man, not police trained, nothing. I was a pilot, and all my experience as a smuggler had geared me to avoid conflict, not seek it out. Aggressive action would not be simple, and it certainly didn't seem logical to take on the most powerful man in the Belt. I started to say that but Bodyguard's expression kept me silent. He was a kzin in midleap and wasn't about to brook any argument. For a moment I considered trying to slip away, but the Goldskins would have a tag on my ident and I wouldn't be able to get off Ceres. Running would label me as both dishonorable and guilty in Bodyguard's eyes, and he would track me down and kill me. I was along for what might turn out to be a very uncomfortable ride.

Unlike me, Bodyguard was perfectly comfortable with direct action, and he knew how to carry it out. Phase one of attack is reconnaissance, and our first reconnaissance was to identify where we might intercept Reston Jameson in order to extract a confession from him. It wouldn't be easy. He had his own retinue of bodyguards, human ones, and his own tunnel farm, which would have more than its fair share of electronic sentries. We called up a map and the scope of the problem became clear. There was exactly one entry point to his complex, a private tube station. We couldn't even get a tube car to stop there without an invitation code, and if we somehow managed to clear that hurdle we'd simply be turned around by the guards. We needed another option, and I couldn't see it.

Bodyguard could. He tapped a talon on the map display. "This tunnel farm is on level one."

"So?"

"Hrrr. So there will be surface locks."

"There aren't any marked."

"I have worked for several wealthy humans. I have learned they are tremendously reticent about every aspect of their lives. There will be much about Reston Jameson which does not appear in the public record. Such a man would not build a lair without a back door. There will be surface locks."

I hadn't thought of that, but . . . "They'll be alarmed."

Bodyguard smiled a feral smile. "Alarms can be defeated." I swear he was looking forward to this desperate little venture purely for the challenge.

My vac suit was on board *Elektra* so I had to rent one. It didn't fit well, and the controls were unfamiliar, an uncomfortable reality for a singleship pilot who was used to intimate and instinctive familiarity with every piece of equipment. Bodyguard had his own suit. The surface of Ceres doesn't offer much more than hard radiation and vacuum, people don't go out on the surface unless they have to, but the lock master asked no questions as he cycled us through and we offered no explanations. It was six kilometers over the surface to the area over Reston Jameson's tunnel farm, four horizons of dead reckoning away. Ceres has no navigational satellites, no magnetic field, and no easy landmarks. The soil has been churned up by the countless tracks of men and vehicles over the centuries so even these are no help. What Ceres does have is a gravity field low enough that you can jump forty meters high. We had a tunnel map that showed surface features like solar arrays and ship locks, and those high slow jumps allowed us to identify enough of them to keep our bearings.

It was vertigo-inducing, but it would have been fun if our mission wasn't so serious. It took us only half an hour to cover the distance, and we hit pay dirt immediately. Bodyguard could get twice as high as I could, so he must have seen it as soon as we left the surface lock. We were maintaining radio silence, on the off chance that we needed to, so he kept his own counsel until we were close enough to see it from the ground.

He waved to get my attention and pointed. I followed his talon. It was a ship lock, and it wasn't on the map. For a moment I thought we were lost and had somehow come back to the main hangars. I turned the map to try and orient myself, and then I realized what I was looking at. Reston Jameson's private ship lock.

That surprised me. I've docked at Ceres many times, cleared in and out through Ceres flight control. I knew the approach funnel cold, I knew the obstacles and the beacons, and I could sketch the three-dimensional traffic-control layer cake blindfolded. This ship lock wasn't in the traffic-control plan. Reston Jameson had clout indeed to keep it off the charts. I looked up and picked up the riding lights of a freighter sliding into the main hangar bay, and visualized the curving low-gee trajectory, wondering how they managed to deconflict the flight paths, and suddenly I understood. Ceres' main hangar is at the equator, and approach and takeoff are both west to east in order to take advantage of Ceres' rotation for velocity matching. A ship coming in to Reston Jameson's lock would use the same approach, offset six kilometers. It would be an open secret in traffic control, but no one else would know the reclusive magnate's comings and goings.

It occurred to me that the crimes I was about to commit in order to clear my name were serious enough to rate to heavy jail time if I was caught. I considered suggesting that we go back, but I thought better of it. If Bodyguard decided I was guilty of killing his client he would track me to the end of the galaxy to put my ears on his belt. I mentally rehearsed throwing myself on the mercy of the court, and followed him toward the lock. The thought crossed my mind that he might have an accident, say with his suit seal. I didn't pursue the idea. I'm not a killer, and that belief had suddenly become important to me.

There was a transpax dome on the surface too, not far from the shiplock, about the same size as Constellation's dome. It seemed Reston Jameson liked to look at the stars himself. I looked up at the star-strewn sky. Watchbird Alpha was sixteen hundred kilometers up there, looking down at me with cameras good enough to pick out an individual in daylight. Somewhere down over the equatorial horizon Delta and Gamma kept their own vigils. I began to wish we'd come at night. I was sweating and couldn't wipe my brow. Dayside Ceres is fifty Celsius, which was enough to make my suit's cooling system run at a steady purr. It was standard night in the tunnels though, and that was what counted. Bodyguard had been unwilling to wait until standard night came into phase with surface night.

I felt dreadfully exposed in the harsh glare on the unrelieved terrain, and I muttered a few choice words about kzinti, after first making sure my transmitter was off. *Scream and leap*. How they'd ever managed to survive as a species was beyond me. I began to wish more fervently that I'd never taken Opal Stone's contract. Bodyguard seemed completely unconcerned as he took one long, practiced leap to the rectangular outline of a personnel lock. The mechanism was a simple pull bar—it was illegal to have a locking mechanism on an airlock, in case someone got trapped outside. Reston Jameson no doubt could have gotten around that restriction, but it seemed he had chosen not to.

And I knew the reason for that. As soon as the lock cycled, the computer would log it. His security teams would be there in a minute or less. Short of drilling through ten meters of rock and regolith we were no further ahead here than we were trying to access his private tube car station.

Bodyguard had come prepared. He drew a variable sword from his day pack, a highly illegal weapon anywhere in Sol System, and extended the blade. The magnetically stiffened monomolecular wire was invisible. I looked for the telltale marker ball that would let him track the tip but there was none. Instinctively I backed up, just in case he wound up cutting me in half by accident. He paid no attention, and with absolute confidence forced the wire into the heavy metal door of the lock. A fine mist of ice crystals began to jet from the incision, growing larger as, with straining muscles, he dragged the force wire around the inner perimeter of the door. The spray had stopped before he'd gotten halfway around; he'd voided the atmosphere to vacuum. A moment later he had a large, roughly square chunk of the airlock door cut out. I had no idea what he intended to accomplish by doing this. He could get away with cutting open the outer door because the lock itself held little atmosphere, but now it wouldn't seal. Tons of air pressure now held the inner door shut and if he tried to cut through it he would explosively decompress Reston Jameson's entire complex, probably launching himself into orbit in the process.

He crawled through the hole he had made and I backed up more to get out of the way of the impending disaster. He stuck his head out and gestured for me to follow him. Somewhat hesitantly I did. Personnel locks are cramped at the best of times. Sharing one with a kzin was downright claustrophobic. I was forced to curl into a ball in one corner while he grabbed the cut-out slab of door and carefully repositioned it where it had come from. Then I had to hold it in position, twisted like a pretzel with fingers straining against the awkward grip my suit gloves afforded while he got a tube of Quickseal from his pack and ran it around the cutline.

Now I understood. When the Quickseal set the outer door would hold pressure again. He could then repeat the process on the inner door without depressurizing all of Ceres. It was an awkward way to cycle through an airlock. It had the advantage of not triggering the alarms by opening the doors. The computer would no doubt log the pressure drop in the lock, but that was a maintenance issue, not a security issue. We were in.

Well, we were almost in. We had to wait an hour for the Quickseal to set properly, an hour I spent in a fetal crouch, half crushed by Bodyguard's weight. I lost all feeling below the waist before he judged it time to go on, and then there were more pretzellike acrobatics to allow him to start cutting the inner door, working with suit lights. The atmosphere hissed in to the lock and I watched the Quickseal carefully for any sign that it might fail as the pressure built up. If it did we would certainly die as we were blasted out that too-small opening, and a lot of other people would die with us as the tunnels depressurized. It was far too late for me back out now. My suit settled on me as the pressure equalized. The Quickseal held, and then Bodyguard was carefully lowering the chunk he'd cut from the inner door into the tunnel beyond. We were in, all the way this time.

I felt my weight surge as we came into the tunnel's artificial gravity field. The passage was dimly lit, standard night on Ceres, and it was opulently appointed. Acres of Persian carpet covered the floor, every kilogram of it imported from Earth, and expensive paintings hung on the walls. We stripped our vac suits and stuffed them in the lock, and Bodyguard Quicksealed the lock door so we could use it on the way out. I checked my tunnel map, and we headed off to the right, towards Reston Jameson's private quarters. The plan was to confront him directly, and as we advanced I could see more and more flaws with that idea. We were screaming and leaping in classic kzinti style. That approach had lost them six wars in a row and eighty-five percent of their empire. I wasn't encouraged by history.

We went down the corridor cautiously, unsure of what might be in wait for us. I'd highlighted a few points on the map where he was likely to be. The first one turned out to be his living quarters. I felt like a burglar, which fit the situation closely enough. There was nothing moving but us, and no alarms went off, but neither was Reston there. That state of affairs was fine with me. I was in no hurry to go forward, and spent some time marveling at the sumptuous furnishing, which made the lavish corridors seem sparse in comparison. There was no sprayfoam, no steel, no plastic. Everything was made of wood or wool or cotton. There was stone, but not the laser-cut basalt I was used to. It was all limestone and marble, minerals that could only have formed in the living forge of Earth. It was everywhere, carved and polished, tiled and inlaid, floors and walls and sculptures. The total mass involved was tremendous, the upship costs incalculable. Here in the Belt, where rock represented all that was common and cheap, Reston Jameson had transformed it into an expression of wealth and power.

And here I was challenging that power like a demented moth hurling itself into a bonfire. Bodyguard was undistracted by the setting. He made a short gesture and went ahead, not even bothering to look to see if I was following. I went with him for lack of a better choice. We found Jameson there, working at a broad desk of polished black stone. He looked up as we came in without surprise. "Good morning. I've been waiting for you."

Bodyguard snarled. "We have come to ask questions on the death of Opal Stone."

Jameson smiled. "I am sure you have."

The kzin's ears swiveled up and forward. I wasn't sure if he could pick up the smugness too. "What is your involvement?"

Jameson shrugged, unperturbed. "I have none."

Bodyguard's lips pulled themselves into a dangerous smile. "I question your honor, human."

"Ah, an insult." Jameson's smile somehow became as predatory as Bodyguard's. "I think at this point it's traditional that I scream and leap to avenge it."

Bodyguard crouched, his talons extended and fangs bared. "If you dare, human."

Jameson made a command gesture to his AI. There was a soft *thwipthwipthwipthwip* and Bodyguard collapsed. Mercy needles, fired from a projector hidden in the camera ball overhead. Kzinti physiology isn't the same as human. Jameson must have arranged mercy slivers made of kzin-specific anesthetic, probably alternating with the standard formula in his defense weapons so they'd work on both species. He really had been expecting us.

He turned his eyes to me. "Captain Thurmond. I hope we can interact less dramatically."

He knew my name, and I knew I was in deep trouble. I looked at the quarter-ton of unconscious carnivore on the expensive carpet. I nodded slowly. *Yes.* I had walked into the lion's den and I was getting exactly what I deserved.

He smiled wide, the predator in victory. "Good. Now tell me what you know."

I shook my head. "Believe me, I don't know anything at all."

His smile disappeared. "You don't expect me to believe that."

I could feel the fear creeping into my expression. I was in way over my head. "I've had a brain blank. They've accused me of killing Opal Stone. I know I didn't do it." I shrugged, hoping that would be enough for him.

"And you think I did?"

"You have a motive . . ." I trailed off. I didn't want to antagonize him.

He smirked. "A brain blank. She's a smart woman, but now I know what she's hiding." He looked away, his eyes distant for a moment, and when they came back to me they were flint hard. He made a gesture. A holo popped into existence, showing Bodyguard and me clambering through the sliced-open airlock door. He'd been watching us since we'd gotten in, maybe from before that. I was so busted.

"I could turn you over to the Goldskins now, but I think I have a better use for you." His voice was smug. Another gesture and pinpricks stitched across my back. I was vaguely aware of the floor coming up to smack me as darkness fell.

I woke up looking at stars. For a moment I thought I was in *Elektra*'s cockpit, and then I thought I was in the Constellation, but as I looked around I saw not my familiar command console or the bar's laser-cut furnishings but exotic flowering plants. The air was humid and rich with the scent of their flowers. There was a throbbing in my temples as the anesthetic in the mercy needles wore off. My extremities tingled and I had a little trouble getting my feet. Bodyguard was watching me.

"Where are we?" The low gravity told me I was still on Ceres, somewhere.

"Hrrr. We are in Reston Jameson's garden dome. I have been here before with Dr. Stone."

"Scream and leap." I couldn't contain my frustration any longer. "See where it's gotten us." I half-expected Bodyguard to scream and leap at me for saying it.

Instead he just twitched his whiskers. "It has gotten us here, obviously." He had taken my sarcasm for confusion.

"It is getting us killed," I said bitterly.

"Then we will have deaths of honor." He seemed unperturbed. I gave up. It isn't that kzinti don't fear death, it's just that they never let it stop them. "I owe you apology and honor debt, Captain Thurmond. You are innocent, as you stated."

"Never mind. We need to get out of here while we still can." I started looking around and noticed that my beltcomp was gone.

"There is no way out."

"There has to be." The dome was perhaps a hundred feet around, full of lush vegetation.

"He has taken all my tools, and the airlock is depressurized."

I had to see for myself. I found the airlock; evidently the

dome was its own pressure zone. As I said it's illegal to lock an airlock, if that phrase makes any sense. There was no lock on this one, but the cycle light glowed amber. Jameson had sealed us in through the simple expedient of pumping down the airlock chamber. It was a cargo lock, three meters on a side. The door opened upward and outward, so though I could open and close the latching bar easily enough the door itself was sealed shut with tons of air pressure. It might as well have been welded. I punched the cycle button to pressurize it but nothing happened, Jameson had disconnected it.

Bodyguard had followed me, and I turned back to him. "Now what?"

He shrugged, a gesture I'm sure he learned in order to communicate with humans. "Now we wait."

I wasn't satisfied with waiting, and so I made a fool of myself exploring the garden trying to find something I could use on the airlock door. Bodyguard watched me with amicable amusement.

"I have already searched for tools."

Nevertheless I persisted in looking. There was nothing else to do, and I hadn't liked the way Jameson said he had a better use for me than turning me in to the Goldskins. Better for him was not likely better for me. Nevertheless it slowly became clear that Bodyguard had been thorough in his assessment. There were a few gardening tools of extruded plastic, some bags of concentrated plant nutrient, a few light metal hangers and the aluminum trusses that supported the twining vines. None of it was sturdy enough to assault the airlock door, and though I vaguely recalled that it was possible to turn fertilizer into some kind of explosive I didn't know how. I couldn't even guess if what was in the bags was the right kind of fertilizer. Even if it was I suspected it would take more than dirt and water to make it explode, and those were all the ingredients I had to hand.

The garden itself was beautiful, and in other circumstances I would have greatly enjoyed exploring it. I'm no expert on flowers, but these were lush and lavish. Some had huge blossoms a foot across, others ornate and intricate folds, everywhere they exploded in a riot of color, climbing on impossibly slender stalks in the low gravity. In the center of the dome there was a respectable telescope, perhaps sixty centimeters. The garden was also an observatory. I'd heard Reston Jameson was an amateur astronomer, though patiently observing the heavens didn't seem to square with the rest of his personality. It had a horseshoe-shaped workbench surrounding it, with a data panel to control its tracking motors. I pointed the panel on, but it didn't respond. I tried manually, but the power had been switched off from somewhere else—so much for getting help over the network. The workbench had drawers underneath it, and I slid one open to reveal an array of lenses and optical instruments of uncertain purpose. Another bigger drawer at the bottom yielded a huge concave mirror, doubtless a twin to the one in the telescope. I quickly checked all the drawers for anything hefty and came up empty.

I remembered the employment offer from Canexco that I'd turned down. *One step better than life in a cage.* I was in a cage now, and I didn't like it. Being an independent has its downsides. I had a brief image of myself trying to batter down the door with an interferometer and turned to Bodyguard. "There's nothing useful here."

"Hrrr." His tail lashed. "We must wait. The airlock is the choke point. We will ambush them when they come in."

I looked at the heavy door and nodded. Bodyguard's lips were twitching back to clear his fangs. Reston Jameson had chosen to cage a kzin, never a good idea. I began to feel sorry for whoever came through the door next. Sooner or later they would have to come for us, and when they did we would be ready. I grabbed one of the plastic garden hoes and began sharpening the end of the handle against the rough surface of one of the stone planters. It was too light to use as a club, but rigid enough to make a serviceable spear. *I'm not a killer.* I'd told myself that but it wasn't really true. Anyone can be a killer if you push them hard enough. Humans aren't any less predatory than kzinti, we're just less open about it.

Bodyguard settled down to wait down in a resting crouch, his big golden eyes locked on the airlock door. I sat beside him, sharpening my weapon. We waited long enough for the sun to rise and slide across the top of the dome. I finished my improvised spear and for want of anything else to do began to make another one. The air warmed noticeably as the sun came up to the zenith, and suddenly I had an idea. I went back to the horseshoe desk and slid open the drawer with the big mirror. There was a wiring harness embedded in its underside, no doubt to drive the piezo-adaptive glass to keep the surface curve wavelength perfect. I picked it up and brought it back, being careful not to let its considerable inertia overbalance me.

Bodyguard looked up from his vigil. "What are you doing?"

"I'm going to see how much sunlight I can put on the door. If we can melt a hole in it the pressure will equalize and we're free."

He twitched his tail dubiously. "Innovative thinking, but I doubt you will command enough energy."

"It's free to try."

He said nothing, and I maneuvered the mirror to catch the sun and spill its concentrated rays on a focal point in the center of the airlock door. The tiny dot of light blazed too brightly to look at directly, and tendrils of smoke curled lazily up as the paint blistered off. The sun is weak out in the Belt, but it was a big mirror, maybe big enough . . .

It was hard to hold the mirror steady enough, but I persevered. Once I flicked the beam spot away and was gratified to see a faint red glow. Steel softens as it heats up, and air pressure provided a steady force against the weakened spot. Maybe enough . . .

After fifteen minutes I had to admit that there wasn't enough heat.

"Let me try this." Bodyguard had pulled out one of the aluminum support tubes from a planter frame. Squinting against the blinding light of the beam spot he stabbed it against the door. It came back melted, but the steel didn't give way.

He held up the melted tube. "You must be close."

I shook my head. "Aluminum melts at half the temperature steel does." I put the mirror down and the red spot faded immediately.

Bodyguard put a paw against the steel. "Hrrr. The door is hot. I suspect you've reached the point where heat is radiating away as fast as you can pump it in."

"Close, but not close enough." I slumped down against a planter and picked up my improvised plastic spear. It didn't seem like much of a weapon to win freedom with.

"There is another mirror in the telescope. If we have half the heat we need, let us gather twice as much sun."

I jumped up. "Of course." I would have kissed his hairy, over-aggressive hide if I thought I could have done it without getting my head bitten off, literally. Twice the mirror might not get us to the melting point, there would be some complex calculus problem involving heat flux and the door geometry and the Stefan-Boltzmann constant to know for sure. I've never been that good at math; it would be easier to just try it.

I bounded over to the telescope and Bodyguard followed me. Closer inspection revealed a problem. Without power the scope had to be forced against its drive mechanism, a gimballed gear train specifically designed to keep it locked in position against any tendency to move it off target. The angle it was at made it awkward to even see how the mirror was mounted in the tube. I wasn't strong enough to force it against the gears, Bodyguard and I together weren't strong enough. We gave that up as not worth the effort and instead I climbed up the mechanism to get a closer look. The tube was steel too, not as heavy as the airlock door, but solid enough to keep the various optical elements in precise alignment with each other, and solid enough to resist attack with the tools we had to hand. The mirror mount itself was a single cast piece, and the bolts securing it to the tube were large and torqued on with the same attention to rigidity. We weren't going to get at the second mirror. Undaunted, I climbed up the tube to see if the mirror could be taken out from the inside, but when I looked down it all I could see was the silver mirror surface. The mountings that held it in place attached from underneath, which made sense because any other arrangement would have blocked part of the mirror.

For a moment I considered throwing something down the tube to break the mirror and take it out in pieces, more to relieve my own frustration than because the shards would serve us much purpose. I resisted the temptation and climbed down.

"We aren't getting that mirror out."

In response Bodyguard hissed and spat something in the Hero's Tongue, slashing the air with his claws. I backed away and didn't try to translate what he'd said. Eventually he calmed down. "We will go back to our ambush."

I went with him and went back to work on my second spear, but I kept my mind busy trying to think up other ways of getting out. Watchbird Alpha was up there, feeding surface imagery to the Goldskins, among others. If we'd been on the surface we could have drawn rescue symbology to attract their attention, a rarely used planetary emergency system I'd learned along with cold-water survival, six different ways to make fire, and a bunch of other planet skills, just in case I ever made an emergency landing on some uninhabited part of a world. Singleship pilots are like boy scouts, prepared for anything.

Only we weren't on the surface, and so rescue symbology wasn't an option and I really wasn't prepared for the situation I found myself in. Bodyguard seemed oblivious to my distraction, his relaxed concentration fixed completely on the airlock door. There was a laser amid the optical instruments, and it occurred to me that if I could figure out how to boresight it with the telescope I could use the scope to aim it at Watchbird Alpha and signal the Goldskins in Morse. I went and looked at it again and proved the triumph of hope over reality. It was a little ten-milliwatt device, good for checking optical systems, but unable to put a visible beam on a satellite a thousand-odd kilometers overhead, and anyway we couldn't move the scope. My eyes went back to the big mirror with the idea of using it as a heliograph but its focal length was only three meters, so getting a spot on Watchbird wasn't an option. There were some flat mirrors in among the lenses, but they weren't nearly big enough, and the sun was already setting.

I went back to the spear again, promising myself that if I managed to get out of this alive I would never again take a contract of questionable legality. No smuggling, no mysterious cargoes, most certainly no brain-blank drugs, and absolutely no kzinti. I would sell *Elektra* if I had to, and work as a rockjack. I went back to sharpening with a vengeance, and was so concentrated on that and my dark thoughts that I didn't hear the airlock cycle. I was yanked back to awareness by a paralyzing kill scream and looked up in time to see a blur of orange fur. Hastily I grabbed up my other spear and ran to follow Bodyguard. I found myself staring into the open airlock and a pair of muscled security thugs with leveled mercy guns. Bodyguard was piled in a heap at the end of the airlock, unconscious. There was a woman there too, her face tense. I dropped my spear. I had no wish to endure another anesthetic headache. One guard covered me while the other shoved the woman into the garden dome, then pushed Bodyguard's unconscious body after her, a heavy and awkward burden even in the low gravity. They smirked and powered the lock door shut. They had come prepared for ambush.

The woman gave me a sardonic smile. "Captain Thurmond. I'd like to say I'm pleased to meet you again, but under the circumstances I'm not."

I looked at her blankly. "Do I know you?"

She came forward and offered me her hand. "I guess the drugs do work. Opal Stone."

I shook her hand, stunned. She wasn't the woman who was at the Constellation that night, but she could have been her sister. "But you . . ."

". . . are on Jinx?" She laughed without humor.

". . . are dead," I finished. I looked her up and down. She had the same build as the woman I'd met in the Constellation, and now that I noticed I could see that she moved the same way, but her face was completely different.

"Reports of my demise have been greatly exaggerated." She looked at Bodyguard's unconscious form and the humor left her voice. "Although they may turn out to be only slightly premature."

"You don't look . . ."

"Plastic surgery, thanks to your ship's autodoc, and the artistic skills of the best plastic surgeon in the Belt."

I sat down on a planter. "Explain please."

She sat down across from me. "I suppose there's no reason to keep it secret now. The escape to Jinx was faked. We took Dr. Helis of the Helis clinic on board. He worked my face through your autodoc. I came back here and went underground until I could get another ship."

Even I had heard of the Helis clinic and the man who ran it. He was merely the best 'doc-driver in the Belt. "But *why*?"

She laughed bitterly. "Why do you think? I sold out Reston. You don't expect to do that and live. He'd track me to the end of the universe to kill me, even from jail. Jinx is no obstacle to him. The only solution is to *vanish*."

"So what are you doing back here?"

"I'm the fox doubling back on her tracks. The hope was he'd believe I was dead, but if he didn't then Jinx would be a dead-end trail. I'm meant to be boarding Nakamura Lines for Wunderland right now with my new face and a hundred million stars in my beltcomp." She shrugged. "It didn't work out that way. Reston's a smart boy."

I looked at her critically. "I liked your old face better."

She smirked. "I don't imagine you'll have to put up with this one for long."

"And what about the blood in my airlock?"

"Leftovers from the operation, drained out of your 'doc. That was to make the Goldskins think you'd killed me."

"*You* framed me."

"Of course." She saw my expression and went on. "Oh, don't feel so bad about it. Without a body there's no case. You weren't going to prison."

"Says you."

"Hey, you volunteered for a brain blank. You knew you were getting in to something deep and you accepted that risk, for which I paid you well. You're a big boy. Act like one."

She had me there, but I was still angry and her attitude didn't help. I stalked off as well as one can stalk in two and a half percent gravity, and went and looked at the telescope. Plants don't interest me, and Bodyguard was asleep. I didn't want to look at her, so the scope was the default.

She came over after a while. "Look, I'm sorry I set you up. I had to do what I had to do."

"You didn't have to do it to me."

She smiled, and despite what I'd said her face was as beautiful as before. "You're a good pilot, you've got a good reputation, and Dr. Helis said you had the right kind of autodoc on board. I needed the best." I looked at her, met her eyes, and I could tell she was used to getting what she wanted by smiling.

I wasn't biting. I went back to looking through the scope. She tried again. "Look, do you want Reston Jameson to win?"

I looked at her. "Win what? Against the rockjacks?" I shrugged. "If I had to choose sides I'd choose the rockjacks, just because I side with independent operators in general. Only I don't have to choose sides. It isn't my war."

"Interesting you should use the phrase 'war.' That's exactly what it is, and like it or not it is *your* war."

I knew what she meant but I was still angry enough to make her drag it out of me. "No. It isn't."

"So how's business been lately?" She arched an eyebrow at me. "Booked right up with contracts?"

"Everyone knows the strike is hurting the economy. That doesn't make it my war."

"Oh no?" She smirked again. "And how many bidders do you think you're going to get for your services when Jameson gets a stranglehold on mining?"

"I can fly outsystem."

"Sure you can. And so can every other singleship pilot once Jameson tightens the screws. Eighty percent of the singleship market in Known Space is in the Belt, and ninety percent of that is in support of the rockjacks. You're all going to find the pickings pretty slim out of the colonies."

"So what's your point?"

"Reston Jameson plans on setting himself up as emperor, nothing less. He's going to break the rockjacks, and once he does that he's going to break the singleship pilots, and once he controls Earth's resource base and the means of transporting it, he's going to de facto rule Earth, and through Earth the colonies."

"That's insane. The UN won't allow it."

"They won't have any choice but to allow it. Earth is completely reliant on space resources, the UN can't afford to have the Belt cut off raw materials. Even if they had a choice they wouldn't act. He's already bought half the Security Council." I looked skeptical and she went on, her tone sharpening. "Who do you think planned this with him?"

"You?"

"Me. We've been putting this together for years, manipulating the market, forcing the rockjacks into a corner so they'd have to strike, and so we'd have an excuse to break them, with Belt government backing. I'm his financial wizard, he couldn't have done it without me."

"So why did you turn on him?"

She bit her lower lip and looked away. "At first it was just a game, at least it seemed that way." She laughed. "We were young, anything seemed possible but at the same time it all seemed so far away." She looked back to me. "Did you ever hear the story of the two soldiers who set out to become generals?"

I shook my head. "No."

"Each one made sure to compliment the other in his absence to their superiors, and slowly but surely they advanced ahead of their peers until they reached their goal. We were like that, we structured the social environment, set up our competition in the Consortium to fail, got ourselves senior positions, and then directorships. It worked better than I could ever have imagined."

Realization dawned. "You were lovers."

She nodded. "Yes, we were."

"So again, why . . . ?"

"Because absolute power corrupts absolutely." She paused, and for the first time I saw real emotion in her controlled, beautiful features. "He doesn't love me anymore, he stopped loving me when he fell in love with power. He's lost it, lost any connection between the ends and the means."

"What does that mean?"

"There's still a threat from the UN, from the Navy. Military intervention could stop us cold, so he has a plan. If Earth doesn't go along with our program he's going to drop asteroids on them."

"The Navy would never let them get close."

"The Navy will never see them coming. He has a thing, a Slaver stasis field in reverse. It just absorbs energy, even neutrino radar. He's had a secret lab working on it for the last ten years." Opal shook her head slightly, as if she couldn't quite believe what she was saying. "Ten years. He never told me. I found out by accident." There was pain in her voice, and it occurred to me that perhaps Reston Jameson's larger crime in her eyes was not his unbridled ambition but his refusal to fully share it with her.

"So you turned him in?"

"Do you think I shouldn't have?"

And I had no answer for that. Her motivations were probably wrong, but it was still the right thing to do. I changed the subject. "Now what?"

"I know Reston. Right now he's setting the stage so that when we turn up dead he can use that for his own ends."

"What ends?"

"Probably to discredit the information I gave the Goldskins, and if he can arrange it, to show singleshippers in a bad light, to ramp up the pressure on the independents generally."

"You think he'd kill us in cold blood?" I asked the question but I already knew the answer. He had a use for us, he'd said, and I doubted it involved any of us being able to tell anyone about what he was doing. His motive for wanting Opal dead was obvious, and the fact that he hadn't kept her isolated from us showed he didn't care what she told us.

"I know he will." Her voice was clipped flat when she said it, and I decided not to ask her how she came to be *that* certain. "We have to get out of here."

"We've been trying." I showed her the spears and the telescope mirror and described our attempts at getting out. "If we could power up the telescope desk we could get a message out over the net."

"It's on a separate circuit. He looks after the details, he's always been good at that."

Bodyguard stirred unsteadily and got to his feet, looking around. "Our plan has failed."

"You must have known that it would."

"I dreamed that you had screamed and leapt beside me . . ." Bodyguard shook his head to clear it and then unsteadily turned his attention on Opal. "Dr. Stone. Welcome back."

She looked at him. "You're the first one to recognize me since I had my face changed."

Bodyguard flipped his ears up, focusing his eyes with an effort. "Oh yes, I can see you have changed your appearance. Your scent is the same. You are in your fertile time."

Opal Stone blushed. I carefully didn't watch. She was still very beautiful. The sun was coming up again. My body was adapted to the Belt standard day reflected in the light/dark cycle of the main tunnel lighting, and the asteroid's quick alternation between night and day was confusing me. It must have been eighteen hours since we'd been caught.

Eighteen hours. Reston Jameson must have his staging set by now, awaiting only the right opportunity to inject our bodies into the volatile political landscape of the rockjack strike for maximum advantage. There would be headlines. "Singleship pilot kills whistleblowing Consortium executive." And there would be rumors, that Opal Stone and I were involved, that we'd plotted to bring down Reston Jameson by falsifying documents. Bodyguard would be dragged into it, because anything connected with the kzinti was automatically suspect around Sol System. Nothing would be proven, but everything would be open to question, and reasonable doubt was all he needed to keep on course to his insane goals. Our time was running out fast.

"You said you could heliograph the Watchbird. . . ." Opal was thinking out loud.

"We'd need a flat mirror, a big one. Plus I'm not sure I could aim it accurately enough; Watchbird is way up there."

"We can have a flat mirror, we have the telescope."

"It's concave."

"Yes, the telescope mirror is concave, and *this* mirror is concave." She tapped the spare mirror. "But what we want is a straight beam of light. So we focus the light from the spare mirror onto the telescope eyepiece, and the optics take that light, focus it onto the telescope primary as a point source at its focus and then we have a beam we can aim anywhere we want."

I nodded. "Clever." It just might work.

Bodyguard turned a paw over, pointing out what I had overlooked. "We cannot traverse the telescope without the workbench controls, and they have no power."

"These are the manual fine adjustments." She pointed to a pair of small, knurled wheels we hadn't noticed when we'd been considering demounting the primary mirror. "It'll take a while, but we can point it anywhere we want."

I looked at Bodyguard. Bodyguard looked at me. I nodded. "Let's do it."

There was a camera body attached to the telescope, with a thick coaxial cable leading to an input jack on the workbench. Opal unlatched it and put in an eyepiece instead, then started laboriously spinning the fine-adjustments knobs. Each full rotation of the knobs moved the scope tube a barely noticeable fraction of a degree. It was going to take forever to line it up on Watchbird Alpha, but we had nothing but time.

No, actually we were rapidly running out of time, but we had nothing to do but try. I mentally urged her to spin faster while I went in search of something to use as a signal shutter so I could pulse the light. Bodyguard pulled down more of the light aluminum plant frames to align the spare mirror with the eyepiece. I finally settled on ripping open a fertilizer bag to use as a shutter, and then wrote down a simple message in Morse. T E L L—L T—N E E L S—G O L D S K I N—O P A L—S T O N E—H E L D—P R I S O N E R—I N—T H I S—D O M E. I started practicing it with my bag. I learned Morse for an emergency but had never had to use it until now. I needed all the refreshing I could get. I didn't bother mentioning myself or Bodyguard, on the theory that the Goldskins would care more about Opal, and that when she got rescued we would too.

Eventually we were ready. Opal had installed the largest aperture eyepiece she could find and Bodyguard carefully arranged the mirror on his improvised and somewhat rickety framework.

We couldn't focus the beam all the way down to a spot, we didn't want to melt the eyepiece or any of the optics, and after some debate we settled on a disk of light half a handspan across. That would also avoid the need to constantly readjust the mirror as the sun slowly moved across the dome. I started signaling, snapping the bag back and forth in front of the mirror to form the dots and dashes of the signal. Morse is virtually dead as a communications medium nowadays, but it's still taught as a backup and hobbyists use it. Hopefully someone would see the imagery and figure out they were seeing a signal, and find someone to translate. It took me about a minute to work my way through the message. I would take a break for another minute and repeat. I could do that seven or eight times before the sun had moved far enough to require shifting the mirror. We kept doing it. There was nothing else to do.

I'd gone through five or six iterations of this and was beginning to worry that we'd run out of sunlight—or life—before anyone noticed. Bodyguard was once again repositioning the mirror when we heard the airlock open. I felt immediate relief and was just about to say so when I saw who had come in. Reston Jameson, flanked by the same two thugs who'd brought in Opal. I dropped the bag and grabbed my improvised spear, a useless gesture.

Jameson had a nasty little smile on his face, and a mercy gun in his hand. "Lieutenant Neels tells me you've been keeping your idle hands busy." He shook his head, more in sorrow than in anger. "I think you've just about outlived your usefulness." He raised the weapon. The anesthetic in mercy needles is mild and overdose-tolerant, but enough of it could still kill. I was about to go to sleep and never wake up. I should have anticipated that he would have bought out the Goldskins. I'd miscalculated and the game was over.

Bodyguard screamed, but he didn't leap. Instead he threw the telescope mirror at them like a heckler throwing a pie at a politician. They all fired instinctively, but the needles just spattered harmlessly against the glass. Bodyguard leaped a half-heartbeat later, his trajectory following his makeshift shield. He probably took a few stray needles, but then he was on them, talons flashing. Jameson and one henchman had gone down when the mirror hit them, the other had dodged out of the way, but the dodge spoiled his aim.

I threw my first spear and screamed and leaped with my second. The thrown spear missed, and then I was looking down the barrel of a gyrojet rocket pistol at Reston Jameson's ice-cold eyes. I saw his finger tighten on the trigger and it would be a much less pleasant end than an overdose of mercy needles.

There was an earsplitting scream and something blurred and orange slammed me to the ground. I heard a soft *zwwwwippppp* and bounced hard in the low gravity and came up to see blood spraying. Bodyguard's attack had taken me out of the way and the mushrooming rocket round had gone in through his stomach and made a hole the size of a dinner plate in his lower back. His momentum had slammed him into Jameson though. The second guard's eyes were full of blood, and Jameson was struggling from beneath the dying kzin's bulk. He still had the gyrojet.

I screamed and leaped again, my spear catching him in the chest, its point digging into his ribs. I braced myself against the edge of the airlock and forced it forward as he struggled to free his weapon arm, his face contorted in exertion and pain. He got his hand free and fired again. I would have died then, but Bodyguard managed to bring a paw up and over and smacked the weapon even as Jameson pulled the trigger. The round *zwwipped* past and pain seared my shoulder, then a half second later the gyrojet sailed over my head. The kill rage swept over me and I shoved hard on the spear. From someplace far away I heard a bloodcurdling scream and realized it was my own voice. Something gave way with a nasty crunching sound and the shaft lurched forward into Jameson's chest. He looked at me with something close to surprise, his once-distinguished features covered in sprayed blood. I didn't wait to watch him die, I let go of the spear and rolled to take on the other guard.

There was another *zzzwwwipp* and I ducked reflexively. I saw the guard's chest explode. Opal held the gyrojet leveled, now covering the guard, but she needn't have bothered. Bodyguard had ripped his throat out in his first attack.

I turned to the kzin. Incredibly he was still breathing, but he wouldn't be for long. There was fur and bone spattered everywhere. His spinal column had been blown out and his legs and lower body sagged uselessly.

"Hang on. We'll get you to an autodoc."

He looked up at me with big green eyes. I hadn't noticed their color before, and I saw in them the certainty of his own death. "Honor is satisfied," he said, his breath rasping. "You fought well, Captain Thurmond."

I wanted to say something, do something but there was nothing that could be done, and he closed his eyes and died right there. I knew in that moment it had been no accident that he'd knocked me out of the way as Reston Jameson fired. He owed me honor debt, for his own accusation that I had killed Opal, and he had repaid it in full.

Honor is satisfied. I found myself shaking, light-headed and nauseous at once.

"We have to get out of here." Opal brought me back to the here-and-now.

I looked up. Three men and a kzin were dead and there was blood everywhere. I was soaked in it myself, and I'd just killed the most powerful man in the Belt. It was definitely not a good time to be me.

"There's a ship here somewhere. I saw the shiplock."

"Reston's courier. I know where it is."

We went straight to the docking bay through the dimly lit tunnels, once having to slip past a lit office where someone was working late on some Consortium project which I had probably just rendered irrelevant by killing Jameson. The ship lock was deserted. Jameson's ship was a converted Hawk-class courier, immaculately maintained, with *Lightning* scribed on her bow above her registration numbers. Inside she was appointed to a level that went beyond luxury into hubris. With hands both bloody and trembling I preflighted her. I did it in record time; the bloodbath in the airlock might be discovered at any moment, and I wanted to be well away from Ceres when that happened, preferably well away from Sol System. The lock pumped down while I ran the checklist, and by the time I was done the doors were sliding open.

I lifted out and called departure control, trying to keep my voice level. They laconically granted me boost clearance. I wasted no time pivoting the thrusters and shoving the throttles forward. *Lightning* responded with smooth, even power, and I realized then that I was abandoning *Elektra*. I would never be back to Ceres now; I was a marked man. *Elektra* would sit in the docking bay until she was sold to cover my debts. My future, whatever it was, lay in the new colonies, worlds where a good pilot with a good ship counted for more than Sol System justice. That hurt. A singleship pilot and his ship have a bond, an understanding, a kind of love that transcends the gap between man and machine. You can't understand that if you haven't felt it. *Elektra* was alive to me, and abandoning her hurt. I took a deep breath, punched in a course for the singularity's edge, and engaged it. The ship surged as the starfield tilted and then we were on our way. I had no other option, and at that I was paying less for my freedom than Bodyguard had. Sometimes being an independent has its downsides.

Opal Stone came into the cockpit. She'd cleaned herself up, replaced her blood soaked clothing with a utilitarian jumpsuit. She looked tired but something had changed, a tension had left her face, and I realized that it had always been there.

"Let me look at that." She took the cockpit medpack from its clips and fussed over my wounded shoulder with saline and sterile swabs and sprayskin. I'd forgotten all about it. It wasn't bad, but it began to throb painfully as the adrenaline wore off.

She was very beautiful. I let her keep fussing, watching the eternal stars. The future was out there.